BEL-TIB NEW MYSTERY
Mystery Scottoline
Scottoline, Lisa
Think twice
31111025839265

P9-DML-194

3/10

DATE DUE

4/12		
JUL 12 2010		
JUL 29 2010		
8-22-10		
Sept 22		
11-04		
APR 02 2011		
MAY 16 2011		

Brodart Co.   Cat. # 55 137 001   Printed in USA

THINK**TWICE**

Also by Lisa Scottoline

THINK**TWICE**

Lisa Scottoline

ST. MARTIN'S PRESS ❄ NEW YORK

This is a work of fiction. All of the characters, organizations, and events portrayed in this novel are either products of the author's imagination or are used fictitiously.

THINK TWICE. Copyright © 2010 by Lisa Scottoline. All rights reserved. Printed in the United States of America. For information, address St. Martin's Press, 175 Fifth Avenue, New York, N.Y. 10010.

www.stmartins.com

ISBN 978-0-312-38075-5

First Edition: March 2010

10 9 8 7 6 5 4 3 2 1

For my mother, with love and gratitude

You have conquered, and I yield. Yet, henceforth art thou also dead—dead to the world, to Heaven, and to Hope! In me didst thou exist—and in my death, see by this image, which is thine own, how utterly thou hast murdered thyself.

—Edgar Allan Poe, "William Wilson"

THINK**TWICE**

Chapter One

Bennie Rosato didn't have anything in common with her identical twin, except their DNA. They shared the same blue eyes, strong cheekbones, and full mouth, but whenever Bennie looked at Alice Connelly, all she could see were their differences. Tonight, Bennie had on a khaki suit, white shirt, and brown pumps, her lawyer uniform. Alice had on tight shorts with a low-cut black top, flaunting cleavage that Bennie didn't even know they had. She made a mental note to look down her shirt, after she got home.

Alice was making dinner and she opened the oven door, releasing the aroma of roasting chicken. "Finally, it's ready."

"Smells great."

"You sound surprised."

"Not at all." Bennie changed the subject. "I like your new house, it's great."

"Yeah, right." Alice turned, carving fork in hand. "Why are you being so condescending?"

"I'm not."

"You are, too. It'll look better when I move all my stuff in, and the rent is low, since the estate can't sell it. That's the only way I could afford it. I don't have your money."

Bennie let it go. "It's good that it came furnished."

"This crap? It's dead people furniture." Alice pushed back a smooth strand of hair, yet another difference between them. She blew-dry her hair straight, and her eyeliner was perfect. Bennie let her hair curl naturally and thought ChapStick was makeup.

She sipped her wine, feeling warm. There was no air-conditioning, and the kitchen was small and spare except for knobby wooden chairs and a dark wood table. A greenish glass fixture gave little light, and cracks zigzagged down the plaster like summer lightning. Still the cottage had a rustic charm, especially set in the rolling countryside of southeastern Pennsylvania, an hour or so outside of Philadelphia.

Alice plopped the chicken on the table, then sat down. "Don't panic, it's organic."

"You're eating healthy now, huh?"

"What do you mean? I always did. So, are you dating anybody?" Alice asked.

"No."

"How long's it been since you got laid?"

"Nice talk." Bennie bit into a potato, which tasted good. "If I remembered sex, I'd miss it."

"Whatever happened to that lawyer you lived with? What was his name again?"

"Grady Wells." Bennie felt a pang. She'd get over Grady, any decade now.

"So what happened?"

"Didn't work out." Bennie ate quickly. It had taken forever to get here from Philly, in rush-hour traffic. She wouldn't get home until midnight, which wasn't the way she wanted to end an exhausting week.

"Who'd you see after Grady?"

"Nobody serious."

"So he's the one that got away?"

Bennie kept her head down, hiding her expression. She couldn't understand how Alice always intuited so much about her. They'd never lived together, even as babies, though Alice claimed to have memories from the womb. Bennie couldn't even remember where she put her car keys.

"So, what's new in your life? Don't give me the official version. I read the website."

"Nothing but work. How about you?"

"I'm seeing a few nice guys, and I'm working out. I even joined a gym." Alice made a muscle of her slim arm. "See?"

"Good." Bennie had been an elite rower in her time, but she'd been too busy lately to exercise. "By the way, I hear great things about the job you're doing at PLG. Karen thinks you're terrific."

"Are you keeping tabs on me, now?"

"Of course not. I ran into her, at a benefit."

Alice arched an eyebrow. "Does she have to report to you just because you got me the job?"

"No, but if I see her, we talk. She knows me, like she knows most of the bar association. She has to, we all support the Public Law Group." Bennie felt a headache coming on. She'd lost a motion in court this morning, and it was turning out to be the high point of her day.

"So what did she say, exactly? She loves to gossip."

"It wasn't like that." Bennie sipped her wine, but it didn't help. "All she said was that they like you. They have you doing office administration, payroll, and personnel, in addition to the paralegal work."

"Not anymore. I quit."

"What?" Bennie said, blind-sided. "You quit PLG? When?"

"The other day. It wasn't for me, and the money sucked."

"But you have to start somewhere." Bennie couldn't hide her dismay. She'd stuck her neck out for Alice and now her friends at PLG would be left in the lurch. "They would have promoted you, in time."

"When, ten years?" Alice rolled her eyes. "The work was boring, and the people were *so* freaking annoying. I'd rather work with you, at Rosato & Associates."

Bennie's mouth went dry. She couldn't imagine Alice at her firm. "I don't need a paralegal."

"I can answer phones."

"I already have a receptionist."

"So fire her ass."

Bennie felt cranky. Maybe it was the headache, which was a doozy. "I like her. I would never do that to her."

. "Not even for me? We're the only family we have."

"No." Bennie tried to keep a civil tongue. Being her sister's keeper was getting old. "I can't fire her. I won't."

"Okay, fine, then think outside the box. You need somebody to run the office, don't you?"

"I run the office."

Alice snorted. "If you ask me, you could use a hand with personnel. Those girls who work for you need a life lesson, especially the little one, Mary DiNunzio. Time for girlfriend to grow up."

"That's not true." Bennie wished she hadn't come. Her stomach felt queasy. Her appetite had vanished. She set down her fork. "DiNunzio's a good lawyer. She should make partner next month."

"Whatever, then I'll be your assistant. I'll take ninety grand, to start."

"Listen, I can't always be the solution to your problems." Bennie's head thundered. "I got you a job, and you quit it. If you want another job, go out and find one."

"Thanks, Mom." Alice smiled sourly. "The economy's in the toilet, if you haven't noticed."

"You should have thought of that before, and you'll find something, if you try. You went to college, and you have lots of . . . abilities and, oh, my head. . . ." Suddenly the kitchen whirled like spin art, and Bennie collapsed onto the table. Her face landed on the edge of her dirty plate, and her hand upset her water glass.

"Aww, got a headache?" Alice chuckled. "Too bad."

Bennie didn't know what was happening. She felt impossibly drunk. Her eyes wouldn't stay open.

"You're such a fool. You think I'd really want to work for you?"

Bennie tried to lift her head up, but couldn't. All her strength had left her body. Sound and colors swirled together.

"Give it up. It's over."

Bennie watched, helpless, as darkness descended.

Chapter Two

Bennie woke up, groggy. She opened her eyes but everything stayed pitch black. She didn't know where she was. She seemed to be lying down. Where was the kitchen? The house? Alice? She couldn't see anything. Was she asleep? She got up and *slam*!

"Ow!" she heard herself say, momentarily stunned. She slumped backwards, hitting the back of her head. On what? Where was she? Was she dreaming? Was she awake? One question chased the next in a crazy circle. It was so dark. If she was asleep, it was time to wake up.

She raised her hand and *bam*! Her fingers hit something hard, above her. She flashed on the dinner with Alice. That had happened, hadn't it? She hadn't dreamed it, had she? Her face had fallen onto the table, hitting her cheek.

Give it up. It's over.

Bennie tried to remember. Had she heard that? Had Alice said that? What the hell? Where was she? The only sound was her own breathing. She raised her arms, cautiously, and hit the thing on top of her. She felt along its surface with her fingertips. It was solid. Coarse. She pressed but it didn't move. She knocked it and heard a rap, like wood. It felt like a top.

A lid.

She didn't get it. She couldn't process it. Her arms were at an angle. The wood was less than a foot from her face. She flattened her arms against her sides. There was another surface under her fingertips, behind her. She spread her arms, running them along the surface behind her. More wood? She shifted her weight down, shimmying on her back. Her toes hit something. Her feet were bare, her shoes gone. She pointed her toes against whatever she had reached. It seemed like a bottom.

It's a box. Am I in a box?

She didn't understand. It couldn't be. She touched along her body from her neck to her knees. She had on her suit from work. Her skirt felt torn. Her knees hurt. There was wetness there. Blood? She told herself not to panic. The air felt close. She squinted against the darkness, but it was absolute.

She felt the lid. Her thoughts raced ahead of her fingers. The top was sealed. There was nothing inside the box. No air, food, water. No hole to breathe through. She forced herself to stay calm. She needed to understand what was going on. It wasn't a dream, it was real. She couldn't believe it and she could, both at once. Was she really in a box? Would Alice come get her out? Would anybody else?

A sense of dread crept over her. She hadn't told anybody at the office where she was going. It was Friday night, and the associates had scattered. DiNunzio had taken Judy Carrier home to her parents' for dinner. Anne Murphy was out of the country for summer vacation, as was Lou Jacobs, her firm's investigator. Bennie's best friend, Sam Freminet, was in Maui, and she wasn't close to anybody else. Nobody would realize that she was missing until Monday morning.

She exploded in panic, yelling and pounding the lid with both hands. It didn't budge. She kept pounding with all her might, breaking a sweat. The lid still didn't move. She felt the seams with shaking fingers. She couldn't tell how it was sealed. She didn't hear a nail or anything else give way.

She pushed and pounded, then started kicking, driving her bare toes into the lid. It didn't move but she kept going, powered by sheer terror, and in the next minute she heard herself screaming, even though the words shamed her.

"Please, Alice, help!"

Chapter Three

Alice dried the Pyrex dish and placed it where she'd found it in the cabinet, then folded the dishtowel over the handle of the oven, the way it had been. She went to the table, straightened the stack of paid bills, and squared the corners, as she had found them.

The name on the mail read Ms. Sally Cavanaugh, and Ms. Cavanaugh would never know that while she was in the Poconos, a random woman had entered her house through an unlocked window and served wine à la Rohypnol in her kitchen. That's what she got for broadcasting her vacation plans all over the local post office. Alice had taken a train from Philly to the little town, scoped it out until she found an empty house, then taken a cab here in the dark, so nobody would see her.

She went to the living room, sliding her cell phone from her shorts. She flipped it open with a thumb and pressed until she found the photo. She had hauled Cavanaugh's things up from the basement, put them back in the living room, and compared the scene with the photo to make sure it was all in order; family and Siamese cat photos on the end tables, quilted knitting bag next to the worn brown chair, bestselling novels stacked on the credenza.

She picked up her black cloth bag and Bennie's messenger bag, then locked the front door by pressing the button on its knob. She twisted the deadbolt to lock, slid up the screen on the window, then climbed onto the porch, closing the window behind her. It was already dark because it had taken her so long to get rid of Bennie. A yellow bug light shone by the door, but no one was around to see her anyway. A thick woods screened the house from view, and it was surrounded by horse pastures. The air was humid and smelled like horse manure. She hurried down the porch steps, her footfalls pounding on the wood. She wasn't sorry to leave the country.

She dug her hand into the messenger bag and found the keys to Bennie's maroon Lexus, glistening in the driveway. She hit the button on the fob, opened the door, and jumped inside. She twisted on the ignition, reversed out of the driveway, then drove onto the private dirt road, spraying dirt and stones. She followed the road as it wound through the woods, passing battered black mailboxes until she reached the main road, then the highway. The air-conditioning blasted cold, and her tank top was finally drying. She'd worked up a sweat dragging Bennie into the backseat.

She hit the gas and relaxed into the ride. Everything was going according to plan. She'd been working at PLG during the day, but started moonlighting with a side business of her own, managing two women who sold Xanax, Ambien, Vikes, and Oxys to housewives at a gym and an upscale boutique. She fell into it when she met her boyfriend Q, who ran a full-scale operation all over the Northeast. He supplied her, but he would've taken a cut if he knew how much she really charged. The ladies who lunch weren't driving their Land Rovers to 52nd and Diamond for their Lexapro. But last week, she'd taken one risk too many.

Men.

Bad boys were her weakness, and though she'd had a good thing going with Q, even the CEO gets boring after a while. She'd hooked up with one of Q's runners, Jimmy, and they had some fun for a few weeks, on the down. But when Jimmy didn't show up to meet her, two nights ago, she guessed what must've happened. Q was a badass and he wouldn't stop until he'd disappeared her, too. He had people everywhere, and if one of his crew ever got ahold of her, she'd beg them not to take her alive. Bottom line, she had to get away, so she decided to become her rich sister long enough to take her money and run. The scam shouldn't take more than a few days. Alice would have killed Bennie but she didn't want to see her face on a dead body, especially not in that horrible suit.

Who still shops at Brooks?

She hit the gas, feeling her pulse quicken as the car accelerated through the dark night, over open road. She stayed the speed limit, but it was killing her. She loved to go fast, she fed on the sensation. She always wanted faster, bigger, better, newer, harder. She moved on when she got bored or restless, she specialized in cutting her losses. Life wasn't a dress rehearsal after all, and Alice lived hers to the fullest. She couldn't help the way she was. It was all because of her childhood, which was too damn good.

She sped along, thinking of her parents, John and Vilna Connelly, proprietors of the Connelly Insurance Agency, in Vineland, New Jersey. They'd lived a small, quiet life, taking good care of her, giving her the requisite pink bedroom in their split-level, sending her to the local public school, and making sure she had all the right lessons, but she never loved them. She didn't feel connected to them at all, probably because she knew inside that she wasn't.

She had grown up feeling apart from them, even before she ever heard the word "adoption." She knew she didn't look like them; she was blond and they were both dark-haired, and she surpassed them in height as early as middle school. The biggest difference was temperament; she was big, loud, and wanted everything, and they were small, meek, and wanted nothing. But every time she had asked them if she was adopted, they'd denied it, and even now, she wasn't angry that they lied, just that they were so bad at it. And when they'd died together a few years ago, in a car accident with a drunk driver, she went to their funeral and could barely squeeze out a tear.

She reached into the messenger bag, fumbled around for a Kleenex, spit on it, and wiped off her makeup. Then she lowered the window to ruin her blow-dry, and by the time she got to Philly, her hair was as curly as Bennie's. She steered into her exclusive neighborhood in Fairmount, near her beloved Schuylkill River. The houses were colonial with painted shutters, and BMWs and

SUVs lined the street. She pulled into a parking space, twisted on the interior light, and smiled at the reflection in the rearview mirror. She looked exactly like Bennie, at least from the neck up.

"Hi, I'm Bennie Rosato," she said, practicing in the quiet car. "Pleased to meet you, I'm Bennie. Bennie Rosato."

She cut the ignition, grabbed her cloth bag and Bennie's messenger bag, got out of the car, and chirped it locked. Two men walked past her, talking, and she kept her head down. She hoped she didn't run into any of Bennie's neighbors because her twin never dressed this good. She reached Bennie's house, a three-story brick rowhouse with shiny black shutters, climbed the front steps, and picked the key that said Schlage as the house key. It slid easily into the lock, and she opened the front door, went in, and let it close behind her. She felt for a light switch, flipped it on, and stopped dead. She had forgotten one thing. Bennie had a big dog.

She stiffened as the dog lifted its head from its paws, got to his feet, and walked slowly toward her. His toenails clicked on the hardwood floor. His head hung low. His tail wasn't wagging, and he didn't look happy. The dog knew she wasn't Bennie, no matter what she looked like.

And in the next second, he started to growl.

Chapter Four

Mary DiNunzio was supposed to go down the shore for the weekend, but she was dying to meet her mysterious cousin, a widow named Fiorella Bucatina, in visiting from Italy. Everybody had crowded into her parents' kitchen, stuffing it like a Marx Brothers stateroom, if the Marx Brothers were Italian-American. No matter how many people came over for dinner, her parents never ate in the dining room, which was reserved for Christmas, Easter, or some other occasion when something really good happened to Jesus Christ.

The kitchen was humid because Mary's parents didn't believe in air conditioners, microwaves, or anything invented after the demise of the Latin Mass. An ancient coffeepot percolated on the stove near photographs of the Holy Trinity—Sinatra, JFK, and Pope John—and a cast-iron switchplate held laminated Mass cards and split fronds of palm. The DiNunzios owned the Kitchen That Time Forgot, and Mary wouldn't have it any other way.

Fresh basil, frying meatballs, and locatelli scented the air, and Tony Bennett was on the radio, but nobody could hear him because they were talking over each other. Mary's father, Mariano "Matty" DiNunzio, hadn't gotten a new battery for his hearing aid, so he was shouting about the Phillies with her boyfriend Anthony.

Her mother Vita stood at the oven in her flowered housedress, stirring a dented pot of bubbling gravy and gesturing with her wooden spoon at Mary's best friend, Judy Carrier. Judy had long ago become an honorary DiNunzio, despite her white-blond hair, Delft blue eyes, and upturned nose, though she always joked that they kept her around because she could reach the top shelf.

Suddenly there was a noise, and everybody turned at the sound of footsteps coming downstairs. Mary couldn't help but feel a tingle of anticipation. "Ma," she said, "is that Fiorella, queen of the witches?"

"*Basta!*" Her mother's brown eyes flared behind her thick trifocals. "No make fun. Donna Fiorella, she has a strong powers, she's a mos' powerful *strega* in Abruzzi!"

"Not stronger than you, Ma." Mary didn't like her mother thinking that her superpowers were inferior.

"*Sì, sì,* yes. Her husband, he had the cancer. Donna Fiorella, she made it go away, *pffft!*"

"But he died, didn't he?"

"*Sì,* a truck, it hit him."

"VEET, I'M SO HUNGRY!" her father shouted, his hearing aid a plastic parenthesis behind his ear. He was dressed for the special occasion in his white short-sleeved shirt and baggy dark trousers. "WHY'S SHE TAKIN' SO LONG?"

"Shhhh, Matty!" her mother said, brandishing her spoon like a lethal weapon.

"I've never met a witch queen," Judy whispered.

"SHE'S NOT A WITCH QUEEN," Mary and her father replied in unison, but only one of them was loud enough to be heard. A union tilesetter his working life, her father didn't share her mother's folkloric beliefs, but he loved her enough to tolerate them. Together a billion years, Mary's parents were the Chang and Eng of married couples.

"Think she'll look like Strega Nonna?" Judy asked. "A little old lady in orthopedic shoes?"

"No doubt." Mary smiled. "I wish Bennie were here. She should see a little DiNunzio magic. Maybe if I had a witch in my corner, it would help me make partner."

Judy laughed. "She's probably still at work. Why don't we call her? She might like a nice home-cooked meal."

"Nah, she's too busy. She wouldn't want to come."

"*Maria,* shhh!" her mother hissed. She'd had her hair done at the corner beauty parlor, where they teased it into a stormcloud to cover her bald spot. She patted it into place as Fiorella Bucatina appeared in the doorway and struck a pose.

The sight of her silenced all the chatter.

Chapter Five

Bennie stopped pounding on the lid, her chest heaving. Her cheeks burned, blood rich. Her heart hammered. Heat thickened the air. Her fists stung, her arms ached. Sweat drenched her, gluing her shirt to her body. Panic lurked beneath the surface of her consciousness, like an undertow. Why would Alice do this to her?

Bennie wracked her brain, thinking back. She'd believed she was an only child until Alice had called from prison a few years ago, saying she was charged with murder and needed a lawyer. Bennie would never forget seeing her for the first time, over a filthy counter in a no-contact interview room. Alice had on an orange jumpsuit, and her hair was short then, scissored into crude layers and dyed a brassy red. Still, Bennie had taken one look at her and had seen a mirror image. She'd been struck dumb, but Alice had spoken with confidence, words that marked a turning point in Bennie's life.

Pleased to meet you. I'm your twin.

Bennie had proved that Alice wasn't guilty in court, but it had been harder to prove that Alice was really her twin. Her mother, Carmela Rosato, was the only parent Bennie had ever known, but by the time Alice surfaced, her mother's depression had worsened to the point that she'd been hospitalized, comatose and unable to speak. Bennie never met her father, one William Winslow, who hadn't stayed around long enough to marry her mother, and she'd had to track him down to verify Alice's story. It had turned out to be true. Their mother had given birth to two babies but kept only one, because she was broke and battling depression, so she'd kept Bennie and put Alice up for adoption. So to Bennie, Alice was a complete and total stranger, who just happened to be family.

Bennie had felt so strange when she learned she had a twin; like being found when she didn't know she was lost. She didn't remember even meeting her father, and her whole life, it had been just her and her mother, alone against the world. In the beginning, her mother worked as a secretary, but in time, her mental illness overcame her, inching over her like a shadow growing longer toward day's end. She'd gotten professional help while she was still well enough to ask for it, and Bennie remembered going with her, and eventually taking her, to a series of doctors and hospitals who experimented with drugs, dosages, and finally, electroshock.

All the time her mother had grown less and less capable, and Bennie had taken care of her, instead of the other way around, even from middle school. The news that there had been two children, twins, helped Bennie understand her mother's downward slide, because such a devoted mother would be wracked with guilt over giving up her own child. Bennie had plenty of guilt herself, when the fact of Alice came to light. She'd tried to compensate for being the one chosen, but Alice had come in and out of her life only to make trouble. Their relationship was tumultuous, but after one big blow-up, Alice finally had redeemed herself. They'd made peace, and Bennie had gotten her sister the job at PLG.

As for your life, it's over.

Bennie still couldn't understand why this was happening, now. She'd had no warning, could fathom no reasons except ancient jealousy. Payback. Resentment. Her thoughts wandered, and she couldn't understand how in God's name she'd let this happen. She should've been on her guard. She should've known better. There was a time, early on in their relationship, when she hadn't trusted Alice at all, even before she'd glimpsed how dark her soul could be. Like a test in school, it turned out that the first answer was the correct one.

In those early days, Bennie had viewed Alice as the typical prisoner who would say or do anything to get a lawyer, and her story about who had really committed the murder was almost a stereotype. The murder victim was a cop who was also her live-in boyfriend, and Alice claimed she was framed for the murder by a conspiracy of corrupt cops. Bennie thought back to how Alice had sucked her into the representation.

At their first meeting, Alice had given her a photo that she said was their father, William Winslow, holding the two of them as babies. She claimed he'd given her the picture during one of his visits to the prison. Bennie had never seen a picture of her father, much less talked with him in the flesh, and even though the man in the photo had light hair and blue eyes, she immediately suspected that Alice was trying to reel her in using the photo, like bait wriggling on a barbed hook.

Alice had followed it up with a second photo, one of her mother. The photo was also allegedly from her father, and on the back it read *To Bill,* in her mother's handwriting. It showed her mother sitting with girlfriends on stools at a luncheonette, at about age sixteen or seventeen years old. Her pretty face was half-turned to the camera, which caught her lively expression, vivid with the mischief of youth.

The picture came as a revelation because Bennie had seen her mother only in heartbreaking decline, but even so, she'd wondered if the photo was a fake and the handwriting on its back a forgery. She hadn't credited Alice's version of its origin, guessing that it had come from one of the other girls on the stools.

She tried to remember at which point she'd lost her objectivity about Alice. Even though Alice's story about the cop's death turned out to be true, and she hadn't killed him, it didn't mean that she wasn't a con artist. And later, something happened that made Bennie wonder if Alice really had murdered someone, at least once in her life. Before now.

Oh my God. I can't breathe.

Bennie inhaled once, then again. Her lungs didn't fill. She opened her mouth but still couldn't get a good breath. Her heart fluttered, arrhythmic and panicky. Reality came back into terrifying focus. How long until she ran out of oxygen? How long could she live without food? How long without water? She had no sense of time. Her watch was gone.

Panic washed over her, drowning any power of reason. She started panting. She couldn't get her breath and she couldn't control herself anymore. She couldn't think of anything but being sealed in a box until she suffocated. Tears of fright sprang to her eyes, and she began pounding on the lid again, then kicking up with her feet and knees. She screamed and hollered and prayed that somebody would hear her or Alice would come back.

She pounded on and on, fighting for her life against the darkness, unyielding.

Chapter Six

Alice backed up against the front door of Bennie's house, edging away from the growling dog. She dropped her bags, shaking as the dog sniffed her sneakers, pressing his nose against the droplets of blood. He growled louder, and when his black lips curled so his teeth showed, she forgot her fear and kicked him. He yelped and sprawled backwards, his back legs slipping out from under him, then her instincts took over.

She went after him, kicking him again and again, connecting twice with his chest, but he ran yelping from the living room. She chased him to the back of the house, where there was a dark kitchen. She flicked on the light, and in the corner was an open door to a basement. She could hear him falling down the stairs, whimpering, so she slammed the door closed behind him. She leaned on the door-jamb, panting and listening. If the dog knew what was good for him, he'd bleed to death. She didn't need a complication like that right now.

She'd never been in Bennie's house and looked around. The kitchen was modern and clean, with white enamel cabinets and shiny black-and-red granite counters. Dog photos lined the window-sill, and a framed rowing poster hung above a rectangular cherry table, set aglow by a glass pendant lamp shaped like a red teardrop. She returned to the living room and checked it out; tan couch with dark end tables, a matching coffee table, an entertainment center that held books, a TV, and a stereo. Bottom line, it was a nice room, but it wasn't her taste at all.

She would have gone for a leather sectional sofa, maybe in black, and cool glass tables with chrome edges. She would have had a much bigger TV and a larger house, for parties. The two of them couldn't be more different, and if they hadn't gotten the blood test, Alice never would have believed they were related, much less twins. She had hardly believed it when she found she had a twin, especially one as useful as a lawyer, supposedly brilliant.

Their father appeared out of the woodwork, when she was in jail, to tell her about Bennie. It turned out that he'd been following both his daughters' lives, even though he never showed himself. He was trying to save her life, and it came at just the right time, before her trial. She went online and read everything she could about the famous Bennie Rosato, and when they sat face-to-matching-face, she claimed to love hazelnut coffee, sports, and big dogs, just like Bennie.

Alice had even pretended to care about their mother, because any idiot could see that Bennie was all about old Carmela. Just like she could hear in Bennie's questions that she wanted to know about the father who left them alone with a mentally ill mother. So she fed Bennie what little information she had about him, filling in the blanks with fantasy. She leaned on the twin thing, which put Bennie on the defensive from day one. She made Bennie feel guilty because she hadn't been abandoned, even though Bennie had the worse childhood of the two, taking care of that crazy mom and flat broke. She'd even tried to convince Bennie that she'd been born underweight as the result of something called "twin transfusion syndrome," where twins share the placenta in the womb, so one twin's blood goes to nourish the other. So it was fate that she would end up standing in Bennie's house, about to take over her life. It was Bennie's own fault, for being such a sucker.

Alice went to the front door, picked up the messenger bag, took out Bennie's wallet and checkbook, then grabbed her black cloth bag and headed upstairs.

She had banking to conduct, after all.

Chapter Seven

Mary blinked as Fiorella Bucatina posed in the threshold, placing a hand on each doorjamb. Fiorella was in her seventies, but her skin was preternaturally unlined, though it didn't look Botoxed or lifted, and her hair, a rich espresso brown, had no gray at all. A chic coif emphasized her lovely, almond-shaped eyes, prominent cheekbones, and Cupid's bow mouth lipsticked a come-hither crimson. She was petite, and her black knit dress showed off curves that could shame a fertility goddess. The woman was no Strega Nonna. On the contrary, she was Strega Sophia Loren.

"Wow," Judy said, and Anthony's mouth dropped open.

"HIYA, FIORELLA," Mary's father said, rising.

Her mother faced Fiorella Bucatina with a nervous smile. *"Per favore,* Donna Fiorella, sit, *per favore. Ti piaci?"*

"Thank you." Fiorella sashayed to the chair and sat down as if it were a throne. Gold bangles jangled on one slim forearm, and she had sensational legs that ended in black slingbacks.

"Donna Fiorella," her mother said, gesturing, "please, meet . . . *ecce mia sposa Mariano e mia figlia, Maria."*

"I prefer English." Fiorella's speech bore no trace of an Italian accent. In fact, she sounded like Queen Elizabeth, or maybe Madonna.

"IT'S A PLEASURE." Her father extended his hand, and Fiorella's red-lacquered nails spread around his fist like talons.

"I had no idea you were so handsome, Mariano."

Her father blushed all the way to his liver spots. "WELCOME. IT'S ALWAYS NICE TO SEE FAMILY."

"It's lovely to meet you, finally." Fiorella smiled seductively, and Mary stepped in.

"Fiorella, this is my boyfriend Anthony and my friend Judy, from work."

"PLEASE, SIDDOWN, EVERYBODY." Her father gestured Mary, Anthony, and Judy into their seats. "FIORELLA, SORRY TO HEAR ABOUT YOUR HUSBAND."

"Thank you, Mariano. This is a very sad time for me."

"IT'S A SIN." Her father's expression fell into sympathetic lines, and his shoulders collapsed like an old house. Her mother winced, then fluttered too quickly to the stove, where she slid a floured sheet of homemade gnocchi into the boiling water. They landed with a steamy *hiss* in the sudden silence. It was a moment slow to pass, and Mary knew they were all thinking of Mike, her late husband, an elementary school teacher who had been killed, and whose death Mary's parents had taken very hard. It had happened years ago, but Mary still thought of him every day, too.

"FIORELLA, HOW LONG WERE YOU MARRIED?"

"Three months. Can you imagine what that was like for me, losing my beloved husband, as a new bride?" Fiorella touched her father's arm, and Mary thought her hand lingered too long, so she interrupted again.

"Were you married before?" she asked

"Enzo was my fifth husband," Fiorella answered, without batting a mascaraed eye.

If her father was shocked, he didn't let it show. "VITA AND ME, WE GOT MORE MILES THAN A CHEVY."

Everybody laughed, including Fiorella, who said, "Mariano, you have such a wonderful sense of humor. If I had been married to you, I'm sure I would have been married only once."

"HA!" Her father went to the stove. "I'LL GET THE COFFEE."

"I love your dress," Judy said, and Fiorella lifted an eyebrow.

"Thank you. It's Armani. Are you interested in fashion?"

"Uh, a little."

"I see that."

Fiorella kept eyeing Judy, or more accurately, her clothes. Judy had come straight from the office, so she still had on her work clothes—an oversized yellow T-shirt, a jeans miniskirt, and red patent clogs. Her hair, cut in its trademark choppy bowl, was dyed only one color today, crayon yellow. Mary was by now used to Judy's eccentric wardrobe, but this morning she couldn't resist telling her she looked like a McDonald's franchise.

"Do you always dress so?"

"Sure." Judy nodded happily, but Mary bit her tongue. She was starting to think that Fiorella was Strega Anna Wintour.

"HERE'S COFFEE!" Her father poured a glistening arc of percolated coffee into Fiorella's cup, then took care of everybody else. "CREAM AND SUGAR'S ONNA TABLE."

Fiorella was still scrutinizing Judy. "I must say, I'm absolutely appalled by your appearance."

Mary felt compelled to defend her friend. "Excuse me, Judy's my best friend, and nobody can criticize her clothes but me."

Her mother froze, and her father and Anthony blinked. Fiorella recoiled, and Mary knew it hadn't come out the way she intended, so she tried again.

"I mean, Judy can dress any way she pleases. She's a genius lawyer and a great painter, and at the office, we value her brains more than her looks."

"I wasn't referring to her clothes, but her health." Fiorella turned coolly to Judy. "Your head aches, does it not?"

"Frankly, yes."

"Someone is thinking ill of you. They are giving you the evil eye."

Her mother gasped. The gnocchi pot bubbled like a cauldron. *"Deo,* the *malocchio?"*

Her father's resigned expression said, *Here we go.* Mary and Anthony exchanged looks because they knew what was coming. Mary's mother could cast off the evil eye, too. In fact, she was probably kicking herself for missing the diagnosis.

But Judy was worried. "Am I going to be okay?"

"Yes, but only if you listen to me. I will keep you safe from harm." Fiorella reached across the table, her bracelets jangling. "Give me your hand, my dear. I can help you. I am the most powerful witch in all of Abruzzi, the witch of all witches."

Mary said nothing, except to thank God that she hadn't invited Bennie to dinner. It would have killed her partnership chances.

Magic was one thing, but crazy was quite another.

Chapter Eight

Bennie lay in the box, exhausted and in pain. Pounding and screaming had burned off her panic. She swallowed hard, her mouth parched. Sweat drenched her. She'd had to go to the bathroom. She remained still, breathing shallowly. She needed to conserve her air and her energy again, so she could try harder.

She wondered where the box could be. People might hear her screaming, unless the box was in the basement of Alice's house. It was the one place that they hadn't gone, but Alice was way too smart for that. Alice was brilliant, despite appearances. Bennie had learned that the hard way a long time ago, when Alice played her during her murder case.

Bennie remembered how she'd started to lose her way, proving Grady right that if she took on the representation, she'd have no professional distance. She'd found out that Alice had been cheating on the murdered cop and she knew it wouldn't have struck a sympathetic note with the jury. So Bennie did what few other criminal defense lawyers would have done. She cut her hair as short as Alice's, and they dressed alike at trial, so they sat at counsel table side-by-side, like a double image. She figured that the jury would see the identity between them and project the goodwill that Bennie had earned onto her less likable twin. That her gambit had worked hadn't made it any less uncharacteristic, and looking back, Bennie realized that during that trial, at some time she couldn't pinpoint, she'd shed her own identity and merged in some uncanny way with her twin.

Now, she couldn't believe how far it had gone. Couldn't believe that she had ever wanted to be with Alice, much less *be* her. It was Bennie's loss of perspective that had put her inside a box that was God knows where, with her very life in jeopardy.

Suddenly, in the quiet, she heard a noise, like a scratching. She waited, then heard it again. It was coming from outside the lid, right near her head. Was Alice scratching on the lid? Why? How? She listened for the noise to come again, but the only sound was her own panting. Then just as abruptly, the scratching returned.

"Stop it!" she screamed. "Let me out! What are you doing? Stop it, stop it, stop it!"

But the scratching didn't stop, so Bennie started pounding with all of her might.

Chapter Nine

Alice found Bennie's home office, dumped the cloth bag on the floor, and sat down at her laptop, switching on the desk lamp. She hit a key and the screen came to life, but it asked for a password. She thought a second. She had no idea what password Bennie used, and she didn't know the name of the dog. She took a guess and typed in their mother's name, Carmela.

INVALID PASSWORD.

She looked through the papers on the desk, but there was no list of passwords on a sheet of paper or random Post-it. The desk had file drawers on the right, and she opened the first, searched through manila folders stuffed with bills, bank statements, and legal papers, but found no passwords file. She went through the second drawer, but still no luck. She sat back in the chair, her gaze falling on an old-fashioned Rolodex. She flipped through the business cards, then on impulse, skipped ahead to P. The first card was handwritten, and at the top it read Passwords.

Bingo.

She skimmed down to Laptop, Home—2424bearmom. She typed it in and the screensaver appeared. She spotted Quicken, clicked it, and read the screen. USABank Household Account, USABank Business Account, and USABank 1717 Building Account. She skimmed the online registers as her heart beat a little faster. There were three major accounts with nine subaccounts, all at USABank. She logged on to the Internet, typed in USABank.com, and clicked Online Banking, but the page asked for her username and password. She went back to the Rolodex, looked up USABank, got the username Bennie Rosato and the password Bearly01, then went back to the bank's site and plugged it in. She clicked onto the main page, where her gaze shot like a bullet to the balance.

Three million dollars and change.

She hadn't known for sure that Bennie was a multi-millionaire, but she wasn't surprised. She clicked on the first account, the Home account that was divided into Personal and Business, and checked the balance—$78,016. The second account, Rosato & Associates, had subaccounts titled Payroll, Expenses, and Travel & Entertainment, with a balance of $2,437,338. She clicked on the third account, 1717 Building, which she knew from the website was Bennie's new office building. It had subaccounts entitled Rent, Expenses, and Miscellaneous, and the balance was $536,393. She checked the bottom of the page, for liabilities.

Zero. None. Nada. *Zip.*

She should have known as much. Bennie didn't have a mortgage for the house or office building, nor loans of any kind, not even a home equity or car loan. Bennie played everything safe, so she wouldn't carry a debt load if she could help it. Everything was bought and paid for, and the girl was a saver, which explained her wardrobe.

Alice considered the implications. All of Bennie's money at USA-Bank was liquid, and the online transfer functions had been enabled, so any or all of the money could be transferred among the different accounts or out of the bank. She wouldn't dream of doing it from a home laptop, not with assets this large, and she'd start tomorrow. She had a plan, which was to set up an offshore account and move the money to it, then leave the country. It would take a few days to accomplish, but she could impersonate Bennie for a day or two, until the jig was up.

She thought a minute. Bennie should have some stock and investment accounts elsewhere, or maybe T-bills and bonds. That money would be more difficult to convert to cash quickly enough, but she opened Outlook and skimmed Bennie's email anyway. There was a note from someone named Sam Freminet, a friend on vacation in Maui, and Bill Pontius of Plexico Plastics, a client who needed to reschedule his deposition, and after the first twenty emails, Alice knew everything about Bennie's work and personal life, emphasis on work. She couldn't find anything from an investment house, another bank, or a stockbroker.

But she'd keep looking.

Chapter Ten

Mary would have been mortified when Fiorella announced she wanted to cast off Judy's evil eye, but she knew that their friendship was strong enough to survive a family exorcism.

"Excuse me." Fiorella glanced around the table. "Everyone but Judy must leave immediately."

"Why?" Mary asked, surprised. Her mother never made anybody leave when she was casting off spells. That was the kind of professionalism that ran in the DiNunzio women.

"You must do as I say or I cannot help your friend."

"Maybe we should forget this," Judy said. "It's just a little headache, a sinus thing. I'm fine."

"No, you are not fine." Fiorella shook her head. "I know better. Please, everyone, leave immediately."

"Mary has to stay." Judy clutched Mary's arm. "I want her here."

"She cannot." Fiorella frowned. "Only you and I may be present."

Mary said, "She'll take her chances, and everybody else can wait in the living room."

"I'll be in the living room, no problem." Anthony rose, but her father looked longingly at Mary's mother, or more accurately, at the stove.

"CAN I GET A MEATBALL TO GO, VEET?"

"*No, no,* go! Come, Matty, Anthony, we go." Her mother lowered the flame under the burners and wiped her hands hastily on her apron. It had taken her three hours to make homemade gnocchi, and now it would taste like wallpaper paste.

Fiorella raised a hand. "Vita, before you leave, bring me what I need."

"*Sì, sì.*" Her mother hurried to the cabinet, extracted a white bowl, filled it with water, then placed it before Fiorella, who merely sniffed.

"Vita, the olive oil should have come first. Get me the olive oil."

Judy shot Mary a look that said, *Is she going to eat me?*

"*Mi dispiace,* sorry, Donna Fiorella." Her mother turned to a shelf over the oven, grabbed a big tin of Bertoli olive oil, and toted it to the table.

Fiorella frowned. "The olive oil must be the best."

"Is all we have, Donna Fiorella." Her mother's hands fluttered to her chest. "Is all we use."

"Leave, Vita." Fiorella sighed heavily as her mother hurried from the kitchen. "Judy, place both hands on the table, with your palms down. Close your eyes. Mary, you, too."

Judy obeyed, but Mary tilted her head down and watched as Fiorella picked up the olive oil and poured some into the bowl. The oil spread over the water, forming a map of Italy, but that could've been Mary's imagination.

Fiorella said, "Judy, I'm preparing what I need to help you, but you must clear your head."

"My head is—"

"Speak only when I tell you to. This is very important. Listen to me and clear your head."

Judy clammed up, and Mary watched as Fiorella stabbed the water with her scary thumbnail and swirled the oil and water together, though they didn't mix. They were like, well, oil and water.

"Now I will begin the prayer for you, for God to deliver you from the evil that threatens you." Fiorella kept stirring the olive oil, making a culinary whirlpool. "I will say a secret prayer, known only to me. It will be in Italian, so you won't understand it, but you are not meant to."

Mary suppressed an eye-roll as Fiorella reached over the table, made the Sign of the Cross on Judy's forehead, and began praying softly, in dialect. Then she seemed to notice a stain on her dress, below her breast, and kept praying as she reached for her napkin, dipped it in a glass of water, and swabbed at the stain. When she had finally blotted it dry, she stopped praying.

Mary frowned, disapproving. Fiorella couldn't deliver a full-strength prayer if she was playing with her Armani. She wasn't a witch queen, she was a designer fraud.

"Ladies, open your eyes." Fiorella's lipsticked mouth curved into a smile. "Judy, you feel better now, don't you?"

"I do!" Judy blinked, then broke into a grin. "Thank you!"

"Yes, thank you," Mary managed to say, but now she was wondering about Fiorella Bucatina.

And she worried that her parents were about to have bigger problems than mushy gnocchi.

Chapter Eleven

Bennie waited for the scratching to start again. It was driving her crazy, and she wondered if that was why Alice was doing it. Her palms stung from pounding on the lid. Her knees ached, her feet throbbed. Urine soaked the back of her skirt. The box reeked of sweat. She had a hard time breathing.

She tried to get a grip on herself. Something about the scratching wasn't like Alice, who always had a purpose for what she did, an angle she was working to get something she wanted. Alice was an excellent planner, she just didn't dress like one.

Bennie remembered at trial, toward the end, the prosecution had produced a surprise witness, the proverbial jailhouse snitch who falsely testified that Alice had admitted she'd killed the cop and later recanted. Bennie was sure that Alice had gotten her to take back her story. She confronted Alice, only to realize that she had engineered both days of testimony, the original confession and the recanting, which left the prosecution's case in shambles. Although Bennie knew Alice wasn't guilty of the murder, she hadn't known Alice had her own back-up plan to ensure her acquittal. It showed Bennie just how long-range Alice's plans could be, and how purposeful.

Bennie frowned, coming out of her reverie to hear a new noise, a rumbling that sounded far away. She closed her eyes and tried to listen. It could have been a truck going by, but it didn't disappear.

Suddenly the scratching started again, but it was faster, which terrified her. If it wasn't Alice scratching, what was it? And what was the rumbling? Were they the same thing, related or not?

She started pounding and yelling again, fighting against the maddening noises, the confusion, and the pain.

Chapter Twelve

Alice walked to Bennie's bedroom, tossed her cloth bag onto the bed, and unzipped it, just to take a peek inside. Packets of twenties, tens, and fives sat jumbled together, wrapped by rubber bands. It was ten grand total, which seemed like chump change after Bennie's millions, but it was all in a day's work for Alice. She'd started embezzling from PLG six months ago, and before she left the other day, she'd grabbed a few hundred from petty cash. The rest was profit from her business. She wondered if Bennie had any cash lying around.

She walked to the dresser, where Bennie's jewelry box sat open like a treasure chest. A passport lay on top, but the first tray held only a few pairs of hoop earrings and two gold bangles. She looked through the trays, but all that was left was silver jewelry, not even the good kind from Tiffany's. She lifted up the tray and found a wad of bills. She grabbed the cash and counted over eight hundred bucks.

Now we're talking.

She searched the top drawer, but all it contained were cotton bras and panties, the kind that came three-in-a-pack at CVS. She opened the next drawer; no hidden cash, only thick T-shirts stacked in messy piles. The third drawer had jeans and sweaters. She went back to the bed, put the money in the cloth bag, zipped it closed, and stowed it under the bed, for later. Then she crossed to the closet and opened the louvered doors. Blue suit, blue suit, khaki suit, khaki suit, and yet another khaki suit. Underneath that, brown and black pumps, and a huge pile of sneakers. She grabbed one of the khaki jackets and tried it on over her black tank, then went to the bathroom and checked her reflection in the mirror. She looked more Century 21 than Bennie Rosato, but it wasn't her clothes that were the problem.

She washed and dried her face, leaving leftover eyeliner on the towel. She wet her hair and rummaged through a bin of wide-tooth combs until she found a clip, then twisted her curls into a messy topknot, checking her reflection again.

It was Bennie Rosato, looking back at her.

Bingo.

Chapter Thirteen

Mary sat in the passenger seat, with Anthony driving and Judy in the back, sticking her yellow head between the seats like a very golden retriever. "Can you believe her?" she said, after she'd told them about Fiorella. "She's no witch queen. What a fake!"

"I don't get you, babe." Anthony maneuvered around the double-parkers endemic to South Philly. "You knew she wasn't for real."

"I know, but I thought she thought she was a witch queen, and now I don't even think that!" Mary was confusing herself. "I don't like her staying in my parents' house, making my mother feel bad about herself. God knows what she's up to. She might steal something."

"Right. Count the spatulas." Anthony hit the gas, turning onto Broad Street, and Judy raised her hand.

"Um, hello. She did cure my headache, Mare. How did she do that?"

"She lucked out. My mother coulda done it, faster."

"Relax. I like your mother better, too. Anyway, if you ask me, the little flower was gettin' her flirt on."

"I know, right? She was hitting on my father."

"Good luck with that." Judy leaned closer. "How is Fiorella related to you anyway?"

"She's on my mother's side, in Italy. I think she's Little Uncle Geno's wife, but he died." Mary had long ago accepted that the DiNunzio family ties were a mystery. Her mother had two brothers, but Mary had thirty-six uncles. In the DiNunzio family, you qualified as an uncle if you were male, a family friend, and lived in the tri-state area.

"Was Geno husband number four?"

"No, two, I think. She gets around, evidently."

Judy snorted. "Who knew widow's weeds had spandex?"

Mary didn't laugh, looking outside the window. The shops along Broad had gone dark, except for the nail parlors and funeral homes, which seemed like the only two growth businesses in this economy. Whoever did nails for the dead would make a killing.

"Don't worry." Anthony patted her leg. "Did you tell your mother what happened with the stain?"

"No, I didn't get a minute alone with either of them."

"You should." Anthony steered the car onto Lombard. "Fiorella's ruining it for all home witches."

Mary didn't smile. "She was supposed to be praying to God to ward off the evil spirits."

"Isn't that ironic, if not heresy?"

"No," Mary and Anthony answered in unison. Mary loved that she didn't have to explain her family to him. His parents lived in South Philly, too, though their house was in Epiphany parish instead of St. Monica's, a two-block distance that made him a foreigner.

Judy asked, "Meanwhile, do you believe in evil, anyway?"

"Of course," Mary answered. "Evil exists in the world. Look at serial killers."

Anthony nodded. "And history. Hitler, Stalin, Pol Pot."

Judy scoffed. "But that's people. Evil resides in people. Anyone, given the right circumstances, is capable of evil. Evil is within us. That's what's so scary about it."

Mary turned around. "You really think that? You're capable of evil?"

"Yes. I'm human, and part of being human is evil, or at least the potential for it. Why, what do you think, Mare?"

All of them fell suddenly silent, and Mary sensed they were waiting for her answer. The car came to rest at a stoplight, bathing them in blood-red.

"I hope you're wrong," she said, in the dark light.

Chapter Fourteen

Bennie braced herself, with a bolt of new fear. All of a sudden, the box had started to vibrate. The scratching and rumbling had grown so loud they blasted in her ears. What was going on? The box shook harder, the noise intensified.

She hollered and pounded on the lid. Something was scratching on the lid. Just then she heard growling. It had to be an animal. Frantic, she pounded on the lid to scare it away, but it kept growling and scratching. The rumbling got louder and the shaking stronger. She kept pounding and screaming and fighting. She refused to die this way, spent, crying, broken, bleeding.

The growling and scratching grew frenzied, faster. It sounded as if the animal was trying to get away from the noise. She pounded harder, her heart hammering, her chest heaving, the wood shaking on all four sides.

Suddenly the scratching and the growling stopped, leaving only the rumbling, deafening. The animal had gotten away but she couldn't. The box shuddered like an earthquake.

She screamed at the top of her lungs as the box shook, rattling her teeth, jolting her bones. She gave way to a terror she could never have imagined, the unknown. She had no idea what was coming toward her. It had the force of a tornado, the power of an express train. The clamor intensified to ear-splitting levels. Her head slammed against the box. Her shoulder banged against the side. Roaring surrounded her, obliterating all other sounds. She didn't know if she was still screaming, because her cries disappeared into its unearthly maw.

Swallowing her whole.

Chapter Fifteen

It was a sunny morning, bright and early, and Alice locked Bennie's front door behind her, dropped the keys in her messenger bag, and trekked down the street, heading to the office in her Bennie Rosato costume: curly topknot, oversized Penn Rowing T-shirt, baggy khaki shorts, and old-school tan Birkenstocks that made her walk like a duck. No wonder her sister couldn't get laid.

She headed down the Parkway to the business district and in no time approached Bennie's building. Skyscrapers lined the street, and people filled the sidewalks, some slinging backpacks even though they were middle-aged, proof positive that they were lawyers. She knew the MO; to an attorney, the weekend was the time to work even harder.

"Hey, Bennie!" called a man, and Alice startled a moment, then flashed him her sister's big, easy smile.

"How've you been?"

"Great! Nice article in the *Journal*!"

"Don't believe a word of it!" Alice shot back, and the lawyer laughed and kept walking.

She powered ahead, channeling Bennie, and it worked like magic. Her duck-walk changed to a stride, and she eyed the lineup of shops and office buildings. Ahead should be number 1717, and though she'd never been to the new digs, she had a hunch which building was Bennie's. Most of the office buildings were modern with reflective windows, but one was smaller than the others, with a smooth limestone front and art deco–type brass plaques. Its entrance was a pair of old-fashioned glass doors, and their shiny brass handles glinted in the sun.

"Big Ben!" shouted a voice behind her. "Where's my hello?"

Alice glanced back, uncertain about the nickname. Behind her, an old man in a turquoise street-cleaner uniform was leaning on a pushbroom, and she waved at him, like Bennie. "Sorry! Didn't have my coffee yet!"

"I hear that!" he called back, grinning.

"Take care!"

"You, too!" Alice suppressed an eye-roll. The test-drive was going well, but she was feeling like a combination Mayor, Girl Scout, and Lawyer Barbie. She crossed the street, and next to the doors of the small building, a discreet brass sign read 1717, so she made a beeline for the entrance, opened the doors, and hit the lobby. A security guard, an older man with bifocals and a blue uniform, sat behind a wooden desk, reading a newspaper.

"That air-conditioning feels good, huh?" he called out, looking up.

"Sure does." Alice managed a smile, but remembered that Bennie used ex-cops as guards, so this geezer was no dummy and she didn't know the building's security procedures. She wiped her forehead. "Boy, is it hot out."

"We shoulda taken vacation this week."

"Agree. I feel like Cinderella." Alice sneaked a glance at the guard's nameplate, STEVEN PALMIERI. She didn't know if he went by Steven or Steve, and she'd have to get the details right. "You want my license and registration, Officer Palmieri?"

"Nah, you're above the law, boss."

"Thanks." Alice walked past the desk.

"But sign in for me, will you?"

Alice froze. She had forgotten what Bennie's signature looked like. It would be on her driver's license, but that was in her wallet and the guard was already pushing the black log across the counter toward her.

"Need a pen?" he asked, handing her a Bic.

Chapter Sixteen

Mary was too nearsighted to read the bedside clock, but it was morning, she guessed around nine o'clock or so. The bedroom was bright, with the curtain over the air conditioner trying vainly to block the sun. Anthony snuggled with his back to hers, and she stayed still not to wake him up. They hadn't made love last night, and she knew why.

She'd been thinking of Mike, running a mental movie of their life together, until the inevitable unhappy ending. Their marriage had been cut short by his death, and even in their few years together, back when she was a rookie lawyer, he'd been so supportive of her, even bringing his grade-school class to the courtroom to watch her. He would have been thrilled that she was up for partner, cheering her every step of the way. Maybe that's why he'd been so much on her mind lately, and thoughts of him popped up at the strangest times, the ambush of true grief. She shouldn't have slept at Anthony's, but she hadn't wanted to make him drive her home so late. She should have known better, after meeting Fiorella, the woman who gave a bad name to widowhood and witchcraft.

Her gaze wandered over the neat modern dresser, bookshelf, treadmill, and a rack of free weights. It was a man's bedroom, and she felt like a hypocrite, in bed with one man, thinking of another.

She heard Anthony turning over, and in the next minute, he ran a palm along her bare shoulder.

"You up, babe?" he asked, his voice soft.

Mary considered not answering. She could pretend she was asleep. She had done it before. "Yeah," she answered after a minute.

"You hardly slept. You still thinking about that witch?"

No, that ghost. "Not really."

"Is it work?"

"Yeah." Mary went with the easy answer. They had been house-hunting, and that played into it, too. Everything was coming to a head at once, but she couldn't tell him that. The truth would cut too deep, and sometimes a lie was merciful.

"What's up at work?" Anthony threw an arm around her, drawing them together. "What's bugging you, the partnership thing?"

"Yes." Mary's thoughts turned to the office. Bennie had told her she'd decide whether to make Mary a partner in September. "She decides in, like, ten days, remember?"

"Sure. You going in today?"

"Yes, I have to. Sorry, I know it's Saturday."

"I figured. Will Bennie be in today?"

"She usually is, but I'm not sure. She never tells anybody anything, you know that."

"So if she's in, ask her. Go for it."

Mary shuddered. She was still intimidated by Bennie, who was older, smarter, and the best trial lawyer in the city. They rarely socialized, and as the boss, Bennie maintained a professional distance from the associates. "We don't really talk, except to say hi. Our practices are so separate, lately."

"So say, 'Hi, Bennie, you gonna make me a partner?'" Anthony kissed her neck. "Just do it. It weighs on your mind. Take a risk."

"But she hasn't even mentioned it. She may not even be thinking about it."

"Trust me, she is. Anybody who has to slice up another piece of the pie is thinking of it. Besides, it shows you have initiative. Ask her. You might be happily surprised."

Half an hour later, Mary was heading to work, standing in a

packed C bus, where the air-conditioning was set to Public Trans-
portation. She'd showered and put on a casual white dress with
flats, but still felt wilted as she slid her hand along the greasy overhead bar, picked her way through the dimpled arms, big bottoms,
and Payless sneakers, then fell into a seat by the window. Her hair
would explode in this humidity. Maybe she shouldn't talk to the
boss today. She didn't have partnership hair.

The bus lurched off, and she looked out a window smeared with
Vaseline, motor oil, or maybe anthrax. They passed a check cashing
agency, a dollar store, and a storefront diner, and she did a double-
take when she spotted a couple at one of the tables. It looked like
her father and Fiorella Bucatina were sitting at a table in the window.

"Pop?" Mary blurted out, standing up as the bus lurched forward. She bumped into a teenager, almost stumbling, then caught
herself on the overhead bar. "Excuse me, sorry."

"No problem."

Mary tried to get off, but a tourist with a suitcase blocked her
way. "Excuse me, I'm sorry, I have to get off."

"Hold your horses," the tourist said, but the bus was already
moving down Broad Street, rocking from side-to-side.

"Wait, please, stop the bus!" Mary wedged her way through the
crowd, but she couldn't reach the front fast enough. The diner re-
ceded into summer haze, so she hung on to the pole and dug into
her purse, found her cell phone, flipped it open, and pressed H for
Home.

"Allo?" her mother answered.

"Ma? It's me, how you doin'?"

"I'm a good, *Maria,* how you?"

"Good, Ma." Now that they had established everybody was good,
Mary got to the point. "Ma, where's Pop?"

"He's a no here. He take Fiorella to St. Agnes Hosp'."

So it was him! "The hospital? Why? What's wrong with her?"

"She cut her finger, onna bread knife."

"Was it bad?"

Her mother made a *pfft* noise. "No."

"Did he eat breakfast before he left?"

"*Sì*, what you tink, I no feed your fath'?"

"And Fiorella, too?"

"Sure, *sì*, why, *Maria*?"

Mary wasn't sure what to say. "Ma, I don't like Fiorella."

"Shh! *Maria*, no say such a thing, be nice, be good, she have such power, she hear."

"She'd hear us, on the *phone*? Mom, that's ridiculous. She's a fake." Mary told her mother what Fiorella did last night during the prayer, and nobody within earshot even looked over when she talked about the evil eye. They weren't all Italian, but every ethnicity had its own superstitions, which was what they contributed to America, in addition to better food.

"Shh, *Maria, basta,* is bad luck, *per favore,* no, shh. She's a nice, she got no family, no no-ting."

The bus was almost at Mary's stop. "Okay, Ma, tell Pop I said hi. I gotta go to work now."

"No work so hard. Is too hot. Come home. Eat."

Mary smiled, touched. Other people had parents who pushed them, but her earliest memory was her mother telling her that reading would ruin her eyes. "Bye, now, Ma. Love you."

"Love you, *Maria,* be good."

Mary pressed END, made her way to the front of the bus, and stepped out into the humidity, where her hair exploded.

Definitely not a good day to talk partnership.

Or maybe things couldn't get worse.

Chapter Seventeen

Bennie didn't know where she was, whether she was conscious or dreaming, alive or dead, but she didn't want it to stop because it was light and golden and she was so happy. Her mother was alive, healthy, and well again, a vision holding out her arms, her long fingers moving and white as bone, reaching for her daughter.

Benedetta, her mother whispered. *I am here.*

Bennie hadn't understood how much she had been hurting, she had been in pain, her heart sick and sore, part of her had stopped living, too. But that was over now and her mother was back, her hair loose and raven-dark, her skin smooth and soft, like when she was young, in the picture.

Her mother was wearing her blue chenille bathrobe, a welcome sight until later, when that was all she wore and she got so sick, and nothing could make her happy or cheer her up or cure her. If Bennie only tried harder, she could make her mother well again, but nothing she did worked, no good grades, no library books read, no spelling bees won, no merit badges, jokes, funny faces, nothing at all could make her mother smile again. But Bennie knew, even when she was little, that her mother was still inside her body and would come out if only she could, and the thing that stopped her was the disease.

Bennie was sitting at the kitchen table, and her mother was cooking pancakes, and she could breathe in the nice baked smell and hear the butter sizzling in the pan. Her mother was showing her how the bubbles popped on the pancakes, a secret clue they were ready to be turned over, and Bennie was standing next to her mother, barely reaching the pan, feeling the heat from the burner near her nose, watching the pancakes flip over so that the golden side came up, all smooth and fresh.

The best part was that they were together again, just the two of them, standing so close that Bennie could smell her mother's tea rose perfume, hear her voice, reach out and touch her soft robe, and she was so happy to have her mother back again for just one pancake breakfast, just one morning, just one day would be all she could ask for. Her full heart told her what she knew was true, that this was surely heaven.

And even though they were both of them dead, Bennie felt that this moment was the only time she felt truly, happily, fully alive.

Chapter Eighteen

Alice accepted the pen from the guard while he watched her, his cop eyes narrowing. Her hand hovered over the log, then she said, "Between you and me, what time did the associates leave last night?"

"Don't know. I wasn't here. Herm was."

"Let's see." Alice flipped the page backwards and ran her finger down the signatures. Her finger stopped at Judy Carrier's signature but she glanced a few lines up at Bennie's, took a mental snapshot, then flipped the page back and scribbled a decent forgery. "When the cat's away, the mice will play."

"The kids work hard, Bennie, and you know Mary's shootin' for partnership. She always comes in on Saturday."

"I know." Alice handed him the pen. "But I gotta whine about something, don't I?"

"Don't we all, Cinderella?" the guard said, and they both laughed as she told him good-bye, walked through the turnstile, and headed for the elevator bank. She found a swipe card in Bennie's wallet and used it over the electronic reader, then glanced quickly at the building directory for ROSATO & ASSOCIATES.

Third floor.

She got inside, and when the elevator doors slid open, she exited and walked through a reception area stuffed with hotel art, blue chairs, shining tables, and a stack of fancy magazines. She came upon a hallway that opened onto a conference room with a table made from a single slab of wood, its edges rough, black bark. It must have cost a fortune, and it was surrounded by soft navy blue swivel chairs, a walnut entertainment center, a plasma TV, and a mini-kitchen in matching walnut. It was classy down to the tartan dog bed that read BEAR, which reminded her to get the dog's body out of the basement before it started to stink.

There were four offices off the conference room area, each with a shiny nameplate: MARY DINUNZIO, JUDY CARRIER, and ANNE MURPHY, and at the end, BENNIE ROSATO. She went into the office, where sunlight streamed through the tall window onto a nubby tan rug, walnut desk, and matching credenza with files. Bronze plaques covered the walls, and the end tables were blanketed with crystal bowls and engraved Lucite.

It's not her office, it's her shrine.

She went around the desk, dropped the messenger bag on the rug, and sat down in the black mesh chair. On the left was a Filofax open to Monday, and the day's only appointment was in the afternoon with Rexco, a potential client she had read about in the email last night. She'd cancel the meeting to avoid any chance to slip up. Suddenly, Bennie's cell phone started ringing in her messenger bag, and Alice dug it out and checked the screen, recognizing the phone number. It was her old boss, Karen Wise, the director at PLG.

Well, how-dee-doo. "Hello, Karen," Alice said into the phone, as Bennie.

"Bennie, how have you been?"

"Great, thanks."

"Sorry to bother you on the weekend, but I left a message last night and didn't hear back from you, and it's kind of important. I won't keep you, but I wanted to let you know that Alice quit on us last week, out of the blue. Just up and left."

"Oh, no." *Do tell.*

"I didn't think you knew. I gather you two haven't spoken recently."

"No, I'm just so busy." *And important. You should see my awards.*

"I thought as much. Alice worked hard and showed such an eagerness to learn, in the beginning. She seemed to lose interest, in time. She started coming in late and her attitude changed."

What a bad puppy!

"She's naturally intelligent and she has a fine legal mind. If she wanted, she could be a great lawyer, like you."

We're about to find out.

"Anyway, here's why I called. There's a problem. I hesitate to even say this, but we think that she might have taken some money from petty cash. It was about four hundred dollars and as you know, it's not as if we have the money to spare, after the last funding cut."

And you didn't notice I embezzled about $1,500?

"One of our other employees saw her leaving the room last, and with her sudden disappearance, well, it seems sort of damning, doesn't it?"

"How terrible, really. Karen, let me send you a check, and please accept my apologies."

"Thank you, Bennie. Again, I'm so sorry about this."

"As am I, but I have to go. Good-bye," Alice said, pressing END. She set the phone down, then heard someone clearing their throat.

She looked up, and standing in the doorway was her toughest test yet.

Chapter Nineteen

Mary stood in the threshold of Bennie's office, trying not to be insecure. The boss owned a coffee mug that read I CAN SMELL FEAR, and she hated it when Mary was insecure. Unfortunately, it only made Mary more insecure, and blotches would bloom on her neck like roses in her own little garden of anxiety.

"DiNunzio, what do you want?" Bennie looked up with her usual businesslike smile.

"Uh, do you have a minute to talk?"

"Only just." Bennie pointed to one of the chairs opposite her desk. "Sit. Talk. Then go."

"Thanks." Mary entered the office, sat down, and crossed her legs, which was when it struck her that it was a huge deal to ask someone to make you a partner, and she hadn't said anything yet, so she could just keep it to herself, for several years.

"DiNunzio, what is it?"

"How are you?"

Bennie frowned. "Fine. How are you?"

"Good. Where's Bear?"

"Home."

"Why?"

"What do you want, DiNunzio?"

Mary found her voice. "I was wondering if you'd made your decision yet, about making me a partner."

"No."

"The answer is no, or you haven't decided yet?"

"No, I haven't decided. I'll think about it and get back to you."

Mary thought the boss was being a little, well, bossy. "We agreed that you'd make your decision by September."

"It's still August. Don't jump the gun."

Mary flashed on what Anthony had said about showing initiative, but it turned out that initiative was overrated. Still, she deserved the promotion, even if she wasn't jerky enough to say so. "I'd like to know more about what you're thinking about it and—"

"Quiet." Bennie raised a palm like a traffic cop. "I can't talk right now. If I said I'll get to it in September, I will."

Mary felt nonplussed. Bennie wasn't usually this abrupt, and she sensed that something was wrong, though she wasn't about to ask. She rose and walked to the door. "Okay, well, I guess we'll talk next month."

"Wait. DiNunzio?"

"Yes?" Mary turned back, and Bennie's expression had changed, her features softening.

"Listen, I hate to get personal, but I should mention that I just heard from Karen Wise that Alice Connelly—you know, my twin— quit her job at PLG. It's just bothersome. I'm so disappointed in her."

"I see," Mary said, concerned. "I knew something was bothering you."

"You did? How?"

"I could just tell. I've worked for you for a long time now."

"Worked *with* me, not *for* me."

Mary blushed. Maybe she really would make partner. "So, do you think you'll hear from her? If she has no job, she'll be needing money."

"That may be true, but it's not my problem, anymore. I haven't seen her in a year or so, and I'm so tired of her expecting me to put her life back together, after she messes it up."

"Remember, she gave you trouble before and she may do it again. She's resentful of you, and you're so successful now."

"I didn't think of that." Bennie looked concerned. "You know, Karen told me that she stole money from petty cash."

"She stole from a nonprofit? That's low." Mary was a twin herself, and she knew from experience that being one wasn't always easy. She and her sister Angie loved each other, but it could be tricky to establish your own identity when somebody else was wearing your face. "Remember, I'm a twin, even though we haven't really talked about it much. So I've been there, to a certain extent."

"Right. I had forgotten."

"People do, since Angie's off always doing missionary work, now that she left the convent." Mary didn't add that she'd never talked to Bennie about her twin because the boss wasn't exactly down with girl talk. "Anyway, I noticed that, in the past, Alice seems to come to you when she needs money, help, or a favor. If she came by on Monday with Rexco here, it might be a problem."

"Then let's cancel the meeting."

"We can't. It took three weeks to get it scheduled. You should see the emails I had to send, back and forth." Mary hesitated, then went for it. She was showing initiative all over the place. "Can I make a suggestion?"

"Sure."

"Maybe we should tell building security to call you if she wants to come upstairs?"

"Do you really think that's necessary?"

"Yes. I'll call Steve and tell him to let us know if Alice shows up, and he'll tell the other guys." Mary felt good, advising Bennie instead of always the other way around. "And, since Alice has been known to be a little . . . rough around the edges, shall we say, maybe you should get a restraining order, just in case."

"Against her?" Bennie scoffed. "Aren't you overreacting?"

"Better to be safe than sorry, that's what you always say."

"But she hasn't done anything wrong."

"She has in the past."

"But she's changed. She's at PLG now and—" Bennie's face fell, and Mary realized that the boss wasn't so different from her, after all. They both tended to see the best in people.

"Let me draft the papers. You'll be good to go, if she acts up. You have to let people take care of you, instead of taking care of them all the time."

"I'll call Steve. I don't need taking care of."

"Don't worry." Mary knew Bennie would say that. "I got your back."

"I'm counting on that, DiNunzio." Bennie smiled. "I don't say it enough, but I really do appreciate you."

"Back at you." Mary turned and left, before she got choked up or otherwise leaked estrogen. It was as if she was seeing her boss with new eyes, understanding her not as a superior, but as another woman.

And on the walk back to her office, she felt, for the first time, that she and Bennie could be partners.

Chapter Twenty

Bennie opened her eyes into pitch blackness. The vision was gone. Her mother had vanished. The good feeling had evaporated. She wasn't sure if she was alive or dead. She felt sick, broken, confused, like she was falling to pieces, her very self shattering and splintering, the center flying apart. There was no sound. The blackness around her was as empty as space. She would have imagined she was floating but for the pain in her body and the stench that brought her back to earth.

She moved her hands, and they hit something hard. She moaned. She was alive and back inside the box. She felt for the wood sides, and they were still there. She was dizzy and faint. Her chest heaved, and a weird sound came out of her, emitted from starved lungs, and she was hiccupping, then spasming until she finally got a breath.

She had to get out of here. She had to save her own life. She slammed the lid with her palm, but it felt different. She raked it with her fingertips and touched something new. There was a ridge in the wood of the lid, that hadn't been there before.

She ran her index finger along the line, tracing it like a route on a map, her sense of touch more acute because of the dark, the pain in her raw finger making it more sensitive. The lid now had a definite crack, running lengthwise, maybe from the shaking. She started banging on it with all her might, and she didn't stop, even when the scratching noise started again.

Chapter Twenty-one

Alice kicked off her sandals, crossed her legs, and took a sip of Diet Coke, which she had with a turkey sandwich from the office refrigerator. Things were going better than she expected, and she could see Mary would be a useful ally. The associate had such an obvious girl crush on Bennie that she could be made to do anything. Mary craved approval, so all Alice had to do to manipulate her was to give her some, but a little at a time. Even now the girl was slaving away on the brief that they'd never need, because Bennie was probably dead by now.

Alice picked up Bennie's phone, skimmed the address list for Building Security, and pressed CALL, which was answered immediately, "Front desk. Hey, Bennie."

"Hi, Steve." Alice remembered how Mary had said the name. "My twin Alice Connelly might come around the office, sometime in the next few days. Let me know if she shows up, would you?"

"Mary already told me, and I sent an email to the guys, and if we see her, we'll call. Too bad Lou's on vacation."

"I know, right?" Alice guessed he meant Lou Jacobs, the firm's investigator, whom she remembered from the trial. Good thing he was out of town, because she didn't need another problem. "Okay, I gotta go."

"You worry about the law, and let us worry about the order."
Steve laughed, then they hung up.

Now it was time to set her plan in motion. She hit a key on Bennie's laptop, and it came to life, asking for the password. She took a quick look at the Rolodex card in her bag, found the right password under Office Laptop, and opened Bennie's email. She remembered the name of Bennie's private banker at USABank, Marla Stone, which she'd come across in the email last night, so she clicked CREATE EMAIL and typed in the first few letters. The program filled in the rest of the email address, and she typed EMERGENCY, CONFIDENTIAL in the re line and continued:

> Dear Marla,
>
> We have an emergency situation. My identical twin, Alice Connelly, has quit her job, stolen money, and may try to impersonate me in order to withdraw money from my accounts when the bank opens on Monday. Of course, she has none of my ID or authority. I want my money transferred immediately to an offshore bank, to preempt any misdeeds. Give me a call on my cell as soon as you get this email. Thank you.
>
> Best,
> Bennie

She proofread the email, clicked SEND, and counted down *five, four, three, two, one,* then the cell phone rang. She picked it up, checking the display. "Marla?"

"Bennie, I got your email. I'm calling from my cell. Goodness, this is bad news, and I assure you that in Wealth Development, our paramount concern is your security and privacy. We would never permit any unauthorized withdrawals from your accounts."

"I wanted to stay ahead of the curve on this. Prepare for the worst and all that."

"Of course, you must!" Marla cleared her throat. "We should transfer your funds to a new temporary account we'll open for you with one of our offshore partners. This way, USABank retains you as a client, until this bad patch is over. We work with the best banks in the Caymans, Singapore, Belize, Andorra, and the Bahamas. This will be easy and quick, too. It's not as if you're seeking to avoid taxes."

Not yet. "So where should we send the money?"

"I favor the Bahamas, since there's been trouble with bank closures in the Caymans, of late. I use Swiss and other European banks when a client has a child in boarding school, for example, in Scotland or at the Sorbonne."

"Could I withdraw from the Bahamas account, as I wish? I have a business to run."

"Yes, easily. You can authorize withdrawals just as you do now, by phone or by calling me and following up with an email or letter, or online. They'd set you up with an online password, too, if you wish. How does that sound?"

Like three million bucks. "Perfect."

"I'll get in touch with the lawyer we use, and he can set that up for you on Monday, when the Bahamas bank is open. Our partner is BSB bank, in Nassau. On Monday, I'll messenger you the paperwork and the signature cards to open the account."

"You can't do it today?"

"Unfortunately, no. I'm in New York today with my family, and the office is closed."

"Understood. How long will this take?"

"Three business days. BSB won't be able to let you use the account until they receive the signature cards with your original signature, but they can open the account as soon as you fax or scan them to me. So I'll send you the cards, and you messenger them back to me. I'll overnight them to Nassau on Tuesday, and BSB will get them on Wednesday. The account will be ready for use first thing Wednesday morning."

"I'd like this done sooner. What if I sent the signature cards to the BSB directly? Then couldn't it open the account a day earlier, on Tuesday morning?"

"Why, yes. I suppose that's more efficient." Marla sounded disappointed at being left out of the loop. "When I send you the cards,

I'll include a DHL package addressed and ready to go. We'll wire your funds into the new account as soon as you scan or fax me the signature cards, and you'll be official first thing Tuesday morning."

"Great, thanks."

"My pleasure. Will there be anything else?"

"Not at all. Thanks again." Alice hung up, pleased. All she had to do was play Bennie on Monday and she could be on a plane to Nassau Monday night. She could pull it off, especially for one business day. She had paralegal training, and she was a scam artist, which was a lawyer without the student loans.

She skimmed Bennie's Filofax, and saw that other than Rexco, there were no meetings, depositions, or other proceedings scheduled for Monday. Alice would sit behind the desk, move papers around, and duck most of the phone calls. She'd have to go through with the Rexco meeting, but it shouldn't be too hard to get up to speed. There would be a case file, and she had read plenty of those. She had drafted pleadings, briefs, and done legal research. Hell, people faked being doctors, and this wasn't brain surgery.

She turned around and opened the file drawer, which was jammed with red accordion files, just like they used at PLG. She checked the first few labels, *Alpha Electronics v. Bersne, Amaryllis Computer v. Ward, Inc.,* and *Babson Metrics v. Teelerson et al.,* then skimmed the case names until she got to *Rexco v. Pattison Dalheimer, Inc.*

She pulled the file, took a slug of warm soda, and got to work.

Chapter Twenty-two

Mary was on the phone, telling Anthony about her conversation with Bennie, but he was sounding less than enthusiastic.

"Honey," he said, "let me get this straight. Bennie turned you down for a partnership, and you feel *more* like her partner?"

"She didn't turn me down."

"She did, for now."

"Only for a week or so."

"Okay, so why do you feel more like her partner? Isn't that ironic?"

"Not really." Mary sipped her coffee, but it was cold.

"Why can't she decide now?"

"Because we said September."

"She's stalling you."

"No, she's not." Mary's good mood wilted. The sun was defeating the air-conditioning in her office, and her gaze flitted over her desk cluttered with Xeroxed cases, empty coffee cups, and the elbow end of a cheese hoagie. "She said she appreciated me."

"But what did she say about partnership?"

Mary wanted to hang up. She'd called him for a break, but she should have called Judy. Sometimes it was hard to choose between best friend and boyfriend, and she should have gone with the ovaries. "Don't be so hard on her."

"I'm not being hard on her."

"Yes, you are. She has things on her mind, problems like everybody else, she just doesn't let it show. She takes care of everybody else instead of taking care of herself." Mary wasn't sure if she was talking about Bennie, herself, her mother, Judy, or all four. Maybe she was talking about every woman she had ever known, or maybe every woman ever born. In the world. And galaxy.

"I don't like her putting you off."

Mary realized she hadn't mentioned her father's breakfast with Fiorella, so she told Anthony that story, too, but he just laughed.

"You're so fired up today, babe. Is this what happens when we don't have sex?"

Mary cringed. "What do you think? Weird or not, that he ate out with Fiorella?"

"Not. They ate after they went to the hospital. What's wrong with that?"

"Why didn't they eat in the hospital cafeteria?"

"Did you ever eat in a hospital cafeteria? Don't think anything of it. Tell me you love me, I have to go to the library."

"I love you, I have to go to the library."

"That's original."

"But it's still funny."

"Whatever you say."

Mary felt stung. "You're being mean."

"No, you are, but I love you anyway."

"Love you, too." Mary pressed END, grateful that he hadn't mentioned house-hunting. She speed-dialed Judy, who picked up right away, sounding weak. "Jude, what's the matter?"

"Somebody's giving me the evil eye and the evil head and the evil stomach. Can we call Fiorella? I need a booster spell."

"She's not home." Mary shook her head. "This is what comes of bringing gringos into an Italian household. You just have the flu."

"In August?"

"It happens."

"It's not that. It's evil, pure evil. What should I do? Should we call Williams-Sonoma?"

"Why them?"

"For olive oil. Fiorella said we needed the best. If we'd had the best last night, I'd be fine today."

Mary let it go. "Do you want me to come over?"

"No, I'm just going back to sleep."

"You sure you're okay alone?"

"Yes."

Mary couldn't hang up just yet. "Jude, you wanna hear a story, or are you too sick?"

"Gimme the headline."

"Alice quit PLG, I might make partner in September, and my father had breakfast with Fiorella at a *restaurant*."

"That's incredible!" Judy's tone improved, which Mary attributed to the curative powers of gossip.

"Which one's incredible?"

"The restaurant."

"I know, right?"

"And you, a partner! Time for the big-girl panties!"

Mary smiled. "Not yet. Maybe."

"Sure you will! And Alice? The bitch is back?"

"Get this. She took money from PLG. She stole from the poor."

"Whoa. She got her Robin Hood mixed up. She's Hood Robin."

"She'll burn in hell."

"Poor Bennie," Judy said, which was exactly the reaction Mary expected, so she told Judy the rest of the story, and they both agreed on the need for a back-up restraining order.

Mary said, "Bennie's not so bad, you know. We judge her too harshly."

"That's so like us."

"She opened up to me, today. She actually said, 'I appreciate you.'"

Judy gasped. "You misheard."

"No. We *confided*."

"No!"

"Yes!"

"Tell me what she said."

Mary smiled. "Then it wouldn't be confidential, but we talked about being twins."

"Well, I'm happy about your partnership. Just remember I knew you when."

Mary felt a twinge. She couldn't believe that she might make partner before Judy, who was so much smarter. "I owe it to you, Jude. You're the one who put me up to it. I never would've asked if you hadn't made me."

"I only encouraged you."

"No, you shamed me into it."

"Whatever. I'm just glad. You deserve it."

Mary felt so lucky, in having Judy as a friend and Bennie as a boss. "You're the best, you know that?"

"Don't get all melty. I'm going back to bed. Watch out for Fiorella, Mare. She could bewitch your dad. See you later."

"Don't be silly, and feel better." Mary hung up, but held the warm BlackBerry in her palm for a minute.

She was wondering how Judy always knew what she was thinking, even when she didn't know herself.

Chapter Twenty-three

Bennie screamed and pounded on the new crack, hoping it would weaken, ignoring the animal scratching and growling on the other side of the lid, trying to get inside. She flashed on a terrifying image of its teeth sinking into her neck, then realized something. If the animal dug through the lid, he could help her break the crack.

She flipped her thinking. The animal wasn't her enemy, he was her friend. He was on her side. She needed it to keep scratching and digging. She started pounding again, this time to taunt him, then began scratching on the wood, digging toward the animal as he dug toward her. Each of them scratched his side of the lid, the animal on the top and her on the bottom, mirror images of each other.

She grunted with effort, reduced to some primal state, merging into her animal self, clawing frantically at the wood, raking her nails along its surface. Something in her snapped when she realized that this was her last chance. She was running out of air.

She clawed and dug and tore, then started pounding, not feeling the pain, not smelling the stink, devolved and focused only on her scratching, fueled by the scratching on the other side.

She wouldn't stop until she was dead.

Or devoured.

Chapter Twenty-four

Alice studied the claims in the Rexco Complaint, and it wasn't difficult. The gist was that Rexco was a national manufacturer of screw-top lids, and three of its employees had quit to go work for a rival company, taking with them the trade secrets for making the lids, which violated Pennsylvania law. A different law firm had drafted the Complaint, and she could see that it wasn't well done, full of typos and bad citation form, which were basic mistakes.

She flipped through the correspondence file and found a letter from Rexco, asking to come to the office for new representation, and another letter, from Bennie, agreeing to the meeting and outlining an overview of trade secret and unfair competition law in the Commonwealth, which gave Alice a complete script for the meeting on Monday.

She knew she'd have to quote some of the cases and maybe use a legal buzzword or two, so she turned to the laptop, logged on to Lexis, and skimmed enough cases to hum a few bars. Then she shifted gears, mentally put the Rexco file away, and got back to her own agenda by logging on to travelocity.com. She couldn't find any direct flights from Philly to Nassau in the evening, so she booked the last flight to Miami, then a connection to Nassau on Monday night, paid for with Bennie's Amex.

"Bennie?"

Alice jumped, then minimized the travel website.

"DiNunzio."

"Sorry to interrupt. You were working so hard, you didn't hear me knock. I wanted you to know that the brief is almost done and I'm going home."

"Already?"

Mary looked apologetic. "It's almost six o'clock."

Give her approval, but a little at a time.

"I'll finish by tomorrow night, so it's ready to be filed on Monday morning. You want me to email you a copy?"

"No, there's no need to. I trust your work."

"Thanks. See you." Mary smiled happily, then left and closed the door behind her, and Alice went back online, looking for hotels in Nassau. There was no Ritz or Four Seasons, but there were decent ones with availability, since it was off season. She looked up the address of the BSB bank in Nassau and booked a hotel near the bank, so she could be there when it opened, then started cruising the web for offshore banks in Switzerland and the Caymans, because she'd have to move the money one more time. By the time anybody realized she was gone for good, the money would be gone for good, too.

When she looked up again, it was eight o'clock. The computer screen glowed, and the hallway had darkened. Outside the window, the city lights were coming up, white squares from office buildings and neon lines on the spiky skyscrapers. She packed the Rexco file in Bennie's knapsack, because no lawyer ever went home without work, then grabbed her messenger bag. She hit the elevator, put on her game face, and walked toward the security desk, where she signed out with Bennie's signature.

Steve looked up from his newspaper, his eyes unfocused behind his glasses. "Good night, Bennie. Like I said, don't worry about a thing."

"Thanks." Alice left and pushed through the old-fashioned doors, and outside it was sweltering, even at this hour. The street was congested, and she hailed a cab, which pulled over quickly. She opened the door and slid into the backseat, sticky on her bare thighs. "No air?" she asked, but the old cabbie shrugged his shoulders.

"Sorry."

She gave him Bennie's address and sat back, letting the hot air blow on her face. The ride wasn't long, and she eyed the couples walking hand-in-hand, going out to dinner and clubs, all dressed up. It was Saturday night and she was horny as hell, but her only date was the Rexco file.

The cab reached Bennie's neighborhood and cruised down the street toward her house, but there was someone sitting on her front step. In the dark, it looked like a homeless guy, but as the cab got closer, she could see that he was a total hunk, tall and blond. He looked too straight to be her type, but he was still hot, even in glasses and a striped tie. She couldn't see his features clearly, but he had light, wavy hair, an old-school white shirt, and his suit jacket was slung over one shoulder.

She handed the driver a ten, grabbed her messenger bag and knapsack and got out of the cab, rearranging her features into the Bennie mask.

The man gave her a wave, obviously mistaking her for Bennie, and rose to meet her, his smile partly in shadow.

She finally recognized him. It was the one who got away. Bennie's old boyfriend, Grady Wells. She remembered him from the trial, where he sat in the gallery to observe one or two days.

"Hey, sweetheart," he said softly, embracing her. "Surprised to see me?"

"Happily so," she answered, hugging him back. The Rexco file would wait. Her Saturday night had fallen into place.

She smelled reunion sex.

Chapter Twenty-five

Mary was trying to make a decision, which wasn't her strong suit. This time the choice was BF or BFF—should she go see her boyfriend or her best friend forever? She hoped to decide on the walk home. The only downside to having a boyfriend was that you were supposed to spend time with them, even when they were cranky.

She had stopped off and done some shopping, but it hadn't helped her make a decision, and now she owned three shirts she didn't need, even at ten percent off. She always bought all the stuff she didn't need on sale, so she could save money as she wasted it, which seemed time-efficient and very partnery.

She sighed, walking in the heat. It was dark, and weekend traffic clogged the street. A couple hurried past her, the guy holding a dry-cleaned tuxedo in a plastic bag. Another couple strolled by, laughing. It was Saturday night, and under federal law, Mary wasn't allowed to spend it with a BFF if she had a BF. But she and her BF didn't have any plans, and a sick BFF trumped a healthy BF, especially if the Phillies were playing, but they weren't. The laws of dating could be so complicated, and it was lucky she had a J.D.

The shops were locking their doors as she passed, and the restaurants beginning to form lines out the door. She was coming to a decision. She didn't think Anthony would mind if she spent the evening with Judy. Maybe he was as bugged as she was, though it wasn't his partnership in question, his boss in trouble, or his parents headed for *Cheaters*. She took her phone out of her purse, pressed A, and waited for him to pick up.

"Hey, babe," he said, breathless.

"How are you?"

"Working away. I left the library to take your call."

"I'm sorry. Do you mind if I don't see you tonight? Judy's sick, and I should go over."

"No problem, I'll just work. Call me later?"

"I won't be done with her until late."

"Okay, I won't wait for your call. Have fun. Are we gonna look at houses tomorrow?"

Uh-oh. "Not sure, yet. I have a lot of work."

"Really? Sunday's a big open-house day, and the weather's supposed to be less humid. It would be fun."

Mary felt a guilty twinge. "I know, but I have that brief to write for Bennie."

"Okay, call me whenever, tonight or tomorrow. Let me know what you want to do." Anthony was silent a minute. "Babe, you mad at me?"

Mary's throat caught. "No. Are you?"

"Not at all. I love you."

"Love you, too. Good night." Mary pressed END, placated. She did love him, and he loved her. They were in love, and nothing was wrong. She pressed J, and Judy picked up, croaking a hello. Mary said, "I'm coming to check on you. What do you need beside Häagen-Dazs?"

"Fresh limes."

"For what?"

"Margaritas, of course."

"See you in half an hour, crazy." Mary pressed END and picked up the pace, satisfied she had made the right decision. Sometimes BFFs were better for Saturday nights, especially when limes were involved.

Half an hour later, one look at Judy, in her gray hoodie and blue gym shorts, told Mary her BFF was sick. Her fair skin was pale, her blue eyes washed out, and a short yellow ponytail sprouted from her head like the Lorax.

"Feeling crummy, honey?" Mary asked.

"Yes."

"Poor thing." Mary closed the apartment door, then trailed Judy into her tiny galley kitchen, where she dropped her purse and briefcase on the café table and set the shopping bag on a butcherblock counter. "Did you sleep?"

"No, my head hurt too much."

"Did you have some soup?"

"I hate soup. I like tequila."

Mary stowed the ice cream in the freezer and unpacked five fresh limes, which rolled around on the counter. "You really think alcohol's a good idea?"

"Yes. Tequila's like Vitamin C, without the Vitamin or the C."

"I can only have one drink. I gotta get up early and finish that brief for Bennie." Mary sniffed the air, which reeked of the turpentine and oil paints that Judy kept in her studio/apartment, which really was a studio and an apartment. "You know, that smell would make anybody sick."

"It's not the smell, it's the spell."

Mary looked over. "Did you just make that up?"

"Yes."

"Then we should get you to a doctor."

"Please call Fiorella."

Mary rolled her eyes. "You, a woman of genius, can't actually believe that you have the evil eye. It's folk medicine. It's what peasants made up to explain their lives, like sacrificing goats."

"What's the harm in calling her? Humor me."

"Fine." Mary went to the table, retrieved her phone, and sat down with it, pressing H. The phone rang, and she hit a button. "I'm putting it on speaker. I wanna hear what she says."

"Good." Judy folded her arms.

" 'Allo?" Mary's mother said, picking up.

"Hi, Ma, how are you?"

"I'm a fine, *Maria,* how you?"

Mary cut the small talk. "Good, but I'm here with Judy, who thinks she has the evil eye, still."

"*Oh Deo!*"

"Can you ask Fiorella to come to the phone?"

"Fiorella? She's a no here. She go viz' her ladyfrien', on Snyd' Avenue. They come back, soon."

"They? Who's they?"

"Your father, he take her."

"And he's not back yet?"

Mary and Judy exchanged looks.

"He drive her."

Mary's mouth fell open. Her father never drove anybody anywhere. Nobody in South Philly ever gave up a parking space unless they were going to their own funeral. "Why didn't she take a cab? You can't park on Snyder anyway."

"What, *Maria,* why?"

"Ma, Fiorella came to visit you, but she's visiting everyone else, with Pop. Did you eat dinner alone?"

"Is good, alla good."

Judy edged closer to the phone. "Hey, Mrs. D, it's Judy. How are you?"

"Good, Judy, you got 'em bad?"

"Mrs. D, can you cure me?" Judy looked hopeful.

"No, no, only Donna Fiorella. She have a great power, greates' power, more great than a me."

"Ma, no, stop that, you're as good as Fiorella." Mary's heart went out to her little mother, eating dinner alone and thinking her superpowers were substandard.

"*Maria,* she's a better, strong, she's a very strong."

Judy asked, "Can we call Fiorella at her girlfriend's?"

"No, *non lo so.*"

Mary was trying to remember the last time her mother had spent a Saturday night without her father. "I don't like you being alone so much. This is wrong."

"Shhh, *basta,* tomorr', you come to church?"

"I can't, I have to work. Sorry."

"Okay, *Maria.* Good night, love you, *Maria,* Jud', love you, God bless."

"Love you, Ma. Bye." Mary hung up, heartsick. "This is ridiculous. My father never leaves the house."

"Correction, he never leaves the kitchen." Judy started cutting limes with a sharp knife, releasing a pungent scent. "I'll help you with your brief, after we have the perfect margarita."

"You got a shot glass instead?" Mary asked, rising.

Chapter Twenty-six

Bennie dug into the lid, pounding and dragging her nails across the wood, reduced to the animal on the other side. She fought the awareness that it was getting harder and harder to breathe. She couldn't fill her lungs and settled for shallow panting, little intakes of breath that could barely keep her going. She knew she needed oxygen because she could feel her brain get funky, her thoughts melting together in odd ways, like she kept thinking she had a giant can opener and was prying the lid off the box, like in the Popeye cartoons where they took the top off the spinach can, leaving a jagged edge. Boy, she was wishing for one of those can openers right now, and if she had one, she knew it would do the trick.

She kept digging, her arms weakening, hurting from the effort of keeping them up. She'd been scratching and pounding on the same spot on the crack, concentrating all her force on three square inches. She could hear the animal working on the same spot, they had the same idea at the same time, only one idea completely occupying their animal brains, which was to get through, to finally reach the other side.

One animal wanting life and the other wanting death.

Chapter Twenty-seven

Alice buried herself in Grady's embrace, on the sidewalk. She loved the feel of a man's arms around her and she brushed her cheek against his strong chin, which had just the right amount of blondish stubble. He smelled like hard soap and hard work, and she was feeling his good-provider vibe. She got so turned on that she had to stop herself from grinding her hips into him. Bennie wouldn't know how to steam up this boy's glasses, and Alice had to stay in character. He was a test she hadn't expected, and she didn't need a monkey wrench thrown into her plans, not when she was this close to getting away.

"Well," Grady said, smiling down at her. "Quite a greeting."

Buckle up, professor. "I'm happy to see you."

"I tried to call you, but that number was disconnected. I assume you got a new one."

"Yes, sorry."

"I know it's impromptu, my arriving unannounced, but my flight got diverted from Pittsburgh and I came straight here from the airport. Call it an irresistible impulse. I thought maybe I could take you to dinner." Grady put an arm around her shoulder. "By the way, this would be a good time for you to tell me you're not married."

Alice smiled. "What a coincidence. I was just about to say that, and I'm not even seeing anyone, either."

"Nor am I. Great minds, huh?"

"Right. Come on in." Alice could see she'd have to get her witty banter up to speed because the felons she dated didn't require conversation. She dug in Bennie's messenger bag for the house key, climbed the steps, and slid it into the lock on the front door. "So, you want to go out to dinner or stay in?"

"You, *cook*?"

Oops. "No, you."

"Touché." Grady stood behind her on the stoop, and Alice hoped he was looking at her ass, if he could find it in the elephant shorts. The front door swung open, and she went inside, but Grady hesitated, frowning. "Oh no. Don't tell me that Bear died."

"Bear?" Alice blurted out, then caught herself as they went inside. Bear evidently wasn't dead yet, because whimpering sounds came from the basement. "No, that's him, but he sounds funny."

"Something must be the matter."

"Bear, Bear?" Alice called out, fake-looking around the living room, but Grady hurried toward the kitchen.

"I think it's coming from the basement."

"Really?" Alice hustled after him for show. "Bear, where are you, pal?"

"Bennie, hurry!" Grady ran down the basement stairs. "He's down here! He's hurt!"

"In the *basement*?"

"I think he's injured." Grady climbed the stairs, holding the limp dog, whose eyes stayed closed, his head hanging down. "Poor guy, he was just lying there, crying at the bottom of the stairs."

"Oh my God." Alice forced a shocked expression. "What happened? You think he fell?"

"Must have. We need to get him to a vet. We can be at Penn emergency in no time. Where's your car?"

"Right down the street. I'll go." Alice bounded out of the kitchen, ran out the door, and hustled down the pavement. She didn't need the dumb dog to screw up her plans, and he'd better die on the way to the hospital. She reached Bennie's car, jumped inside, started the engine, and double-parked in front of her house just as

Grady appeared on the sidewalk with the dog. She got out and opened the back door so he could set the dog on the backseat.

"How's that, old boy?" Grady gave the dog a soft pat, and Alice suppressed an eye-roll.

"Great, let's go," she said, and Grady jumped in the passenger seat. She hit the gas and shot to the end of the street, where she realized she had no idea how to get to Penn Vet. It sounded like they'd been there before, and it was something the real Bennie would have known. She stopped the car and faked a beginner sob. "Can you drive? I'm too upset."

"Sure, sorry, I should have thought of that." Grady jumped out and ran around to the driver side, and Alice switched places with him, turning her face away to hide her not-tears.

"This is so horrible." Alice tried to cry.

"I always knew this day would come. But not yet, not tonight." Grady hit the gas and steered around the corner, sped across the Parkway, and headed for Eakins Oval, then took a right over the bridge.

"I walked him before I went to work, and he seemed fine."

"Don't blame yourself. He's old, he probably lost his footing and fell." Grady hit the gas, running the light. "The door to the basement was closed. You must've closed it, not realizing he was down there."

"I guess he didn't make any noise. He never makes a fuss."

"Such a good dog."

"The best dog in the world." Alice felt trapped in a greeting card or maybe a fuzzy puppy calendar.

"Don't worry." Grady steered past Victorian rowhouses with Greek frat signs. "You know how good they are at Penn. Remember when he ate the tennis ball?"

No. "Yes."

"They got him through that, they'll get him through this." Grady tore through Powellton, running two red lights, then twisted the car onto Spruce Street and hit the gas. There wasn't much traffic, the University area was empty for summer, and nobody was on the street.

"We lucked out on the traffic."

"I'll say. Hang on!" Grady zoomed up the street and at the top, steered into an empty parking lot in front of a modern building. The sign read UNIVERSITY OF PENNSYLVANIA VETERINARY HOSPITAL, and he cut the gas and put on the emergency brake. "You get the door, I'll get Bear."

"Okay." Alice jumped out of the car, ran around to the backseat, and opened it while Grady scooped up the dog in a fireman's carry. They hurried to the building, hustled through the lobby, and made a beeline for the emergency room. The registration desk was on the right, and a young female vet student behind the glass rose, concerned.

"Car accident?"

Alice shook her head. "No, he fell down the steps."

"Has he been here before?"

"Yes. It's Bear, my dog. I'm Bennie Rosato."

"Stay right there." The vet student hurried out of sight, and Alice wondered if vets could tell if a dog had been kicked, like doctors could with abused kids. Quickly a vet appeared with a large assistant, who took Bear from Grady and carried him away, back through the swinging EMPLOYEES ONLY doors.

"Thank you so much." Alice watched them go with pretend emotion, and the student vet smiled in a sympathetic way.

"We need your permission to do an X-ray to see if he has any broken bones and to make sure he didn't ingest a foreign object. We'll let you know as soon as we learn anything. We'll pull his records, and I'll bring you the intake form later."

"Thanks, take good care of him," Grady said, as the vet student hurried off. He turned to Alice, and in the light, she could see how handsome he was, even with glasses. His eyes were large and light gray, his crow's feet gave him a relaxed, almost intellectual look, and his hair was thick blond curls, like a halo. Plus he had a small nose, a strong jaw, and the most kissable mouth she had ever seen on a lawyer.

"I'm so worried." Alice bit her lip. Tears magically filled her eyes. "I don't want to lose him."

"Everything's going to be all right," Grady whispered, taking her in his arms. "I'm so glad I'm here."

"Me, too," Alice said, holding him tight.

The only thing better than reunion sex is comfort sex.

Chapter Twenty-eight

Mary sat across from Judy on the floor, her back propped against the wall and her bare legs stretched out in front of her, on the worn hardwood floor. Her feet were bare, and she forgot where she left her shoes. She was comfortable, if only because of the third margarita. On the floor between them sat fragrant containers of lo mein, a red foil bag of spare rib bones, two dirty paper dishes with undersized plastic forks, and a hot laptop.

Judy picked up the tequila bottle, squinting at the label. "Mare, what does *reposado* mean? It's Spanish."

"Obviously, it means delicious."

Judy smiled. "Good one."

"My humor improves with drink."

"So does your brief writing."

"To us." Mary raised her tumbler. "We did an excellent job."

"We always do. The lo mein helps."

"Every brief we've ever done together, we order lo mein."

"It's our secret weapon."

Mary felt a warm rush. She loved hanging out with Judy. Her paintings leaned against the wall in vivid stacks, and the shelves held old coffee cans of washed paintbrushes and wooden boxes of oil paints. Somehow it looked right, even coordinated, with a big white four-poster with a funky gauze canopy. Judy was so talented in so many ways, and Mary would always be a little in awe of her.

Judy smiled. "You're getting all melty again. What's going on with you? You're even more emotional than usual lately."

"I know, right?" Mary's throat went thick. "I'm not sure why."

"Is it partnership? You worried about making it?"

"Yes, but it's not only that. It's Anthony, and the house thing. It's hard, all of it together."

Judy frowned. "I thought you were excited about the house. He was telling me about one you saw on Bainbridge, the trinity."

Mary felt that twinge again. "It needs tons of work, and it's so dark inside."

"Tell me what's going on."

"Looking at houses with him, and moving in together, that's great, but there's questions to deal with. Can we look at houses out of our price range? What if I can afford a nicer house than he can? Do I put him on the deed? Is it weird if I don't?" Mary thought a minute. "And what do we do, after we move in? Am I his landlord? Do I ask him for half the mortgage each month?"

"Lots of hard questions." Judy looked serious. "You tell me. What do you want to do?"

"If I make partner, the difference in our income, the disparity, it's just ridiculous." The more Mary thought about it, the more uncomfortable she felt. Even telling Judy made her feel like she was ratting out Anthony. "He's living on his savings, writing his book."

"You guys talked about this, right?"

"A little."

Judy shrugged, and melting ice tinkled in her tumbler. "So maybe you need to talk about it more."

"That will embarrass him."

"How?"

"Because it makes him feel bad that I make more money than he does."

Judy half-smiled. "I think he's aware of that."

"So why rub it in?"

"How do you know he feels bad?"

"I can tell." Mary's chest tightened. "If we go out to dinner, he'll try to pay, so that means we can't go anyplace nice. He'll let me split it sometimes, but that's always uncomfortable. I give the waiter my credit card, and Anthony gives me the cash, and the waiter always brings the credit card back to him."

"Always a wonderful moment." Judy wrinkled her nose.

"Yeah, great, huh? So now we're getting a house together, and he's going to live with me, and it's going to get weirder if I make partner. I don't know what to do. You would think after dating all this time we'd have figured this out, but we haven't."

Judy took a sip of her drink. "I'm lucky, with Frank. He loves being a contractor and his business is doing terrific."

"Everything's good when the boy makes more than the girl."

"Hey." Judy winced. "You know money isn't a big deal with me."

"I know, sorry, I didn't mean that about you. It isn't with me either. But it is with men, at least with Anthony. They still measure their self-worth by their salaries."

"Unlike women, who measure it by their hair, faces, and bodies." Judy smiled. "He's writing a book, and when he gets published, he'll have money."

"If it gets published. It's hard, especially a biography in an academic press. And what if it doesn't, or if the advance is super low? It will make him feel terrible."

"He'll go back to teaching."

"He could. He says he'd like to talk to Penn."

"Okay, so there you have it."

Mary knew it wasn't that easy. Anthony had been a professor at Fordham when she met him, on his sabbatical in Philadelphia, but he'd left to stay with her. She couldn't help but feel as if she owed him.

"You love him, don't you?"

"Yes, but, the other night, you know . . ." Mary rubbed her forehead. She wished she hadn't had any tequila. As a drunk, she was a downer.

"Mare, it's okay to love Anthony. It's okay to go on." Judy smiled, sadly. "So be happy. Okay?"

"Okay, right. Will do." Mary checked her watch. "Well, I guess it's time to go."

Judy cocked her head, sympathetic. "You can stay here if you want. I'll give you the bed and I'll take the sleeping bag."

"Thanks, but no. I'm supposed to decide whether to look at houses tomorrow and call Anthony to let him know."

"So decide, and call him."

Mary could easily go house-hunting. The brief was done, and her only other option was church. "I can't decide."

"So talk to him about that, then. Call him, right now."

"You want me to drunk dial my boyfriend?"

"Maybe that's what *reposado* means," Judy said, with a crooked smile.

Chapter Twenty-nine

Bennie had no strength left. Her arms lay useless at her sides. She could barely stay conscious. The animal kept growling and clawing his spot, but her body was admitting defeat. She lay there, gasping for breath, hiccupping for oxygen, reduced to an organism trying to survive.

Her chest barely moved in and out, and she was beyond pain and fear. Her will was slipping away. A calm washed over her, and an acceptance. Her thoughts turned to Bear, then the office and the girls, Mary, Judy, Anne. She hated to leave them, and she regretted not telling them how much she really loved them, but it was too late now. She was suffocating to death, and she couldn't pound, claw, or scream anymore. It hadn't worked. At least she went down fighting.

Her heart started beating harder and faster, pounding in her chest, and she started writhing in the box. She tried to stay still, to conserve whatever oxygen she still had, but she couldn't stop twisting and turning. The only sound she heard was her own gasping, her chest buckling but never expanding, her lungs never filling, there was nothing to fill them with, nothing left at all.

She started coughing, and her head felt like someone had taken an axe straight down the center of her brain, and she couldn't think a single thought, her heart thumping too many beats a minute, and she realized that this would be how she died, in darkness, filth, and urine. She had always thought she was better than this, but in the end, she wasn't, at all.

The coughing stopped, or she stopped hearing it, and she drifted back in the darkness, in a vacuum that was her lungs, and maybe her very body would turn itself inside out or pop, then she was thinking of her mother again, and finally she found herself remembering the one who got away, the man she loved truly. He was the love of her life, she knew it now, with absolute certainty, and every beat of her heart.

And it made it worse to know it only now, when her heart was, at last, stopping.

Chapter Thirty

Alice rested her head on Grady's shoulder on the car ride home, her eyes closed, playing her part. The stupid dog hadn't died yet, although the vet had told them that they'd know more in the morning, after they'd run all their tests. She hoped for good news, when she would have to imagine something sad enough to make her cry, like not getting laid for another week.

"Here we are," Grady said softly, parking in front of Bennie's house and twisting off the ignition. "I know you're upset because you didn't yell at me for not using my blinkers."

Oops, again. "You got a bye, this time."

"Hang in." Grady patted her bare knee, and Alice felt a rush of warmth. She got out of the car, and he materialized at her side, put an arm around her shoulder, and helped her to the front door. She'd always gone for bad boys, but she could see the appeal in a Boy Scout, especially Bennie's Boy Scout.

Alice reached into the bag for the keys, opened the door, and they went inside, where he closed the door, and she dropped the bag on the couch, faking a sad face. "It's so quiet, with Bear not coming to the door. I should've known something was wrong when he didn't meet me."

"You were distracted by my surprise visit." Grady smiled tenderly at her, and she faked a simpy smile back.

"I know, I was so shocked to see you."

"I'd love to stay tonight, but if you want to be alone, I understand."

"I'd love you to stay. Actually, I need you to stay." Alice flashed him another simpy smile, which must have worked because he wrapped his arms around her again.

"Good, because I need you, too," he whispered into her ear, and Alice nestled her cheek against his white shirt, soft from a day's wearing. Underneath she could feel the hard muscles of his arms, which got her juices flowing. He seemed a few years younger, and who knew Bennie was a cougar?

"I hope he's okay." Alice pressed her body into his, though it was too soon for any major moves.

"I wonder if we should have stayed at the vet's."

"We're not helping him by moping around in the waiting room." *We could help him more by having great sex.*

"I love him, too."

"I know you do." *Feel my hips?*

"He's an old guy, but he's a fighter."

And I'm a lover, so what are we waiting for?

"Listen." Grady broke their embrace, holding her away from him and looking into her eyes again. "I don't want you to think I'm barging back into your life, expecting everything to be the way it was between us."

How was it between us, again?

"I know we still live in different cities, and we both work too hard. None of that's changing anytime soon."

Like I care. I'll be in Nassau by Monday night.

"I've been thinking about you so much lately. I Google you all the time, I've been wanting to email. Truth is, I have called your cell. I knew you had changed the number."

You, devil, you. Kiss me.

"What I'm saying is, it's not an accident that I'm here. I had to see you."

Great. Now will you take that shirt off?

"I think we ended it too soon. We made a mistake, and I'm hoping we can give it another try. We can play it by ear."

Shut up and grow a pair!

"Nobody's mattered to me since you, and nobody could. I feel like you're the one who got away, Bennie."

Bingo! "I feel the exact same way," Alice said, matching his tone, after he finally stopped talking. "Forget the past. Let's not even talk about it anymore. We're both here now, and single, so let's live in the present."

"You really want to give it another try?" Grady asked, his sexy lips curving into a smile, and Alice couldn't take it anymore. She rose on her tiptoes and kissed him fully.

No tongue, yet. Remember, keep your tongue to yourself.

Grady kissed her back, his lips warm on hers, and he pulled her to her toes in a way that made her forget the no-tongue part. She kissed him more deeply, her hands clinging to his back, and she could feel his shoulder blades flexing under his shirt, which drove her crazy.

"I missed you," Grady said, coming up for air, and Alice could see he had the look of love. She kissed him again, and the idea that she was about to screw Bennie's boyfriend got her so excited that she yanked his shirt out of his pants in back and ran her hands underneath to his shoulders, aroused by the warmth of his skin.

"Let's go upstairs," Grady said huskily, releasing her embrace and taking her by the wrist. He tugged her up the stairs, and they hit the darkened bedroom, where he picked her up and tossed her backwards onto the bed. She kicked off her Birkenstocks, tore off her T-shirt, and was about to take off her bra when he crawled on top of her, stopping her hands.

"You know that's my job." Grady reached around her back, unhooked her bra, slipped her out of it, and tossed it aside. "Some things you never forget."

Alice kissed him and threw her arms around him, pulling him on top of her, loving the feel of his shirt against her bare breasts. His hands moved to her nipples, which set her on fire. She couldn't wait to feel him inside her and she knew she'd be better than Bennie. She had his shirt off in record time, throwing it over his back, and her fingers flew to unhook his waistband and unzip his pants.

"Down, girl!" Grady chuckled. "What's got into you?"

Oops. "I'm happy to see you, is all."

"Right answer." Grady moved to unfasten her baggy shorts, but Alice unzipped his fly.

"Beat you."

"God, you're so . . . different."

"Don't be silly." Alice warned herself to back it down. She leaned over and kissed him slowly, setting a more relaxed pace, so he wouldn't be suspicious. "You can't even remember how I was."

"I know, it's been too long." Grady caught her hands when she went to take off his boxers. "I don't have a condom. Do you?"

"It's okay." Alice went for his boxers, but Grady stopped her again.

"This, coming from you?"

"Let's just do it. Just this once." Alice freed her hand, reached between his legs, and slipped her fingers inside his boxers. She hit paydirt, but there was a problem. There was no ignition, and she wondered if Grady's body knew something that his brain didn't— that she wasn't the real Bennie. "Okay, you're right, wait a minute."

"Good."

"Be right back." Alice rolled over, groped the night table for the drawer, and stuck her hand inside, feeling around for condoms. She could tell the difference between a Trojan and a Durex by feel, but all she could find were pens and pencils.

"Any luck?"

"Stay tuned." Alice jumped out of bed, ran for the bathroom, flicked on the light, and tore open the medicine chest. No condoms. She rummaged through the trays and found combs, vitamins, and mint dental floss, but there were no condoms anywhere.

"How we doing?"

"Almost." Alice flicked off the light and hurried across the bedroom to Bennie's dresser. She rooted through the underwear, but nobody who wore CVS panties would have a box of condoms. She hurried back to bed and threw her arms around Grady, who let her pull him on top of her again.

"Well?"

"Forget it, please, please, please." Alice kissed him, writhing beneath him, and getting hot all over again when he finally responded, grinding into her. But there were still no signs of life in the southern hemisphere.

"I'm sorry, let's just rest." Grady stopped and propped himself up on an elbow, looking down at her. She could see the outline of his head, and his shoulders.

"I can try—"

"No, please. I guess this is all happening so fast. Too fast."

"True, that." Alice made herself relax. She didn't know if this happened all the time with him, and she had to be careful not to arouse his suspicion, if she couldn't arouse anything else. "Okay, we'll just rest."

"I guess there's a first for everything, even this."

"Right. It happens."

"Not with you, though. We never had a problem before." Grady sounded puzzled, but she didn't want him wondering.

"Look, it's been a terrible night. You're probably thinking about Bear, and you must feel exhausted from the flight. Don't worry about it. I'm upset about Bear, too."

"I know you are, sweetheart." Grady hugged her close, and Alice snuggled against his chest.

"Good night."

"Good night," Alice said, trying to sound sleepy. He definitely believed she was Bennie, which was good.

Because if he started suspecting anything, she'd have to kill him.

Chapter Thirty-one

Mary was up early Sunday morning, showered and wrapped in her bathrobe, pressing floppy contacts into her eyes, feeling terrific despite the tequila. She had fallen asleep easily, which was euphemistic for passed out on her bed, and had awakened with new resolve. Today was a day in which she would confront her problems rather than avoid them. If she was going to be a boss, she'd have to start acting like one.

She slicked her hair back into a ponytail, padded out of the bathroom, shed her bathrobe, and slipped into clean underwear, a fresh white cotton tee, a blue cotton skirt, and leather sandals, then picked up her BlackBerry and waited for Anthony to pick up.

"Hey, babe," he said, characteristically cheerful, which touched her.

"So, you still want to look at open houses? I found some good ones online and in the paper."

"Good, let's do it. Judy feeling better?"

"Nothing a hundred proof didn't cure. I'll be at your place by noon, so that we can start by one o'clock, okay?"

"What about work? That brief you had to do?"

"The brief is *reposado,* which is Spanish for legally sufficient, though it can also mean really delicious."

Anthony laughed. "*Reposado* is a type of tequila and it means 'rested.'"

"That's just how I feel. See you at one."

"Love you," Anthony said, but she hung up before she could tell him, which was an accident. She slipped the BlackBerry into her back pocket, grabbed her purse, left her apartment, and grabbed a cab to South Philly. She had to make a stop, first.

She got out of the cab in front of her parents' house, waved to the neighbors, and went up the stoop to the screen door, with its fake-Gothic D in aluminum. She remembered a time when everybody on their block had a D on their front screen, and growing up, she had thought it stood for Door, until she realized it was DiCrescenzo, D'Antonio, and DeJulio. The neighborhood had changed since then, but not the DiNunzios. She opened the door and went inside.

"Ma, Dad?" She dropped her purse on the chair and walked through to the kitchen, which was packed with her father and her favorite octogenarians, his friends The Three Tonys—Pigeon Tony Lucia, Tony-From-Down-The-Block LoMonaco, and Tony "Two Feet" Pensiera—all of whom were sitting at the table, enchanted by resident temptress, Fiorella Bucatina.

"*Maria, 'allo, Maria!*" Her mother was at the stove making meatballs, and the air smelled like saturated fats.

"Hi, Ma." Mary kissed her, catching a whiff of AquaNet and fresh bread crumbs. "I thought I'd drop in and see you and Pop."

"Good, alla good." Her mother set the meatball in the hot oil, where it sizzled aromatically. "Everybody come here aft' church, for base-a-ball game."

"I understand," Mary said, but she didn't. Her father never watched the Phillies with anything but his cigar.

"HEY, KIDDO!" Her father grinned, and Mary went over and gave him a kiss on the top of his head.

"Hi, Pop, hello everybody." She flashed smiles all around, and everybody smiled back except Fiorella.

"Good to see you, Mary." Fiorella's black eyeliner looked fresh, her lips glistened cherry red, and she wore a new cleavage-inducing black dress, which was perfect for church, if you were Mary Magdalene.

"MY TURN, FIORELLA!" Her father moved his coffee cup aside and placed his hand on the table. "MY TURN!"

"Here, Mariano." Fiorella picked up her father's veined hand, cupped it in hers, and ran a crimson fingernail along one of the lines in his palm.

"What's going on?" Mary asked, but it was rhetorical. She got the gist, she just couldn't believe the gist.

"Shhhh!" Tony Two Feet's eyes danced behind his Mr. Potato-head glasses. He went by "Feet," making him the only man in South Philly whose nickname had a nickname. And nobody had any idea how he got either one. "Fiorella can tell the future from your hand."

"Really?" Mary glanced at her mother, who kept frying meatballs, her flowered back turned.

"Yeah," Feet answered. "She told me I'm gonna come into money. All I gotta do is put ten bucks on Willy Nilly, in the third at Monmouth. He's a twelve-to-one long shot, but he's gonna win."

Tony-From-Down-The-Block waved a baggie filled with salt, or maybe crack cocaine. "And she said my prostate's gonna clear up if I drink this, in hot water."

"How nice for you both," Mary said, watching Fiorella run her talons around her father's thumb.

"Mariano," Fiorella purred, "this is your heart line. You have a good heart, a wonderful heart."

"THANK GOD. IT'S THE LIPITOR. MY CHOLESTEROL'S 203."

Feet elbowed him. "Too bad your weight isn't," he said, and they all laughed except Fiorella.

"Mariano, caro, I wasn't being so literal. Your heart line governs your emotions, and love." Fiorella kept stroking his hand, and The Three Tonys watched like the little-old-man version of see no evil, hear no evil, speak no evil.

"LOVE?" her father repeated, and Mary boiled over, hoisted him up by his arm, and wrenched him out of his chair.

"Pop, come with me. I need to talk to you for a minute."

"WHY?" her father asked, bewildered, and across the table, Pigeon Tony looked up, his baby-owl eyes round with confusion. If he could speak English, Mary knew he'd call her a party-pooper.

"But I want to hear his future," Feet said.

"Me, too." Tony-From-Down-The-Block frowned. "You're going to mess up the magic, Mare."

Only Fiorella remained calm, withdrawing her hands. "We will continue when you return, Mariano."

Her father allowed himself to be tugged out of the kitchen, past his wife, through the dining and living room, and outside. Mary closed the D door behind them and they stood on the stoop in the hot sun. She could smell that he was wearing cologne, and it wasn't even a Holy Day of Obligation.

"Pop, what do you think you're doing? Letting Fiorella touch your hand like that? Driving her around? What about Mom?"

"WHAT ABOUT HER?" Her father shrugged in the thin white shirt he always wore to church. "YOUR MOTHER WANTED ME TO DRIVE HER."

"I saw you at breakfast with her, at a restaurant. Did Mom ask you to do that?"

"SHE GOT HUNGRY AFTER THE HOSPITAL." Her father blinked against the brightness. "WHAT'S THE BIG DEAL?"

"Fiorella wants you to be hubby number six."

"ARE YOU NUTS?" Her father rubbed his tummy like a summertime Santa. "SHE COULD DO A LOT BETTER THAN A FATSO LIKE ME."

"That's not the point, and she can't tell your fortune, she just wants to touch your hand. She's flirting with you, Pop, and you're flirting back!"

"MARE, I'LL FORGET YOU SAID THAT." Her father wagged a thick index finger at her, and she couldn't remember ever having angry words with him, especially not outside. The neighbors stopped washing their stoops, garden hoses hanging from their hands and cigarettes dangling from their lips.

"But Pop—"

"*BASTA!*" Her father showed her a palm, then opened the screen door, and went inside.

Leaving Mary to face the neighbors, suddenly not *reposado* anymore, at all.

Chapter Thirty-two

Bennie opened her eyes into white light, so bright it hurt her eyes. She didn't know where she was or what was happening. She blinked, lying still, in confusion. She wasn't coughing anymore, nor was she gasping. She could breathe. Odors of filth, urine, and sweat filled her nostrils. They told her she was still in the box, but she was alive, which meant that the light could be a hole in the lid.

"My God in heaven," she heard herself say. The animal must have made the hole, finally scratching his way through, along the long crack in the lid. She felt a sort of gratitude, and wonderment. She passed her hand over her eyes a couple of times, blocking and un-blocking the light. She left her hand in the air, catching the light in her palm. She spread her fingers slightly, and a single shaft of bright-ness shot toward her, like a glowing wand onto her hand.

It's the sun!

She tried to think, to reason. The box must be outside some-where, and the animal was gone now. If it was nocturnal, it would be back tonight. She felt a familiar bolt of fear and slammed the hole with the heel of her hand. Pain shot down her arm, but she ignored it. If the animal had made this hole, she was going to make it larger and bust through it. It was her only chance, and she had to do it before the animal came back.

She pounded on the hole with her palms, pressing upward with all her might. Her hands hurt so much, but she couldn't stop. She wanted to live. She didn't feel hunger or thirst. She visualized breaking through the lid, powering through to the sunlight.

And survival.

Chapter Thirty-three

Alice opened her eyes to sunlight, pouring through the bedroom window. She buried her head back in the pillow, then remembered that Grady had spent the night. She turned over, but his side of the bed was empty. She checked the bathroom, but he wasn't there, either. She sat up in bed and looked at the clock.

Damn!

She had overslept. She was supposed to be worried about the dog, and sleeping late didn't fit the story. She jumped out of bed, put on a fresh Bennie outfit, found the Birks by the dresser, and hurried downstairs, fluffing up her hair, which still had the barrette. When she hit the ground floor, she smelled bacon, so she slowed her pace and walked into the kitchen, rubbing her eyes.

"Hey, you." Grady turned from the stove, came over, and gave her a hug. He had changed into jeans and a navy Lacoste shirt, revealing a torso that tapered to a trim waist. He looked so sexy she almost forgave him for his failure to launch.

"I had such a headache I couldn't sleep, all night." Alice broke their clinch and looked at him, pained. "That must be why I overslept. I really want to get to the hospital."

"Relax. I called and they said he was hanging in. They'll give us the details when we get there." Grady smiled. On the counter behind him was a plate of bacon, and an empty frying pan sat on the burner next to a carton of brown eggs. "You want coffee? The bacon is extra crispy, the way you like it."

"How nice, thanks." Alice loved her bacon extra crispy, which proved that she and Bennie had exactly one thing in common.

"I was waiting until you came down to start the eggs. How do you want them?"

Alice had no idea how Bennie liked her eggs or coffee, and details like that could tip her hand. "You know, I'm sorry, I'm not hungry."

"But we didn't have dinner last night."

"I'm too upset to eat. Why don't we just go, see how he is?"

"But you love bacon. I've seen you eat entire pigs."

"Not this morning. I'll get my bag." Alice left the kitchen for the living room, looking for Bennie's messenger bag.

"Let me put the eggs away," Grady called from the kitchen, where suddenly the telephone rang.

"Don't pick up," Alice called back. She didn't need another test. She found the bag and went to the front door. "We have to get going."

"Okay."

The phone stopped ringing, but there were clicks that sounded like an old-fashioned answering machine, and Alice stopped, her hand on the knob. Did Bennie have an answering machine? Who still had an old-fashioned answering machine? How had she missed it? In the next second, a woman's voice started talking, amplified.

"Bennie?" It was Mary DiNunzio. "I got the brief finished for Alice's restraining order, with Judy's help. I hope you won't need it, but it's good to have. I'll email you a final tonight. See you tomorrow. Take care, bye."

Oh no! Alice couldn't believe her ears. She opened the front door like the call was nothing, but it was the last thing she needed. Now Grady would know that she was back in Bennie's life. If she kept making little slips, it could give him reason to wonder whether she really was Bennie. Alice told herself to play it cool, but Grady came slowly out of the kitchen, his brow knit and his eyes concerned behind his glasses.

"Does she mean Alice Connelly?" he asked. "Are you getting a restraining order? What's going on?"

"Nothing, really. You know DiNunzio. She's overreacting, big-time."

"What happened?"

"I got a call that Alice quit her job, is all." Alice reminded herself to stay the course. Until now he had no reason to suspect anything, and she couldn't let Mary's phone call ruin everything. "She wanted to get a restraining order, just in case."

"Why did she quit?"

"I'll fill you in on the way. Let's go." Alice walked out the door, and Grady followed, puzzled.

"Has she threatened you?"

"No, but DiNunzio wanted to have it in place, in case she did."

"I didn't even know you two were in contact. Last time I heard, Alice had skipped town, after you were nice enough to prove her not guilty, for free."

"Can we not talk about this now." Alice locked the front door, and when she turned around, Grady was frowning. She hurried down the steps and passed him on the sidewalk. "Let's go, we have to go."

"You sound like you're not taking this seriously. Alice is danger-ous."

Thank you. "No, she's not."

"She's a sociopath."

Flatterer. "Don't be silly."

"You always underestimated her. You trust her when you shouldn't."

You got that right. "I don't trust her, not completely."

"Bennie, why didn't you tell me about this last night? This is big news, and you didn't even mention it."

"I was worried about Bear, and I still am. You drive, okay?" Alice tossed him the keys when they reached the car, and they got inside. She didn't need all these questions right now. It was just her luck that Grady picked this weekend to hook up with his long-lost love. She flashed on that saying about the best-laid plans.

And I didn't even get laid.

Chapter Thirty-four

Mary was losing hope that she and Anthony would find a house, ever. They'd seen four in their price range, but all of them fell short of Curb Appeal! and New Fixtures! and Five Years Young! The one they were about to see was the "reach," which she realized was code for perfect when she saw the façade of the lovely brick townhouse, three stories high, with glossy black shutters and matching window boxes, bright with pink and white snapdragons.

"Welcome, folks, I'm Janine Robinson," the realtor said, opening the door. She was an older woman, nicely made up, though her linen pantsuit had folded into an accordion. Mary had done her time in linen, and it was time for everybody to agree that linen wasn't good for anything except irons.

"Hello," Anthony said, introducing them both, which provoked the typical response from Janine the realtor:

"How long have you two been married?"

"We're not," Mary answered, since it was her turn, and Anthony stepped into the entrance hall, his hands linked loosely behind his back.

Janine smiled, toothily. "Oh, are you getting married?"

"No, we are going to live in sin." Mary's favorite old-time euphemism was "shacked up," but only Tony-From-Down-The-Block used that one. Nobody trying to sell you a house ever said you were shacking up, even if you were.

"Are you working with anyone?" Janine asked, which Mary knew was another euphemism, for will-I-be-getting-a-three-percent-commission-or-six?

"No, we don't have a broker. We're on our own."

"Come with me, I'll show you around, then I'll let you two wander upstairs."

"Great, thanks." Mary stepped into the living room, where something funny happened. She had never lived in any house as nice as this, but it felt instantly like home.

Janine was saying, "Fully renovated living room, new parquet floors, authentic crown molding, southern exposure, everything a young couple could ask for . . ."

Mary zoned her out. She had memorized the listing, and any idiot could see that the room was flooded with light, unusual for the city, and that its colonial proportions had a historic grace. The windowsills were a foot thick, begging for a window seat or a housecat. She and Mike used to have a cat, but she pressed that thought away.

Janine continued, "Here you see the dining room, also spacious, with windows that overlook this charming courtyard. The brick patio is new, and the plantings are specimen, a miniature cypress and several yew bushes."

Yew? Yay! Mary peeked into the courtyard, captivated. She could imagine sitting outside, reading in an Adirondacks chair. She'd never had a house with a real backyard. Her parents had had a concrete pad for their trashcans, where her father had once tried to grow a fig tree, required for Italian men of a certain generation.

"The kitchen, over here, has also been fully renovated, all stainless steel, and you can see it's fitted for a gourmet. Viking Range, Sub-Zero refrigerator, KitchenAid trash compactor, all top-of-the-line." Janine gestured to the glossy tan countertop. "This, of course, is granite, and all of the plumbing is Perrin & Rowe, which comes directly from London, England."

Mary stared at the sunshine reflecting on the stainless steel. It was a dream kitchen, plus she could get an excellent tan.

"I'll let you find your way upstairs. There's a nursery up there, next to the master." Janine picked up a fact sheet. "Anthony, take this. Your girlfriend looks too smitten to read it."

"She is?" Anthony turned with a bemused smile.

"Not yet," Mary said, to preserve their bargaining position. Her neck blotches alone would drive the price sky-high.

Janine handed them both her business card. "Don't wait too long on this listing, folks. I had a crowd in here today, even with everybody away. This one won't be on the market much longer."

"Thanks," Mary said, slipping the card into her purse. She and Anthony left the kitchen and went upstairs in silence, as was their custom. Neither wanted to influence the other, and she suspected that the realtors eavesdropped. They went into the master bedroom and closed the door behind them.

"Can you believe this place?" Mary whispered, and Anthony started laughing.

"I know. I don't need to see the rest."

"Me, neither!" Mary's heart leapt with happiness.

"We should go."

"What?" Mary didn't understand. "We should buy it!"

"*What?*" Anthony looked at her like she was nuts. "Do you know how much this place costs?"

"I know it's expensive, but do you like it?"

"Did you see this?" Anthony held up the fact sheet, like a teacher holding up a flunking exam, and Mary was the worst student in class.

"I know the asking price from the listing."

"You didn't tell me."

"I told you it was a reach."

"It's not a reach, it's Everest!" Anthony laughed, but Mary didn't.

"Do you like it?"

"Of course I like it. What's not to like, except the price and the location?"

"What's wrong with the location? It's right off Rittenhouse Square, the best location in Center City. I can walk to work, you can walk to the library or the train."

"I know, but—"

"But what?"

"Come on." Anthony puckered his lower lip. "It's a bit much, don't you think?"

"No, I don't think. What's that mean?"

"Over the top. It's so much more than we need."

Mary blinked. "What is? It's a house, and we need a house."

"Do we need a gourmet kitchen? Most of the time, we eat take-out."

"Now we do, but we don't have to," Mary said, starting to feel bothered. "We won't always do that. We can make nice meals."

"But we won't, and we didn't even see the rest of the house."

"I know, and we'll look, but it's already perfect for us, I can just feel it. Why shouldn't we have a nice house, if we can?"

"But we can't, babe." Anthony's expression darkened, and his lips pursed. "*I* can't."

Mary swallowed. They were finally going to have this conversation, so she spoke from the heart. "Don't worry about it, I can afford it," she said, softening her tone.

"What are you saying? It's a reach even for you, isn't it?"

"I know that, but I can afford it."

"So what does that mean, in practical terms?" Anthony asked, pained. "I can't afford to buy this with you. I don't have even half of this down payment."

"Then I'll buy it. I'll put down the whole amount, and you keep your money."

"Babe, I can't even afford half of what this monthly mortgage would be." Anthony looked stricken. "It might be within your reach, but it isn't in mine."

"Then don't pay anything. Here's what I think." Mary finally had clarity. She should have talked to him about this a long time ago, like Judy said. "I can afford the whole thing, and I want you to live with me. It doesn't matter who pays."

"It does to me." Anthony's expression went cold. "I can't do that, I can't let you do that. I'd feel kept."

"But you're not. Somebody has to make more than somebody else, and it happens to be me. It just happens."

"Not to me."

"Yes, to you." Mary tried to moderate her voice. "It'll be my name on the deed, if you don't mind, but no one has to know. We love each other and we live together, that's all."

"I can't do it, babe." Anthony thrust the fact sheet at her, and Mary gave up, throwing it to the ground.

"Then how do I win? I can't win!"

"It's not about winning and losing."

"Women make that deal every day, and nobody thinks it's weird!"

"It's not a deal, either. No man in the world would feel comfortable with that arrangement."

"I know one who would!" Mary shot back, angry, and she didn't have to explain who she meant. Anthony went red in the face, his dark eyes glittering with bitterness.

"I'm not him, and I'm not buying this house."

"Well, I'm trying to make partner in a law firm, and I can't be less than I am so you'll feel good about yourself!"

Anthony looked stunned, and even Mary couldn't believe what she'd said. It was true but unsayable, which was a category she hadn't known existed, until now.

"Then buy it, *partner*." Anthony turned away and walked out of the bedroom, his steps echoing in the large, empty house.

Chapter Thirty-five

Bennie pummeled the bright little hole, over and over again. The animal's constant scratching had thinned the wood around it, and the lid was splintering along the crack. She picked at the edges of the hole with her fingers, then she bashed the wood until painstakingly, excruciatingly, and infinitesimally, she was widening the hole, its golden circle like her own personal sun.

It was the size of a dime, and she was aiming for a quarter, and so she kept going. She had to finish before the animal came back. Her face was soaked with sweat, perspiration drenched her entire body, and though she could breathe, the air in the box had grown hotter. She hit harder, and suddenly, something fell through it onto her face. She blinked and shook it off, reflexively. It felt like dirt, and then she understood.

I'm buried alive.

She forced herself not to panic. She started pounding again, but her hands were bloody and every blow hurt, so she hooked her hand inside the neck of her cotton shirt and yanked hard. It tore the shirt down the front, and she wrenched the fabric back and forth to rip it to the bottom, ending up with a bandage, of sorts. She wrapped it around her right hand, pressing it into the open wound with her chin. The pain brought tears to her eyes, but she got back to work, pounding and picking.

She stayed strong thinking of Grady. If she got out of this alive, she would call him and tell him that he was more important than work, more important than anything. That she thought about him every day, he was always in the back of her mind, and that she had called his office once and hung up, like a teenager. She'd even Googled him to see what cases he was working on, she'd read his articles and briefs online. She would beg him back.

She stuck her finger through the hole to keep widening it, grabbing the edge and wiggling it up and down to break off more and more pieces of wood. There was no other way to keep going, and she hit the lid again and again with her bandaged hand, powered by the sheer will to live.

And the memory of a love she'd left behind.

Chapter Thirty-six

"Hi, I'm Bennie Rosato, here about my dog, Bear." Alice stood at the reception window, with Grady, and the vet student behind the plastic shield was different from last night's. He looked young, with a tiny black goatee and a neck tattoo of a bar code, which Alice guessed passed for a bad boy, among graduate students.

"Hold on, are you *the* Bennie Rosato?" he asked, his dark eyes lighting up. "My girlfriend's at the law school, and she took your class in appellate advocacy last year. She loved you. Her name's Sherry Quatriere. Do you remember her?"

"Lemme think a minute."

"Dark hair? Dreadlocks? She's Jamaican."

"Of course. Sherry. Give her my love."

"I'll tell her, she'll be so excited. Let me go check on your doggie." The vet student jumped up. "Why don't you take a seat over there?"

"Thanks." Alice turned, and she and Grady walked over to the waiting area, which was empty except for a lady with a plastic cat carrier on her lap. They sat down in the plastic bucket seats next to a wall of memorial plaques in honor of dogs and cats, which proved to Alice that there really was a sucker born every minute.

Grady saw her looking at them. "Don't read them. They'll make you sad."

"I know." *What a waste of money.*

"I've been thinking, I was supposed to leave tonight, but I'd like to stick around for a couple of days. Between Bear and Alice coming back into your life, what kind of boyfriend would I be if I blew out of town?"

No! "But don't you have to be somewhere?"

"I have a deal tomorrow in Pittsburgh, an employee buyout of some trade magazines, but I could get my partner to fill in. I'll tell him it's a family emergency. As far as my other matters, I have my laptop and I can work anywhere. Set me up in an office at the firm, I'll be fine."

Alice remembered that saying about keeping your enemies closer, then looked at him with grateful eyes. "Would you really do that, for me?"

"Of course." Grady leaned over and kissed her gently on the cheek, then there was a noise to the left as the EMPLOYEES ONLY doors banged open. A vet emerged and walked toward them, carrying a clipboard. His expression was serious, and Alice's hopes soared.

"How is he?" she asked, rising, and so did Grady, slipping his arm around her shoulder.

"Please." The vet waved them into their seats. "Please. Sit."

Bad news! Alice sank into her seat with Grady's arm around her.

"He has a hematoma on his spleen, a result of his fall. It didn't show up on the X-ray but it did on the ultrasound. We can do surgery, but there can be serious complications, especially in a dog his age. I can't say for sure that he'll survive it, and the surgery is expensive. It could cost between three and five thousand dollars."

Hell, no. Gas him now. If you don't, I will. Got a hose?

"Our records show that you don't have any insurance. I don't know if you want to put him through that, or if you want to undertake that kind of expense." The vet faced Alice, all earnest. "You can let him go, or see him through the surgery and hope for a good result, though the odds are very low. It's a difficult decision."

It's a no-brainer. Alice acted like she was bravely holding back tears, and Grady leaned over to the vet.

"Doc, what would you do, in our position?"

"People always ask us that." The vet smiled sadly. "Bear isn't my dog, but I know how much you love him. Any decision you make will be the right one, because there are no wrong answers."

Done deal. Alice was about to give the mutt the thumbs-down.

Grady asked, "Can we see him?"

"Of course, and if you do decide to put him down, you can be with him."

Complete waste of ten minutes.

The vet led them out of the waiting room, through the doors, and into a huge room filled with examination tables, medical equipment, and vets in white coats and green scrubs, attending to animals in cages on three sides.

"Where is he?" Grady asked, and Alice hung back, playing the bereaved mother.

"Here." The vet pointed to one of the large cages on the bottom, where Bear lay on a white blanket. His eyes were closed, and a plastic tube snaked from his front leg out of the cage to a bottle attached to the bars. He looked half-dead, and Alice felt like celebrating.

"Poor guy." Grady crossed to the cage and knelt down.

"I know." Alice stood behind him and tried to tear up—*$5,000, $5,000 $5,000.* In the next minute, her eyes were wet.

"Bear?" Grady called softly, and the dog raised his head slowly, and looked up at them. Then, all of a sudden, he freaked out, barking in fear and trying to get up. His back legs scissored, and his front clawed the blanket, yanking out the IV tube.

Alice knew he was reacting to her, but Grady leapt to his feet, flustered as the vet tried to calm the frantic dog, and two vet techs rushed over to help.

"Grady, back off," Alice said. "He doesn't remember you. You're upsetting him. Let's get you out of here." She took Grady's arm and hurried him through the double doors to the waiting room.

"I'm so sorry." Flushed, Grady raked his hair back with his hands. "I thought he would know me. He did last night."

"Last night he was barely conscious. Don't feel bad. Maybe it's the drugs they gave him."

"No, it was me." Grady pouted like a little boy, and Alice wished she could kiss him right there, tongue included.

"It wasn't your fault."

"Yes, it was. I shouldn't have gone in. He didn't look good at all, did he?"

"He looked awful." Alice blinked away her bogus tears.

"He seems even older than yesterday, if that's possible. How old is he?"

"It's been a long time since you've seen him. He's really aged."

"Poor old guy." Grady gave Alice a hug, and she let her arms encircle his waist, looking forward to a rematch.

"I hate to see him suffering like that."

"I know." Grady released her and looked into her eyes. "So what do you want to do? He's your dog, it's your decision."

"I know what to do. The right thing."

"Really?"

"Really." Alice managed a shaky smile.

It could be a whole new thing. Grief sex.

Chapter Thirty-seven

Mary sat cross-legged on her bed, working in her Donovan McNabb jersey, gym shorts, and glasses. The air conditioner rattled, a hot coffee cooled on the night table, and her brief glowed on her laptop. All systems were go except her brain. She kept thinking of Anthony and whether she should call him. She wished she could take back some of those awful words.

She didn't know if she was right or wrong. She didn't know if a house mattered more than a man, or if it was a house that she was standing up for. It was confusing. She hadn't known the words would come out of her mouth until they did, but when she heard them, they sounded true. She was standing up for herself, right?

She put it out of her mind and read the last paragraph of her brief for the umpteenth time. The facts section was empty because Alice hadn't done anything bad yet, but the case law in the legal section needed editing. She had to email the brief to Bennie tonight, then get to work on her own clients. She'd brought in five new ones last week and she had tons to do.

Then buy it, partner.

She forced herself to refocus and deleted a word, trying to smooth out the writing, then her mind wandered and she picked up her BlackBerry. There were new emails from clients, but none from Anthony. No texts or calls from him that she'd missed by accident. She thought about calling him but she didn't know what to say, and texting him would be so middle-school. Instead, she called Judy, who sounded out of breath, with salsa music blaring in the background.

"What's that?" Mary asked. "You at a club?"

"No, home. Frank is teaching me how to samba."

"Frank can *samba*?"

"Oh, there's nothing that man doesn't know."

Mary smiled. "Catch you later. I just wanted to see how were feeling."

"No more evil eye."

"Congratulations, see you tomorrow." Mary pressed END and set the phone back down.

She stared at the computer, feeling night falling like a closing curtain. She was betwixt and between, lost between apartment and house, associate and partner, boyfriend and late husband. She thought about calling her parents, but they'd ask about Anthony and she was the worst liar in the bar association. She would bet her father was hurt about what she'd said to him, but she couldn't take that back, either. She wished she could talk to her sister, who was on yet another mission, a twin trying to prove she was unique.

Her gaze fell on the brief, and she wondered what it was like to be Bennie and have a twin who disliked you. It would be like warring with your very self. Bennie didn't deserve that kind of pain, not after all she'd done for Alice.

DiNunzio, I appreciate you.

She read the paragraph again, reenergized. She didn't have time for a pity party. She was a professional and she had a job to do. Bennie was her client, and anybody who wanted to hurt her would have to get through Mary.

She took a slug of warm coffee and got busy.

Chapter Thirty-eight

Bennie counted *one, two, three,* and the wood splintered with a cracking sound. The hole had gone from a quarter to a fist, and it had blackened like a solar eclipse, so she knew it was dark outside. The animal would be back soon. She pounded harder than before, smashing the heel of her palm against where the wood splintered. It cracked again. She grabbed the wood with her bandaged hand and pressed up. The piece broke, but was still hinged to the wood.

"HELPPPPP!" she screamed. She didn't know how far underground she was, but it couldn't be that far, judging from the light through the hole. Maybe somebody could hear her shouting. She wrenched the wood back and forth until she could tear the piece off. She thrust her arm through the hole, threw the chunk of wood out, and started all over again.

She pounded on the hole, ignoring the pain. She had to get free, she felt it like a wild desire, a natural force that fueled her, propelling her upward. She didn't smell the filth anymore, only the earth that kept falling inside the box, shaken loose. She heard the splintering again, busted off another piece and pressed it backwards, grunting with exertion. It gave way and broke off, widening the hole to the size of her shoulder. She let the wood piece fall and started pounding next to it, bashing as hard as she could. The animal could come back any minute.

Sweat poured over her face but she kept breaking the hole until it was almost big enough for her head. Dirt fell onto her eyes, and she heard a shuffling above. A shadow chased across the hole, maybe three feet from her face. The animal was back, growling. Terror struck. Her throat and face lay exposed. She shrieked.

Suddenly the animal jammed his snout through the hole, frenzied and growling. Jaws snapped inches from her nose. Saliva dripped on her cheek. She squeezed herself against the side of the box. She screamed again and again.

The animal rammed his snout farther down, frenzied. His breath reeked of carrion. She kicked the lid to scare him, but he kept coming, driving her against the side of the box. She fumbled for the piece of wood she had dropped. She prayed it had a jagged edge.

She heard somebody roaring, like a war cry, and it was her. Her fingers found the wood piece. She stabbed the animal, slicing his lip. He writhed in pain. His head got caught in the hole. He couldn't back out. It was do or die for the both of them.

The animal bit down. Sharp teeth raked her fingers and ripped her bandage. She stabbed again. She cut his nose, and he roared in protest, throwing his head this way and that, the movement trapping his head inside.

She stabbed again and again, finally jamming the knife into his mouth, where it stuck. His terrified yelp gave her an opening. She punched his snout again and again. The animal backed out of the hole yelping in distress.

She reached up, grabbed the edge of the hole, and wrenched the wood back and forth frantically until it cracked off. Still the hole wasn't large enough for her. She attacked the hole again, desperate. Another piece splintered off, a skinny shard shaped like a spike.

Yes.

Dirt fell in the box. The animal yelped and cried on the surface, about a foot over head. A circle of black sky glimmered above her.

She waited for the right moment. The animal ran back and forth over the hole. The cries and scuffling came closer.

Go.

She launched herself upward, leading with the spike. Her head exploded through the hole to the surface. The animal screamed. It was a skinny wolf, brown and gray in the moonlight. But she felt like a wolf now, too. Lethal, primal. She embedded the wood in the fur of his underbelly, his skin hot against her knuckles.

The wolf whipped his head around, his canines bared. The whites of his eyes showed terror and fury. She let her arm drop, and the wolf bolted away, yelping.

She scrambled out of the hole and reached the surface, panting hard. Listening for the wolf. His cries sounded farther and farther away. She felt an urge to go after him, hunt him down, and finish him off. She ran a few steps but she suddenly didn't have the strength.

She fell to her knees and collapsed, utterly exhausted. Bloodied. Shaking, as her adrenaline ebbed away, leaving her lying face-down in the grass. In the middle of an open field, under a night sky and a full moon.

Alive.

Chapter Thirty-nine

Alice sat in the passenger seat of the car, trying to look stricken. She couldn't make herself cry, so she aimed for numb with grief, which was more like Bennie anyway. Luckily it was dark, so no Academy Award performance was required. Grady steered the car from the Penn campus, heading home in silence, his eyes glistening like a complete loser.

"I know how hard a decision that was for you," he said, his hands on the wheel.

"We did the right thing. It's selfish to make him suffer."

"That's true, but it's the passing of an era."

No, it's the passing of a dog, dude.

Grady hit the gas as the light was about to turn red, and the Lexus cruised forward in light traffic. "You know what's bugging me?"

Let me guess. Why you can't get it up?

"It's bugging me that he'll be alone while they put him down. All by himself."

Oh, please. "I can't stay with him. I couldn't take it."

"I know." Grady slowed the car, cranked the wheel to the left, and made a U-turn. "I want to be with him. I want him to know that we loved him. Wouldn't you feel better, knowing I was with him?"

Alice suppressed an eye-roll. "But you upset him."

"Maybe I just surprised him. He used to be my buddy, remember, we ran together? I'll go and be there with him, so he's not alone."

Alice tried to think of the Bennie-like response. She didn't want to make him suspicious, after Mary's phone call. "Okay. I really appreciate it."

"Good. I just hope I get there in time."

"Me, too." Alice forced a little hiccup that would sound like a stifled sob. "This is really great of you."

Grady hit the gas, slid his cell phone from his back pocket, and flipped it open. "Perfect. My battery's dead."

You're telling me.

"I didn't charge it last night. Do you have your phone with you? I want to call the hospital and tell them not to do anything until I get there."

"Good idea." Alice fumbled in Bennie's messenger bag, but there was no BlackBerry. "I forgot it this morning. I was too distracted. Sorry."

"That's okay, we're only a few blocks away. Hang on." Grady sped up Spruce Street, running a red light, and they were at the vet hospital in less than five minutes. He parked in the emergency parking, cut the ignition, and placed a comforting hand on her shoulder. "You sure you're okay here?"

"Yes."

"I'll tell him you love him."

"Thank you." Alice was so bored with all this talk about the stupid dog. "Sorry I'm not coming in."

"Try to rest, and hang in there." Grady gave her a quick kiss, jumped out of the driver's seat, and jogged to the entrance of the hospital, disappearing inside.

Alice breathed a relieved sigh. She switched on the radio and found a hip-hop station playing Usher, then Justin Timberlake and Ludacris came on, and if they played anything sexier she'd be rocking the car all by herself. Finally Grady reappeared at the hospital exit, leaving with his head down. She snapped off the radio and pretended to be dozing as he hustled toward the car and opened the door. She faked waking up and looked at him.

"I can't believe it," she said, drowsily. "I must have fallen asleep."

"You're exhausted from last night." Grady gave her a hug, and she could feel wetness on his cheek.

"Was it horrible?"

"Let's not talk about it, okay?" Grady's voice sounded husky. "You go back to sleep, and I'll get you home."

"Whatever you say." Alice let herself slump backwards in the seat. She looked out the window as they steered from the parking lot and drove home in silence.

No talk and no sex. We're practically married.

Chapter Forty

Mary shifted on the bed, her concentration refocused. The laptop had gotten hot so she had to rest it on a pillow, and its bright screen glowed in the darkening bedroom. She read the legal section one last time, then leaned back with a sigh of satisfaction.

Maybe I deserve to be a partner after all?

She lifted the computer and pillow off her lap, set it aside, and reached for her coffee, but it was long gone. She glanced at the clock, which told her that she'd spent way too long on the brief, especially when she had so many of her own cases. She logged on to her email and wrote to Bennie:

I'm attaching the brief. Let me know what you think, and I appreciate your kind words today.

She signed off with "Best, Mary," because "Love, Mary" would get her fired, then attached the brief and clicked SEND. Anthony popped back into her head, the thought sent from the boyfriend lobe, which seemed to be waiting for her to finish work. She checked her BlackBerry. No email from him, no text or calls. He was waiting her out, playing love chicken. Or maybe he was letting himself cool down, or he had just gone to sleep.

The realtor's business card was sitting on the bedspread, and she picked it up and ran a thumb over the blue embossed letters. She flashed on the house, which was perfect. True, it was a reach, but even her father had said it made sense to step up when you found the house you really wanted. Should she buy the house? If she did, would that be the end of them, or could they work it out?

She felt a pang of love and longing, and this time it was for Anthony. She wanted to live with him, and at times, she wanted to marry him. He was special, and years of dating had taught her that good men are harder to find than good houses. So why lose him for four walls and a roof? She didn't need a gourmet kitchen for spaghetti and meatballs.

But why do I need his permission to buy something I want?

A hard nub of resentment lodged in her chest, and she knew it wouldn't go away if she gave up the house. It would only grow, impinging on her heart, and in time she would blame him for a decision that she herself had made. She read the business card again and picked up her BlackBerry.

Wondering.

Chapter Forty-one

Bennie stood up as soon as she had the strength, swaying unsteadily. The moon shone surprisingly bright. The air smelled sweet and clean. A breeze caressed her battered body, rustling the tatters of her clothes. She wiped blood, tears, dirt, and sweat from her face, looking around the field.

It was dark around her, with no houses in sight. The grass had been cut for hay and lay in humped rows. In the distance was a tall treeline and a hulk of farm machinery. She remembered the shaking she'd felt in the box, the tornado she'd heard driving over her. It had been a harvesting machine.

It struck her then what must have happened. The hay in the field must have been tall when Alice had buried the box, but she wouldn't have known that it would be cut at the end of the month. The harvesting machine, and the wolf, had saved Bennie's life.

She started walking, wobbly and weary, looking for a road. Her bare feet aching, her hand trailed its bloody bandage. She didn't want to think about what she looked like. She hadn't eaten in forever, her throat was dry and parched. She felt dizzy and weak.

She heard the screech of a faraway owl. The loud knocking of a woodpecker, echoing over the field. Crickets everywhere. She passed a herd of deer lying in the short grass. They spotted her, startled, and took off, their back hooves flying, white tails upright as surrender flags.

She kept walking, using the hayrow as a guideline. Above shone the stars, their whiteness brighter out in the country. They pierced a velveteen sky, a glittery whitewash of stardust. She remembered looking at the stars so long ago, when her mother was still alive. She had thought that her family was fixed as the constellations, but she'd been wrong. She'd learned that stars changed and so did families, hers when it belatedly acquired its darkest star.

She walked through another field, passing immense rolls of hay, lined up together like houses, two stories high. She followed the rows of mown hay when she could and her sense of direction when she couldn't, stumbling and halting but going ever forward, and she saw a black ribbon of paved road that snaked along the fields, its canary yellow divider phosphorescent in the moonshine.

She almost cried with happiness. She staggered over, reached the shoulder, and walked next to it in the grass. It was only a matter of time until someone drove by. She'd call the cops and find Alice, no matter where she tried to hide. She'd charge her, prosecute her, and lock her away for good. Twin or no. Sister or no. Blood or no.

Her pace quickened, heedless of her sore everything. And when she spotted a pair of headlights coming down the road, she thanked God.

For salvation.

And for vengeance.

Chapter Forty-two

Alice trailed Grady into the house, acting grief-stricken, and he hugged her as the door closed behind them.

"I know what you need," he said softly. "Remember my specialty, from our Vermont trip? When you saw that deer and got all upset? I'll make it. You haven't eaten all day."

"Thanks, but I'm not hungry."

"Not at all?" Grady pulled away from her, surprised. "It'll cheer you up. Do you have the ingredients?"

"I doubt it." Alice was playing the odds. Whatever the ingredients were, Bennie wasn't the homemaker type. "But I should get to work, I have a new client coming in tomorrow. Rexco. It's a big meeting and I should prepare."

"You can't work now, you know that." Grady touched her cheek tenderly. "Why don't you go up and rest? I'll bring you dinner in bed. Is that bodega still on Spring Garden?"

God knows. "Yes."

"I'll go get the stuff and be right back." Grady gave her a quick kiss, then went to the front door. "You're going to go rest?"

"Yes. Promise." Alice flashed him a smile, and he left.

As soon as the door closed, she dropped the smile. Something was bugging her and she felt antsy. Hinky. She should have known about the Vermont thing. She hoped Grady wasn't getting suspicious. She fetched the messenger bag and went upstairs to the home office. She scattered the Rexco file around the desk and fired up the computer so it looked like she'd been working. Then she went to the bathroom and switched on the light, checking her reflection.

I don't look sad, I look horny.

She wet a bar of soap, worked up a lather, and rubbed a little into her eyes. They stung like hell, and tears flowed. She rinsed and dried her face, but spilled water on her shirt by accident. She crossed to the dresser and opened the middle drawer to find something dry. She grabbed yet another oversized T-shirt. VESPER ROWING, it read, and she was slipping into it when she spotted something strange outside.

She went to the window. She didn't have the best view, and her eyes were killing her, but it looked like Grady was on a pay phone, down the street. It was too far away to be sure it was him, but she thought it was his blond hair and he was holding a paper bag in his left hand.

Who used pay phones, except people whose cell phone batteries had run out, or who had something to hide? Or both?

She watched him hang up the phone and hurry toward the house, so it was definitely Grady. Her thoughts raced. If he had stopped at Bennie's on impulse, he probably hadn't told his friends or family where he was going. And if he'd asked his law partner to cover for him on a family emergency, then his office didn't know he was at his old girlfriend's. Odds were, no one knew Grady was here.

Perfect.

Alice grabbed a wad of Kleenex from a box on the night table and flopped face-down on the bed, burying her face in the pillow as if she'd been crying. In the next minute, she heard the front door open and close downstairs.

"Come on up!" she called out, forming a new plan. If Grady didn't mention that he'd made a phone call, it could mean he was getting suspicious of her.

Boyfriend might have to get dead, after all.

Chapter Forty-three

Mary put the realtor's card back down on the bedspread. Anthony hadn't called, but she wasn't about to stand on ceremony. Partners didn't play power games, except when it was billable.

She speed-dialed him and listened to the phone ringing. Once, twice, three times, then his voicemail came on. The sound of his voice gave her a familiar pang, but she didn't give in to a love attack. She thought about leaving him a call-back message, but she didn't want to do that either. Why hadn't he picked up? Was he blowing her off?

She put down the BlackBerry. Maybe he was in the bathroom or the shower. She got up, stretched her legs, and went to the bathroom. She emerged a few minutes later, made a beeline for the BlackBerry, and speed-dialed him again. Still no answer. She could feel herself start to simmer. When the voicemail came on, she no longer felt a pang when she heard his voice.

Would it kill you to pick up?

She felt grumpier by the minute. She had a right to buy a house if she wanted one. Anthony should be willing to talk about it. Who was he to not take her phone calls? They said they loved each other, didn't that mean anything? At the very least, it should mean I-take-your-calls-even-when-I'm-pissed-at-you.

She picked up the laptop on its pillow desk and logged on to her email, killing time before the next phone call. She'd gotten two zillion emails from clients and she kept opening them without really reading them, preoccupied. Anthony could at least pick up. His mother spoiled him. He was the darling of the family, just because he wasn't on parole.

When she figured about fifteen minutes had passed, she called him again. No answer. She found herself boiling over, but when the beep came on, she restrained herself and hung up. She would give him one last chance. And by the way, she was sick of always being the one to make up after they fought.

She tried to return to her email, but she'd worked herself up too much. She called Anthony and listened to the phone ring again. Frustrated, she picked up the realtor's card and called her cell, and the call was answered in the middle of the first ring.

"This is Janine Robinson."

"Hi, it's Mary DiNunzio, and we met today at the open house. I came with my boyfriend."

"Yes, I remember you. How can I help you?"

"I'm sorry to bother you after hours, but I've been thinking about that house all day. I wanted to ask you a few questions, like how long it's been on the market and—"

"Let me stop you right there. I already have two offers on the listing."

Mary's mouth dropped open. "You mean two people have already put in bids?"

"Yes, exactly."

"Does that mean I couldn't have the house, even if I wanted it?"

"You weren't working with anyone, correct?"

"I have no broker." Mary could almost hear Janine running the numbers in her head, coming up with a boatload of dough.

"I can tell you, confidentially, that neither of these bids is for the asking price. You're free to make an offer, and I can come to your house with the paperwork. Do you live in the city?"

"Yes. How much time do I have to decide?"

"I'm in the car as we speak, driving to meet with the owner. If you give me the word, I'll stop by my office, pick up the papers to bring over to you, and take all three offers to the owner."

"At *this* hour?"

"Yes. If you're going to make an offer, it will have to be within the next half an hour. I warned you, houses like this don't come along all the time. In fact, the best listings are going off the market. Sellers are figuring that the prices will go back up in a few years, when the economy rebounds. Are you looking for a decent house in the next three to five years?"

"Yes." *I want a baby and a house and a husband, but not in that order.*

"Then you'd better act now."

Mary swallowed hard.

Chapter Forty-four

"Help! Help!" Bennie hurried to the white pickup truck that was pulling over to the side of the road. The door on the driver's side opened, and a man stepped out, a shadowy figure behind a tiny flashlight beam, jittery as a lightning bug.

"Somebody there?" he called out, and as he got closer, she could see that he was a small, older man in a mesh John Deere cap and a white T-shirt. She stutter-stepped to him, her knees finally buckling, and he caught her, dropping the flashlight. "Good Lord, lady! What in the hell?"

"I'm sorry, I'm so tired." Bennie sagged against him, and he almost fell over.

"You stink to high heaven! Is that blood? What happened here?"

"My twin buried me in a box and there was a wolf. I almost died and—"

"*Buried* you? With a wolf? Are you crazy, lady?" The old man struggled to support her, and Bennie tried to rally, straightening up.

"I need to get to the police and tell them about Alice."

"Hold on now. Put an arm around me. You're a sight! Cover yourself, I'll get you to a hospital, sure enough."

"No, please, let's call the police. Do you have a cell phone?"

"Lady, I can't hold ya. Put your arm 'round my neck. You need a doctor." The old man took her upper arm and wrenched it around his shoulder.

"We have to call the police, do you have a cell phone?"

"My wife does. Lady, please. Walk to my truck, would ya?" The old man half-lifted and half-steered her to the pickup, and Bennie couldn't seem to stop talking, the words spilling like a torrent.

"We can use your wife's phone and call, then the cops will come and find Alice, she won't get away."

"Here we go." The old man led her to the truck, opened the door with difficulty, then helped her inside. Her foot grazed a chainsaw that sat on the floor, filling the cab with a gasoline odor. She practically fell into the seat, and he closed the door. "Now stay here. I'm goin' back for my flashlight."

Bennie slumped in the filthy truck, wondering where his wife was with her cell phone. Clothes sat mounded next to old newspapers, coiled rope, empty bags of Doritos. There was a can of orange soda in the cupholder, and she upended it, but it was empty. She searched for another can, tossing aside some newspapers and receipts, but couldn't find anything to drink.

"Got it," the old man said, returning to the truck. He opened the door and sat inside, with a grunt.

"I'm so thirsty. There's nothing to drink, do you have any more?"

"Drink?" The old man twisted on the ignition, setting a large key ring jangling. "Some pop in the holder."

"It's gone, and I'm so thirsty, I haven't had a drink in so long." Bennie tried to think. "What day is it? I last had a drink on Friday."

"Oh, so that's the deal here." The old man chuckled, and the truck took off. "You like to drink?"

"What day is it, is it Saturday night?"

"No, it's Sunday night. So, you need a drink? Sounds to me like you had enough. Lord, what a stink, if you don't mind my sayin'."

"I need a cell phone, where's your wife?"

"At home." The old man pointed to the pile of clothes on the seat. "I got some shirts there. You wanna put one on? Cover your unmentionables?"

"Oh, yes." Bennie looked down, and her bra was exposed. She sorted through the clothes in the dark. "I'm just so tired, and I can't see, where is the cell?"

"Take the blue one on the top." The old man steered with one hand and handed her a work shirt with the other. "So you been drinkin', that it? I didn't see no car aroun'. Somebody drop you off 'n leave you there?"

Bennie struggled into the shirt, willing her brain to function. "I'd really love a drink."

"Hang on." The old man rummaged in his door pocket while the truck cruised down the dark road. "I bet you and your boyfriend were on a bender, then he dropped you off? Or are you a workin' girl?"

"What, no, I work in Philly and I need something to drink—"

"I never met a girl like you and I never been to Philly, neither. Now calm down, I know what you need." The old man produced a flask from inside the door, twisted off the cap, and passed it over. "Wet your whistle. Don't think the doc will mind. You're already lit up like the Fourth of July."

"What is it?" Bennie asked, but it smelled like whiskey. She held the flask with difficulty but was so thirsty she took a big gulp, then coughed. The truck turned onto the highway, and by then she had taken a second swig and a third, sucking on the bottle. She knew she'd get drunk but she suddenly didn't care. "Do you have any more?"

"You got a wooden leg, lady?" The old man chuckled. "We're almost there. Be patient now."

"I will, do you have any more?" Bennie felt groggy and it was hard to think. "We need to get Alice."

But the old man just laughed and slid the flask from her bloodied hands.

Chapter Forty-five

Alice stifled a fake sob as Grady sat down beside her on the bed, leaning over.

"How you doing, sweetheart?" he asked, stroking her hair.

"Don't look at me." Alice peeked at him with one eye, hopefully bloodshot. "I look awful."

"No, you don't, you look beautiful. You are beautiful."

"I tried to get some work done, but no dice."

"Forget work, for now." Grady's hand moved down her back, and he rubbed it lightly. "I knew you were going to crash. You were holding together too well."

"I feel silly. He was just a dog and I have so much to do."

"Don't feel that way." Grady segued from rubbing her back to kneading it with strong fingers, but Alice told herself not to get turned on.

"I miss him already."

"I know. Me, too. You'll feel crummy for a while, there's no avoiding it and no denying it." Grady kept kneading her back. "My mother used to say that you have to let bad news sink into your bones. You absorb it, and all the losses and setbacks in your life become a part of who you are."

Oh give me an effing break.

"How about I go downstairs and make us something to eat? If you're still awake when I'm finished, it's there for you. How's that sound?"

"Good, great. Thanks."

"No problem." Grady eased off the bed, and if Alice was going to find out about his secret phone call, this was the time to see if he'd tell her or hide it.

"You were gone so long, I was a little worried. Did you have trouble finding the bodega?"

"No, it was where it always was, with the same surly guy behind the counter. I forget his name."

Strike one for boyfriend. "It's not the best neighborhood around that store. I thought something might have happened."

"Nah, I'm fine." Grady walked toward the door, his tone suspiciously casual.

Strike two. "I'm just being paranoid. I don't want any more surprises today."

"No way." Grady was leaving the room, his footstep heavy on the hardwood at the threshold.

"You sure it's okay with your office, you staying here?"

"Don't worry so much. I'll check on you in about half an hour. You want the light on or off?"

Strike three. "Off, please."

"You got it." Grady shut the light, and the bedroom went dark, leaving Alice alone with her thoughts.

So he hadn't mentioned the phone call. The person he'd called was probably Mary. He could have followed up on her call, or worse, warned her of his suspicions. She didn't know if he had reached her, but she couldn't take any chances. She had her gun with her, but it would be too noisy. She was good with a knife, but he was strong. The clink of pots came from downstairs, so he had already started to cook his stupid specialty, which gave her an idea.

What's good for the goose is good for the gander.

She got out of bed, dug underneath for her cloth bag, and got what she needed.

Chapter Forty-six

Mary hung up with the realtor, confused. It was all happening too fast. She had never Acted Now. On the contrary, she specialized in Delaying, Second-Guessing, Doubting Herself, and Stalling Whenever Possible.

She called Anthony, but the phone just rang and rang, then the voicemail clicked on again. This time she left a message: "The house that I love is available, and I have to make a decision right away. Please call me back." She pressed END, feeling her grumpiness go into overdrive.

Still asking permission, partner?

If he wouldn't pick up the phone, it would serve him right if she bought the house. One fight, and he walks out of a master bedroom that wasn't even theirs. And why do they call it a master bedroom, anyway? Why not a mistress bedroom, especially if a woman bought the house? The world was sexist, including Anthony. He couldn't handle it when the discussion was anything but academic. The man could talk Dante, but not down payment. Well, they had come to the point of no return.

Buy the house!

She felt a stab of heartache. If she bought the house, she could lose the guy.

Don't buy the house!

She had to make a decision, and fast.

So what's it going to be?

She told her inner voice to shut up. It was time to stand on her own and decide. It was her money and her love life, and it would be her house.

She sat still on the bed, listened to her heart, and said a little prayer, and in the next minute, her mind cleared, and she knew what to do. It wouldn't be easy, but it was her choice.

And because of that, she knew she could live with the consequences, come what may.

Chapter Forty-seven

Bennie heard voices around her and felt the sensation of being lifted and borne forward. She opened her eyes, and a nurse in blue scrubs was rolling her into an examining room with medical equipment. They stopped when another nurse in pink scrubs appeared, and Bennie tried to stay awake, but couldn't. She wanted to call the police and go find Alice, but she could barely stay awake long enough to listen to what they were saying.

"What do we have here?" one nurse was asking the other.

"A Jane Doe. Not an emergency. A farmer found her in a field, drunk. BP and other signs are normal. I started the drip and tried to get her to talk to me, but she kept passing out. Vomited on herself. God, she stinks, doesn't she?"

The other nurse said, "Hmm, looks like a dog bite on the right hand. She'll need a shot, and we'll clean her up. She looks like she's been in a fight, from her hands. Odd. Definitely smells like she tied one on. I'll take blood, for a tox screen."

"That right hand looks broken, doesn't it? I'll get her on the sked for X-ray. That's the farmer's shirt she's wearing, with her skirt. He thinks she'd been with her boyfriend. She was almost topless when he picked her up."

"Jeez, think it's a rape? Should we call the cops, get a kit?"

"Triage put in a call, but the cops are on skeleton, with vacations and all. Playtime for everybody but us, eh?"

"Everybody's gone to the moon. You know that song? My dad loved that song. Wow, she has nice veins. She must work out."

"I don't think we need the rape kit. It's so intrusive, and her skirt's not ripped or anything. Undies intact, no other signs."

"Good. Did she tell the farmer she'd been assaulted?"

"Not that he told us, so no. No ID, wallet, handbag, phone. She didn't give him any other information except that she was from Philly."

Bennie felt her right hand being manipulated, and miraculously, it didn't hurt at all. She opened her eyes. "I'm feeling no pain."

"Understatement of the year," the nurse in pink said, setting her hand down. "What's your name? Do you remember how you hurt your hand?"

"Uh huh." Bennie wanted to tell them about Alice, but it was hard to form coherent thoughts. "I drank too much and . . . Alice put me in a hole."

"What? Can you repeat that? Are you on any medication? Miss? Miss?"

Bennie felt herself doze off.

"Miss, did you take any street drugs? Miss?"

"Wicker." She'd been trying to say whiskey and liquor, but it came out wrong.

"Did you take street drugs of any kind?"

"No, no, no."

"Are you on any medication?"

Bennie wanted them to call the cops but couldn't make the words. "I want to get . . . Alice. I have to tell you about Alice. We have to—"

"Miss, what is your name?"

"Bennie."

"Bonnie?"

"Bennnneeee!"

"Stay calm, don't shout, I hear you. Penny, what's your last name?"

Bennie let it go. "Rosato."

"Risotto?"

"Rosato."

"Arzado? Okay, Penny Arzado."

Bennie nodded. Close enough. It didn't matter. She had to get Alice. Throw her in prison.

"Penny, do you have health insurance? Do you know what kind of insurance you have?"

Bennie couldn't answer any more questions, or listen. She had to go to sleep.

"Penny, talk to me. Penny?"

Chapter Forty-eight

Alice went downstairs to the kitchen, where Grady was cleaning up. It smelled like something good was baking, but she couldn't tell what, because there was nothing on the stovetop and no ingredients on the counter.

"Hey sweetheart." Grady turned from the sink, drying a bowl. He set it down with the dishtowel and gave her a hug. "You didn't have to come down. I told you, I was bringing it up."

"I thought I'd keep you company, maybe have a drink."

"Okay, good." Grady released her and brushed a stray hair from her forehead. A look of pain crossed his eyes, deepening his crow's feet. "I'm sorry all this happened, especially tonight. We're in the kitchen when we should be upstairs."

You, man, you.

"I'm sorry about last night, too. You know I have a better track record than that."

"I know." Alice reached up and gave him a Bennie-like peck. "I want a rain check."

"You got it." Grady grinned, his relief so obvious that she doubted he suspected her. Still, she wasn't about to change her mind. He had officially became a loose end.

"I forget if I have any wine." Alice opened the cabinet above the refrigerator, but it held a stack of reusable shopping bags. She moved to the next cabinet, but it contained plastic bags of brown rice, a few cans, and boxes of spaghetti. "God, my head is killing me. I can't even think where I put the wine."

"You don't want wine with this anyway, do you?"

Oops. "Tonight, I want wine with everything."

"I got milk, if you change your mind." Grady opened the oven door, releasing the delicious smell of baking brownies.

"I'll get it." Alice went to the refrigerator, turned her back to him, and seized her opportunity. Quickly she picked up the milk carton, popped off the cap, then grabbed a glass from the overhead cabinet. She poured the milk into the glass, then dropped the roofie into the drink. She took another glass from the cabinet and filled that one, too, taking her time so the roofie would have a chance to dissolve.

"Looks like we're good to go."

"I'll get napkins." Alice opened a drawer, retrieved two napkins, and set them next to the plates. She felt as if they were playing house, except that mommy was about to kill daddy.

"Would you get the ice cream, too?"

"Sure." Alice went to the freezer, got a new tub of Cherry Garcia, and closed the freezer door. She took a scooper from the silverware drawer and set it all on the table, figuring that the roofie should be dissolved by now.

"These look great, if I don't say so myself." Grady cut the brownies. "Of course, we won't wait until it's cool, because otherwise we won't be able to burn the roofs of our mouths."

"Hear, hear," Alice said, because it sounded like Bennie. She picked up both glasses and carried them to the table, making sure to give herself the one without the drug.

"Am I good or am I good?" Grady wedged two brownies out of the dish, put them on the plates, and brought them over, then they sat down.

"You are good." Alice took a big bite of hot brownie, which was delicious. "Amazing."

"Thank you." Grady popped a brownie into his mouth. "Not bad. Did you burn the roof of your mouth?"

"Yes."

"Good."

"Agree." Alice set down the brownie and took a drink of milk. *Got Rohypnol?*

"So, brownies for dinner. Unorthodox, yet terrific." Grady kept chewing, showing no sign of reaching for his milk.

"Very terrific." Alice could barely stand more stupid banter. She was afraid to speak for fear of saying the wrong thing and she was fresh out of brownie conversation.

"Starting to feel better?" Grady asked. He kept not drinking his milk, and she wondered if he'd seen her slip the pill into his drink.

"Absolutely, thanks."

"Brownies are nature's cure-all. Your words."

"I'm right, as usual."

"You having ice cream?"

"Not yet." Alice couldn't wait any longer. "How can you eat a brownie without milk?"

"Ugh. When have you ever seen me drink a glass of milk? You know I hate it."

Damn! "How quickly they forget, huh? What's your name again?" Alice laughed, hiding her flub.

"Out of sight, out of mind." Grady grinned crookedly, and Alice smiled, again. So he didn't drink milk. Now she would have to figure out another way to drug him. She sipped her milk.

Trying to remember which drawer had the butcher knives.

Chapter Forty-nine

Mary signed the last copy of the sales agreement, exhilarated and nervous, both at once. She was finally buying her own house, and it was a dream come true. On the downside, she didn't know how Anthony would react and she'd never spent so much money in her life. When she saw how much of her mortgage payment went toward interest, she decided that the line between federal banking and organized crime was way too fine.

"Well done." Janine gathered the papers into a stack. "And your check? Can't forget that."

"No, we can't, can we?" Mary opened her checkbook, made out a check for the earnest money, and handed it over. "Ta-da!"

"Happy?"

"Yes. Very." Mary couldn't help but clap. "I bought a house! All by myself!"

"Good for you!" Janine laughed, her lipstick fresh after all these hours, though the same couldn't be said for her linen suit. "But I have to warn you, your offer hasn't been accepted yet and there's still lots to do."

"Like what?"

"We have to schedule the inspection within ten days, and there's plenty of other details I'll go through with you, if they accept."

Janine stuck the check and the thick packet of agreements in a manila envelope. "I'll be back to you as soon as I can."

"Do you think it will be tonight?"

"It could be, and if I have an answer, I'll call you right away. What time do you go to bed?"

"Call me anytime. I doubt I'll sleep much, anyway." Mary's head was already swimming with thoughts of paint chips and swatches, rug samples and curtains. A homebody at heart, she'd dreamed of her first house like some girls dream of their wedding day. And wedding days weren't something she wanted to think about right now.

"The seller has forty-eight hours to either accept or reject our offer."

"Gotcha." Mary walked the realtor to the door. "I should've known that, being a lawyer."

"A partner, even?"

"Not yet, and don't jinx me." Mary opened her apartment door, and Janine gave her a businesslike hug.

"Good luck!"

"Thanks," Mary said, surprised to find herself welling up.

She closed the door and stood there, savoring the moment, alone. In the movies, she would have felt bad because she didn't have anyone to share it with, but in reality, she didn't mind. It was her moment, only. She'd worked for this moment every day since law school, and it had finally come to pass, because she willed it so. She had changed her life with the stroke of a pen. And a very large check.

Ring! It was her cell phone, and she ran back to the kitchen, where she'd left her BlackBerry. She picked it up and checked the display. Anthony, read the screen, and Mary braced herself.

"Hello?" she said, pressing the green button.

"Hey." Anthony sounded subdued. "Sorry I missed your call. I was at my mother's, fixing her sink."

Mary swallowed hard. "Sorry if I got hysterical. I needed to make a decision, and I did."

"So?"

"I made an offer on the house." Mary's mouth went dry. "I hope you understand. If you want, I'll come over and we can talk. It's probably not a conversation we should have over the telephone."

"Well, I'm happy for you." Anthony's tone softened, and Mary could hear the genuine emotion in his voice.

"Thanks."

"You should be proud of yourself. I'm proud of you, and I'm sorry for what I said in the house today and the way I spoke to you."

"I'm sorry, too," Mary said, biting her lip. She almost rather that he'd yell at her or be angry. She heard a new resignation in his voice, and a finality.

"We have a major issue that we should explore, and I think you're right, we shouldn't do it over the phone. Let's give this some thought, then we can talk about it another time. Does that sound good?"

Gulp. "Sure, you free for dinner tomorrow?"

"I think it will take me a little longer than that. I need some perspective. I think we need to take a break."

Mary felt stricken. Suddenly she heard a beep on the phone that meant another call was coming in, but she wasn't about to interrupt him. "I don't think we need a break."

"We do. I do."

"For how long?"

"I don't know. I'll call you."

"Anthony, are we breaking up?"

"I don't know. I'm sorry. I have to go. I'll call you. Bye."

Mary hung up, anguished. It was one thing to tell yourself you can accept the consequences, but another when they actually happen. Still she wouldn't take the decision back, even now. Buying the house was either the best or the worst thing she had ever done.

Does being me cost me you?

The BlackBerry beeped, signaling that someone had left a message. It could have been Janine or a client, so she pressed a button for voicemail and a message came on.

"DiNunzio, it's me."

It was Bennie, but she sounded strained.

"Don't worry, I'm fine, but I'm calling you from Pellesburg Hospital, which is God knows where. I need you to feed and walk Bear.

Ask my neighbor next door, with the red shutters, for my house key. Then call Marshall and tell her to cancel all my credit cards. Call me back and I'll tell you the details. I don't know the hospital's main number, just call me back."

Mary pressed END, bewildered. Bennie was in the hospital? What happened? Was it some kind of accident? What was she doing in Pellesburg, wherever that was? And why all this stuff with the credit cards?

Mary checked her phone log, which showed the last call, so she pressed the number and a woman answered, "Pellesburg Hospital."

"I'd like to speak to Bennie Rosato. She's a patient there."

"Thank you." There was a clicking sound, then the operator said, "We have no one here by that name."

"I'm sure she's there. She just called me a minute ago."

"Sorry, but I show no listing for a Bennie Rosato, and in any event I couldn't ring a patient's room at this hour. We don't permit calls after ten."

"But she just called me."

"I show no one by that name, and as I say, we do not permit patients to receive calls after ten. Call tomorrow morning after eight o'clock."

Mary felt confounded. "But she said it's an emergency. That I should call her back."

"Please call back in the morning. Those are the rules."

"Thank you," Mary said, and hung up, worried. If Bennie said it was an emergency, it had to be an atomic bomb. She felt honored that Bennie would call her for help. They really had turned a corner in their relationship.

Partners!

Chapter Fifty

Bennie left a message for DiNunzio, then hung up the bedside phone. Her head was clear, and so was her mission. She had to get Alice. It wouldn't be easy to find her, now that she had such a head start, but it was all Bennie could think about. Being in that box had changed her, she could feel it. Something had happened to her. She felt different, inside.

Her right hand was in a splint wrapped with an Ace bandage, and her left was bandaged in gauze, but she wrestled with the thick guardrail to put it down and threw off the cotton coverlet. Cuts and bruises covered her legs, her feet were swollen, and two toes on each one had been bandaged together. She swung her legs out of bed, leaned on the IV stalk, and was standing up, painfully, when a nurse entered the room and rushed over.

"No! Please, don't get up." The nurse looked about fifty years old, and had concerned brown eyes, a graying braid, and white scrubs with dancing kittens. "You're not ready to walk around yet and you'll disturb the IV."

"I need to get to the police. I can't wait any longer." Bennie knew she sounded abrupt, but it was as if she couldn't help it. She wasn't herself.

"We called them, twice. We called in triage, and so did my supervisor. Please, sit down." The nurse pressed on her shoulder, firmly, and Bennie sat back on the bed, for the moment.

"What did the cops say? Why aren't they here?"

"They said they'd come and take your statement as soon as they could. We have only a small force, not like a big city." The nurse checked the IV and rolled the metal stalk back into place. "Right now, you must be still. I'm surprised you're even awake."

"Will you call them again, or ask the supervisor to?"

"I will, and if they arrive in the meantime, I'll show them right in. Do you remember the last time you ate or drank anything?" The nurse reached into a metal basket on the wall and retrieved a blood pressure cuff.

"Friday night, at dinner with my sister. She gave me a drug, then she tried to kill me. She buried me alive in a box, in a field—"

"I saw something like that in your file. You told that to triage, in the ER." The nurse wrapped the cuff around Bennie's arm. "How did you injure your hand? You have a small break."

"I had to get out of the box, then there was a wolf. It attacked me and I had to fight it off."

The nurse lifted an eyebrow, pumping the black rubber bulb. "You were under the influence when you arrived. Do remember what you had to drink?"

"Whiskey. The man who picked me up gave it to me."

"I see." The nurse cocked her head, eyeing her watch and listening for the telltale tick, then she released the bulb and the cuff deflated. "Your blood pressure is quite high. Did you use any drugs of any kind, whether prescription or street?"

"As I said, my sister drugged my wine, without my knowledge. I don't know what she gave me, but it knocked me out. She's my twin and she's jealous and resentful of me." Bennie could see the nurse didn't believe her, but was too polite to say so. "When can I get out of here? I need to see the police. I really am a crime victim. This was attempted murder. She stole my car and my wallet, too."

"You will not be released tonight. Doctor's orders. You're under observation until we have your vitals back to normal and you're stabilized." The nurse tried to press her down toward the pillow, but Bennie stayed sitting up.

"I want to leave. I can discharge myself."

"Please, if you try to get out of bed again, I'll have to call security." The nurse pursed her lips. "Please, cooperate. We already called the police. They'll be here as soon as possible."

"I have a better idea." Bennie picked up the telephone receiver, but there was no dial tone and she hung up. "What's the matter with the phone?"

"Calls are not permitted after ten o'clock."

"But I just called one of my associates."

"Then you got your call in under the wire. Now, please, if you would cooperate, you'll be discharged a lot sooner. We have you scheduled in the morning with a social worker, for an evaluation."

"I don't need an evaluation!" Bennie couldn't help but raise her voice. "I need the police!"

"An evaluation is routine in a case like yours."

"There *is* no case like mine!" Bennie tried to get up, but the IV stalk started to fall over and while she went to catch it, the nurse was taking the plastic top off a syringe and inserting its needle into the IV tube.

"Please, remain calm. I'll speak to my supervisor and I'll make sure she calls the authorities again. Now you just get some rest, you hear?"

"No, stop! What are you doing? What is that?" Bennie got the answer in a minute. She felt as if snow were suddenly falling on her brain.

"It's a light sedative to help you sleep. It was ordered by your doctor in case you became agitated. Please, try to rest."

"I didn't see a doctor! I have to get Alice!" Bennie tried to remember a doctor, but her thoughts were adrift. Her body relaxed, and the nurse was already lifting her legs back into bed, tucking her in, and putting up the guardrail.

"We'll get that all taken care of for you, you'll see," she said, turning away and leaving the room.

Chapter Fifty-one

Alice was sitting in bed with Grady, clothed and fake-reading the Rexco Complaint. It was time to put boyfriend to sleep, so she set down the correspondence file. "You know, I could really use a drink. How about a nightcap?"

"What would you like?" He looked over the top of the Sunday newspaper. "I'll get it for you."

"No, I'll go." Alice rose, stretching her arms. "It'll do me some good to get up. What can I get you?"

"Nothing, I'm fine."

No, you're not. "Join me. I'm having wine."

"Okay, wine, if you can find it. Water, if not. You sure you don't want me to go?"

"No, thanks. Let me. You were so great today."

"You, too. You're the trouper."

"Thanks." Alice flashed him a smile, left the bedroom, and padded downstairs. She searched the cabinets until she found a bottle of merlot and went digging for a corkscrew. She found one, opened the bottle, grabbed two glasses, and poured the wine about halfway.

She checked behind her to make sure she was alone, then took the roofie from her pocket, broke the pill into two halves, and dropped them into the glass on the right. She grabbed a spoon, stirred the wine to dissolve the roofie, then took both glasses upstairs. She would wait until Grady had passed out to go back for a knife. She didn't want to risk being caught with a knife on her, if something went wrong.

"That was fast," Grady said, looking up with a smile.

"The brownies called to me but I resisted." Alice handed him his glass, and they raised it in a toast.

"To the end of a truly terrible day."

"To the end." Alice sipped the wine, while Grady did the same. "Nice. Dry."

"Agree."

"Well." Grady set down the paper. "I'm beat."

"Want to turn in?"

"It's kind of early, isn't it?"

"Not really." Alice leaned over and gave him a soft kiss, pressing her breast into his side.

"Whoa. Smooth move." Grady reached for her and kissed her, sending a warm rush through her body. His hand slipped under her T-shirt and slid over her breast, caressing it in his warm palm. She was about to catch fire when he turned into a dead weight.

"Grady?"

"Wha?" He tried to lift himself up on his hands, but he was already halfway asleep. "I'm sorry."

"Sure, that's okay. You look sleepy." Alice eased him back onto the pillow, took off his glasses like a good girlfriend, and watched his eyes close.

Suddenly the cell phone rang on the night table, and she jumped for it, annoyed. The screen read Mary DiNunzio, and Alice walked out of the room with the phone. "DiNunzio, what's up? I'm busy."

"Oh, sorry. I'm calling you back."

"I didn't call you."

"Yes, you did. You called me from the hospital. I just got your message."

Uh-oh. "My what?"

"You left a message. You asked me to call you back at the hospital, and I did, but they wouldn't let me speak with you. They said they didn't have a patient by that name. What's going on?"

Alice's thoughts raced ahead. Did Bennie get out of the box? How did she live? "DiNunzio, I'm home. I didn't call you or leave a message. It must have been Alice, posing as me."

"Oh my God, how could I have been so stupid?"

"You're not. We sound exactly alike."

"You know, I *thought* her voice sounded funny. I assumed she was just upset or sick. She said she was in Pellesburg Hospital."

Alice suppressed a bolt of anger. She should have put a bullet in Bennie's brain. Pellesburg was near where she had buried the box. Between Grady dropping in and Bennie coming back from the dead, Alice needed a Plan B.

"She said that I shouldn't worry, and that I should get your house key from the neighbor with the red shutters and go in and walk the dog."

"That's her idea of a funny joke, but it's not mine, not today. I had to put Bear down today."

"That's terrible." Mary moaned. "You must be so upset."

"I don't want to talk about it, and I wonder how she knew. I hope she isn't stalking me, the freak. What else did she say?"

"That I should call Marshall to cancel the credit cards."

"Obviously, don't do that. She must be trying to screw me up."

"Of course." Mary paused. "But why would she call me, instead of you?"

"She's pretending to be me, so she can't call me, right? She's underestimating you, DiNunzio."

"I wonder what her game is."

"Criminal impersonation, right? She called you pretending to be me, so I bet she's about to try and keep that up. It's a good thing you were heads-up enough to draft a restraining order. She's playing into our hands."

"Right! You think she'll show up at the office, pretending to be you?"

"She might, but we're ready for her." Alice was already seeing a way to work this to her advantage. "We should file a complaint for criminal impersonation with the police. It should come from you, since she spoke to you, and I can make a statement if they need it."

"Will do."

"Good, now, here's what else I need you to do. Get the restraining order brief in final, sign and file the papers, then call the court in the morning and ask for an emergency hearing."

"Okay."

"Be up at six. Call me then. If she tries to call you, don't answer. She's playing mind games with you." Alice paused, for effect. "And DiNunzio, I'd like you to be my partner."

"Thank you so much!" Mary practically cheered. "My God, it's so hard to believe that this is finally happening, after so many years, starting way back before I even came to work for you, way back to law school. I never thought I'd see this day, but it's really here!"

"Congratulations. From now on, we're Rosato & DiNunzio."

"I'm so honored! I know I'm not the lawyer you are, but you've taught me everything I know. I owe it all to you."

Whatever. "Way to go."

"Thanks again, so much, Bennie."

"Thanks, to *you*." Alice hung up as she walked back to the bedroom, where Grady was out cold, his head to the side. She couldn't kill him now, with Bennie on the loose. It was too risky, and she had bigger problems.

She had to cover her tracks before it was too late. If she moved fast, she could get it done and be back at the house before Grady woke up. She was still on track to take the money and get out of the country, and nothing could stop her, not even Bennie. She couldn't let anything stop her, because if she did, Q would find her and kill her.

She ran downstairs, took the messenger bag, and flew out the front door.

Chapter Fifty-two

Mary worked bent over her laptop on her bed, powered by an adrenaline tsunami. She was a partner now! She'd have her name on a law firm. She'd own something other than a blow dryer. She felt so charged up, she worked in fast forward. She'd called the police about the criminal complaint, but she'd have to go in the next morning to file it formally, so she'd redrafted the brief, adding the new facts about the fake phone call from Pellesburg Hospital, which strengthened their case. She'd tried to find precedent on point, but couldn't. Still, what they lacked in authority would be made up by the equities, and she knew they had a winner.

She went onto the court's website, pressed a button to file the papers electronically, then hit PRINT. She stretched, surprised to see it was already getting light, then checked the bedside clock—5:30 A.M. She had to call Bennie by six. She pulled off her McNabb jersey and gym shorts, then went to the bathroom, jumped into the shower, and shampooed quickly. She didn't have time to shave her legs.

Partners don't waste time on dumb stuff.

She finished up and dried off quickly. She combed out her hair, ran for the BlackBerry, and called the chambers of the emergency judge, where she left a message requesting a hearing. Then she called Bennie and filled her in, her heart pumping.

"Well done," Bennie said. "Call me when you have the hearing time, and I'll see you in the office when I get there. If you see Alice anywhere near the building, avoid her."

"Don't you think we should hire extra security? You know Meyers, that security firm we use? I bet we could get the same guys."

"No, find a new one instead. The old ones weren't the best in town, and we need heavy artillery."

"I'll get on it and see you at work. Bye." Mary hung up, happy. She was actually influencing Bennie. Maybe this would be the shape of things to come. She went to her closet to get dressed for court. She flashed-forward to standing up for her partner, as a partner, for the first time ever.

But not before she ran back to the bathroom, to shave her legs.

Chapter Fifty-three

Bennie woke up to the sounds of people talking in the hospital hallway. It was bright outside the window on the far wall, so it must be morning. She still felt different inside, though she knew what she had to do. She sat up, shifted over, and picked up the receiver from the bedside phone. When the operator answered, she said, "Can you tell me the number of the local police, or connect me?"

"I'm sorry, we're not permitted to make such calls."

"Can I call 911 from this phone?"

"No."

"Then will you call for me, please?"

"I'm sorry, we're not permitted to contact 911, either. If there's a problem on your floor, you can contact the nurse."

"How about the Philadelphia police?" Bennie had a homicide detective on her speed dial, but she didn't have her cell phone. "You can call information for the number of the detective division—"

"Sorry, but I'm not permitted to place any such calls. Please tell your nurse the problem, and she can help you."

Bennie hung up, tried a different tack, and called her office. It went to voicemail, which surprised her. It seemed late enough for Marshall to be at her desk, and when the voicemail beep sounded, she left a message: "I'm going to be in late today, and we have a problem. Alice has reared her ugly head and she has my wallet. DiNunzio, please take care of Bear, and Marshall, please cancel my credit cards. Talk to you later."

Bennie hung up, threw off the covers, and put the guardrail down. It wasn't easy with the splint on her hand but she managed to peel off the cloth tape holding her IV, pull the needle from her vein, and stop the bleeding with her bandaged left hand. She was swinging her feet out of bed when a nurse walked by, then hurried in to stop her.

"My goodness! You—"

"Don't even say it. I'm discharging myself. Do you know where I can get some clothes?" Bennie hobbled to the door, but the nurse stood in the way, folding her arms. She was different from the one last night, heavyset with short black hair, a pinched look around her mouth, and a businesslike manner.

"Your social worker will be up any minute. Once you speak with her—"

"You can help me get clothes, or you can move out of my way."

"If you would just wait—"

"No more waiting." Bennie tried to get around the nurse, but another woman came out of nowhere and blocked the threshold. The woman was thin and little, lost in a voluminous denim dress, and she had an officially sympathetic smile as she extended a hand.

"Hello, I'm your caseworker, Melissa. I heard you wanted to leave, but you can't until we speak."

"If you lend me clothes, I'll speak to you."

"Fine. Please, sit down, and we can have a chat, Ms. Arzado." The social worker gestured to a nearby chair, and Bennie sat down.

"My name is Bennie Rosato, not whatever you called me, and I have to see the police."

There was a commotion behind them in the hallway, and two uniformed cops appeared at the nurses' station. The social worker and the nurse turned around, and Bennie stood up, gathering her gown behind her.

"Come in, gentlemen!" she called out, relieved. She didn't have any more time to lose, and fifteen minutes later, she had finished an egg burrito and had given a statement to Officers Villarreal and Dayne, who sat in chairs opposite her.

"A wolf?" Officer Villarreal repeated, raising a thick black eyebrow. He was about thirty years old, with a wide, fleshy face, dark brown eyes and a ready, if skeptical, smile.

"I think it was, a wolf or a coyote. Do you have them around here?"

"Probably."

"So I saw one."

"We understand that you were drunk when you came in."

"The pickup driver gave me whiskey."

"He says he found you that way."

"So he lied, but it doesn't matter. The issue is attempted murder. My sister tried to kill me. She has my car, my wallet. I want to prosecute her."

"And she's your identical twin?"

"Yes, and her name is Alice Connelly." Bennie knew it sounded nuts. If she hadn't lived it, she wouldn't have believed it, either. "Please, get me to a computer and we can verify this easily. You'll see that I'm a trial lawyer, and she was a defendant in a murder case I tried." The cops looked at each other, but Bennie rose, covered her butt, and went to the door. "There has to be a computer somewhere."

The social worker hurried after her. "I suppose we could look at one at the nurses' station."

Bennie was already heading towards the nurses' station, ignoring the other nurses and orderlies, looking at her funny. She walked around the high counter to an empty computer and was about to hit the computer keys with her splint when the social worker stepped in front of her.

"Please, allow me. Do you want to get on the Internet?"

"Yes. Please. Google my name and Alice Connelly." Bennie spelled her name, the social worker plugged it in, and a long list of blue links appeared. Bennie pointed to the top one. "Try that."

"Let's see." The social worker clicked the link, and Bennie couldn't have asked for more. Side-by-side were pictures of her and

Alice, looking identically happy, under the headline, TWINS WIN. The social worker gasped. "My, my!"

"How about that?" Officer Villarreal smiled, but Officer Dayne remained reserved, saying nothing.

Bennie looked over at the social worker. "Can you lend me some clothes, please? Now?"

Chapter Fifty-four

Alice twisted her hair into a topknot, then clicked the barrette into place while Grady slept like the dead. She slipped into a khaki suit, white cotton shirt, and brown shoes with low heels, then checked her reflection in the bedroom mirror. She looked like Bennie, no makeup, no frills. It was almost criminal for a lawyer to go to court this way.

She got the messenger bag from the chair, then went under the bed and pulled out the cloth bag. She unzipped it and transferred as much money to the bag as she could carry without it looking suspicious. She shoved the gym bag back under the bed, went to Bennie's jewelry box, took her passport, and stowed that in the messenger bag, too.

Grady was finally waking up, even though he'd conked out in his clothes. She couldn't leave him here, now that Bennie was alive, so she squeezed his shoulder. "Grady? Grady? Time to get up."

"What?" His eyelids fluttered, and Alice turned on the bedside lamp.

"Wake up. We have to get ready. I need your help, with Alice."

"What's going on?" Grady opened his eyes and shifted upward onto his elbows. "Is she here?"

"No. I'll fill you in on the way to the courthouse."

"Man, did I conk or what?" Grady sat up, shaking his head. "I fell asleep in my clothes?"

"Sorry to rush you around, but I figured you'd want to come to court."

"Sure, yes, I'm up." Grady slipped on his glasses and got out of bed as the BlackBerry rang.

"Excuse me a sec." Alice went to the messenger bag and found the phone. It was DiNunzio. "What's happening?" she asked.

"I'm on my way back from the Roundhouse." Mary sounded excited. "I filed the complaint for criminal impersonation, and they didn't need your statement. We have an emergency hearing on the restraining order set for eight o'clock."

"Good girl." Alice watched Grady stumble around the bed, stepping over the discarded Birks.

"Should I meet you there or pick you up in a cab?"

"Pick us up, but not in a cab." Alice would have to leave the money bag in the car. She couldn't take it into the courthouse, through security. "Call a hired car, and it can wait for us after court."

"Okay, I'll be there in fifteen minutes. But who's 'us'? You said 'us.'"

"We'll have co-counsel today."

"What? Who?"

"My other partner," she said, smiling at Grady.

Chapter Fifty-five

Mary had to pretend she wasn't nervous, so she couldn't scratch the blotches under her high-necked white blouse. She sat in the second pew of the packed gallery with Bennie and Grady, waiting for their case number to be called. It wasn't easy to get a restraining order, because courts are loath to restrict a person's civil liberties without a convincing showing of threat. Mary had only gotten one or two restraining orders in her career, and even they were a long time ago—and her boss wasn't the client. She sent up a prayer to Saint Jude, patron saint of lost causes and lawyers who were in over their heads.

The Honorable Francis X. McKenna was presiding, a bald, blocky, ruddy-faced judge in his sixties with steel-rimmed glasses and a permanently even temper. He was known to be compassionate and smart, but there was an outside chance he could deny their restraining order. There hadn't been any physical threat to Bennie, which was usually necessary.

The courtroom was old, with a dull gray marble bench, high ceilings painted a fading cerulean blue, and a brown Emerson air conditioner that rattled in a tall, mullioned window. The bar of court was made of dull mahogany, its top rail supported by ornately carved spindles, and behind it were the mismatched wooden desks of the law clerk, court crier, and court reporter, who went about their business, filing papers and tapping away on the stenography machine, their faces professional masks. Suddenly, the judge ruled, and the court crier rose and called for case number 53263, which was one away from theirs.

Mary watched as one restraining order after another was issued to the women and children of the City of Philadelphia, each one telling its own horror story of fathers attacking children, boyfriends stalking girlfriends, and grudges taken out on beloved pets. It made her feel even worse, but she told herself that they were getting what little justice the law could offer.

She glanced over at Bennie, who smiled back at her. Bennie had gotten a million restraining orders in her day, but she hadn't tried to interfere when Mary had fumbled her way through filling out the forms in the Clerk's Office. But that was Bennie Rosato for you.

"DiNunzio," Bennie whispered, patting her hand. "Have faith in yourself. I do, in you."

Mary felt a surge of gratitude, and when the court crier called out their case number, she felt taller than she ever had before. She went to the podium, stood before the judge, and said, with pride:

"May it please the Court, I'm Mary DiNunzio, of Rosato & DiNunzio."

Chapter Fifty-six

Bennie sat in the police cruiser, parked outside of Alice's house. The day was sunny and hot, and it was sweltering in the car, but Officers Villarreal and Dayne had made her wait while they'd gone inside. She'd led the cops to the house, though she knew that Alice would have flown the coop by now. Oddly, it looked as if she'd left her front door unlocked, because they had walked in easily.

Bennie felt strange, sitting where criminals usually sat, in the backseat behind a perforated metal grate. It only added to her feeling of not being herself, and she had on clothes unlike any she'd ever wear, a blue tank top with glitter around its plunging V-neck, tight jeans shorts, and shiny gold flip-flops. The outfit was all that the social worker could scrounge up at the hospital, evidently left behind by a country hooker, if not Daisy Duke herself.

The cops emerged, Officer Villarreal frowning in the sunlight and Officer Dayne behind him. He was the older of the two, thin and taciturn, playing up his elder-statesman role. They walked to the cruiser, and Officer Villarreal went to see her in the backseat, since he was the nice one, who did all the talking.

Bennie shifted to the half-open window. "She's gone, huh?"

"Not exactly." Officer Villarreal eased the brim of his cap upward on his forehead. "Alice Connelly doesn't live here. The house belongs to someone else."

"That's not possible." Bennie tried to think. It was the right house. She'd remembered the address. "I was in this house. This house belongs to Alice Connelly."

"You're confused."

"No, I'm not," Bennie shot back. "Let me go in. Let me look around. I have to see it."

Officer Villarreal scowled. "Only if you conduct yourself appropriately and the homeowner agrees."

Officer Dayne interjected, "This isn't a game, Ms. Rosato."

Bennie inched to the window. "I swear, it's Alice's house. Please let me out, I want to see it."

Five minutes later, Bennie was looking around the kitchen, dumbfounded. The chairs sported flowery pads, and family photographs sat on a table, and there was even a window air conditioner. She realized instantly that Alice had merely used the house and told the officers as much, though they withheld judgment. They introduced her to the homeowner, one Sally Cavanaugh, an older woman with bright eyes, short gray hair, and a loose-fitting shift that read SO MANY BOOKS, SO LITTLE TIME.

Bennie turned to her. "Ms. Cavanaugh, were you at home on Friday night?"

"No, I was on vacation, in the Poconos. I came home early because the weather was bad."

"Where there any signs of forced entry? Broken screen, an open window?"

"Not at all." Mrs. Cavanaugh gestured at the cops. "As I told the officers, this is just the way I left it. Everything's in order. I never like to come home to a messy house. It's too depressing."

"Can I see your wineglasses?"

"Why not?" Mrs. Cavanaugh went to the cabinet and reached for a glass in the front row, but Bennie stopped her with her bandaged right hand.

"Wait, they could be evidence."

Officer Villarreal came over. "Wouldn't she have washed them before she put them back?"

"Yes, but how careful could she have been? She didn't expect me to live, and she could have washed them by hand. If you test them, I'll bet you'll find some latent prints and drug residue."

"*Drugs?*" Cavanaugh's hand flew to her mouth. "Uh-oh. We used those glasses last night."

"What?" Bennie asked, dismayed.

"My book club came over, and it's time to pick the books for the year, and well, you know how that goes." Cavanaugh smiled sheepishly. "Janey gets a little carried away, and so do I. We had some vino to smooth things over."

"So you washed the glasses?"

"Of course. I did wash them by hand." Cavanaugh turned to the cops. "What type of drug was it?"

Officer Villarreal answered, "Nothing to worry about."

"Are you sure?"

"Absolutely. May I ask, do you have a paper bag?"

"Yes, right here." Mrs. Cavanaugh fetched one from a stack behind the microwave and handed it to him.

"Thanks." Officer Villarreal accepted the bag and reached for the wineglass, but Bennie grabbed a paper napkin and handed it to him.

"You might want to use this."

Cavanaugh said, "Yes, I saw that on *Law & Order*. Wait'll I tell my book club. We're going to read a mystery this month, and now we're in one."

Officer Villarreal put the glasses into the bag. "Thank you very much, Mrs. Cavanaugh, and we're sorry to have bothered you." He turned to Bennie. "Time to go."

"No, I'd like to see the rest of the house, and I have more questions."

"We do the police work in Cambridge County. Thanks for your help, though."

"It'll just take a minute. There might be clues as to where Alice went."

"I said, we have to go."

"But we need to find her. God knows where she could be, by now. We're here, and if we looked around and—"

"No." Officer Villarreal put a heavy hand on Bennie's shoulder, steered her to the door, and ushered her outside, where he handed the evidence bag to Officer Dayne and stowed her in the backseat, his smile cooler. He had given her a chance in the hospital, but he was losing faith.

"Why don't you call the farmer who found me? You talked to him already. Ask him where he picked me up, then I can show you the box she buried me in, in the field."

"We're a step ahead of you, Philly."

"You mean we're going now?"

"Yes."

"Then we need to find Alice, as soon as we're done."

"Please, sit back." Officer Villarreal closed the cruiser door, went around the front, and got in, twisting on the ignition.

Bennie shifted toward the metal divider. "Also, Officer Villarreal, could you call dispatch again about my car? Maybe it's been spotted."

"We already put the APB out. If it turns up, we'll hear about it."

Officer Villarreal accelerated, Officer Dayne manned the police radio, and Bennie sat back, left to her thoughts. The box in the field would prove her story. The cops would see the tunnel, the broken lid, the pieces of her clothes. They might even find blood samples, hair, and fibers that could lead them to Alice.

Officer Villarreal hit the gas as they sped along one-lane roads for almost twenty more minutes. Humid air blew into the backseat as they whizzed past clapboard farmhouses, tall blue silos, soybean fields, and black Amish buggies, their drivers' faces hidden under the brims of straw hats, their bay horses lathery with sweat. She noticed a commotion down the road, where police sawhorses blocked the street and traffic was being detoured. An array of cruisers, newsvans, and pickup trucks sat parked along the side, until the road veered out of sight. Over the ridge, a hazy gray cloud puffed into the blue sky like a random thunderhead.

"What's going on?" Bennie asked, and Officer Villarreal slowed to a stop in front of the roadblock, put the cruiser in park, and turned around, his eyes hard.

"Why don't you tell us? We're less than a mile from where you were found."

"I don't know what you mean. Why are we stopping? Let's go see the box."

Officer Dayne snorted. "The box, eh?"

Officer Villarreal shook his head, his lips flat. "We can't go any farther. It's the biggest fire we've ever had in the county. Somebody torched a field of hay rolls. It's a disaster."

Bennie was stunned. She couldn't process it fast enough.

"The fire burned all night. We only got it put out an hour ago. It took fire trucks from thirty different counties, and police from all the surrounding counties. That's why it took so long for us to get to you. Five firefighters sent to the hospital, so far, for exhaustion. No fatalities, luckily. So far, it burned up almost three hundred acres, untold property damages, $140,000 in lost hay and near $75,000 in equipment. An almost-new John Deere harvester burned up."

Bennie flashed on the hay rolls, then the harvester she'd seen, parked.

"There's no houses around here, or people would have been killed."

Bennie knew what must have happened. She felt sick inside, not only for the lost evidence, but for the damage. Alice had scorched the earth to destroy the evidence of that box.

Officer Villarreal took a deep breath. "Now, Ms. Rosato. Do you want to tell us what *really* happened last night?"

Chapter Fifty-seven

Alice strode to the security desk, followed by Grady and Mary, and flashed a smile at Steve. "Good news, pal. We're just back from court, where Mary got a restraining order against Connelly, so she's not permitted within a hundred feet of us, the tenants, the clients, or the building."

"Good. If we see her, we call the cops, then you."

"Also, we ordered extra security, to backstop you. Rothman Corporate." As Alice spoke, she slid the log book toward her, forged Bennie's signature, and signed Grady in, as her guest. "They should be here any minute."

"We know those guys. They're retired cops, too, most of 'em from the Fifth."

"Now, I still have a business to run, and new clients, Rexco, coming in at two o'clock. Keep it low key if nothing is going on." Alice slid the log book to Mary. "Sign yourself in, champ, and give Steve a copy of the court order."

"Will do." Mary opened up her canvas briefcase, withdrew a few copies of the order, handed them over, and signed herself in. "One is for you, and the Rothman guys will need one, too."

"Thanks." Steve started to read the order, but Alice gave a little rap on the desk, a Bennie move.

"Gotta go," she said, moving toward the elevators. She hoisted her purse and the messenger bag, heavy with money, to her shoulder, then swiped her card and hit the button. Grady met her eyes for a minute, and his expression looked strained, but she couldn't read his thoughts. She hoped that he couldn't read hers either, because she was trying to figure out how to stage his accidental death in a building lousy with security.

Maybe if I got him up on the roof?

The elevator pinged, and they all piled inside.

Alice had never met the firm receptionist, whose nameplate read Marshall Trow. She looked like a sixties throwback with a long braid and a Mexican peasant dress, and when she spotted Grady, she broke into a big smile.

"Grady! Great to see you again!"

"You too, Marshall!" Grady gave her a quick kiss. "How've you been? How's the baby? She driving yet?"

A rustling came from the hallway, and Judy Carrier bounded toward them in a tangerine T-shirt, baggy blue capris, and hot pink clogs, with her short hair dyed red as a Christmas ball. Alice didn't know what to make of the girl. Either she was colorblind or insane.

"Grady!" Judy met him at the reception desk, and he lifted her off her feet.

"Nice hair!" Grady set Judy down, ruffling her red locks. "You a fire engine?"

"I'm totally primary." Judy whirled around on her clogs, and Alice wondered how to get the girl up to the roof, too.

"So you've all heard that Alice is back in the picture. We have a restraining order in place, but if she manages to get up here, call the cops immediately. I don't want to cancel Rexco and I'm not going to let her mess up my life." Alice spotted the envelope from USABank, marked Personal and Confidential, on the receptionist's desk. Inside would be the signature cards to open the Bahamas bank accounts. "Marshall, any messages and mail for me?"

"Oh, right. Sorry." The receptionist picked up the packet and placed a stack of pink message slips on top. "Marla said you should call her, ASAP."

"Will do." Alice took the stuff and turned to Grady. "I have a spare office, since Anne Murphy is on vacation. You want to use it to check your email or get some work done?"

"Yes, but hold on, aren't you forgetting something?" Grinning, Grady gestured at Mary.

"Oh, wait. Of course." Alice suppressed an eye-roll. "Everyone, I'm proud to announce that Mary DiNunzio has become a full partner in the law firm of Rosato & DiNunzio."

"Awesome!" Judy jumped up and down, then Mary and Marshall joined in, and the three women celebrated together while Grady laughed.

Alice wondered if she could have a party on the roof and shove everybody over the side.

But not until after she'd called USABank.

Chapter Fifty-eight

"Can you believe it?" Mary asked, now that she and Judy were be-hind closed doors, in her office.

"No, I can't believe it!" Judy's fair skin flushed with happiness. "You're a partner! Tell me everything! How did it happen? When did she tell you?"

"Wait. It gets better." Mary couldn't stop smiling. "I bought a house! If they accept the offer."

"*What?*" Judy's eyes almost fell out of her face. "You *what?*"

"It's gorgeous, it's right in town, and I made an offer! In only one day! Just like that!"

"It's unbelievable! A house? So you and Anthony worked it out!"

Mary deflated instantly.

"What?"

"I think we might be over," Mary answered. It wasn't until she heard the words aloud that she realized they could be true. "Can you believe it? Just like that."

"What happened?"

Mary told her the story, beginning with the fight in the master bedroom and ending with the phone call on Sunday night. She got through the entire thing without shedding a tear, because if she met the Rexco people crying over her boyfriend, she'd be not only fired, but shot.

"This is terrible." Judy sat down. "Do you think he really means it?"

"Yes." Mary knew it was true. She felt it inside. "Do you think I did the right thing?"

"Yes. You have every right to buy the house, and if you waited, you would have lost it. He'll come around, he has to."

"No, he doesn't."

"But you didn't do anything wrong, and he can't punish you because you bought something you wanted. Or because you wanted something he couldn't buy. Money has nothing to do with love."

"Except in the real world, where you buy things."

"It's not fair to you." Judy frowned.

"It's not about fairness. He's ashamed. That's how he sees it, and it's not going to change." Mary's cell phone rang in her purse, and they locked eyes.

"I bet it's him," Judy said.

"I bet it's not." Mary dug in her purse, retrieved her BlackBerry, and checked the display screen. "Told you." She answered the call. "Hey Ma."

"*Maria, e vero,* you and Anthony, no more?" Her mother sounded as if she'd been crying, which made Mary feel even worse.

"We're taking a break, Ma. We needed some space, that's all."

"What means space?"

Mary tried to think of the Italian words for needing space, but Italians never needed space. Italians hated space. They loved closeness, with a side of spaghetti.

"Wait, your father, he wants to talk." There was a pause, then, "MARE, WHAT'S GOING ON? ANT'N'Y'S MOTHER TOLD CAMARR MILLIE WHO TOLD THE BUTCHER THAT YOU BOUGHT A HOUSE!"

"I made an offer on a house. They didn't accept yet."

"WHY? YOU WANNA MOVE, YOU SHOULD MOVE HOME."

"I'm too old for that, Pop."

"WHERE'S THE HOUSE AT?"

"In town."

"CENTER CITY?" he asked, like, NEPTUNE?

"Yes, and by the way, I made partner, too."

"HOLY GOD, MARE! YOU MADE PARDNER, AT THE COMPANY? THAT'S GREAT! CONGRADULATIONS, KIDDO!"

Mary smiled while her father shouted the news to her mother.

"SO WHAT'S THE DEAL WITH ANTHONY?"

"It's a long story, Pop."

"WE GOT TIME."

"I know, but I don't, not right now." Mary had to get ready for Rexco and she hadn't worked any of her own cases this weekend. She probably had thirty calls to make before five o'clock.

"WE'RE NOT INTERFERING, BUT ANTHONY LOVES YOU."

"I know, Pop."

"HE'S A REALLY GREAT GUY."

"I know that, too."

"WE LOVE HIM. SO DOES CAMARR MILLIE, THE BUTCHER, AND FATHER TOM."

"Our priest? How does he know?"

"HE'S A PRIEST, MARE. HE KNOWS EVERYTHING. YOUR MOTHER'S ASKIN' ME TO ASK YOU, DOES THIS MEAN NO GRANDCHILDREN?"

"Ask Father Tom, he's so smart."

"MARE, BE NICE."

"Sorry, but—"

"DON'T BE SO HARD ON ANT'N'Y. GIVE HIM ANOTHER CHANCE. PEOPLE ARE PEOPLE."

"Pop, you got it backwards. I didn't break up with him, he broke up with *me*."

"WHAT? HE DID? WHERE DOES HE GET OFF? YOU'RE THE BEST THING THAT EVER HAPPENED TO HIM!"

Mary smiled. She knew her father would turn on a dime, if he knew the truth. He always sided with her, and she was glad they weren't fighting anymore. "Talk to you later, okay?"

"FORGET ABOUT HIM, HE'S NUTS. WE LOVE YOU, DOLL."

"Love you both. Bye." Mary pressed END, with a sigh.

"Anthony will come around," Judy said, with certainty.

But Mary knew better.

Chapter Fifty-nine

Bennie sat across from Officers Villarreal and Dayne in a clean, brightly lit interview room that smelled of fresh paint, evidently, white. There was no window, and the carpet was thin, brown, and all-purpose. Modern, if mismatched, chairs held the cops, and Bennie was behind a plain wooden desk, its surface uncluttered except for a telephone and a stack of blank statement forms. Oddly, she felt as if she were a CEO, not a suspect, and in some parallel universe of her own office.

"I had nothing to do with the fire," Bennie was saying. She could see they doubted her, but she wasn't intimidated. Nothing could intimidate her, after the box. She felt stronger than ever before. "Think about it. I was in the hospital at the time."

Officer Villarreal scoffed. "We don't know for sure what time the fire started, yet. As best the Chief can tell, it started last night, sometime after you were picked up."

"If it started after I was picked up, I didn't start it."

"That's not necessarily true. The fire started with an accelerant, but we don't know what kind yet. Depending on how the fire was set and how fast it spread, the Chief told us it wouldn't have gotten into high gear until two or three hours after you were gone. There's nobody living around there, so nobody could see when it started.

Nobody noticed it until it was blazing, full-blast. You could have set that fire."

Officer Dayne leaned back in his chair, crossing his arms over his chest and saying nothing, but Bennie wasn't talking to him, anyway.

"Look, I gave you a reasonable explanation for the fire. My sister started it to destroy the evidence of the box. Why would I start a fire? What possible reason would I have?"

"Why were you drinking?"

"I told you, I wasn't. The farmer gave me the liquor." Bennie gestured at the telephone with her good hand. "Call him and ask him why he lied. I don't know why he lied, but he did."

"I know Bradley and his wife, June. They've lived here forever, his father farmed the same land. My parents know them, too. They're not the type of people to go around lying on other people."

Bennie thought a minute. "Did you interview him, personally?"

"Yes."

"With his wife?"

"No. Bradley was in the living room, June was in the kitchen."

"Could she hear you two, talking?"

"I suppose so."

"So Bradley didn't want to tell the truth in front of his wife. He didn't want to say that he gave some strange woman, who was half-naked, a flask of whiskey. He didn't want to admit, to a couple of cops whose parents are friends of his, that he drinks and drives, or that he drinks at all. Maybe he has a drinking problem, he's trying to quit, you don't know." Bennie pointed to the phone. "Call the Philadelphia police, the Homicide Squad. I know two of the detectives, Azzic and Holland. They were involved with my sister's trial and they'll tell you all about her. She's the one you should be worried about, not me. She's the one you should be questioning, not me. Please, call the Roundhouse."

"I'm not calling the Philly cops."

"Do it, or I will." Bennie reached for the phone, but Officer Villarreal beat her to it, picking up the receiver.

"Fine. Good. You want me to call, we'll call." Officer Villarreal called information, reached the Homicide Division, and introduced himself. "I'm out here in Cambridge County and I wanted to talk to a Detective Azzic or Holland. Huh? They're on vacation?"

Bennie rose. "Then ask for the inspector or the deputy inspector. Tell them it's me."

Officer Villarreal said into the telephone, "Can I talk to the inspector or the deputy inspector? I'll hold, thanks."

"I want this on speaker." Bennie leaned over, pressed a button on the phone, and walked around the desk as the call went live.

"Deputy Inspector Johnson," said a voice Bennie didn't recognize, but she wasn't deterred.

"Deputy Johnson, this is Bennie Rosato, a lawyer in town. We haven't met."

"No, I started last month. Relocated from the department in Milwaukee."

"I'm a well-known lawyer, and I have a twin sister named Alice Connelly, whom I represented in a murder trial. Detectives Azzic and Holland worked the case, and they could give you the background. Are they in?"

"No. They're on vacation until after Labor Day."

"Can they be reached?"

"Don't know. Why, what's this about?"

"On Friday night, my sister drugged me and buried me alive, trying to kill me."

"Excuse me?"

Officer Villarreal interjected, "Deputy, we're trying to get to the bottom of this. We're out in Cambridge County and we picked up Ms. Rosato, who seemed to think you could verify her bona fides."

Bennie interrupted, "The issue is that we need to find Alice Connelly. She could be anywhere at this point. She's guilty of attempted murder and grand larceny, because she also stole my car. She even set a fire out here, to destroy the evidence."

"Is this some kind of joke?"

"No, not at all," Bennie shot back. "I'm being questioned in connection with a crime I didn't commit while a killer goes free. I can't seem to convince anybody out here that Alice Connelly is worth investigating, so it made sense to call you."

Officer Villarreal turned, angrily. "We're investigating, Ms. Rosato. We may not be big-time, but we manage. Why do you think I'm making this phone call? Why do you think I took the wineglasses? Why do you think we drove you all over Creation?"

"You're accusing me of setting a fire. You're investigating a fire, not attempted murder."

"That fire caused major loss of property and damage to—"

"Folks?" On the speakerphone, Deputy Johnson cleared his throat. "Excuse me, can I break in? Ms. Rosato, you say that this woman tried to kill you by burying you alive. Where did this take place?"

"In a field, in Cambridge County."

"Well, if you're a lawyer, you would know that the Philadelphia police have no jurisdiction over an attempted murder in Cambridge County. Our jurisdiction ends at the city line."

"I know you don't have jurisdiction, but I'm out here with no way to convince these people that I'm not spinning stories. That's why it's important to try and reach Detectives Azzic or Holland, even on vacation. They won't mind. In fact, they'd be angry if I didn't. If you call them and tell them to find Alice, they'll be all over it."

"Even so, your friendship with two detectives doesn't confer jurisdiction on your case." Deputy Johnson paused. "Ms. Rosato, if you were attacked in Cambridge County, the local constabulary is who you need to be talking to. Thanks very much for your call. Take care, all."

"Thank you, Deputy Johnson," Officer Villarreal said, hanging up. He turned to Bennie, his jaw set. "I don't agree with your saying we're not investigating. We are investigating. Part of your story rings true, but some of it stinks to high heaven."

Officer Dayne stood up, his eyes narrowing. "Cut the crap, Ms. Rosato. You were found drunk in a hay field that burned up the next day. You set that fire. Maybe you did it for kicks, you're a pyro, you got problems, I don't know. Or maybe you and somebody else partied too hard and sparked it, by accident. It would be easy, with a cigarette and a bottle of whiskey."

Bennie looked from one cop to the other. She actually understood their position. They weren't going to help her, and neither were the Philly cops. She was on her own. She'd hunt down Alice herself. She went to the door.

"Where do you think you're going?" Officer Villarreal asked, frowning.

"You don't have enough to charge me on this fire. You have no evidence that I committed a crime."

"We will when the Chief completes his investigation, in a day or two."

"You won't know if he finds a burned-up box out there, either. Not for a day or two."

"There's no burned-up box," Officer Dayne interjected, but Officer Villarreal waved him off.

"So?"

"So I have a day or two to find Alice. I need to call a cab, because I'm leaving."

Officer Villarreal cocked his head. "Where are you going?"

Officer Dayne said, "You can't leave the county."

"Unless you arrest me, I sure can, and you know it." Bennie took a pen from the desk and scribbled her phone number and home and office addresses on a statement form. "Here's where I am. Call me when you find the box."

"Hold on." Officer Villarreal blinked, uncertain. "I don't know about this—"

"Then lock me up right now, and I'll call a lawyer. I own a law firm, so the price is right. In the end, I'll win."

Officers Villarreal and Dayne exchanged glances.

"I thought so." Bennie opened the door and walked out of the interview room.

Chapter Sixty

Alice was pretending to work in Bennie's office, with the door closed. She tore open the USABank envelope, skimmed the instructions from Marla, then took out the signature cards. She opened the desk drawer, found Bennie's checkbook, then set the register on the desk as a handwriting sample. She forged Bennie's name on the signature card, then did the six others.

She signed the paperwork, scanned it in her desk scanner, and emailed it to Marla at USABank. She found the DHL envelope, put the cards inside, and sealed the envelope. She bent the envelope in half and stuffed it in Bennie's purse, which was sitting on the floor, in front of the locked drawer that held the money bag. Then she called USABank.

"Marla?" she said, when the call picked up. "It's Bennie Rosato. How are you today?"

"Just fine. Did you get the signature cards?"

"Yes, thanks, I'm done. I scanned and emailed them to you and put the hard copies in the DHL envelope. I'd like you to wire the money to BSB right away."

"I will. Wait a minute, I see your scanner copies coming into my email, right now. After I wire the funds, your account will be open at BSB, but you can't use or withdraw any of the money until to-morrow, when they get the original signatures."

"Understood. Please make the transfer after we hang up. My sister has already begun impersonating me." Alice filled her in quickly on the details. "And now I have a restraining order against her. I think it's prudent to expedite things."

"Of course, I'll make the wire transfer as soon as we hang up. Thanks so much for entrusting your business to USABank and its partners, in such a difficult time. You know how much we value our relationship."

"I do, thanks." Alice hung up, then pressed information, got the number of the TV station, and waited until the call con-nected. It was a little risky to call the media, but she had to pre-empt Bennie, who might go there in desperation. Alice had to keep the upper hand, especially now that Bennie was on the loose.

When the phone was answered, Alice asked, "May I speak to Emily Barry, please? Tell her it's Bennie Rosato."

"Yes, please hold."

Alice didn't have to wait long.

"Bennie!" Emily said, picking up. "It's great to hear from you. We haven't spoken since the Connelly trial."

"Thanks for taking my call. You did some of the best reporting on that case, so you were my first choice of reporters." Alice paused for effect. "I'd like to give you some information, but it has to be off the record. You can't attribute it to me."

"You have my word."

"I have reason to believe that Connelly is up to her old tricks."

"Like what?" Emily sounded excited. "Sleeping with crooked cops, or otherwise whoring it up?"

Jealous, much? "No, impersonating me. We had one incident over the weekend, and I can't tell how far she'll go."

"How can I corroborate? You know I need a second source."

"We filed a police complaint and just got a restraining order."

"Perfect. That's public record." Emily started taking notes, the keyboard clacking away. "But why are you telling me this? You never leak. I used to have to pull teeth to get you to talk."

"Honestly, I'm afraid of her." Alice went to victim mode. "I'm doing everything I can to protect myself from her, just in case she comes to the office and tries something. But I need more help. If you run the story, everybody in the tri-state area will be looking for Alice, and I'll be a lot safer. After all, she's not hard to spot. She looks exactly like me."

"I get it. *Very* smart."

"Thanks. Gotta go," Alice said hastily, because her doorknob was twisting. Someone was coming into her office, and she hung up and put the checkbooks away just as the door opened.

A woman was standing in the threshold, and Alice had no idea if she was another lawyer, a client, or an old friend, so she plastered on a fake Bennie-smile.

"Hello!" Alice said, rising. "Great to see you!"

"Really?" asked the woman, arching an eyebrow.

Chapter Sixty-one

Mary hurried from the reception area toward Bennie's office, her heart in her throat. Her parents had surprised her at work with Fiorella, who had wandered off. It never ended well when The Flying DiNunzios came to Rosato & Associates. Her worlds weren't meant to collide, but to remain separate, maintaining order in her own personal galaxy.

"Stop, no!" Mary reached Bennie's office just as Fiorella was opening her door.

"DiNunzio?" Bennie said, uncertain, from behind her desk, and Grady emerged from Anne's office.

"What's going on?"

"Oh, nothing really." Mary grabbed Fiorella by the arm. "Fiorella, this is my partner, Bennie Rosato, and her friend, Grady Wells."

"Nice to meet you, Fiorella." Grady extended a hand, but Fiorella barely looked at him, keeping a cold eye on Bennie.

"Bennie is a name?"

Bennie shrugged. "It's Benedetta, but I go by Bennie."

"Why? Why would you do such a thing?"

"I'm pleased to meet you, too." Bennie held out a hand, but Fiorella didn't take it, so she let it drop and turned to Mary. "I didn't know you had guests, DiNunzio."

"My parents dropped in to celebrate my making partner and putting an offer on a house. Did I mention that?"

"No. Congratulations."

"Thanks." Mary edged backwards with Fiorella, who wouldn't stop glaring at Bennie. Her forehead knitted, and her mouth set like granite, if granite wore lipstick.

"Hey Mare." Judy came to the rescue, out of breath. "Bennie, I see you've met Fiorella."

"*Benedetta!*" Mary's mother joined them, throwing open her arms and hugging Bennie. "*Benedetta, mille grazie,* I'm a so hap' you make *Maria* the boss."

"I'm happy to do it," Bennie said, smiling, and Mary released Fiorella only long enough to pry her mother off, juggling DiNunzios like sharp knives.

"BENNIE! CONGRADULATIONS ON MAKING MY DAUGHTER A PARDNER!"

"My pleasure," Bennie said, a moment before Mary's father bear-hugged the breath out of her, and Judy had to step in to peel him off, too.

Grady laughed. "It's great to see you both. You should be very proud of your daughter."

"WE ARE, FROM THE DAY SHE CAME OUTTA THE EGG! COME TO LUNCH, ALL A YOUSE!!"

"No, thanks," Bennie answered. "I have to prepare for a meeting this afternoon."

"You." Fiorella fixed a dark gaze on Bennie. "I was drawn to your room, to *you*. I feel something here, with you. This, I see. This, I know."

"Pardon me?" Bennie asked, confused, and Fiorella pointed at her with a red-lacquered index finger.

"You are evil, Benedetta."

Judy gasped, and Mary's career flashed before her eyes. She grabbed Fiorella's arm, but the older woman swatted her away.

"You are a woman of great power," Fiorella said, her words heavy with theatrical portent. "But my power is greater than yours. My power comes from God. Yours comes from the Devil!"

"No, please!" Mary yanked Fiorella backwards, and so did her horrified mother and father.

"*Per favore,* no, Fiorella, *per favore, Oh Deo,* no!"

"FIORELLA, ARE YOU NUTS?"

"I curse you, Benedetta Rosato!" Fiorella shook her fist in the air, even with three of them dragging her backwards.

"Sorry, she thinks she's a witch queen," Judy explained, then she piled on Fiorella, who struggled against all of them.

"I *curse* you, Benedetta! I will defeat you! I will! You are no match for my power! I am the queen, not you!"

"*Oh, Deo!*" her mother exclaimed, then prayed in rapid Italian.

"FIORELLA, YOU CAN'T PUT A CURSE ON A LAWYER! THEY SUE YOU!"

Mary clapped her hand over Fiorella's mouth, and they all carried her into the reception area past Marshall, who pushed the elevator button.

"Mary, where do you get these people?" she asked, incredulous.

"Where else? They're family."

Ping! went the elevator, and they all hustled inside.

Chapter Sixty-two

Bennie shifted in the backseat as the cab turned onto her street. They pulled up in front of her house, and the cabbie finally closed his cell phone. He'd yammered away the entire ride to the city, but she'd been too preoccupied to care. She couldn't wait to take a quick shower, change out of her absurd get-up, and go find Alice.

"I'll run inside and get my money," she said. They'd agreed on a fare of $300, and she had the cash in her jewelry box.

"Don't know how you people live here, on top of each other." The cabbie braked, and the engine shuddered into silence.

She got out of the cab and went to her neighbors, the Mackeys, to get her extra keys. She didn't know how she'd explain to them her cuts, bruises, or tarty outfit, but no matter. She walked up their stoop, rang the bell with her splinted finger, and waited, but no answer. She rang again, but still no answer. Maybe Mary had already picked up the keys, anyway.

She climbed down the steps, went to her own house, and tried the front door. Bear knew her step, and she waited for him to start barking, but he didn't. That must mean that Mary had taken him to work with her, so she went back to the cab, where the driver was getting out of the front seat.

"Miss, is there a problem?" he asked, worried.

"I need to call my office to get my keys. Can I use your phone?"

"I ran out of battery when we hit the city."

"Wait here. I have another idea." Bennie went down the street and to an alley that ran behind the rowhouses on the block, including hers. She knew she had an old window to the basement, and she could bust it to get in. The alley was narrow, flanked on either side by back fences, and the cobblestones that made up its floor dipped in the middle, collecting rainwater and moss.

She walked to her own fence, a brick affair that contained her patio. She jumped up and tried to reach the top with her left hand, but she fell back, wincing in pain. Her right hand hurt, and her flip-flops had almost no purchase. She tried again, jumping higher, and made it the third time, flopping over the wide ledge. She was catching her breath when she heard someone shouting.

"Hey, you!" A woman's voice echoed across the backyards. "What do you think you're doing? I'm calling the cops!"

"Wait, no!" Bennie raised her head, but the motion threw her off-balance, sending her falling off the wall. She landed on the cobble-stones, pain arcing through her skull. Her hand throbbed, and for a minute she thought it couldn't get any worse, until the cabbie was standing over her, his hands on his hips.

"You're trying to beat me out of the fare! You think I'm dumb 'cause I'm country?"

"No, wait," Bennie started to say, getting up, and the cabbie yanked her to her feet by her arm.

"I want my fare! This took up my whole day!"

"Wait, listen, I have to get into my house. There's a window—"

"Hell, no! You're not gettin' away with this!" The cabbie tugged her through the alley, to the sound of nearby sirens.

"Listen, I'm a lawyer, and we can straighten this all out."

"A lawyer? What a load of bullcrap! Is that why you dressed like that?"

"I'm telling you, you'll get your money." Bennie looked down the street as a Philadelphia police cruiser shot toward them, its siren blaring and its lights flashing red. The cruiser cut the siren, and two uniformed officers emerged and hustled over. One was heavy and one was thin, and she flashed on Officers Villarreal and Dayne.

"Officers," Bennie began, "I live here, and as soon as I get in my house, I can pay this driver."

"Bullcrap!" the cabbie interjected. "She doesn't live here. She's not anything she says she is. I picked her up at the police station, and she's trying to beat me out of the fare. You ever hear of a law-yer wears sequins?"

"Both of you, relax." The heavy cop raised his hand, then turned to Bennie. "You say you live here?"

"Yes."

"Which house is yours?"

"That one, 2133." Bennie pointed with her good hand. "If I can get in the back window, I can get his money."

"I understand." The cop nodded. "Let's see some ID, Miss."

"I don't have any, on me." Bennie considered telling him the story, but tabled it for now. "Look, if I had to, I could go to my law office, get the keys, come back, and let myself in. Maybe I should do that, instead."

The cabbie scoffed. "Don't let her out of your sight, Officer! She's a liar, plain and simple. If I told you what else I think she is, I wouldn't be the gentleman I am. She owes me three hundred dollars!"

"Three hundred?" The cop's eyes widened under the bill of his cap. "Okay, I've heard enough. Let's go downtown, folks."

Chapter Sixty-three

"What was *that*?" Alice followed Grady into her office, uneasy. She felt shaken by Fiorella Whoever, but couldn't let it show. Even though the curse was crazy, did that woman really know who she was? How? Alice didn't need any more surprises. The money had already been transferred, and all she had to do was conduct business as usual, keeping a lid on any suspicions for just a few more hours.

"I don't know what that was. Something Italian, with a British accent?" Grady walked around her desk, sat down in her chair, then bent over and popped up with the yellow DHL envelope, to the Bahamian bank.

Oh no! "I must've dropped that." Alice reached for the envelope, but Grady was already reading the address.

"BSB? What's this, you representing them?"

"Yes."

"I didn't know you were doing banking matters. That's tricky, especially offshore. What's the case?"

"A small litigation matter. Contract dispute."

"Who's your local counsel in Nassau? I've used Lawrence Bastone. He's pretty good and he won't undermine you with the client."

"I forget, I'm still freaked by Fiorella." Alice had to get out of this conversation. She took the DHL envelope and set it aside. "You ever see anything like her?"

"No, she was a natural force, like a volcano. Mount Etna. Vesuvius. Pompeii."

"Or merely delusional."

"On the contrary, I think she had your number."

Gulp.

"You *are* evil." Grady smiled, in a sexy way.

"You got that right." Alice kissed him, teasing him with her tongue. She let her fingers slip to his thigh, then slide to his crotch. He'd forget about BSB bank if his blood went elsewhere. "I am evil, I just don't look it. Nobody knows what I'm capable of, except you."

"Keep it that way."

"I will." Alice pressed herself into his lap, feeling the hardness there. His hand moved to her breast, and she knew she was home free.

Chapter Sixty-four

Mary wondered how things could be so right and so wrong, in the very same day. She may have won her first motion as a partner, but the only restaurant open for lunch this early was Japanese and her parents never ate anything but Italian. The waiter served their sushi on a sampan, and the DiNunzios recoiled as if it were a garbage barge.

"IT DOESN'T LOOK LIKE FISH TO ME, MARE."

Her mother, still in her topcoat, shrank from the table.

"It is fish. It's special fish." Mary didn't mention the uncooked part. She figured it wouldn't help her argument.

"Mr. D, try it!" Judy chirped, reaching for her chopsticks. "You'll love sushi. It's delicious!"

"Ugh." Fiorella turned up her Roman nose. "I dislike sushi."

"Really." Mary couldn't hold her tongue another minute. "Well, if we hadn't had to flee my office, because somebody at the table screamed at my new partner, then we could have waited until noon and had eggplant parm, which we all love."

Fiorella didn't reply.

"FIORELLA, SHE'S RIGHT. YOU SHOULD SAY YOU'RE SORRY FOR WHAT YOU DID."

"*Sì*," her mother said softly, and Fiorella turned to Mary.

"I'm sorry. Let's move on and forget this matter."

"Not so fast. I understand if you don't like Bennie. My mother didn't either, the first time she saw her." Mary turned to her. "Remember, Ma? You called her evil, too."

Her mother nodded, chuckling. "*Sì, sì, e vero.* I no like Benedetta. She work *Maria* too hard. Alla time, work, work, work."

Mary smiled, turning back to Fiorella. "Bennie is really a good person. She taught me everything, and even though she didn't make it easy on me, I'm a better lawyer for knowing her. I'm a better person for knowing her."

Fiorella sniffed. "You are naïve."

"You don't know her. Or me."

"Perhaps we can agree to disagree."

"Fine," Mary said, stiffly, and Judy picked up her water glass.

"Now, for a toast to our girl Mary, who made partner today! Congratulations!"

"CENT ANN'." Her father raised his glass, and her mother did the same, smiling sweetly at her.

"*Cent ann', Maria, te amo.*"

"I love you guys." Mary raised her glass. She wasn't about to let Fiorella ruin this day, for any of them. "Thank you all very much, for everything. This wouldn't have happened without my wonderful family or my best friend."

"Brava!" Judy said, and they all took a sip.

Mary looked over at her mother, who was shifting uncomfortably in her chair. It was on the small side, and with the bunchy coat, she was wedged inside its arms. "Ma, why don't you take your coat off?"

"No, is h'okay."

"You'll feel better, don't you think?"

"*Sì, Maria,* h'okay." Her mother stood up and shrugged off the coat, surprising all of them. She wasn't wearing her usual flowered dress or the blue one she wore to Mass. Instead, she had on an obvious knockoff of Fiorella's sexy black Armani. Unfortunately, she was shaped like a meatball, with breasts. She modeled the dress, flushing red, then sat down.

"Ma!" Mary said, quickly. "Wow! You look so nice! Where did you get that dress?"

"*Grazie, Maria,* I made."

"You did a great job!" Mary should have guessed as much. She looked over at her father and flared her eyes meaningfully.

"YOU LOOK SO GOOD, VEET!"

"Mrs. D, you're awesome!" Judy grinned, and her mother smiled happily, which was reward enough for Mary.

Nobody but Mary noticed that Fiorella said nothing.

Chapter Sixty-five

Bennie sat in her second interview room of the day, across from another set of odd-couple cops, the husky Officer Pete Mora, who took her statement on an IBM Selectric typewriter, and the gaunt Officer Kevin Vaz, who gazed at her from behind his aviator glasses.

"So that's it," Bennie said, finishing her saga. If they thought she was crazy, they didn't let it show. "They're busy investigating the fire in Cambridge County, and your Deputy Johnson says you don't have jurisdiction to help me find Alice Connelly."

"He's correct. We don't."

"Do you know Azzic and Holland?"

"No, we're just humble uniforms." Officer Mora shifted forward. He was about thirty years old, with large brown eyes, a smooth chin, and a wide nose. His shoulders were broad, pulling at the seams of his summer uniform. "What about our friend the cabbie? That is our jurisdiction."

"I would have paid him when I got into my house. Do you know anybody on the job in Cambridge County?"

"No, but given the fire, I'm sure the county will make it a priority."

"It's a question of their effectiveness, not their will."

"I never second-guess other departments." Officer Mora unrolled the statement from the typewriter. "Now, as for the cab driver, you say you can get the money and you'll also produce proof that it was your house you were breaking into."

"I have a copy of my deed at the office and I can have it messengered here." Bennie took a sip of vending-machine coffee, holding the cup with two hands. "The Cambridge County police said they put an APB out on my car, a Lexus, but can you check into that?"

"I'll do that for you." Officer Vaz stood up wearily and stretched. He was the older of the two, with a graying mustache, but was trim as a marathoner, with lean limbs and a black runner's watch that slid around on his wrist. "I gotta check the front desk, anyway. I'm expecting a message. My first grandchild."

Officer Mora nodded. "Don't count on Mike to bring it to you. He's back and forth to the can, on those meds again."

"They ain't gonna help." Officer Vaz's gaze shifted to Bennie. "What kind of car did you say it was, again?"

"Burgundy Lexus, last year. I don't know the plate."

"Be right back." Officer Vaz left, and Officer Mora handed her the statement, with a Bic ballpoint.

"Your autograph, please."

"Sure, thanks." Bennie read and scribbled her name on the statement, then handed it back to Officer Mora. He was stapling the papers together when the door opened and Officer Vaz stuck his head inside, motioning.

"C'mere a sec, would you, Pete?"

Mora turned. "You a grandpop yet?"

"No, c'mere."

"Sure." Officer Mora rose and left, and Bennie stood up, tugging down her shorts. She was almost glad the cops hadn't recognized her because she'd never live it down. Her breasts were practically falling out of the glittery top, and she hadn't waited around for the social worker to find her panties. Not only was she dressed like a hooker, she was undressed like one.

Officers Mora and Vaz reentered, but something was wrong. Concern crossed Officer Mora's eyes, and Officer Vaz's ennui had vanished.

"Why don't you take a seat, Ms. Rosato?" Officer Mora retook his seat with a sheaf of new papers, while Officer Vaz stood in front of the door.

"What's the matter?" Bennie sat down, and her shorts rode up.

"We have a few more questions." Officer Mora held the papers in his hand, close to his chest. "Did you call a lawyer named Mary DiNunzio from a hospital in Pellesburg, in Cambridge County?"

"Yes, why. How do you know that I called DiNunzio?"

"Did you identify yourself to her as Bennie Rosato?"

"Yes, of course, in the message I left for her." Bennie didn't like the way this was going. She'd been in enough interviews to know when they turned into custodial interrogation. "Is there a problem?"

"Ms. DiNunzio has filed a complaint against you, for criminal impersonation."

"What are you talking about? You must be mistaken."

"Here's a copy, filed this morning." Officer Mora glanced back at Officer Vaz, then handed over the papers, and Bennie read the complaint, incredulous. It was all there, the message she left for DiNunzio, as well as a sworn statement that the woman DiNunzio heard from was Alice Connelly.

"This is crazy. It was me, not Alice."

"Ms. DiNunzio's statement is that she worked with Ms. Rosato at the office on Saturday."

"I wasn't at the office on Saturday. I was buried in a box in Cambridge County."

"Ms. DiNunzio says that Ms. Rosato—"

"I'm Ms. Rosato. I'm Bennie Rosato."

"You'll see a supporting statement there, filed later by Ms. Rosato."

"But I didn't file anything," Bennie said, but it was already beginning to dawn on her what was going on. She had assumed that Alice would run away, after trying to kill her. Instead, she was trying to take Bennie's place. It was inconceivable.

"See for yourself." Officer Mora reached over, flipped to the back page, and pointed with a thick finger. "Here's Ms. Rosato's statement, saying that she worked with Mary DiNunzio, at the offices of Rosato & Associates, and that she didn't call Mary DiNunzio on the evening in question." Officer Mora looked up, his eyes cool. "You called this Mary DiNunzio, pretending to be Bennie Rosato. You also represented to us that you were Bennie Rosato. That's criminal impersonation, Ms. Connelly."

"No, it isn't. I'm Bennie Rosato. She's the fraud. She's impersonating me."

"Do you have someone we could call, to verify what you're telling us?"

"No." Bennie flipped through the possibilities. Her closest friend, Sam Freminet, was in Hawaii on vacation. DiNunzio and Carrier had been fooled, and Lou was gone, too. None of her clients knew her personally.

"I'm hereby informing you that you have the right to remain silent. If you cannot afford a lawyer, one will be provided for you—"

"You don't have to warn me, I know my rights. I'm Bennie Rosato. I'm a lawyer."

"You have no ID. No proof."

"Of course not, because she took it. She drugged me and tried to kill me, then stole my car and took my place."

"How about your doctor? Your psychiatrist?" Officer Mora's tone turned gentle. "Have you ever been hospitalized for a mental disorder?"

"Of course not."

"Okay, stay calm." Officer Mora glanced at Officer Vaz, and Bennie could see that they thought she was nuts. She would have tried to convince him that she was telling the truth, but being in that box had changed her. Now she wanted to get Alice, her own way. The criminal complaint didn't matter. In fact, it helped. Now she didn't have to hunt Alice down. She knew exactly where Alice was. At Rosato & Associates.

"You know, I think I understand what happened." Bennie stood up, masking her emotions. "I want to call a lawyer. I want to exercise that right. He knows my doctor, too. They can help me."

"This way, we can use my desk." Officer Mora opened the door, Officer Vaz stood aside, and Bennie followed, apparently quietly. The cops led her into the cluttered squad room, which was empty, luckily, probably because of the vacation scheduling. The path to the door was clear. Nobody was at the front desk. Two uniformed cops stood at the back of the room, talking near the file cabinets. The cops led her toward the right, away from the exit, but suddenly she bolted left for the door.

"No, stop!" Officer Mora shouted.

"Freeze!" Officer Vaz yelled, but Bennie was already out of the room and slamming the door behind her. She slipped off a flip-flop, folded it in half, and shoved it under the door, ignoring the pain in her hand. The flip-flop wouldn't hold forever, but it would for now.

She took off, barreling down the hallway, full bore. She knew the Roundhouse like the back of her hand. She bolted down the exit stair, losing the other flip-flop as she raced downstairs. She half-sprinted, half-tumbled down the flights, taking the stairs three at a time, hitting the landing.

She banged through to the lobby, where she caught her breath. There were a few cops and administrative staff going this way and that, and they'd stop her if she ran. She sashayed through the lobby, swinging her hips like a hooker who'd been upstairs for questioning. Nobody noticed that she was barefoot because their eyes never left her glitter.

The exit was only ten feet away. She prayed she'd make it to the door before Mora called down to the security desk, which was staffed by a female cop behind bulletproof glass.

She flashed a grin at a young male cop, who smiled back. She twitched her hip at another male cop, who acknowledged her with a nod.

Suddenly the phone on the security desk started ringing, the female cop picked it up, and Bennie was out of time.

She sprinted for the door, darted out, and bounded like a wolf through the parking lot to the street.

A split-second later, police sirens exploded into sound.

Chapter Sixty-six

Alice kissed Grady in the desk chair, straddling him. His fingers found the buttons on her blouse, undoing the first, the second, and the third, then he slipped his hand inside her shirt and underneath her bra again, teasing her breast with his thumb. Her cell phone rang, bringing Alice back to earth, and she shifted off his lap.

Grady moaned. "Can't you let it go to voicemail?"

"No, it could be Rexco." Alice recognized the number on the display as the TV station's main number, so she climbed off and walked over to her door. "Hello?"

"Bennie, it's Emily. A stringer I use just called me. The police scanner is reporting that your sister escaped from the Roundhouse."

Shit! "Alice got away from the cops, when?" Alice repeated, for Grady's benefit, and he jumped to his feet, adjusting his pants around the crotch.

"Probably fifteen minutes ago. She might be heading your way, and I was worried about you."

"And you wanted to make sure I'm here, so you can send a camera."

Emily chuckled. "A girl's gotta make a living. See you in five minutes. I'm on my way."

Grady walked over. "Who was that?"

"A reporter." Alice hung up and buttoned her blouse. "Alice might be coming this way."

"Don't worry." Grady touched her arm. "We've got her stopped six ways from Sunday."

"Will you go tell Marshall? I'll call security downstairs."

"Sure." Grady tucked in his shirt, opened the door, and left while Alice called the Rothman security detail on the number Mary had emailed her.

"Bennie Rosato here," she said, when a man picked up. She went to her office window and looked down at the sidewalk in front of the building, where she saw a burly guy in a suit, answering a cell phone. "Are you out front, wearing a gray suit?"

"Yes. Name's Bob Taylor. How can I help you?"

"We have a problem." Alice scanned the traffic below, but didn't see Bennie. It was almost lunch hour, and the street was clogged with traffic and the sidewalk with businesspeople. "I got word that my twin sister Alice Connelly escaped from the police about fifteen minutes ago. She might be headed this way. Your job is to keep her away from me, my people, and my building."

"We will, ma'am. We have five men here, and more coming. We can handle her."

"Call me the moment you see her. Serve her with the court order."

"Will do, ma'am."

"Thanks. Bye." Alice hung up and called the security desk downstairs.

"She *escaped* from the Roundhouse?" Steve said, astounded, after she'd told him. "That never woulda happened in my day."

"Stay inside and keep order in the lobby. Make sure the tenants or clients can come and go. If she gets through the Rothman guys, call me immediately."

"Nobody's getting through them, they're a defensive line. One played for Penn State."

"Thanks, bye." Alice kept looking out the window, her eyes sweeping the street. The only good thing about this development was that it would make everybody forget about that crazy Fiorella. Suddenly Marshall came up behind her, then Grady, who pointed to the far right.

"There she is!" he said, and they all turned.

"That's *her*?" Alice couldn't believe what she was seeing. Bennie was hurrying toward the building, her expression deranged, her blond hair flying in all directions. She had on a blue top that barely fit and tiny shorts. Both her hands were bandaged, and she was barefoot. Nobody would believe her now. She really was playing right into Alice's hands.

Marshall gasped. "Alice looks totally crazy. Is she crazy now?"

Grady shook his head. "That's a yes."

Alice hid her delight. "I guess she always was, I just didn't want to see her that way."

They all watched as the Rothman guards surrounded Bennie, penning her like a stray dog. She gestured wildly, trying to push past them, but they closed the circle swiftly. People on the street reacted by scattering, or laughing. Suddenly a white TV newsvan pulled up, its doors slid open, and a crew jumped out with videocameras on their shoulders. Emily Barry emerged from the front seat, smoothing her red hair.

"Here comes Film at 11," Marshall said, but Grady pointed to the right.

"Forget the TV people. Look who's coming, over there."

Alice looked over, cursing silently.

Chapter Sixty-seven

Mary was walking back to the office with her parents, Fiorella, and Judy, when their way was blocked by a growing mob, gawking at a homeless person making a fuss on the sidewalk. She led them around the crowd toward the building, but when she got closer, she did a double-take. The homeless person was Alice Connelly, raving like a lunatic. She was dressed in her usual skimpy clothes, but she had bruises all over and her hands were bandaged. Rothman security guards surrounded her like a forest of Sequoias.

"Judy, that's Alice!" Mary pointed.

"Oh my God!" Judy's mouth fell open. "What happened to her?"

"Let's get my parents out of here. They never met Alice, and I don't want them to."

Ten feet away, Alice yelled at the top of her lungs. "*I'm* Bennie Rosato! This is my building! I own it! She can't keep me out of my own building!"

"Ms. Connelly!" boomed a huge Rothman guard. "You're being served with a court order, requiring you to remain a hundred yards away, at all times." He pressed the order into her hand, but Alice threw it back in his face, and still he kept talking. "We have informed the police that you're attempting to enter the premises unlawfully, and they should be here any minute."

"She will not get away with this! Not while I draw breath!"

The crowd surged forward, gawking and laughing. TV cameras kept rolling. Police sirens blared in the distance. Mary's mother was too short to see what was going on, and her father shielded her and Fiorella with his arm, shocked.

"YO, AIN'T THAT BENNIE? MARE, WHAT THE HELL'S SHE DOIN'?"

"No, Pop, come this way." Mary tugged him by his arm, but he couldn't hear her over the noise.

"BENNIE! OVER HERE, BENNIE! NEED HELP?"

"Pop, no! That's Bennie's twin, not Bennie!" Mary shouted, too late.

"DiNunzio?" Alice struggled harder against the Rothman guards, kicking and biting so fiercely, she was able to move them closer to the building. "DiNunzio, it's me, Bennie! That's Alice up there! She tried to kill me!"

"Stay away from my family!" Mary held up a straight arm while Judy hustled her parents and Fiorella away.

"DiNunzio!" Alice shouted. "That was me who called you from the hospital! Remember, I wanted you to walk Bear!"

"You're sick!" Mary got mad. "You know how much Bennie loved that dog, and the day he died, you called her about him! That's disgusting!"

"Bear's *dead*? What?"

"Help!" Mary shouted, and the Rothman guards regained control and dragged Alice backwards.

"Ms. Connelly, you're not permitted within a hundred yards of Bennie Rosato, Mary DiNunzio, Judy Carrier, Grady Wells—"

"*Grady?*" Alice screamed. "DiNunzio, where's Grady?"

Suddenly two Rothman guards appeared at Mary's sides, took her by the elbows, and hurried her toward the building. She spotted another one helping her parents and Fiorella into a cab, and a third escorting Judy to the building. The Rothman guards left Mary in the lobby, and she joined Judy at the security desk, gathering with Steve and Herman. They were all catching their breath when they heard a new surge of noise from the crowd, and Mary

turned around just in time to see Alice stick her splint into the eye
of a Rothman guard, then break free and run off.

"She's getting away!" Mary said, shocked. "They didn't stop her!"

"They can't." Steve shook his head. "Rothman isn't supposed to
restrain, and the cops will pick her up in no time. She embarrassed
them by escaping, and they're not about to let that happen. You
okay?"

"Fine. That Rothman guard will need a doctor. Should we call
one?"

"We will, but they're tough, those guys. Get 'em a bullet to bite
on."

Mary looked at Judy. "Did my parents get in the cab, safe and
sound?"

"Yes." Judy wiped her brow. "They were upset, though. You
might want to call them when we get upstairs."

"I will." Mary managed a smile. "They'll never come in town
again. Sushi, and now this."

"I know, right?" Judy smiled back. "Let's go up and see how
Bennie is. Thanks, everybody."

"Yes, thanks, guys." Mary walked Judy to the elevator bank,
swiped her reader card, and hit the UP button. They went into the
elevator, and when the doors closed, she rested against the side
wall, decompressing. "That was a scene, huh?"

"Yeah, I'll say."

"I'm so glad we got that court order. It saved our asses, and Bennie's."

"You think?"

"I know. Don't you?"

"Maybe." Judy shot her a look, uncharacteristically grave. "I
have a question for you."

"What?"

"What if that was really Bennie, outside? And the woman upstairs is really Alice?"

"Huh?" Mary looked at her like she was crazy, because she was,
if she thought that. "You're kidding, right?"

"Not really." Judy's eyes were troubled, and her mouth formed an unsmiling line. "What if?"

"That's absurd. Alice got to you with her mad scene. It's like Bennie told me, she plays mind games."

"It's not what Alice said." Judy's tone grew quiet. "It's what Fiorella said."

"Please tell me this is a joke," Mary said, incredulous. "Fiorella's even nuttier than Alice. She's a fake witch queen."

"Fiorella said that Bennie was evil, the first time she met her."

"For which she apologized, at lunch. Fiorella's crazy, a drama queen."

"Really? What if she called it? What if she had it right, the first time? What if that really is Alice, in our office, masquerading as Bennie?"

"Are you insane?" Mary stood up, recovering. "Then where's Bennie? Is she that crazy lady outside, dressed exactly like Alice?"

"It's possible."

"No, it isn't. Why? How? I was with Bennie on Saturday, and she didn't look like that. She looked normal, like herself."

"They're identical, Mare. Maybe you were with Alice, and thought it was Bennie."

"Judy." Mary rolled her eyes. "Why are you saying this?"

"Because of something Fiorella said to me, before I put her in the cab."

"What did she say?"

"Family meeting." Judy pressed the red button with her thumb, and the elevator stopped.

Chapter Sixty-eight

Bennie barreled down the street, ignoring the pain in her feet. Sweat streaked her face. Her heart pounded hard. Her thighs pumped strong. She ran past a Burberrys, a Starbucks, a Kiehl's. People on the sidewalk stopped talking, watching as she streaked past, driven by instinct. Her only thought was to escape. Police sirens blared in the distance, and she tore down the cross street, leaving Center City behind. She pounded past well-kept rowhouses to Lombard, then Bainbridge, Naudain, and beyond. The neighborhood changed, and the sidewalks emptied. The brick rowhouses became run-down, the parked cars broken down. Trash and garbage reeked in the heat. The sirens grew distant.

She took a left onto one of the narrow sidestreets, sprinting past boarded-up windows and lots strewn with rubble and glass. Her eyes swept right and left as she ran, looking for a place to hide. People could be calling 911 from the houses. She had to get off the street, fast. She spotted a corner tavern up ahead. It would do, for now. She slowed her pace to a fast walk, passing women drinking beer on a stoop. She had almost reached the tavern when she heard a shout.

"Yo, wait up, Al!" a woman called, from behind her.

Bennie kept walking.

"Hey, it's me, Tiffany! Al! Alice!"

Alice? Bennie turned to see one of the women from the stoop hustling toward her, unsteady on Candies sandals.

"Yo, wait!" The woman reached Bennie, out of breath, and she had a sweet, almost deferential, manner. Her streaky brunette hair was cut in raggedy layers, and a fiery sunburn blanketed her turned-up nose. She had on a flowered camisole and shorts, and after she looked Bennie over, her small mouth formed a perfect circle of surprise. "Whoa, what the hell happened, Al? I almost didn't recognize you."

"I know, right?" Bennie decide to play it by ear. If Alice was pretending to be her, then she would pretend to be Alice.

"You get in a fight or somethin'? Why you runnin' like that?"

"It's a long story."

"Caitlin's been lookin' for you. Kendra, too. Where you been?"

"Around." Bennie couldn't risk being on the street. "Hey, can I get a drink at your place?"

"Sure." Tiffany beamed. "I'm right around the corner. Let's bounce."

Chapter Sixty-nine

Alice was standing in the lobby with Grady and Marshall when the elevator doors opened on Mary and Judy, who entered the reception area. They seemed unusually quiet considering the ruckus, and Alice wondered what had happened to them outside. She had to keep them on the reservation.

"Are you guys okay?" she asked, going over. "DiNunzio, you all right?"

"Thanks, we're fine." Mary flashed a weak smile.

"We saw everything from the window. Way to go, out there. You really went toe-to-toe with Alice."

"But she got away, did you see?"

"We did. I hope they get her quick. She's obviously off the grid and she needs a shrink."

"I know, right?" Mary glanced at Judy, who averted her eyes, a movement Alice didn't miss.

"Carrier, how are you? You look upset."

"I'm fine, too."

Marshall gave Mary a sympathetic hug. "It looked like Alice was yelling at you. I thought she was going to attack you. What happened?"

"She was just ranting and raving. The Rothman guys had her."

Alice sensed something was still bothering them, but she couldn't defuse it until it was out in the open. "DiNunzio, what did Alice say to you?"

"Nothing, really."

"Like what? Tell me."

"What we discussed, like she's Bennie and you're really Alice. That she owns the building and we can't keep her out, the whole nine."

"Nice try." Alice fake-laughed. "More mind games, eh?"

"Exactly."

Marshall laughed. "You'd think if she was going to try to be Bennie, she'd at least dress the part."

Grady nodded, smiling crookedly. "What, you never saw my girl in a bra, in public?"

They all laughed, including Mary. "Grady, she went ballistic when she heard you were up here. She must think you're hot."

Grady nodded. "Of course she does. She has good taste. It's in the DNA."

"Very funny." Alice faked a final smile. "As if she could fool you, or any of you, for that matter."

"Not me, I'm smarter than I look." Mary squared her shoulders, and Alice gave her a pat.

"DiNunzio, it's just what you said. She's trying to run a scam that she's me, and your restraining order worked like a charm. Thanks, partner."

"You're welcome."

"Now let's go get ready for Rexco. They'll be here in twenty minutes. We have a big client to reel in, yes?" Alice got Mary moving toward the offices, with Grady following. Marshall went to the reception desk to answer a ringing phone.

Judy brought up the rear, dragging her feet. "The only thing I don't get is what Alice gains by making a scene in front of our building."

"You're right, Carrier." Alice kept moving, her tone casual. "She gains nothing."

"Then why does she do it?"

"She just wants to jerk me around, and that's enough for her. She's so jealous, she can't control herself or forward her own agenda, like find a job on her own, or get a life. She thinks everything I have, I got at her expense."

Mary shook her head. "Plus, it does hurt us. Wait until what happened out there hits the TV news and the Internet. It's such bad publicity for the firm. I bet we get calls from the clients."

"You're right." Alice gave her another pat on the back. "But don't worry about it, DiNunzio. She can't keep us down. Let's go get ready for Rexco."

"Let's do it!"

Alice could feel everybody cheer up as they walked back to their offices.

Everybody, that is, except Judy.

Chapter Seventy

Mary went back to her office with Judy on her heels, closing the door behind them. She had a million things to do and they had discussed this already in the elevator, but Judy stood in front of her desk like a dog with a bone.

"Mare, don't you get it? Fiorella said, '*That* is a good woman,' and she pointed to Alice, outside. Doesn't that mean anything to you?"

"No, like I said, Fiorella's Italian. She's dramatic. Ever hear of Verdi? Rossini? Puccini? See a pattern? I should know, I have the same infection."

"No." Judy shook her head. "It's amazing that she said that, and she was looking right at Alice, or Bennie. Nobody out there would've said *that* was 'a good woman.' Every single person thought Alice was crazy."

"Fiorella's the crazy one." Mary rubbed her eyes irritably. She'd never even disagreed with Judy, much less argued with her.

"Listen, I hear you. I didn't think anything of it, either, at first." Judy shrugged. "I mean, I know that Fiorella isn't a witch queen, even if she cured me."

"Good, we agree on something."

"But she is intuitive."

"She's a woman. It comes with the ovaries."

Judy didn't laugh. "So it got me thinking. What if?"

" 'What if' is meaningless. You're smarter than what if."

Judy frowned: "What does that mean?"

"It means this is speculation, not fact. You're usually the logical one, not me."

"Hear me out, one last time."

"Fine, shoot." Mary glanced at the phone messages scattered in a sliding pile on her desk. All of them were from her clients, individuals with small matters, and on these child-size blocks, she had built a client base that had made her a partner. None of the messages was from Anthony, nor had he called on her cell.

"Let's say something happened over the weekend, something we don't know. Bennie, or Alice, or whoever was out there, said that Alice tried to kill her. I heard that, you heard that."

"Yes, I heard it. It's part of her scam. It's a lie."

"No, assume for these purposes, that's not a lie. Assume it's the truth."

"Okay." Mary's gaze fell on her stack of correspondence, all the tri-folded letters neatly opened and paper-clipped to their envelopes, a three-inch stack of tasks that needed her attention. She could work all day and night and never do them all.

"So what if Alice tried to kill Bennie over the weekend, but she didn't succeed and then she came back to take her place?"

"Who came back to take whose place?"

"Alice. Alice came back to take Bennie's place."

"First question." Mary didn't have time for this. Rexco would be here in fifteen minutes. The phones at reception were ringing nonstop. "Bennie has all her stuff. Messenger bag, phone, clothes, keys."

"Alice could've taken it from her, and did you notice she doesn't seem all that sad about Bear?"

"Bennie's not the type to blubber all over at the office. It would be unprofessional." Mary couldn't take the conversation seriously when there was so much real work to be done, and she felt the weight of her new responsibilities. "Look, of course she's Bennie. She looks like Bennie, she walks like Bennie, she talks like Bennie."

"Sometimes your own mother can't tell the difference between you and Angie."

"Grady would know the difference. Do we need to go there?"

"He hasn't seen her in a while, so it wouldn't be that hard to trick him." Judy's eyes narrowed. "What if Alice is taking Bennie's place, right here, before our eyes?"

"Second question. Why would Alice do that? Why would she want to be a lawyer? Nobody wants to be a lawyer. Lawyers don't even want to be lawyers!"

"I don't know, but neither do I know why Alice would be outside, trying to ruin Bennie's business. I don't know anybody who would risk arrest just to destroy somebody else."

"I do. Alice. She's self-destructive."

"Not really. Alice is all about self preservation. She fought tooth and nail not to be convicted of murder. Besides, she and Bennie had reconciled. So why would she give Bennie a hard time now? Did you ever think about that?" Judy leaned farther over the desk. "You know what I saw on her face, out there? Desperation. Didn't you see it, too?"

"Yes, I did. Alice is desperate to ruin Bennie." Mary started when the intercom buzzed on her phone, a signal that Rexco had arrived. She grabbed a fresh legal pad. "I have to go."

"How about if we think of a test?"

"What you mean?" Mary searched on her desk for a pen without teethmarks. Partners didn't chew their pens. She could tell Rexco that she had a puppy.

"There's years of things that Bennie knows about and Alice wouldn't. We all have a history, a shared history, and it excludes Alice."

"So what?" Mary went to the door, her chest tightening with impatience.

"So let's think of something that would test her. A case we had, a client we loved or hated, or a point of law. There are so many possibilities." Judy's eyes lit up, but Mary couldn't join her enthusiasm, which suddenly seemed childish.

"It's not a game."

"I know that. I didn't mean it that way." Judy's forehead creased. "Look, it's a good idea. We should think of some reference that only Bennie would know, then we wait for the chance to spring it on her and see if she knows what we're talking about. If she does, it's Bennie. If she doesn't, it's Alice."

"I don't have time to do that, and I don't want to." Mary put her hand on the doorknob. "Hasn't Bennie been through enough? Her sister is terrorizing her and her dog is dead. Cut her a break."

Judy looked mystified. "Why are you acting so weird?"

"I'm not."

"Yes, you are."

"Judy, really!" Mary threw up her hands. "There are real clients out there that we have to sign and real dollars we have to bring in. All of us."

"Whoa. You've been drinking the Kool-Aid." Judy edged back, frowning, and Mary felt stung.

"That's not fair."

"Did you ever think that if she's Alice, she's co-opted you? All those compliments she's dropping, like 'great idea' this and 'great idea' that? She doesn't really mean it."

"Thanks." Mary started to go, but Judy touched her arm, her face reddening.

"I'm sorry. I'm not saying you don't deserve it, I'm saying she could be manipulating you, if she's Alice."

"No, she's not. She's Bennie."

"You said so yourself, on the phone, how strange it was that she complimented you. Then she made you a partner, and overnight, you got so far on her side, you won't even consider there's another side."

"On this, there's only one side," Mary shot back, and Judy recoiled, confused.

"Really?"

"Yes," Mary answered, and through the open door she could hear Bennie greeting the Rexco people in the lobby. "I really have to go."

"Okay, whatever. Go."

Mary walked out, feeling a wrench in her chest. Wondering if she were leaving her best friend, as well as her boyfriend, behind.

Chapter Seventy-one

Bennie followed Tiffany into a basement apartment that reeked of stale cigarette smoke. The living room, stifling and windowless, contained a worn brown couch, a plaid fabric chair, and an old TV. A wrinkled Bon Jovi poster hung over a café table that held a black laptop, magazines, and gum wrappers. Empty glasses and full ashtrays dotted cheap end tables.

"Sorry it's so hot." Tiffany climbed up on the couch and turned on an air conditioner installed into the wall, then jumped down, with a grin. "Better, huh?"

"Yes, good."

"It'll be cold fast, you'll see. I got Bud Light, okay?"

"Fine." Bennie didn't thank her, because Alice wouldn't have.

"Sit down, make yourself comfortable. Want a sandwich, too? I got ham and cheese, okay?"

"Fine." Bennie sat down on the couch, taking a load off her feet, which throbbed, dirty, swollen, and cut. Her hand ached from hitting the guard. "You got any Advil?"

"Yep, sure. How'd you get so busted up?"

"If I told you, I'd have to kill you."

"Ha!" Tiffany laughed too loudly, as if she were sucking up, and Bennie wondered why.

"I could use some Band-Aids or gauze, for my feet."

"I got that. I even have the expensive kind, with the goop." Tiffany scurried out of the room. "Be right back."

The air conditioner rattled away, and Bennie felt like herself again, or at least, the new normal. She suppressed thoughts of Grady, Bear, and the associates, and focused on Alice. If the girl wanted to take over her life, she might be able to do it for a short while, with all the ID, checkbooks, and house keys. She probably still had the Lexus, too. But Bennie didn't understand why. Alice couldn't fake being a lawyer for long and she wouldn't want to, because that was work. The only thing the girl really cared about was money.

Bennie rose, went to the laptop, cleared the clutter, and sat down. She palmed the mouse as best as she could, clicked to the Internet, and typed in USABank.com. The bank's splash page came on, and she logged in with her username and password. The screen changed with a message that read, **Invalid username and password.** She hoped it was a typo, then retyped her username and password. The screen changed again, and she got the same error message. She typed in the information one more time. The new screen read, **Sorry, you have been locked out of this account. Please contact customer service to reset your password**.

She put it together, keeping a lid on her fears. Alice must have found the passwords in the Rolodex and gained access to the bank accounts. Bennie ran the numbers in her head. She kept roughly three million dollars liquid, more than usual, but sensible given the economy, and she had a substantial retirement account which couldn't be liquidated easily. Alice could do anything she wanted with the money, including withdraw or move it, but she wouldn't have much time, now that Bennie was back.

"You got a cell phone?" she called out to the kitchen.

"Yeah, sure." Tiffany returned with a can of beer, and a white-bread sandwich on a flimsy paper plate. She set the food on the beat-up coffee table and pulled a cell phone from her pocket, handing it over. "Be my guest. I'll get you the Advil and the Band-Aids, I couldn't carry it all."

"It can wait." Bennie rose and flipped open the phone. "Can I have some privacy?"

"Sure, I'll go outside, catch a smoke or somethin'." Tiffany fetched her purse and left the apartment as Bennie pressed in the phone number for Marla Stone, her contact at USABank.

"Hello, Marla? It's Bennie Rosato."

"Oh, hello." Marla sounded cold and distant. "I didn't recognize the phone number."

"It's not my phone and—"

"As you know, I can't discuss this account with you over the phone, unless you send me an email with written authorization and the password."

Oh no. "Marla, this is me, Bennie. We don't have a password on this account. We talk on the phone all the time about my accounts."

"I'm sorry, I cannot discuss your account with you without email authorization and password."

"Marla, we didn't agree to anything. My sister Alice is impersonating me. You've been dealing with her, not me."

"I'm sorry."

"Marla, this really is Bennie. I know—" Suddenly the line went dead, and she redialed. The phone rang and rang, but the call wasn't answered. She had to try another tack. She called information for the main number of the bank, let the call connect, and asked the operator for the head of private banking. "I need to speak with Russ Baxter, please," she said. "This is Bennie Rosato."

"I'm sorry, but he's on vacation this week."

"Who else can I speak to? I have an emergency problem with my account. My sister is gaining unauthorized access—"

"Ms. Rosato, I have instructions to transfer all calls regarding your accounts to Marla Stone. Would you like to speak with her?"

"I've already spoken with Marla and she hasn't been able to help. Who does Baxter report to?"

"Mr. Baxter heads our private banking unit. We all report to him."

"Who's the president of the bank, then? I met him once at a benefit. Isn't his name Ron Engel?"

"I'm sorry." The operator paused. "I have been instructed that if you call, to transfer you to Marla and only to Marla."

Bennie hung up, her thoughts racing. Alice must not have emptied her accounts yet, because she'd be gone if she had. It would probably take her two or three days to get that accomplished, and Bennie had to stop her, but was stumped. She couldn't go to the cops or the bank. She couldn't rely on the law for justice. She was on her own. If Alice was crime, then Bennie was punishment.

Suddenly Tiffany opened the door and walked inside, wreathed in cigarette smoke. "Sorry, you done your call?"

"Sure." Bennie handed her back the phone.

"Thanks." Tiffany flopped onto the couch, crossing slim legs, both with ankle tattoos of blue butterflies. "I'm surprised to see you on the run, Al. I heard you got a regular job, and all. You really come up in the world since the joint."

"I know, right?" Bennie picked up her can of beer, popped the top, and took an icy-cold swig, sitting down. She wanted to keep Tiffany talking because more information might help. "It sucked, inside, huh?"

"Totally. 'Course you ran the show, even then. I was happy for you when you got off on that murder rap. You really didn't do it, huh?"

"I didn't. Imagine that."

"Go figure." Tiffany laughed. "I went by the shop and saw Caitlin, and she asked me had I seen you. She said Kendra didn't see you and you didn't come by the shop, neither. Said she was lookin' for you all week, callin' for you everywhere. Didn't she call you?"

"Don't know." Bennie wolfed down her sandwich. "I left my cell somewhere. That's why I needed yours."

"I can take you to see Caitlin at the shop. You know how she is. High maintenance."

"Good."

Tiffany hesitated. "Listen, Al, I would really love to come work for you. I swear, I could do a good job. You got Caitlin at the shop and Kendra at the gym, but you can have me at the lunch truck. Who cares where the money comes from? It's all green."

"How do you see yourself, working for me?"

"Easy. You'd be surprised at how many guys come to the truck, looking to score. Construction guys, painters, masons, all the trades. Men need Oxys, too. Not just housewives."

"You think?"

"Sure! The guys who come to me, they got aches and pains, from real work. They talk about it all the time, rotator cuff this, pulled whatever, that. You think they can't use a Vike or an Oxy? They can, sure as shit. None of 'em sleep that good. They need Ambien, Xanax, whatever. I could make you a killing."

Bennie listened, drawing conclusions on the fly. Alice and her cop boyfriend used to run a drug business, selling crack through boxers' girlfriends out of a boxing gym. She had sworn to Bennie that she'd changed, but her only change had been to sell prescription drugs, where the addicts were better-dressed.

"Will you think about it? Caitlin said no, but she's not the boss. So, will you?"

"Yes." Bennie rose. She had to get to Alice, and now she had a next step. "Lemme grab a quick shower before we go see Caitlin."

"Sure." Tiffany got up. "I'll show you the bathroom. Advil and Band-Aids are there, too. Anything else I can get you?"

"Yes, fresh clothes, shoes, and a coupla bucks."

"No worries."

"Plus a gun," Bennie said, surprising even herself.

"For real, Al?"

"Do I look like I'm kidding?"

"Sorry, can't help you there."

"Forget it," Bennie said, but she wouldn't. She was already taking the splint off her right hand.

Chapter Seventy-two

Alice crossed the reception area, pasting on a smile to meet the Rexco people. "Gentlemen," she said, reaching out to shake hands. "I'm Bennie Rosato. So glad you could make it."

"Hans Mescal, good to meet you." He shook her hand, and he wasn't how she had pictured him, from the file. He had hooded blue eyes behind his steel-rimmed bifocals, a brushy white mustache, and a gray suit that fit badly, showing that he was a tightwad, for the boss of a Fortune 500 company. He introduced the other men, and they all said a round of hellos, but Hans acted as if he was the only one who counted, and Alice took her cue.

"Hans, everyone, please, come this way." She led them into the smaller, enclosed conference room, which had been stocked with hot coffee, fresh fruit, and cinnamon buns, and Mary was already waiting with a legal pad.

"Welcome, everybody," she said, smiling like the first day of school.

"DiNunzio, introduce yourself to Hans and the others, and let's get started. Hans, please, sit by me." Alice turned to Hans, gestured him into the seat at her right, and sat down at the head of the table. They all settled, and she began. "Let's get started. We all know the problem. Your employees made off with your trade secrets and lit out for the West Coast. You went to McGarity & Boston for the complaint, but they're not up to the task. You're a big enough company that every law firm in town wants your business, but I want it the most."

Hans cocked his head, listening.

"In fact, I want it so much that I'm willing to be unconventional in my billing practices."

The older man next to Hans frowned. "We don't usually talk fees before we talk substance."

"Why?" Alice never took her eyes off Hans. "The law is clear. You need a restraining order, and any court would give you one. You've probably already interviewed Morgan, Lewis, and Dechert, all the big boys. They've told you the same thing, right?"

The older man said, "But do you think the order should—"

Hans lifted an index finger, silencing him. "How unconventional, Bennie?"

"You can buy a restraining order from any of us, but they're expensive. Generally, a law firm has to drop everything, conduct discovery, and draft papers on the double. Yours would require two lawyers, full-time, for the next three weeks, through the preliminary hearing. It all adds up. The other firms were talking seventy-five to eighty grand for next month, correct?"

"Yes."

"We'll do it free. *Free,*" Alice repeated, when she saw Hans's eyes widen.

"Why would you do that? What's the deal?"

"If you're satisfied with the job we do, then you let us represent you for the next year, on all litigation matters. If you don't like our work, you walk away."

"That's quite a risk."

"No, it isn't. We're the best lawyers in town." Alice looked over at an astonished Mary. "Right, partner?"

"Right!"

"So what do you say, Hans?" Alice felt a little charge. She wouldn't be around to pay this debt anyway, and an admiring smile was spreading across the CEO's face.

"I didn't expect this, I must say." Hans stroked his mustache. "You think long-term. You have confidence in your team. I heard you were unorthodox."

"You heard right. Do we have a deal?" Alice extended her hand, and Hans shook it.

"Done," he answered, nodding.

"Wonderful." Alice gestured to Mary. "I should have mentioned that Mary here has just become my new partner, and she'd be more than happy to field any technical questions you may have."

Mary looked surprised but recovered with a game smile. "I sure would, gentlemen. Any questions?"

After the meeting, Alice led them out to reception, said good-bye to Hans and the others, and had Mary pack them into the elevator while she went back to her office. She saw that Grady wasn't in his, so maybe he'd gone to the bathroom, which gave her an opening. She hustled into Bennie's office, shut the door, and called the number for USABank.

"Marla, it's Bennie," she said, when the call connected. "I wanted to check in before the day ended. I'll send the signature cards out tonight. Did you wire the money?"

"Yes, it's all sent, as were the scanned signature cards. All of your money has been transferred to BSB, and your Bahamian accounts are open, pending receipt of the hard copies."

"Excellent."

"By the way, Alice called me earlier but I refused to discuss anything with her, as per our agreement."

Damn! "Why didn't you call and tell me?"

"I did. I spoke with Marshall, but she said you were in a meeting."

"Oh, sorry." Alice thought a minute. So Bennie had figured out what she was up to, but she didn't know the details and by the time she figured them out, Alice would be out of town, a step ahead of her, and Q.

"Bennie, you should also know that someone, undoubtedly Alice, tried to access your accounts online. She was denied because she didn't have the new password. You have to reset it yourself online, and I sent you an email with instructions to that effect."

"Thanks." Alice logged on to her email, skimming the boldfaced names until she found one from USABank. "I see, okay. Thanks. Gotta go."

Chapter Seventy-three

Mary entered the coffee room, where Grady and Judy were standing in front of the Bunn machine, feasting on leftover cinnamon buns. They looked up, and if Judy was still mad at her, it didn't show because her mouth was full of carbohydrates.

"How'd Rexco go?" she asked. "Apart from the food, which rocks."

"Amazing. We got 'em."

"How?" Judy asked, and Grady leaned against the granite counter with a Styrofoam cup of coffee while Mary told them the story. By the time she was finished, Grady looked charmed, but Judy's smile flattened.

Mary felt tense all over again. "I think doing it free was a great idea, don't you, Grady?"

"Brilliant." He grinned. "I *love* that woman. She's so damn smart."

"Sure is." Mary felt like he was a kindred spirit. "She's not afraid to take a risk, either. The client loved her, you could tell."

"I'm sure." Grady smiled, sipping coffee. "Do I have to give him a beatdown?"

"No." Mary laughed, if only to cover Judy's silence, which Grady didn't seem to notice.

"I'm glad we got some good news, after that debacle with Alice.

Marshall said the clients have been calling all afternoon. Report-ers, too."

"Any word on if the cops got Alice yet?"

"None."

"Too bad," Mary said, and Judy seemed to come to life, looking over at Grady.

"Was Bennie upset by that scene with Alice?"

Grady blinked. "Sure she was. Couldn't you tell?"

"Not really, but I don't know her as well as you do."

"She seemed upset to me."

"She didn't to me, and she didn't seem that upset over Bear, ei-ther. Was she?" Judy kept her tone light, but Mary knew she was pumping him.

Grady shook it off. "She's not the type to bleed all over, or in front of you guys. At home, she was a basket case. She cried her eyes out."

Mary glanced over at Judy, not bothering to hide her triumph. "Bennie doesn't show her emotions, especially at work. She's a private person. I respect her for that."

Judy didn't appear to be listening, wiping her sticky fingers on a napkin. "Grady, let me ask you a hypothetical. Is it possible that the woman who made a scene on the sidewalk really was Bennie? And not Alice at all?"

"Pardon?"

Mary felt stricken. "Grady, she's just kidding."

"No, I'm not," Judy shot back, and both women flanked Grady, catching him in the crossfire. "Think about it, Grady. What if we've mixed them up? Fiorella thought we had."

"Fiorella?" Grady set down his cup. "That crazy lady? What does she have to do with anything?"

Judy waved him off. "Forget Fiorella, she's not the point. What if that woman out there really was Bennie, and that woman in the office down the hall is Alice?"

Grady looked from Judy to Mary and back again, astonished. "Are you serious?"

"Yes," Judy answered.

"No," Mary answered, at the same time.

"That's impossible." Grady looked nonplussed, his forehead creased, and his eyes were vaguely pained behind his glasses. "Of course it's Bennie, in her office."

"How do you know?"

"I know my own girlfriend."

"Would you?" Judy lifted an eyebrow under her maraschino bangs. "You haven't seen her in a while. Does she seem different to you, in any way?"

"*Judy!*" Mary said. "You're being so inappropriate."

Judy touched Grady's arm. "Prove me wrong. Give her a test. Think of something that only you and Bennie know about, something intimate, and ask her about it. See if she knows it. If she does, she's Bennie. No harm, no foul. But if she doesn't, she's Alice."

"You mean this, don't you?" Grady released his arm, obviously uncomfortable. "That's a very strange notion you have there. Is your hair dye sinking into your brain?"

Mary felt as if she didn't even know Judy anymore. "He's right, stop it."

Judy's head snapped around. "Mary, did you just tell me to 'stop it'? I thought we were friends."

"We are."

"Then why are you ordering me around?"

"You're being disloyal and unkind, and I want you to cut it out."

"What if I don't?" Judy's blue eyes hardened like ice. "What are you going to do about it? Are you going to fire me?"

"Of course not."

Grady interjected, "Ladies, stop. Please, don't fight—"

Ignoring him, Judy asked, "How about telling Bennie on me, Mary? Would you tattle on me?"

"I don't know."

"You *don't?*" Judy frowned, raising her voice. "If you're my friend, you wouldn't tell. But now that you're a partner, maybe you would. Choose, Mare. Who are you? Friend or partner?"

"I don't have to choose."

"To me, you do. Make a decision—for once."

Ouch. Mary stood toe-to-toe with Judy, opposed for the first time ever. "Do you want me to tell her?"

"I dare you."

"Fine!"

"Good!" Judy threw down her napkin and headed for the door. "This time, I'll walk out on *you.*"

Chapter Seventy-four

Bennie walked down South Street with Tiffany, on the way to see Caitlin at the shop. They were only ten blocks from the business district, so she kept an eye out for the police and was wearing a disguise, of sorts. She'd borrowed sunglasses, tucked her hair into a Phillies cap, and had on a nondescript gray T-shirt, navy shorts, and old Keds, blending in with the summer tourists thronging to the hip restaurants and trendy shops.

"It's cool down here." Tiffany exhaled a cone of Marlboro smoke, acrid in the humidity. "But you can't park, and it's way expensive."

"Right," Bennie said, rather than say the wrong thing, and Tiffany tossed the cigarette to the curb as they approached an upscale boutique with a preppy pink sign that read PRINCIPESSA, above a ritzy glass entrance.

"There's Caitlin." Tiffany grabbed the glass handle. "Let's go in."

Bennie started to follow her through the door, but they were stopped at the threshold and pushed out of the shop by an attractive young woman in a striped shirtdress, with short blond hair. Presumably, she was Caitlin, though she looked more suburban housewife than pill pusher, even with a scowl wrinkling her upturned nose.

"Get out, Tiffany!" she hissed. "I told you never to come here."

"Alice wanted to see you, and I gave her a ride."

"Where's Alice?" Caitlin looked over at Bennie, and her eyes widened as if she'd seen a ghost. "*Alice?* Oh my God! Is that you?"

"Yes, hi."

"Jeez!" Caitlin glanced over her shoulder, slipped out the shop door, and hurried them both to the side, in front of a restaurant. "I thought you were dead!"

What?

"Where've you been? Why are you dressed like that?"

Tiffany interjected, "If she told you, she'd have to kill you."

Caitlin ignored her. "Alice, wait here. I'll tell Janey I got a call from Danny's school." She turned, ran back inside the shop, and closed the door behind her.

"See what I mean?" Tiffany frowned. "She has a thing against me. Use me, will you?"

"I'll think about it," Bennie said, though now that she'd met Caitlin, she could see why Tiffany didn't fit into Alice's business plan.

Caitlin reappeared, hoisting a Kate Spade purse to her shoulder and shooing Tiffany away like a roach. "Go, please. I'll take Alice home."

"Okay, okay." Tiffany edged backwards. "See ya, Al."

"Later," Bennie said, like Alice.

Caitlin was already hailing a cab, which pulled over immediately, thanks to her cute face and skinny legs. Up close, her eyes were round, an unusual green-brown, and her pretty mouth glossy with pink lipstick. She even smelled expensive, like floral perfume. They climbed inside the cab, and it lurched into traffic as Caitlin gave the driver an address that Bennie remembered was Alice's.

"So, Alice, where were you?" Caitlin turned to her, tense. "We had no pickup, and we sold out of what we had left. Q called me at the shop looking for you, and he's furious. He cursed me out when I said I didn't know where you were. I had to tell Janey he was my brother and I don't even have a brother."

Bennie didn't remember Alice talking about someone named Q. She stayed quiet and absorbed the information.

"I didn't sign up for that. I don't want to deal with that. He scared me half to death. I have kids!"

Bennie was already revising what she'd thought earlier. If Alice had to get away from this guy, Q, then that must be why she'd tried to kill Bennie. So it didn't start out being about the money, but it was ending up that way.

"Where were you? Kendra and I were worried." Caitlin waited for an answer, and Bennie slipped into Alice's mindset, which was surprisingly easy. She was already thinking of Caitlin and Kendra as a darker version of DiNunzio and Carrier.

She eyed Caitlin, coolly. "You weren't worried about me. You were worried about your job."

Caitlin blinked, one beat of her perfectly lined eyes. "Okay, right. What do you want me to say?"

"Try the truth."

"I need the money, and I didn't know what to do, with you gone. I didn't know whether to take my cut, and you weren't around to ask, so I did. I gave Kendra hers, too." Caitlin's tone turned lecturing. "We're running a business here, at least you are, and we all need the extra money. But it's not my life, and I don't want it to cost me my life. Or jail, or anything like that."

"Okay."

"You're the one who came to me, saying you were ahead of the curve, that you saw this market that wasn't being served. You said it was like any other business, but it's not. Not when I have to answer to a gangster like Q, or whatever his real name is."

Bennie let her talk, and Caitlin wouldn't be stopped anyway, having a meltdown.

"You said you were a professional. So you can't disappear for a week or sleep around. You think I don't hear you on the phone with Jimmy, whoever he is? If you keep fooling around with him, you could both end up dead!"

"You finished yet?"

"One last thing. You pissed off our supplier, so how do you expect us to stay in business?"

"Leave that to me."

"I can't deal with this level of stress. I get constant grief from my ex, always late with the payments, and then he gives the kids the check on Sunday, which he's not supposed to do." Caitlin rubbed her forehead with French-manicured fingers. "It's back-to-school time, and I had to take my cut to make a Staples run. You know how much those JanSport backpacks cost? And Book Sox are five bucks a pop."

"Book Sox?"

"They're things that cover the kids' textbooks."

"We always used paper bags." Bennie smiled, and so did Caitlin, finally calming down.

"So did we. Anyway, what happened to you last week?"

"I met somebody."

Caitlin shook her head, disapproving. "Who?"

"Nobody you'd know, obviously."

"What'd you do?"

Bennie shrugged, offhand. "We partied."

"Well, did you have a scratch party? Your legs are a mess."

"Don't ask."

"And your hand? It looks cut. Did he cut you or something?"

"Of course not." Bennie glanced out the cab window, watching the skyscrapers pass, then the tall brick townhomes of Society Hill. "Bottom line, I drank too much, we played some games, and I had such a good time that I don't remember where I left my wallet, keys, or phone."

Caitlin snorted. "So how are we going to get into your apartment? The super?"

"Obviously."

"So you don't have your car keys, either?"

"No." Bennie paused a minute. Everybody had an extra set of car keys. "I must have an another set somewhere."

"You do, in your dresser. Remember, you lent them to me, that time my car was in the shop?"

"Oh, right." Bennie held on to the handstrap as the cab steered out of town toward I-95, heading north.

"So where's your car?"

"Hell if I know."

Caitlin rolled her eyes.

"You gonna ground me, Mom?"

Caitlin smiled again, begrudgingly. "Anyway, we did so well that we were out of product by Sunday. Everybody's crazy busy, with school starting. I'm not the only mom who's stressed out. Look." Caitlin slipped a hand into her purse and passed Bennie a stack of wrinkled bills wrapped with a pink scrunchie. "This is three thousand dollars, and we already took our cuts, like I said, and you have to trust me we didn't take more, because you know we wouldn't. We had a great weekend, one of the best ever."

"Good." Bennie tucked the money into the cheap brown purse she'd gotten from Tiffany.

"You need to get us a new supplier. This business is too good to let it go, and it'll only get better come the holidays, with all the shopping and cooking. A visit from the in-laws will drive anybody to Xanax." Caitlin laughed at her own joke. "Also, the Lexapro was gone by noon on Saturday, and I think we should increase the price on the Norco, the hundred-milligram, when we start up again. These women have money, and we can get $45 a pop."

"I'll think about it."

"Fine." Caitlin pulled a cell phone from her purse, flipped it open and pressed a button. Into the phone, she said, "Kendra, I found Alice. Yes, she's fine. Meet us in ten minutes at her place. Get the key from the super, would you? See you." Caitlin hung up, looking over. "By the way, how did you end up at Tiffany's?"

"What's the difference?"

"You're not going to take her on, are you?"

"No." Bennie looked out the window as they sped in silence onto the highway, whizzing past immense warehouses blanketed with ads. They got off, took a left onto the main boulevard, and navigated a warren of well-kept apartment buildings. Finally they pulled up in front of Pembroke Arms, a new brick low-rise that was presumably Alice's. Caitlin handed a twenty to the cabbie, and Bennie got out of the cab just as another attractive young woman walked toward them, her sleek ponytail swinging.

"Alice!" It was Kendra, but she could have passed for a fitness model, tall and lean in a black stretch top that read PERSONAL

TRAINER, which she wore with bike shorts and bouncy Nikes. Her brown eyes were wide-set and animated, her nose small, and her smile dazzling. "I was so worried about you! What happened?"

"Tell you another time."

"We sold out this weekend, but we had a problem with Q."

"So I heard."

"Can you hook us up with somebody new?"

"Yes, I have it covered."

"Hey, I saw you on TV at the gym, when I was with a client. What were you doing at your sister's office? I missed what you said. We had it on mute, and I couldn't stop to read the closed captioning."

Caitlin turned around, surprised. "You were at your sister's?"

Bennie shrugged if off. "I asked her for a loan and she said no, so I embarrassed the hell out of her."

"I'll say." Kendra waved a key. "Your super would do anything for me. Whose apartment do you want to see next?"

"Let's go." Bennie fell into step behind Kendra and Caitlin, so they wouldn't realize that she didn't recognize her own apartment, and they entered the lobby, let themselves into the main door, then walked beyond the elevator bank and down a plush carpeted hall-way, passing 1-C, 1-E, 1-G, and stopping at 1-I, where Kendra slid a key into the doorknob and twisted the lock.

Bennie figured it was Alice's, so she pushed on the door, and it swung open into the apartment.

The women froze at the sight.

Chapter Seventy-five

Alice grabbed the messenger bag, tucked the bright yellow DHL envelope inside, and hurried around her desk. She had to get that envelope to the Bahamas, and according to the DHL website, the closest drop-off box was in the lobby of Mellon Center, eight blocks away. She checked her watch. It was three thirty, and the last pickup was four. She'd have to hustle.

She left her office, glancing over her shoulder, but Grady wasn't at his desk. She hurried ahead and heard talking in the coffee room, so she avoided that doorway, jogged toward reception, and gave Marshall the high sign.

"Be right back," Alice said, then punched the elevator button and ducked inside when the doors slid open. They were almost closed when a hand popped between them and bounced off the black safety bumpers. The doors sprang back immediately, and Judy was standing there, out of breath.

"I caught you!" Judy pushed her way into the elevator, and Alice tensed as the doors closed, with the associate inside.

"What do you want, Carrier?"

"Where are you going?"

"I have to run an errand. What is it?"

"Mind if I go along? I want to talk to you."

"About what?" Alice asked, as the elevator slid downward.

"A case I'm working on."

"Let's talk when I get back."

"I can go with you. I'd like to."

Alice started to wonder what was up. The kid was never this pushy, and her tone of voice sounded higher and thinner, like she was nervous. "I'd rather you stayed at the office. It's bad enough that I have to run out."

"But I can use some fresh air, after today."

The elevator reached the lobby, the doors slid open, and Alice stepped off the elevator, blocking the way. "Carrier, go back upstairs and mind the fort."

"The fort is fine."

"Then mind my boyfriend."

"I want to go with you." Judy didn't budge. The security guards looked over, starting to eavesdrop.

"I don't want you to. Mommy needs some me time, got it?"

"Okay, but before you go, I want to ask you something, for this brief I need to finish right away." Judy's forehead wrinkled. "Remember when we were working on that case with Marta Richter? We were of counsel? It was winter, during a blizzard, a couple of years ago? I forget the case name. Do you remember it?"

Alice had no idea what she was talking about. It seemed like an odd question. "How can it matter what the case name was?"

"I guess it doesn't, I was just thinking, oh, right, I remember now, it was Steere, that was the defendant's name. Elliott Steere." Judy nodded. "Anyway, you told Marta that she was in breach of, like, five ethical canons under the CPR."

Alice tried to remember what CPR stood for.

"Remember that?"

"Hardly." Alice checked the ornate clock on the lobby wall—3:45. Now she'd have to run.

"I was wondering if you ever reported Marta to the Disciplinary Board. I wanted to cite you as precedent."

"That's hardly good precedent."

"It's good enough for me. Did you report her?" Judy looked at her directly, with her clear blue eyes, and Alice realized it wasn't a question. It was a test, and she was about to fail.

"Carrier, what case are you working on, that you want to know this?"

"Cypress Construction. I have a similar situation. Kind of."

"Did you check the Steere file?"

"Why? Don't you remember?"

"Sue me, but I don't, and I've got other things on my mind. We can discuss it later." Alice crossed the lobby to the exit, but Judy dogged her steps.

"Where are you going? What's the mystery? You always tell us where you're going, so we can find you."

"No I don't. You just think I do." Alice was getting worried. The guards were listening. "Now get back to work."

"Okay," Judy answered uncertainly, then turned and went back to the elevator bank.

Alice blew out of the building, passed the Rothman guards, and hurried up the street, her thoughts churning. She had to get out of town as Bennie, especially after that scene on the sidewalk, and Judy was starting to be more of a problem than Grady. It was only a few hours until her flight, but one phone call could blow her cover. And Q would put all the pieces together.

Alice picked up the pace, running like it was a matter of life and death.

Because it was.

Chapter Seventy-six

Mary walked into the reception area, looking for Judy. She hated being in a fight and she had to set it right. She asked Marshall, "Did you see Judy?"

"Yes. She just went down the elevator with Bennie."

Uh-oh. "Where were they going?"

"I don't know, I was on the phone. It's been crazy, between reporters and clients. All I know is I saw Bennie leave and Judy go after her."

"Were they fighting?"

"No, why would they be?" Marshall answered, with a frown.

"No reason." Mary was already heading for the elevator bank and punching the DOWN button. "I'll be right back."

"What's going on?"

"Nothing, really."

"So where are you going?"

"To get them." Mary jiggled the button, impatient.

"Sheesh. This is the strangest day ever." Marshall answered a ringing phone, and Mary gave up on the elevator. She bolted for the exit stairway, pushed open the door, and ran down the stairs, hitting landing after landing. She was out of breath by the time she reached the first floor and pushed through the door that dumped her into the lobby.

"Did you see Bennie and Judy?" Mary called to Steve, who looked up from his newspaper.

"Yeah. Bennie told Judy to go back up to the office, and Judy got in the elevator. But then she came back down again and went after her."

"Which way did they go?"

"That way." Steve pointed, and Mary ran for the door and hustled outside the building and onto the crowded sidewalk. Pewter gray clouds cloaked the sun, and humidity thickened the air. Rush hour was starting, and people streamed toward the subway, PATCO, and suburban trains.

She jogged past the Rothman guards, hurrying down the street and threading her way through the crowd, scanning right and left. Judy was tall and her hair cherry red, so she should be easy to find. Mary was on the lookout for a walking ice cream sundae.

She saw bald heads, fauxhawks, and weaves. Blondes, brunettes, and cornrows, but no Judy. She darted across the street and looked to the right, then spotted a head as red and round as a Tootsie Roll pop. It was Judy, two blocks down the street, waiting at a traffic light as a SEPTA bus rumbled through an intersection. Mary looked one block farther and spied Bennie, who was the only person running through the crowd. From the looks of it, Judy was stalking Bennie.

Mary took off. Up ahead, the SEPTA bus passed through the intersection, and Judy started moving, keeping a half a block behind Bennie.

Mary slid her cell phone from its holster and speed-dialed Judy on the fly. The call connected and the phone rang, but Judy didn't pick up or break stride.

Mary slid the phone back, put on the afterburners, and took off, pumping her arms. Bennie kept running, way ahead, and Judy reached Market Street, hot on the trail.

Mary ran harder, closing the gap between her and Judy from a full block, then to half. She lost sight of Bennie but Judy stopped at the corner, blending into the crowd.

"Judy!" Mary yelled, huffing and puffing.

Judy turned around at the sound, and Mary reached her at speed, falling into her arms and almost sending them sprawling.

"Don't stalk Bennie! You're gonna get fired and I don't want to work there without you! I'm sorry for what I said, I am!"

"I'm sorry, too!" Judy hugged her and set her back on her feet. "But this is the weirdest thing ever!"

"Why are you following Bennie?"

"She's not Bennie!"

"She is!"

"No, trust me. This woman *cannot* be Bennie Rosato." Judy gripped Mary by the arms, her blue eyes bright with zeal. "She told me she was going to run an errand, but she went into the Mellon Center!"

"So?"

"What errand can you run in Mellon Center? It's an office building. There's no drugstore or anything like that."

"That doesn't mean anything. There's Mellon Bank. Maybe she banks there."

"No, she's at USABank. We all are."

"So maybe she's meeting a friend. Like you said, there are tons of law firms in there. Ballard, Spahr, and plenty of others. She knows tons of people."

"That's not it." Judy shook her head, her mouth set. "She didn't say she was meeting a friend. If you're going to meet a friend, you say that. If you're going to run an errand, you say *that*."

"I don't know—"

"Think about it, Mare. She never goes out during the business day if it's not billable. And guess what else? I gave her a test and she blew it. She *forgot* the Steere case. How could you forget Steere? It was one of our biggest murder cases."

"She forgot the case?"

"Well, the name of the case."

"Jude, that's not the same thing."

"She also said she doesn't remember if she reported Marta to the Disciplinary Board." Judy's eyes narrowed. "A second test, flunked! If she were Bennie, she would have remembered that. Admit it. We all hated Marta. We *prayed* they'd discipline her."

Mary could understand how it seemed strange, but still. "When did you ask her?"

"When she was leaving."

"Oh. Then, of course, she was preoccupied. She's having a rough day, don't you think?"

There was a voice behind them, and they both froze.

Parting the foot traffic on the sidewalk, her arms folded, stood a very unhappy Bennie Rosato.

Chapter Seventy-seven

Bennie surveyed the living room in Alice's apartment, which had been ransacked. A TV lay face-down on the floor. Cushions were flipped over on a corduroy couch. A coffee table had been upended, and a ginger lamp lay smashed on the wood floor. File drawers hung open in a small desk, scattering bills and papers. A surge protector lay on its side, its wires unconnected to anything, and an open Mac laptop had been cracked like a clam shell.

"Oh my God!" Kendra's eyes widened. "It had to be Q."

"Oh no." Caitlin shook her head. "I bet he robbed you."

"Damn it to hell!" Bennie said, not wanting to say more, yet. She followed Caitlin into an adjoining bedroom, which was also destroyed. Shoes and papers lay scattered around, dresser drawers hung out, spilling clothes onto a blue rug. The closet doors stood open, the clothes shoved to one side on the rack, and the shelf on top held shoeboxes that had been opened, their lids off.

Kendra bit her lip. "He was looking for money."

"Of course he was." Caitlin was already on her knees, peering under the bed. When she looked up, her expression was resigned. "He found it, too. It's gone. Ten thousand dollars, and your gun, too."

My gun. Bennie masked her surprise.

"Told you so." Caitlin rose, brushing off her knees in disgust. "You take too many chances, Alice. Not only do we have to find another supplier, we only have three grand to buy pills with. He's trying to put us out of business."

"She's right, what were you thinking?" Kendra frowned, and Bennie reacted, as Alice.

"Quit your whining!" she shouted. "I'm the one who's a sitting duck here! Q's trying to kill me, not you!"

"I'm sorry, I didn't mean it," Kendra said, instantly putting up her hands.

"Yes, you did." Bennie eyed Kendra, hard. "How do I know it was Q who robbed me, and not you? You knew where I keep the money. You knew I was away. The super loves you, you said so yourself. Did he let you in this week? Did you take the money?"

"Alice, no." Blood drained from Kendra's face. "I would never rob you. I would never rob anybody."

Caitlin interjected, "Alice, come on. It's not her, it's Q. You cheated on him with one of his own guys and embarrassed him in front of everyone he knows and everyone who works for him. He's a thug right, so what did you think was going to happen? You're lucky to be alive."

"Screw you!" Bennie shouted at Caitlin, and the words came more quickly than she expected. "Are you working with Q, now? You could be. You talked to him on the phone. Did you tell him I was gone? Did you tell him to come here? Take the money and the gun, then toss the apartment, to make it look like someone else did it?"

"No!"

Suddenly Bennie shoved Caitlin backwards, an explosion of violence she didn't know was in her, until now. "You didn't cover for me. You could've told him you saw me, that I was sick or something."

Caitlin backed up, shaken. "I'm sorry, I didn't think of that. I was worried about you, I just didn't think."

"Shut up!" Bennie pointed to the door. "Get out! You're fired. I don't need you. I'll find another, better worker. Suburban housewives are a dime a dozen, and everybody needs Book Sox, right?"

"Alice?" Kendra said.

Bennie turned, and froze.

Kendra was pulling a gun from her purse.

Chapter Seventy-eight

"Walk with me, ladies." Alice took Carrier and DiNunzio by their arms and got them moving, having mailed the DHL envelope. "We need to talk, since you guys seem to be following me, for some reason."

"No, we weren't," Mary said, quickly.

"I was," Judy corrected. "I think you're acting strangely and I'd like to know why."

"How am I acting strangely, Carrier?" Alice powered them through the businesspeople, who flowed around them in the opposite direction. The sky was darkening, and an older man looked worriedly at the clouds.

"Well, what errand were you running, in Mellon Center?"

"I wasn't running an errand."

"You said you were."

"I lied."

Mary looked over, in surprise.

"So what's the truth?" Judy stopped on the sidewalk, and Alice turned to face her.

"I went to meet somebody, a man I've been seeing. I didn't plan on Grady coming back into my life. He did that on impulse. So I had to break up with someone, now that he's back."

"Why didn't you just call him?"

"I don't dump men on the phone. Do you?"

"But you weren't gone long enough. I saw you go into the building, like, five minutes ago."

"I ran into his partner in the lobby, and he told me he wasn't there. So I'll have to catch him later or maybe settle for a phone call, when Grady isn't around."

Mary's neck erupted in blotches. Bennie never shared this kind of personal information with them and still wouldn't have, if Judy hadn't made her. "That explains everything, to me."

Judy swallowed visibly. "It does. Sorry."

"Good, now I have some questions for you." Alice wanted to flush Judy out. If the associate didn't come clean, she wouldn't survive the night. "Why did you follow me in the first place? What were you thinking?"

"It's been a bad day, I know, and I . . . was worried about you."

Yeah, right. "Why didn't you simply tell me that?"

"I was going to, but then Mary came, and you, right after."

"You're sure that's it?"

"Absolutely."

"Nothing else?"

"No."

You just signed your own death warrant.

Mary interrupted, "Looks like rain. We'd better get back."

"You're right, DiNunzio." Alice got the girls walking again. "Tell you what, Carrier. I'm having dinner tonight with a biotech company from Dublin, Ireland. I'm meeting the CEO, the general counsel, and an operations type. This just came up today, and I'd love to get their business. Do you want to come with me?"

"Sure." Judy sounded pleased, which was just what Alice wanted.

"Good. It will be a late night, though. They're expecting me to show them around. They've never been to Philadelphia, and I have to show them how much fun we are."

"No problem. My boyfriend's away on a job. What company is it?"

"It's a fairly complicated parent-sub relationship. I'll let you know before the meeting."

Mary interrupted, "I'll take Grady to dinner. How about that?"

"Thanks." Alice squeezed Mary's arm. "Make him pay. Order the lobster."

"You're on." Mary smiled as they hurried along. Suddenly it started to drizzle, and everybody on the sidewalk picked up the pace, fumbled for umbrellas, or covered their heads with purses.

"Haul ass!" Alice shouted, and the women half-ran and half-scooted down the crowded sidewalk, hustling all the way back to the office in the rain. They hurried past the Rothman guards and through the doors, then emptied into the lobby, out of breath, laughing, and slightly damp.

Steve looked up from the security desk. "You guys need some paper towels?"

"No, thanks." Alice led the girls to the elevator bank, swiped her card, and punched the button with a wet hand.

Mary grinned. "I can't keep up with you two. My legs are too short."

"You did fine, stumpy." Judy's soaked hair was red as blood.

Alice ushered them into the elevator when the doors opened, and pushed the button. They prattled on about hair, and she zoned them out, alone with her thoughts. The rain was a lucky break because it would get darker sooner, and she and Judy would have dinner at a restaurant down by the Delaware River, where there were fewer people and plenty of back alleys.

The elevator doors slid open, and the women dripped into the reception area, where Marshall and Grady were standing. Grady turned, smiling. "What happened to you guys?"

"We went on a field trip, girls only." Alice walked over and kissed him on the cheek. "I'm taking Carrier to dinner tonight, so you're dating DiNunzio, okay?"

"Great!"

"We'll be out late with an Irish client, so don't wait up. Now let me get back to my office. I have to make one more call before the end of the day."

"Go ahead," Grady said, and Alice left them in reception. She went down the hallway, entered her office, and closed the door behind her, then walked around the desk, opened the bottom drawer, and moved aside some correspondence. Underneath, where she had hidden it, lay her revolver.

She picked it up and checked the chamber. It housed six bullets, which was five more than she would need for Judy. She clicked it back into place and aimed it at the air, imagining her target.

"Bang!" she whispered.

Chapter Seventy-nine

Mary spent the next hour or so at her desk, returning calls, answering emails, and tackling the day's correspondence. Her cell phone started ringing, and she slid it from her holster, thinking immediately of Anthony, but the screen showed the realtor's number.

"Hi, Mary," Janine said, "the owner has your offer, and they're considering it."

"That's all? I offered the asking price." Mary sighed just as Grady popped his head into her open door, and she waved him into the chair opposite her desk, where he sat down, silently.

Janine was saying, "I think they'll accept, but there are other offers, so don't start celebrating. They have three days to accept, and it's prudent to take the full time."

"I don't want to get into a bidding war."

"I'll call you when I know something. In the meantime, we have to line up an inspector, and I'll email you with a referral."

"Thanks." Mary pressed END and set the phone down.

"The house?" Grady asked. "It'll come through."

"I hope so. It cost me my boyfriend."

"Wanna talk about it? I'm here." Grady looked sympathetic, but Mary didn't know him well enough to cry on his shoulder.

"Nah, thanks. I'm fine." She reached for her computer mouse.

"Let's look online for a restaurant. What would you like? Chinese? French? Steak? They're gonna be out late."

"I know, Bennie gave me the house keys. I'm supposed to put them in the flowerpot for her, then go to sleep." Grady rose and came around the desk. "On a different point, this thing Judy's talking about, that somehow Bennie is really Alice. You don't agree with her, do you?"

"No." Mary looked up. "Why?"

"It's odd." Grady leaned against the credenza, slipping his hands into his pockets. His shirtsleeves were rolled up, and his striped tie loosened. "I've been thinking about it ever since Judy said it."

"Really?" Mary was starting to wonder if the world had gone nuts.

"It's like when someone asks you if you hear water dripping, and you don't. But then, after they mention it, it's all you hear. You're listening for it, then. You understand?"

"You mean you agree with Judy now? You said you didn't."

"I know, I didn't." Grady's brow knit in confusion. "But now I'm thinking about it."

"Why?"

"Because of some things that happened last night, between Bennie and me. Little things, like she gave me a glass of milk and she knows I hate milk."

"Not a smoking gun."

"But it was an old joke between us, because she loves milk so much."

"So she forgot. You haven't seen her in a couple of years. Do you remember which drink she absolutely hates? There is one."

Grady's expression went blank. "Uh, no."

"Root beer."

"Touché."

"Plus, you surprised her with your visit, didn't you? Your coming in probably threw her for a loop." Mary was thinking about the man who worked at Mellon Center. "She's just off her game."

"Possibly."

"Definitely."

"So Judy's completely wrong?"

"Yes." Mary's cell phone rang and she checked the display screen, hoping again for Anthony, but no luck. "Excuse me, it's my parents. I'll just be a minute." She pressed the green button and said, "Hi."

"*Maria, Maria!*" It was her mother, in tears.

"Ma, what's the matter?"

"Your father, he's a *cheat* with Fiorella!"

"*What?*" Mary asked, shocked.

"He's a with Fiorella! Come home, *per favore, Maria! Tornare a casa!*"

"I'm on my way," Mary said, springing to her feet.

Chapter Eighty

Bennie's heart stopped when she saw the gun, but Kendra turned it around and handed it over.

"Take this, Alice," she said, her tone softer. "You need it more than I do right now. Sorry about what I said. You're right. We were being selfish."

Caitlin looked over. "Ken, you have a gun? Why?"

"Protection," Kendra answered. "The gym's open late and sometimes I have to lock up."

Bennie examined the gun, a new Beretta, sized for women. It was a peace offering, and even Alice would have shown some remorse in the circumstances. "Sorry I did the freak, guys. I'm a little jumpy, with the apartment and all."

"I'm sorry, too." Caitlin dug in her purse and came out with a baggie full of white capsules. "Here. Take your chill pill. You'll feel better."

Whoa. "Not in the mood."

"Come on, we know how you get. Take the bag."

Bennie felt them watching her, waiting. She had never taken a drug in her life, but she didn't want them to doubt her. She put the gun in her pocket, plucked the bag from Caitlin's hand, and popped a capsule in her mouth, swallowing it dry.

"Just the one?"

"Listen, you guys should go. I'll call you as soon as I have another supplier."

"Please don't wait too long," Caitlin said, and Kendra nodded.

"Alice, seriously, I rely on the extra income. I've lost clients because of the economy. I need to make up the difference."

"I hear you." Bennie walked to the door, opened it, and gestured them out to the hallway. "I'll be in touch. Don't worry."

They left together, and Bennie closed the door, her gaze traveling over the disarray. The shattered lamp, the strewn papers. It felt strange, standing in Alice's place as Alice, having drugs and a loaded gun. She imagined Alice in her place, as her. And now they had switched businesses, too.

Her gaze fell on something bright amid the debris near the desk, a red book sliding out of a thick manila envelope. She went over, picked up the envelope, and looked inside. It wasn't like the bills and printed papers; next to the book was a packet of letters. She slid out the book, which turned out to be Alice's college yearbook, her name stamped in fake gold on its pebbled cover. Papers were wedged inside like a bookmark, and she opened the yearbook to the page, moving them aside.

Senior Class Monster Mash, read the top, above photos of couples slow-dancing, in Halloween costumes. Her eyes went immediately to Alice, drawn there because it was like looking at a photo of herself, in costume. Alice was dressed as Alice in Wonderland, in a blue smock with a white pinafore, and was dancing with a tall boy in a rabbit outfit, complete with top hat. He was handsome, very tall, with dark, lively eyes and a wide smile, though he had a jagged scar on his right cheek. Under the photo, the caption read ALICE AND HER MAD HATTER.

Bennie sat down on the couch with the yearbook. She had never seen a photo of Alice from her college days and flipped through the yearbook for more candids. There were none, so she went to the senior pictures in the back, finding Alice in the C's. Again, her face was exactly Bennie's, and under the picture, the caption listed no activities, though there was a personal note that read "Hugs and kisses to Biggest Dave, TLF."

True love forever?

Bennie paged through the senior pictures, starting back at the A's, looking for Biggest Dave. It took her until she got to the G's, when she found a senior photo of the Mad Hatter, recognizable because of the scar. His name was David Gamil, and he'd played Intramural basketball and been in ROTC. Under his photo, the caption said, "Alice, you are my wonderland, TLF." In the margin of the page, he had written, All my love always and forevermore, in neat printing.

She blinked, surprised that Alice was capable of a normal love relationship. She paged idly through the book, noticing something else. There were no other handwritten notes from friends with their pictures. She turned to the inside front cover, then the inside back cover. There were no written notes by friends, anywhere. She thought a minute, then looked up from the yearbook and scanned the tables and shelves in the living room. There were no photographs, even on the floor, and there hadn't been any in the bedroom. Alice had no friends, and neither of them had any family, except each other.

Bennie thought of her own house. She didn't have any photos of anybody else around, either, except Bear. That was why Alice could so completely take over her life, with nobody the wiser. Because nobody really knew Bennie that well at all. She looked down at the yearbook in her hands and noticed the blood drying on her hand, where she'd taken the bandage off. She wished she could see it at cell-level, down to her very twisted DNA. It was Alice's DNA, too. They both had good blood and bad blood, but how much of each?

She pressed the thought aside and went to the packet of letters, which looked like ten of them in a thick rubber band. She tugged the first letter from the pack, and the envelope was addressed to Alice, at this address. The postmark was foreign, with Arabic writing. She slid out the single page of notebook paper, which read:

Dear Alice, It's so great that you got back in touch with me, even though I'm deployed here, on my third tour. The military lets us have a Facebook page, but we have to keep it PG-13.

Ha! I thought about you a lot over the years and am so happy
you have a new job, and came through everything okay . . .

Bennie's eyes skipped to the bottom of the letter, and it was
signed, Love, Dave. So Alice had gotten back in touch with Dave
Gamil, from college. Surprised, Bennie checked the date on the letter. It was two years ago, about the time Alice had started at PLG.
She thumbed through the rest of the envelopes, and they were saved
in chronological order. She went to the second letter, which was
dated two months after the first.

Dear Alice, I love your letters and packages, they remind
me of home, college days, and mostly you, and how happy we
were. All the guys are jealous that I get such great cookies,
too, but you're not supposed to send the Playboys. I gave them
away, because I'm thinking of you more and more . . .

It showed Bennie that Alice had a good side and that she hadn't
been wrong to trust her. It was so hard to believe, now, after the
box. Bennie opened the next few letters:

Dear Alice, I love you, and you have changed everything for
me, even in this hellhole. I'm so happy that we got our old flame
rekindled. I never used to care about getting home soon, with
my folks gone. But now I wish I could get this job done and see
you tomorrow . . .

Dear Alice, I think of you all the time, day and night, and
so much of my time here is just sitting and waiting, then all
hell breaks loose. My buddy Mojo says it's like baseball, hurry
up and wait. We have an operation coming up soon, but don't
worry . . .

Dear Alice, I am so sick of this place sometimes! I sweated
through my armor and I stink like hell, and all I want to do is
finish my job, go home, and take you to bed. I look at your

picture a lot, and Mojo says his wife is more beautiful but he thinks tracer fire is beautiful . . .

Bennie skimmed the next few, which were love letters, then came to the next-to-last one:

Babe, I know this isn't the kind of thing to do in a letter, but I love you and I can't wait until I'm home and I don't want it to be in email, so here goes! WILL YOU MARRY ME? PLEASE SAY YES! We would be so happy together and we could raise a basketball team of our own . . .

Alice, engaged? Bennie stopped reading. She couldn't believe it had gone this far. She put the letter back in the stack, and the motion dislodged another envelope from the back, which fell to the rug. She picked it up and opened it, but there wasn't a letter inside, just a newspaper clipping. The clipping showed a photo of David Gamil in uniform, with the same scar on his cheek and the same lively look in his eyes. But it was an obituary, and the beginning read:

First Lieutenant David N. Gamil, USAF, of Paramus, New Jersey, who served with the 6th Security Forces Squadron, was killed in action on March 20, when enemy forces attacked his vehicle with an improvised explosive device, near southern Baghdad, Iraq. . . .

It was awful news, the loss of a wonderful young man, and she could only imagine the pain Alice must have felt. Bennie checked the date on the newspaper; March 21, just last spring. She looked back at the last letter, his proposal, and it was dated March 19.

She tried to process what she had learned, with the pill taking the edge off her emotions. It must have been Dave's death, about six months ago, that set Alice back and caused her to revert to form. That was about the time she'd lost interest in her job at PLG, started selling drugs, and sleeping with Q. Alice must have been grief-stricken, off-balance and self-destructive.

But no.

Bennie came out of her reverie. There was a difference between explaining and explaining away. What Alice had done could be explained, but it couldn't be explained away. Not anymore, and not again. The box had changed everything, and there was no going back anymore, no way of forgiving.

Bennie got up, letting the yearbook and letters fall to the floor. She found her purse, put the pills, money, and the gun inside, then went to the bedroom, tore it apart until she found the extra car keys, and left the building.

Cold rain pounded on her face and shoulders, making her more alert. She didn't know if Alice had left her car here, but there hadn't been one in the driveway at the house, she remembered now. She pulled the car key from her pocket and pressed the button on the fob. Down the street, a red Toyota came to life.

She went to the car, got inside, started the engine, and didn't have another thought until she found herself downtown, parking around the corner from her building, with a view of its entrance. People with umbrellas hurried this way and that on the sidewalk, flowing around the private security guards, still on duty. She didn't know when they got off, but it didn't matter. She would follow Alice anywhere she went and take her when they were alone.

She turned off the ignition, looked up at her office window, and caught a glimpse of Alice, moving around her office. It made her want to scream, which must mean that the chill pill was wearing off. She didn't know exactly what it was, but she was beginning to see why it sold so well. She dug in her purse, pulled out another pill, and popped it into her mouth. She didn't want to feel angry. She didn't want to feel anything at all.

Sooner or later, she would get Alice alone.

And it would all be over.

Chapter Eighty-one

Alice grabbed her coat and the messenger bag, hurried down the hall to Judy's office, and stuck her head inside. "Carrier, ready to go?"

"Yep. Did Mary and Grady leave? I got caught on the phone."

"Yes, let's go."

Judy glanced out of her office window, where sheets of rain streaked the glass. "Should we wait for the storm to let up?"

"We can't." Alice picked up Judy's striped umbrella. "Here."

"Okay, great." Judy got up, grabbed her kilim purse, and came around the desk. "We're meeting the client there, right?"

"Yes. Come on."

"Where are we going?"

"It's called Roux. Been there?"

"No, but I've heard it's cool, trying to gentrify the neighborhood down by the waterfront, right?"

"Right."

"I'm in favor."

"Good." Alice led her down the hall to reception, where Marshall was working. "You still at it, girl?"

"I still have a few things left, with all the distractions today."

"Thanks, but go home."

"I will, soon."

"We're out of here." Alice went ahead to the elevator and pressed the button. Outside, the sky had gone dark with the storm, and cars clogged the street. She flagged down one of the Rothman guards.

"How you doin', Ms. Rosato?" he asked, raising his voice to be heard over the downpour.

"Did you hear if they caught Alice?"

"No, I'll keep you posted. By the way, Bob's fine."

Alice frowned. "Who's Bob?"

"One of our guys, the guard your sister punched."

Whatever. "Good. We're going out, meeting new clients."

"You want protection? I can spare a man."

"No, thanks, it wouldn't look right. I'm reasonably safe, now that the cops are looking for Alice."

"So when should we leave here? Our contract says ten o'clock."

"Perfect. Thanks."

"You're welcome." The guard's eyes shifted to the street. "Hold on, I see a cab." He waved it down, and when it stopped, Alice opened the door and told the cabbie the address.

They lurched into stop-and-go traffic, and Judy turned to her. "I went online and researched the biotech industry in Ireland, for some background info. I learned a lot."

"Good for you."

"I couldn't research this client, because you didn't get back to me with its name."

"I was busy, sorry." Alice made up a name. "It is Genlynn Enterprises."

"Gotcha." Judy went into her purse and pulled out an iPhone. "I can look it up right now, online."

"No, don't." Alice stopped her hand. "Let them tell us. Clients love to talk about their business, and we don't want to sound like we studied."

"Oh." Judy blinked. "Even if we did?"

"Right. Why don't you tell me what you found out, generally, to give us some context?"

"Sure, well, it's really interesting. Wyeth is the big dog in Dublin, in biotech, and they have a campus south of the city . . ."

Judy lectured on, and Alice zoned out as the cab headed east toward the Delaware River. They reached Columbus Boulevard and turned right, passing the well-lit big-box dance clubs and party-of-twelve tourist restaurants. They took the curve, leaving the lights and excitement behind, and steered toward the more deserted section of the Boulevard. The Walt Whitman Bridge loomed ahead, and on the right, train cars that read HAPAG-LLOYD AND HAMBURG SUD stood on rusted tracks.

Alice looked for the restaurant on the left, on the riverbank. They passed old-time municipal piers, then a huge ship with a peeling black hull and three red smokestacks, like a busted *Titanic*. She spotted Roux dead ahead and scanned the surrounding area. Next to it was some kind of abandoned distribution center, with a rubble-strewn parking lot, empty except for a few tractor trailers without the truck cabs. It was a dark, lonely stretch, with ancient RESTRICTED AREA signs hanging on saggy concertina wire.

Alice felt satisfied. There would be plenty of places to leave a body, so that it wouldn't be discovered until morning.

"How'd I do?" Judy asked, when the lecture was over.

"Perfect." Alice smiled. "Just perfect."

Chapter Eighty-two

Mary hurried inside her parents' house, left Grady in their living room, and made a beeline for the kitchen, which looked different from ever before. There was no food on the table, and nothing bubbled on the stovetop. Tony Bennett was silent, and there wasn't even the sound of coffee percolating. The room was empty except for her mother, who sat slumped in her chair, her hand in her chin, her body a forlorn pile of flesh and spandex.

"*Maria,*" she said, her voice choked and quivery, and Mary rushed over, sat beside her, and hugged her tight, breathing in her faded perfume.

"It's gonna be all right, Ma."

"No, no." Her mother looked over, her gaze red-rimmed behind her bifocals and her rookie mascara making dark quarter-moons under her eyes. "Fiorella come, and everyting go bad."

"Ma, it can't be. You and Pop love each other."

"*No, Maria.* He no love me no more." Emotion mottled her papery skin, and red tinged the tip of her nose. "He *cheat*!"

"How, Ma? What happened?"

"Your father, he *kiss* her, inna restaurant!" Her mother's eyes brimmed with tears, but Mary couldn't believe it was true.

"That's impossible, Ma."

"*No, e vero.*"

"How do you know?"

"Johnny, he works inna museum, he's a grandson from the TV man down a block." Her mother pressed a balled-up Kleenex to her nose. "Johnny, he call the TV man onna phone, and the TV man tell Camarr Millie, and she tell Camarr Franny, and she call me."

Mary felt mortified for her. "What restaurant? What museum?"

"*Non lo so,* I dunno. He take Fiorella, inna city. Art museum. She want to go. Anywhere she want, he take her, alla time."

"*Kissed* her?" Mary still couldn't believe it. "It's just a rumor, gossip. Pop would never kiss another woman, never."

"No, no." Her mother squeezed her hands together, squashing the Kleenex, and Mary hugged her closer.

"Ma, I'm sure there's an explanation. Pop loves you. You have the best marriage ever. Everybody knows that."

"No more, no more. Ever since operaysh . . ." Her mother's voice trailed off, and Mary knew what she meant. Her "operaysh" was her operation. Her hysterectomy.

"Where is he?"

"*Non lo so.* He's a suppose to come home for dinn'. He no come, he no call."

Suddenly there was a commotion in the living room, and Mary heard the screen door slam closed, then her father talking to Grady.

She and her mother looked toward the living room.

Chapter Eighty-three

Bennie found a parking space down the street from Roux, having followed Alice and Carrier here from the office. Their cab was still idling, and the valet waited at its back door to meet them with a golf umbrella. They were evidently going to dinner together, and she would wait until they had finished and Alice was alone. The red Toyota sat behind a boxy white truck, so it couldn't be seen from the restaurant.

She cut the ignition, freezing the wipers in place. The engine shuddered, and the defrost wheezed into silence. Raindrops ran in rivulets down the windshield, but if she shifted to the left, she had a view of Roux's entrance, its blue awning flapping in the storm.

She looked around. She'd never eaten at Roux because she didn't like the neighborhood, which was too industrial, even cheesy. A strip club sat across the street, flashing a sign that read BACHELOR, BACHELORETTE, AND DIVORCE PARTIES! Busted cyclone fencing failed to cordon off empty lots, and the municipal piers were no longer in use, had gone to seed.

She thought ahead. It wouldn't be long until dinner was over, and it would be darker by then. The storm showed no sign of letting up. There wouldn't be anybody out on the sidewalk, or anywhere nearby, and in between the Toyota and the restaurant was the back of a distribution center, with a loading dock shaped like a hub. It looked abandoned, too, with only a few tractor trailers rusting in place. There were no streetlights at all.

She listened to the thrumming of the rain and rubbed her eyes. She was so calm, she knew it was the drug. It didn't feel as if she were going to kill Alice. It felt as if she were performing a series of tasks that would result in Alice's death. The deed would ruin her, but she wasn't thinking about that now. She couldn't go back to her old life, anyway. A snake couldn't wriggle back into its skin. A cicada couldn't crawl back into its husk.

She wasn't Bennie Rosato anymore. She'd passed the point of no return.

She pulled out the gun.

And set it on her lap, waiting.

Chapter Eighty-four

Alice climbed out of the cab, hoisted the messenger bag on her shoulder, and stepped onto the slick asphalt, ducking under the umbrella offered by the valet. Rain thundered on its nylon and sprayed underneath. She turned to Judy, as if she'd forgotten something. "Damn, I left my cell phone at the office, and I need to call Grady."

"You can borrow mine." Judy stepped under the umbrella, then reached in her bag, produced her iPhone, and handed it over. "Here."

"Thanks." Alice pressed in her office number as the valet escorted them to the restaurant, but right before they reached the curb, she let the iPhone drop into the filthy water flowing in the gutter. "Oh no!"

"My phone!" Judy scrambled to pick up her phone, but it came up dripping wet, its end cracked and screen gone black.

"I'm so sorry, I'll get you a new one." Alice let the valet usher them inside Roux, then left Judy behind to struggle with her phone, in vain. The restaurant had a French country vibe, and candles glowed against golden walls. The place was half empty, either from the weather or the vacation week, and Alice found the maitre d' while Judy joined her.

"It's dead," she said, with a frown.

Bad choice of words.

They were seated at a table not far from the door, and half an hour later, Alice was craning her neck, pretending to check the entrance for the Irish biotech client. Then she eased back into her chair, shaking her head. "Not here yet," she said. "The weather must have held them up."

"Probably." Judy checked her watch. "It's been a half an hour."

"That's annoying, and we rushed down here for nothing. Make a note, and we'll charge them."

Judy frowned. "You're sure it was tonight, right?"

"Positive. They called today."

"Too bad we don't have a cell."

"We're snakebit." Alice picked up the menu. "I'm hungry. Are you?"

"Yes, but should we call them? I'm sure there's a pay phone, or we can use the restaurant's phone."

"I don't have the number, and I wouldn't want to do that, anyway. Why make them feel bad about being late?"

"What about calling the office to see if they called?"

"Nobody's there to answer. Marshall's gone by now. If they want to reach us, they're smart enough to call the restaurant." Alice opened the menu. "Let's get a bunch of appetizers while we wait."

They ordered food, the waiter brought it, and Alice had lobster bisque while Judy tucked into a goat-cheese-and-beet salad. They made small talk, with Judy doing most of the talking. If the associate still harbored any suspicions, the wine seemed to smooth them over. They finished the appetizers, and Alice signaled for the check. "I gather they're not coming," she said, pretending to be miffed. "Let's skip dinner and go. I've got work to do, at home."

"Shouldn't we wait longer?"

"No. Something must have gone wrong."

"Do you want to ask the waiter if they called, again?"

"I will, but I'm sure he would have said something." Alice reached for her wallet. "Grady will be happy I got home earlier than I thought."

"Good." Judy rose, taking her napkin from her lap. "I should use the bathroom."

"Me, too." Alice got up with her. She wasn't about to let the girl out of her sight.

Not when she only had fifteen minutes to live.

Chapter Eighty-five

Mary looked up as her father appeared in the doorway to the kitchen, the shoulders of his windbreaker dappled with raindrops. She felt her heart break for her mother, because she could tell from his face that the rumor was true. His forehead creased with guilt, and his pained eyes focused completely on his wife.

"Veet?" he said, too upset to talk loud, for once.

Mary looked back at her mother, so stiff and small, her head tilted down as if her neck had frozen in place. She was staring at the wet ball of Kleenex clutched in her hands, saying nothing. Her silence had a depth of its own, and Mary had never seen her so still. It reminded her of an Italian proverb her mother always quoted, *Dolori sono muti.* Great griefs are mute.

Mary rose, turning to her father. "Pop, can this really be true? What were you thinking?"

Her father's lips parted, and his gaze remained on her mother. "Veet, what you heard, I'm so, so sorry. It didn't mean anything."

Her mother didn't look up, still silent, and Mary went to lawyer mode.

"Pop, what did you do? You were *kissing Fiorella*?"

Her father raised a finger, hushing her, and he took a step toward her mother. "Veet, I did not kiss her. We were eatin' and talkin' and all of a sudden, she leaned over the table and kissed me, on the cheek. But it was wrong, I know that, and I kind of came to my senses, and I said it was time for her to go back to Italy. She's goin' back tonight."

Mary said nothing, and her mother remained frozen.

"I'm so sorry, Veet. It's like, I don' know, somethin' came over me." Her father threw up his hands, and they fell back to his sides with a flapping sound. "She made me feel all handsome and strong. It's like a los' my head for a while, but now I'm back and I'm sorry. I'm so sorry."

Mary's throat caught, and her father looked over at her.

"Mare, you were right. I was flirtin' back. It's wrong and it's disrespectful of your mother and it's a sin, and I'm sorry to you, too."

Mary felt his words touch her heart, but his wrong was ultimately against her mother, and only she could absolve him. "Pop, where is Fiorella now?"

"That's a whole 'nother story." Her father sighed, shaking his head. "After this happened, I said we should come home so she could pack, and we were on our way to the car and all of a sudden she said she got a bad feeling, like something bad was happening to Bennie."

"Bennie, *my* Bennie?" Mary asked, surprised, and out of the corner of her eye, she saw her mother raise her head.

"Yes, and she wouldn't stop worrying about her, so I went to a pay phone and called your office to ask you if Bennie was okay, and Marshall said Bennie and Judy went out to dinner and you went home, so I came here."

"Where's Fiorella now?"

"She's gone. Before I could stop her, she gets a cab and jumps in. I think she went to the restaurant."

"What restaurant?"

"It was named Kangaroo, or something like that."

"Roux?"

"I think that's the one. Marshall heard Bennie tell Judy where they were goin'."

"Pop, no!" Mary's head exploded. "Bennie and Judy are meeting new clients there. Fiorella will ruin it!"

"Jesus, Mary, and Joseph," her father said, and her mother moaned.

"I have to warn Bennie." Mary slid out her BlackBerry, speed-dialed Bennie, and let it ring, but there was no answer. She speed-dialed Judy, but it went to voicemail. "Maybe we can still catch Fiorella. South Philly's closer to the restaurant than the Art Museum."

"*Andiamo!*" her mother said, already on her orthopedic shoes.

Mary hurried them from the kitchen, grabbed Grady on the fly, and went to rescue Bennie.

Chapter Eighty-six

Bennie glanced at the dashboard clock, glowing in the dark. It had been over an hour, and they had to be finished with dinner soon. The sidewalk was deserted in the downpour. The storm blew full force, the rain driving on a slant, bouncing off the sidewalks, washing down the gutters and thundering on the hood of her car.

She held the gun while she watched the entrance, planning her next step. Alice and Carrier would come out. They would either share a cab or not. If they shared a cab, she would follow it until it ended up at her own house, with Alice. If they didn't share a cab, she would follow until Alice got out, probably at her house. And then it would be done.

Finally, the door to the restaurant opened, and Carrier emerged, followed by Alice, who put up an umbrella covered with crazy, colorful stripes. It had to belong to Carrier, and before, it would have made Bennie laugh. The women shared the umbrella, which hid their faces. Carrier's yellow clogs practically glowed in the dark, and Bennie recognized her own brown pumps on Alice's feet. Still she remained detached, waiting and watching.

Alice looped a hand through Carrier's arm and they walked abreast, together under the umbrella. Carrier raised her right hand for a cab, but there weren't any. The traffic had let up, and it wouldn't be easy to get a cab down here. For some reason, they headed toward the Toyota, which Bennie didn't understand. It didn't make sense to keep walking away from Roux to catch a cab, and if they got much closer, they could see behind the truck and Alice would see her own car.

Bennie ducked down in the driver's seat and peeked above the steering wheel. Rain ran in jagged rivulets down the windshield. She could barely make out Alice and Carrier, walking together, approaching the deserted stretch in front of the empty parking lot, with the dark loading dock.

She felt a tingle of alarm, without knowing why. Alice had an oddly close hold on Carrier's left arm. Carrier's right arm was up, waving for a cab. Then Carrier and Alice appeared to be talking under the umbrella, and in the next second, Carrier's hand went down and Alice seemed to be pressing her toward the loading dock.

Something was wrong.

Carrier was in trouble.

Bennie grabbed the gun, cracked the door, and sneaked out, crouching so she couldn't be seen. A van whizzed by and sprayed her with dirty water and gravel. She scrambled forward, still crouching along the side of the parked cars, and in four more cars, she'd reach Alice and Carrier.

One.

Two.

Chapter Eighty-seven

"Ouch!" Alice pretended to stumble on the sidewalk, hanging on to the heavy messenger bag while she reached down toward her soggy foot. "I slipped, my ankle hurts! I think I twisted my ankle."

"Oh no!"

"Ouch, help!" Alice fumbled the umbrella, which dipped suddenly. Cold rain drenched them. "Take the umbrella, quick! I need to sit down."

"Got it!" Judy grabbed the umbrella and covered them. A stiff wind whipped off the river, blowing rain everywhere. "Let's go back to the restaurant. We can get help there."

"No, I can't walk that far." Alice looped an arm around Judy's shoulder and gestured toward the loading dock. "Go, there, please, ow! I can't walk another minute. It's killing me. Help me get over there and sit down."

"Where?"

"Over there, on that ledge, at that loading dock." Alice pointed. "Then you can go back to the restaurant and get help. Carrier, hurry, I need to get weight off this thing!"

"There, you sure? It's so dark back there."

"So what? I'm in pain. Ow!" Alice cried out, then slid her hand in her pocket for the gun. "Carrier, hurry. It's killing me!"

"Okay, hang on." Judy hustled them across the slick asphalt lot, juggling the umbrella while Alice weighed down her other arm. They staggered to the loading dock, but suddenly a security light went on, probably a motion detector, drenching them in a pool of brightness.

"Oh, ouch!" Alice howled in fake pain. She hadn't planned on the light shining directly on them, but they were still shielded from the street by the parked cars and trucks. She eased onto the concrete ledge, holding Judy for support with one hand, and with the other, sliding her gun from her pocket. "Here, right here! Judy, help!"

Judy paused. "What? You called me Judy. You never call me Judy."

"So what? Help me!"

"You're not Bennie!" Judy's expression changed, her eyes widening with the realization. "I *knew* it!"

Suddenly there came a shout from the street, and they both turned to see a tall silhouette running toward them, out of the rain and darkness.

It was Bennie.

Alice seized Judy, yanked her backwards off her feet, and drilled the muzzle of the gun into her forehead. "Stay still and shut up!"

"Help!" Judy cried out, but Alice pressed the trigger, making a fateful *click.*

"I said, shut up!"

"Please, no!" Judy went rigid just as Bennie ran into the light, raising a gun.

"Let her go!" Bennie shouted, and Alice laughed.

"*You* have a gun, counselor? *You* gonna shoot *me?*"

Judy whimpered, the gun at her temple, her terrified eyes shifting from one look-alike to the other.

"Let her go!" Bennie shouted again, but Alice only laughed again.

"Drop the gun or I'll shoot her."

"No!" Bennie looked down the barrel and saw her own face. "Drop the gun, Alice. Or I'll shoot *you.*"

Chapter Eighty-eight

"Please, faster!" Mary said to the driver as they sped down Columbus Boulevard. She sat on the edge of the passenger's seat, with Grady and her parents in the back. Rain pelted the windshield, but Mary finally spotted the red awning of Roux. "There it is! Pull up. Hurry!"

"Okay." The driver slowed behind another cab, and all of a sudden its back door opened. Fiorella scooted out and scurried toward an empty lot next to Roux.

"Fiorella!" Mary pointed. "Where the hell is she going?"

"That's her!" her father cried, as Mary flung open her door, blinking against the rain.

"Stop! Let me out! Let me out!"

"Hold on!" The cab lurched to a halt, and Mary jumped out and ran after Fiorella. The cold rain hit her like an ice shower and she could barely see where she was going. There were lights down to the right, toward a loading dock, and Fiorella hustled toward it like a much younger woman, her stilettos stutter-stepping across the shiny asphalt.

"Fiorella!" Mary yelled, into the storm. Rain drenched her face and clothes. Grady and her parents were shouting, behind her.

Mary plunged into a dark aisle between two tractor trailers, running through it like a cattle chute, using her hands against the wet steel to keep her balance. She heard shouting from the loading dock, where she could barely make out Fiorella and some dark figures beyond her, illuminated by a pool of light.

Mary froze when the figures came into focus. Bennie had a gun on Judy, and Alice had a gun on Bennie, in a terrifying stand-off. Time slowed down, and Mary heard her heart thudding in her ears. Grady and her parents stopped next to her, making a horrified tableau.

Mary looked again, in confusion. Suddenly she didn't know which woman was Bennie. Her brain struggled to process it on the spot. Both of the women looked like Bennie, but neither could be Bennie, because Bennie would never pull a gun on anybody.

Then she realized one of the women had to be Bennie, and one had to be Alice, and she knew exactly who was who.

Because Bennie would never pull a gun on Judy. Ever.

So Bennie was really Alice.

Judy had been right, all along. And now she was about to die for it.

Chapter Eighty-nine

Bennie kept her gun aimed at Alice, who was dragging Judy backwards, away from the loading dock and toward the pier. An immense ship sat anchored next to them in the darkness, and beyond it glimmered the Delaware River, its black water choppy with wind and rain, its reflection of the city lights a dark kaleidoscope.

"Let her go!" Bennie advanced slowly, her gun raised. "This is between you and me."

"Stop!" Alice moved farther backwards, out of the security light and into the shadows beyond. "One more step and she's dead!"

"If you hurt her, you're dead!" Bennie left the light, blinking rain from her eyes, and followed Alice onto the pier.

Suddenly, the security light went off, plunging them all in total darkness. She could see Alice and Judy only in silhouette, against the fog of the sky and the brightness of the opposite shore.

"Stop or I'll kill her!" Alice shouted, but the time for talk was over.

Bennie raised her gun, aiming at the silhouettes in the black and the rain. She was a decent shot but couldn't take a chance, not yet.

In the next instant, there was a scuffle on the dock.

A gun went off, and Judy screamed.

And all hell broke loose.

Chapter Ninety

Alice was dragging Judy off when all of a sudden, the girl kicked her in the shin with her clog.

The gun fired, and the bullet found its target.

Judy screamed, and hot blood spattered everywhere.

Alice shoved her off the dock, sending her over the side, her arms pinwheeling. The girl screamed all the way into the darkness until she hit the water with a splash.

Alice tore down the dock in the rain, the messenger bag thumping at her side. She heard shouting behind her. She heard another splash. She knew what it was. Bennie had gone after the kid. She'd save Judy rather than catch Alice. They all would. Fine with her.

She ran harder. She spotted another pier to the right. She could run that way and double back to the Boulevard. But the cops would be searching there in no time. Her heart was pounding, her chest hurt.

She was almost at the end of the pier, which pointed at the dark water like a finger.

She ran to the very end, took a deep breath, and jumped into thin air.

Chapter Ninety-one

Mary screamed, anguished. She ran to the pier, tears streaming down her face. She reached the spot where Judy had gone over the side and almost fell in looking for her in the gloom. Grady caught her from behind and stopped her.

"Stay back!" he shouted, but Mary was hysterical.

"She got shot! Alice shot her!"

"I know, calm down. Bennie's down there! Stay here! I'll go!"

"Grady, help!" Bennie called from the depths, her frantic cry drowned by the rain.

Grady dove into the blackness beside the ship, disappearing.

Mary heard a splash. She kept watching. She could make out three heads below in black water.

"*Maria, Maria!*" her mother cried, hurrying up from behind her, and Mary held her close, heaving a great sob.

"Oh, Ma. It's Judy. Judy, Ma."

"Oh, no, *Deo, Maria.*" Her mother hugged her, and Mary tried to shield her from the rain, cradling her tight.

Fiorella stood behind them, soaked. "Your father ran to the restaurant to call 911."

"Thank God." Mary tried to control herself, hanging on to her mother like a little girl, not sure who was comforting whom. She looked down, watching the heads in the water, scared to death.

Then she heard her mother praying and joined her.

Until the sirens came.

Chapter Ninety-two

Bennie kept Carrier afloat by treading water and holding her under the arm on one side, with Grady helping on the other. Still the girl had lost consciousness. Her head fell back, her eyes closed, and her mouth flopped open, her jaw slack.

"I got her!" Grady shouted. "You okay?"

"Yes!" Bennie shouted back. Rain fell everywhere. Sirens sounded far away. She didn't know if they'd get here in time. It didn't look good. "What should we do? Can we get her up, on land?"

"Don't see how!" Grady looked up. "Too damn high."

Bennie could see that Carrier was losing blood. She patted her cheeks, trying to keep her alive, but her skin had taken on a terrible pallor. "Stay with us, girl! Stay with us!"

The sirens grew closer, and there was a new sound, the rumbling of an engine, coming from out on the water. Bennie looked down-river. Two police boats were speeding toward them, cutting through the storm.

"Look, help!" Grady shouted.

"Swim to them!" Bennie and Grady kept a hold on Carrier and swam away from the pier, stroking past debris, floating oil, and rotting fish. The current flowed stronger mid-river, and they struggled to stay above water.

"Help! Over here!" Grady waved frantically.

"Help! Help!" Bennie hollered.

Mary and the others screamed to the police boats from the pier. Sirens blared closer. Red lights flashed as cruisers hit the Boulevard.

"Thank God!" Grady shouted, joyful.

Bennie could see they were losing Carrier. Her eyes fluttered open, then rolled back in her head, the whites looking sightless at the sky. Rain fell mercilessly on her upturned face.

"Help!" Bennie shouted, wishing, now more than ever, that she had killed Alice.

But her gun was probably on the bottom of the river, and Alice had vanished into the storm.

Chapter Ninety-three

Alice swam against the wind and storm. The chop slapped her in the face, rain poured onto her head. She swallowed a gulp of gritty water, then spewed it out. Police boats sped toward the pier but they were already well behind her. She was getting closer to the Jersey side, swimming hard.

The river reeked, and plywood floated by with a nail sticking up. She felt something slither around her leg and kicked it off. Oil dotted the surface of the water. Gunk stuck in her teeth, tasting disgusting.

The current pulled her downriver. She fought it, keeping the bright lights of the Camden waterfront to her left, trying to swim straight. Her heart pounded, water chilled her skin. Her messenger bag weighed her down, too heavy to float. She kept putting it back on her shoulder, pulling it along by its strap as she swam.

She glanced back. The storm grayed her view. She could see the flashing red of a police cruiser. They'd gotten there quick. They'd look for her first on land.

She swam harder, her thoughts churning. The money had already been transferred to the Bahamas. All she had to was get there and take it out. It was almost hers.

She swam even harder, with new energy.

Chapter Ninety-four

Mary sat in the hospital waiting room, trying to come to terms with what had happened. The paramedics hadn't let anybody in the ambulance, so the only thing she knew was that Judy had been rushed into the emergency room. The doctors hadn't come back yet.

Her gaze wandered over the wallpaper, a baby blue print that provided an intentionally soothing backdrop for landscapes in muted pastels. Ancient magazines covered the coffee table, and the TV was mounted in the corner, playing on mute. She couldn't watch it. Judy could be dying at this very minute.

She felt pure dread, and her parents, anguished and bedraggled, weren't speaking to each other. Fiorella had gone to the ladies' room, but her presence lingered like an unwanted ghost.

Her mother looked at the TV with her chin tilted up, blinking behind her bifocals. Her gray hair was wet, exposing her bald spot, and she watched *Seinfeld* with apparent absorption, though she couldn't have any idea what was going on since there was no closed captioning. Her father kept his head down, his shoulders sunk into his damp windbreaker and his hammy hands folded in his lap.

Her attention shifted to Bennie, who was sitting next to Grady, talking in low voices with two Philly cops. Her blond hair lay in wet tangles on her shoulders, scratches covered her arms and legs, and an oddly girlie purse hung from her shoulder. She seemed distant and didn't make eye contact with anybody, even Grady, though she'd called Judy's parents, who were flying in from San Francisco, and her boyfriend Frank, driving home from his job site.

Mary felt a sadness so deep she could drown. Judy was bleeding. Bennie was bleeding in another way, less obvious. Her parents were bleeding, too. She didn't know if anybody could be healed. The pieces of her life had been reconfigured, and she didn't know if they would ever fit together, ever again. Especially if something happened to Judy.

Suddenly Fiorella entered the waiting room, smoothing her wet hair back, though its chic cut was ruined. She had no lipstick on, and her wet raincoat covered her black dress. She walked over to Mary's mother. "Vita," she said, coolly. "Good-bye, I'm going home."

Her mother turned from the TV and eyed Fiorella with a look that could kill. "*Bene,*" she said simply.

"I must collect my things, from your house. I'll take a taxi."

"*Certo.*" Her mother dug in her purse, produced her house keys, and handed them to Fiorella. "Go. Now. Leave under mat."

"Thank you, and I should say that—"

"Go! Leave!" Her mother pointed at the exit, her cheeks flushed with sudden emotion. "You are powerful woman, Donna Fiorella! You are not good woman. Not good woman at all!"

Fiorella flinched, took the keys, then turned to Mary and her father. "Good-bye, all. Many thanks for your hospitality."

Her father said nothing, and neither did Mary.

In the next minute, an ER doctor appeared in the threshold to the waiting room, in blue scrubs and a puffy hat with the Phillies logo.

Fiorella turned, the cops looked over, and Bennie and Grady rose.

Mary stood up, her knees weak. "Is she okay?" she asked, her mouth gone dry.

And the doctor slid off his hat.

Chapter Ninety-five

Bennie was relieved that Carrier would be fine, but she didn't feel any other emotion, except regret that Alice had gotten away. Evidently Grady was back, but she couldn't deal with him right now. He, DiNunzio, and her parents were group-hugging, and she didn't join in the celebration. She'd taken another pill in the ladies' room and stood off to the side, near Fiorella.

"Ms. Rosato?"

"Yes?" Bennie came out of her reverie, as a uniformed called to her, entering the waiting room as if he had news. "Did you get her?"

"Did you?" Mary repeated, clustering with Grady and her parents.

"No, but we have a lead," the cop answered. "We checked the airport, and there's a Bennie Rosato ticketed on the last flight to Miami, with a connection to Nassau, in the Bahamas."

"When's the flight?" Bennie asked.

"In half an hour."

"The airport's twenty minutes away. We have to go now."

"Hold on, it's taken care of." The cop held up a warning hand. "My captain is coordinating with the TSA and the FBI. We're holding the plane, claiming weather delays, and we're already setting up a stake-out. The minute she shows up, we'll arrest her. The A.D.A. is meeting us there."

"Nassau?" Bennie's thoughts raced ahead. "The Bahamas have offshore banking. She has my bank accounts and my ID. She changed all the passwords. She's moving my money to the Bahamas."

"You're right." Grady's eyes flared an alarmed blue. "I saw a DHL envelope in her office, going to BSB. She told me she had a new banking client."

"That's it then." Bennie flashed on her call with Marla. "I need to talk to someone at USABank."

"It's after hours."

"I'll want more than a teller. I met the president of the bank once. Ron Engel. He lives in Society Hill." Bennie turned to Grady. "Do you have a cell phone?"

"No, it got wet."

"Here." A cop handed her a phone, and Bennie flipped it open and called information for Ron Engel.

"I'm sorry," the operator said. "That number is unlisted."

"This is a police emergency." Bennie handed the phone back to the officer. "Please get the number and the address for Ron Engel. We have to talk to him."

"Hello?" the cop said, putting the phone to his ear on the fly.

Bennie hustled out of the waiting room, ahead of Grady and the cops.

Chapter Ninety-six

Alice kept swimming, getting her second wind. Her legs went rubbery but they were still churning. Her arms wind-milled. She was only fifty feet from Jersey. She swam ugly but she was getting there, stroke by stroke.

The fifty feet became forty, then thirty, and she looked up, wondering how to get up onto shore. There were dark industrial buildings ahead, with a crumbling stone wall lining the riverbank. She couldn't see more through the rain. She swam like a demon, ignoring the downpour. She closed in on the stone wall, ten feet, then finally five.

She treaded water for a minute, her chest heaving. The wall crumbled in parts, and she finally reached it, grappling the edge with her fingertips. It felt slick and cold, and she groped for a ledge between the stones. She found one and tried to hoist herself up. The messenger bag was a dead weight but she couldn't let it go. She slipped back down, splashing into the water.

She tried again. Her fingertips raked the stone. She found a grip and pulled herself up with all of her might. She started climbing, wedging her hands and toes into the cracks. She clawed her way to the top and flopped exhausted on top of the wall, then rolled over it into the mud and scrambled to her feet.

She hurried out of the shadows and ran across a parking lot. It was a deserted industrial stretch, and she hurried past abandoned cars rusting in place. She ran along the street, and ahead shone the lights and attractions of the Camden waterfront. Rain ricocheted off the asphalt. Stones dug into her soles but she kept running. There wasn't much traffic, and a minivan sped past her, spraying water and grit.

A sign read WIGGINS PARK AHEAD, but it looked too far away. She didn't have time to waste. She had to get to the airport. She couldn't keep up this pace much longer.

A cab turned the corner, slowing at a stop sign, and she bolted for it, tore open its back door, and shouted at the woman passenger, "Get out!"

"Hey! What?" The young girl edged backwards in fear, her short dress riding up. "Help!"

The cab driver twisted around, startled. "Lady, what're you doin'? This is *my* cab!"

Alice yanked the girl out by her elbow, then slammed the door closed. "Drive! There's five hundred bucks in it for you!"

"Bull!"

"Drive, I said!" Alice stuck a hand into her soggy messenger bag, where the bundles of money sat in a pool of water. She grabbed one and waved it at the cabbie, spraying him. "It's wet but it's green."

"Whoa!" The cabbie hit the gas. "Where we goin'?"

"To the airport, and hurry."

Chapter Ninety-seven

Mary stood at Judy's bedside while she rested, a greenish oxygen tube snaking her friend's nose, an IV running to the back of her hand, and a plastic wire traveling to a clip on her index finger. She had gone into shock, but the bullet had only pierced her shoulder and she was going to be fine. Mary sent up a thankful prayer as her mother smothered Judy's face with kisses.

"Ma." She placed a hand on her mother's soft back. "If you keep this up, she'll need more oxygen."

"*Jud', Jud', ti amo.*" Her mother smoothed Judy's bright red bangs from her forehead. "*Ti amo.*"

"Thanks." Judy smiled and her weary gaze shifted to Mary's father, who was attached to her hand more securely than the IV. "I love you guys."

"WE LOVE YOU, TOO, KIDDO." Her father patted her hand, and Mary smiled.

"Jude, your parents are on the way, and we told them you were okay. We caught them right before their plane took off."

"Good. Thanks." Judy sighed, and her eyes fell on Mary, at the foot of the bed. For a minute neither of them said anything.

"I'm so sorry," Mary said, softly.

"What for?"

"For not believing you. For giving you such a hard time. For being such a bad friend. For almost getting you killed."

"Guilt city." Judy reached for her hand. "You don't have anything to be sorry about."

"Yes I do."

"No, you don't. It's okay. Friends fight."

"Not us."

"Once every ten years, even us. That's how we know we care. Agree with me, would you? I'm perforated, for God's sake."

"Okay. I agree." Mary nodded.

"Where's Bennie and Grady?"

"Off, after Alice."

"Good." Judy's gaze shifted toward the door, which was opening.

They all turned to see who was coming in, including Mary.

Standing in the threshold was Anthony.

Chapter Ninety-eight

Bennie, Grady, and two cops, Officers Stern and Rigton, crowded onto the front step of the Society Hill townhouse, and the door was opened by a tall, bald man in a red plaid bathrobe, whom they'd clearly gotten out of bed.

"I'm Ron Engel, folks," he said, extending a hand. "Officers, good to see you. Please excuse my appearance. Do come in."

"Ron, hello." Bennie had spoken to him on the phone but he'd insisted on seeing her in person. "Do you remember me? We met a few months ago, and I'm a private client of yours."

"I remember you, yes. Come on in out of this weather." Engel let everyone in to a well-appointed anteroom with a cherry console table, a sculptural ceramic lamp, and a Persian rug. "I made some calls to my team in private banking, in reference to this matter."

"What's happening?" Bennie asked. Grady stood next to her, but she didn't pay him any attention. She wasn't the woman he remembered anymore, anyway. "Ron, is Alice moving my money and how can we stop her?"

Officer Stern looked over, frowning under the wet bill of his cap. "Miss Rosato, we agreed we'd handle this."

"You are," Bennie shot back. "So am I."

"To begin, I spoke with Legal about it." Engel glanced at Officer

Stern. "Officer, are we sure this is the real Bennie Rosato? I wouldn't want to expose the bank to any liability."

Officer Stern nodded. "This is Bennie Rosato. We expect to have Alice Connelly in custody tonight. At this juncture, she's a fugitive from a charge of attempted murder, among other things."

"Murder?" Engel's graying eyebrows flew upward, and Bennie ran out of patience.

"I need to stop her from transferring that money."

"We can't. I've checked, and all of your accounts were already wired to BSB on Nassau."

"All my accounts? Everything?"

"Yes." Engel's lips set. "The bank is not liable in this matter, because, as you know, Miss Connelly presented all the proper identification and she—"

"I'm not going to sue you," Bennie interrupted. "Can't we call the Nassau bank and prevent the transfer? Right now?"

"No. No one's there, and the transfer is electronic and instantaneous. It goes through, regardless. It already has."

"That's impossible. I don't have an account there."

"Yes, you do. She opened one. It will be opened automatically the first thing tomorrow morning, and the money's already in it. We do it all the time for private banking clients." Engel cocked his graying head. "USABank is merely a stakeholder in this matter. We had no choice but to transfer the money when properly instructed to do so—"

"Ron, there has to be some way to undo that transfer."

"Please." Engel held up a hand. "We can't undo the transfer, but we can freeze the accounts. We'll send an email that will instruct BSB, the Bahamian bank, not to permit any withdrawals or transfers from any of the accounts. I'll follow up with a phone call personally, first thing on Tuesday morning."

"Will that prevent her from withdrawing it, for sure?"

"Yes. BSB is our partner bank. If we instruct them that the legality of the transfer is in question, they'll put a hold on the accounts." Engel frowned. "No one pushes millions of dollars across a counter that easily. That's not how it works. She can only transfer the money by presenting herself at the bank, and after we freeze the accounts, the funds won't be available to her."

"If she shows up there, what will she be told?"

"That the accounts are frozen."

"Alice will go down there, anyway. She'll try to find a way to withdraw the money."

Officer Stern said, "No, she won't, Bennie. We'll pick her up tonight. She won't get on that plane."

Engel gestured. "There you have it, Bennie. Your ultimate solution is with the authorities. That's what Legal tells me, too."

Bennie thought something felt wrong. Her brain stalled, and she wondered if it was the pill working, or if she needed another. She looked at the cops, from one to the other. "What if you don't stop her?"

"We will." Officer Stern was confident. "We'll leave right now. She won't get past us. She can't."

"Then let's go," Bennie said, on fire.

Chapter Ninety-nine

Alice handed the cabbie back his phone and perched on the edge of her seat. The car wasn't going any faster than a crawl, and it was making her crazy. She had to get to the airport. "Can't you go any faster?" she asked, again. "I told you, rock this crate!"

"Rain's terrible. Can't see a damn thing. Doin' my best."

"Do better."

The cab lurched forward, and Alice thought ahead, taking a mental inventory. She had an ID, passport, and money, but she was pretty sure her gun hadn't survived the swim.

"I need to buy a gun," she said.

"There's a gun shop, but it's not on the way."

"No good. You know anybody who could meet us on the way with one? There's a hundred bucks in it for you."

"Lady, you can't take a gun on the plane, anyways."

"Let me worry about that. You know anybody or not?"

"Matter o' fact, I do." The cabbie looked in the rearview. "I got one."

"Of course you do!" Alice almost cheered. "Let me see it."

The cabbie seemed to stall, his eyes on the road.

"I'm not gonna shoot you, grandpa."

The cabbie reached under the seat, straightened up, and passed her a revolver, its dull muzzle glinting in the darkness.

She pushed out the chamber and gave it a slow whirl. Six round gold circles smiled back at her. "I'll give you two hundred bucks."

"S'worth three."

"Okay."

"You expensin' it?" the cabbie asked, chuckling.

"You're a funny guy, you know that?"

"Tell my wife, would ya?"

The bright lights of the airport lay ahead, in the distance. "We almost there?"

"Sure enough."

Alice smiled. Home, free.

Chapter One Hundred

Mary's emotions came rushing back at the sight of Anthony. His eyes were troubled and his expression dark with concern.

"ANT, HOW YOU DOIN'?" Her father gave him a bear hug, and her mother waddled after, clucking.

"Ant'n'y, what's a matta, you no love my *Maria* no more? You no happy no more?"

"Ma!" Mary's head exploded. "Please!"

"It's . . . not like that, Mrs. DiNunzio," Anthony stammered, and Judy waved from the bed with a weak grin.

"Yoo hoo! I'm over here and I'm fine, thanks."

"Hiya." Anthony walked to the bedside. "So you're alive. Way to go."

"I know, right?" Judy smiled. "Nice of you to come."

"It's all over the news, did you see?" Anthony gestured at the TV in the corner, but it was off. "Anyway, how are you?"

"I've been better."

"Does it hurt?"

"Not yet."

"They said you were shot. When do you get out of the hospital?"

"I don't know."

"Is there anything I can do?"

"Not really. The troops are here, and Frank's on the way."

"Great." Anthony shifted his feet, plainly uncomfortable. "Well, I guess I'd better go. On the news they said you were critical."

"I am," Judy said, and everybody laughed except for Mary's mother, who couldn't follow the conversation.

"Okay, well, see you all." Anthony gave Judy a peck on the cheek, then turned awkwardly away. He went to the doorway and paused on the threshold. "Judy, hope you feel better soon."

"I will, thanks."

"Good-bye." Anthony left, closing the door behind him. Everybody fell quiet a minute, and all the heads turned to Mary.

"They got a cardiac unit here?" she asked.

Chapter One Hundred and One

Bennie leaned forward in the backseat of the cruiser, where she was sitting with Grady, her purse in her lap. A long line of red taillights snaked ahead of them, and they were barely moving. "Can't we go any faster?" she asked, through the metal grate.

"No. It's the traffic and the weather."

"Can't we use the siren?"

"It's not procedure. The plane isn't going anywhere, and we don't want to tip her off, either."

"You got all the flights covered, right?"

"Yes. We know what we're doing. Sit back and relax."

Bennie tried to stay calm, and the traffic finally loosened. The cruiser broke free, accelerating as a minivan and an SUV cleared out of the fast lane.

Grady patted her arm. "We're almost there. You feeling okay?"

"Fine."

"How's that hand? It looks kind of raw."

"It's fine." Bennie boosted herself up in the seat. Just ahead, the bright lights of the airport cut through the rain, making a halo in the dark sky.

"Go, go, go," she said under her breath.

Chapter One Hundred
and Two

"Go, go, go," Alice said under her breath, boosting herself up in the backseat. The cab turned onto the ramp to the airport, leaving the highway traffic behind.

"Finally, eh?"

"Hurry, hurry, hurry."

"I'm on it."

Alice opened the soggy messenger bag and withdrew the droopy bills, including the fare and the gun. She unstuck her wet blouse from her shirt, smoothed back her hair, and got ready to hustle. Only a few cars were parked in front of the terminal, dropping people and luggage off. There were no cops in sight.

The cabbie hit the gas, and she felt a smile spread across her face. She was almost out of the country, safe from Q, the cops, and Bennie. She'd have enough money to go anywhere and do anything. She'd be free.

The cab pulled up in front of the terminal. "Here we are. Safe travels."

Alice got her bag and handed him the wad of bills. "Remember, you didn't see me."

"Didn't see who?" The cabbie laughed.

Alice blew out the cab door.

Running into the terminal.

Chapter One Hundred
and Three

Mary and her parents looked over as a nurse bustled into the room, her smile bright despite the late hour.

"Party's over!" she said, cheerily. "I cut you a break, but it's time to go."

Mary frowned. "Too bad Frank didn't get here in time."

"It's fine." Judy waved her off. "Thanks for coming."

"Your need to rest, Miss Carrier." The nurse took a blood pressure cuff from a plastic basket affixed to the wall. "I have meds for you, too."

Mary gave Judy's arm a quick pat. "You gonna be okay, all by yourself?"

"Yep." Judy looked up, her blue eyes washed-out. "How about you, without Anthony?"

"Sure." Mary managed a smile as her parents took turns kissing Judy.

"My, my." The nurse laughed, wrapping the black cuff around her upper arm. "You got any face left?"

"See you, honey." Mary picked up her purse and waited for her parents, who trundled out of the room, their faces falling as if they'd checked their trouble at the door. She slipped an arm around her mother, and they walked past the nurses' station.

"Poor Jud," her mother said softly, and her father shuffled behind, alone.

Mary couldn't remember the last time her parents hadn't walked together, and they went down the elevator as a somber threesome, the triangle of their family reconfigured. Nobody said a word as they left the hospital, where Mary hurried them past the reporters, shielded them from the videocameras, and shouted a steady stream of "no comments." She hailed a cab, stuffed them inside, and got in. The cabbie took off, and Mary gave him their address, which was when her mother finally spoke.

"*Maria,* stay home, tonight. Stay home."

"Sure, Ma," Mary answered. She knew her mother was hurting, but she couldn't see her expression in the dark. They passed under a street lamp, and it flashed like a strobe light, exposing rather than illuminating them.

They rode the rest of the way in silence, and Mary listened to the raindrops thunder on the roof of the cab. Fog clouded the windows, walling them inside. They reached South Philly, crawling through the rainswept streets, and she didn't bother to check her BlackBerry. Anthony hadn't written, called, or texted. They were really over.

The cab pulled up in front of the rowhouse with the D on its screen door, where her father opened his wallet, and her mother let out a tiny sigh.

"Home sweet home," said the cabbie.

Chapter One Hundred and Four

Bennie hurried out of the police cruiser with Grady and the two cops, hitting the pavement running. They ducked into an unmarked door at a side entrance of the terminal, then hustled down a series of corridors, passing two airline employees catching a secret smoke. They reached a steel door that read SECURITY and went inside, letting it close with a metallic *clang!*

TSA employees, uniformed cops, airport personnel, and two men in blue FBI windbreakers filled the room, which was dimly lit and surrounded on three sides by sixty-odd surveillance-camera monitors, their flickering images glowing in front of a long, gray counter dotted with coffee cups and an open box of picked-over donuts.

Bennie glanced at the screens. "Which one is the monitor for the Miami flight?"

"There." An airport security guard pointed to the middle screen, on the far right. "Miami is at Gate 3, Terminal A. It's waiting to board. She's booked on a connection to Nassau, and that's delayed, too, because of weather."

Bennie eyed the grainy images, changing every second, with time and date tickers running along the bottom of the screen. They showed women sipping drinks, men tugging roller bags, sleepy toddlers with stuffed bunnies, a teenage boy checking an iPod dial, a little girl toting her own bedpillows, and business types with Blue-tooths in their ears, talking to the air. None of the travelers were Alice.

"See her?" the security guard asked.

"Not yet."

Grady added, "I don't either. She had on a tan suit today."

"She's your identical twin, right, Ms. Rosato?" The security guard glanced up, then returned to the screen. "They sent us a photo."

"Yes, but she might have disguised herself somehow, guessing we'd be on the lookout. There's plenty of stores in the airport where she could pick up a fresh set of clothes."

"Most of them are closed this late."

"She'll find an open one, or she'll beg, borrow, or steal new clothes."

"A disguise won't help her. The seat is booked under her name, or rather, your name. She'll have to identify herself to board."

"Of course. Has she checked in yet?"

"No."

"Even this late, she hasn't checked in?" Bennie watched the screen, puzzled. "Isn't that strange?"

"Not really," answered a TSA employee, standing with the cops. "If she called the airline or checked the flight status online, she would've seen that it was delayed."

"So we won't know who she is until she tries to board, as me. Is that right?"

"Yes, and the airline won't board her. Nobody wants trouble on the plane. They're cooperating with us, and we're all on the same page."

"Is it a full flight?" Bennie kept her eyes on the screen.

"No."

"So what's to stop her from buying a ticket with cash and going on as somebody else?"

"That would take ID."

"She could have fake ID."

"We'll see her get on, right here." The TSA employee gestured at the Miami monitor. "As soon as we ID her, she'll be apprehended and arrested. The cops already have a team in place, waiting in the security office in Terminal A. They'll go as soon as we give them the word."

Bennie nodded. "Did you circulate her photo to other ticket desks, for other airlines, so they could be on the lookout, too?"

"No." The TSA employee frowned. "We had no reason to, and no time, anyway. This flight was already ticketed to a Bennie Rosato."

"Maybe it's a decoy. Maybe she's setting us up." Bennie ran through the possibilities. "What if she took another flight, to somewhere else? Flew to Nassau direct or went another way? Changed it up at the last minute?"

"She can't. There are no more direct flights to Nassau on any carrier. Besides, she doesn't know that we know about her ticket."

Suddenly something on the Miami monitor caught Bennie's attention. A group of tall teenage boys headed en masse toward the gate, lugging backpacks, plugged into earphones, and wearing baseball caps worn low over their eyes. They were all too tall for them not to be a basketball team, but one of the boys in the back was looking right and left, for no apparent reason. He wasn't walking with the others, and no one was talking with him. His cap had a telltale bulge that could have been hair, tucked underneath.

"Look at him." Bennie pointed. "The one in the back."

"Hello?" The TSA employee snorted. "They're boys. It's a boy's beach volleyball team, from California. I have the manifest."

"She could be dressed as a boy. Her hair's under her cap. See it?"

"My God, you're right!" The TSA employee turned excitedly. "Tom?"

"That's her!" Officer Stern said, moving toward the door.

"We made her!" somebody shouted into a Nextel.

"We're on, people!" Officer Rigton and the other cops bolted for the door, with Bennie and Grady on their heels. They tore down one corridor, then another, finally bursting through doors that let them out in the terminal, which was engulfed in a melee. People shouted, screamed, and ran for cover. A team of uniformed cops shouted for them to get down and streaked ahead to the Miami gate.

Bennie ran right behind them and when she reached the gate, all the travelers had scattered, hiding under seats or behind desks while a scrum of uniformed cops had piled on Alice, struggling at the bottom. The cops got off the pile one by one, dragging Alice to a standing position. They wrenched her hands behind her back and turned her around.

Her hat fell off, and her hair shook free.

It wasn't Alice, but a terrified teenage boy, with long hair.

"I'm sorry, I'm so sorry!" he yelled, his eyes wide. A new *Transporter* DVD lay on the floor, at his sneakers. "I'll give it back, I swear!"

Chapter One Hundred
and Five

Alice hurried through the terminal in her bare feet, her clothes soggy, but there was no one around to see. The hallway was deserted, and she hustled past a janitor pushing a trashcan on wheels. She hustled around a corner, her messenger bag heavy with wet money, the gun in her purse. She didn't have to go through security because she was flying private, having charged the trip on Bennie's Amex, which nobody had thought to cancel yet.

She hustled to the gate, manned by a female flight attendant in a red RentJet uniform. The cops were probably at the Philly airport, but she'd skipped the flight booked to Miami, called a private company from the cab, and chartered a jet out of this regional airport, in Jersey. The Philly police didn't have jurisdiction here, even if they'd had the time to notify the area airports.

"Hi, I'm Bennie Rosato." Alice flashed ID at the flight attendant, who barely looked at it, instead eyeing her clothes.

"I'm Willa. My goodness, you really did get caught in the rain, didn't you?"

"Yes, it's awful tonight."

"I picked you up a complete set of clothes, per your request. A simple T-shirt, shorts, sweatsocks and sneaks. You know, you could have driven right up to the plane."

"I didn't know. I don't fly private that much."

"Well, we're glad to have you tonight. In weather this bad, people cancel and fly commercial. One was a Bahamas route, so we didn't have to file a new flight plan. Please, come this way." The flight attendant led her out the door under a red canopy and gestured toward a handsome African-American man running toward them, also in a RentJet uniform. "Here's my crewmate to take your bags."

"I don't have any. This trip is impromptu."

"Then he'll help you on board and we'll get underway."

"Good, because I'm in a hurry." Alice smiled at the man, who came toward her, opening a red umbrella.

"I'm Knox," he said, in a Caribbean accent.

"Where are you from, Knox?"

"Nassau. That's why I work this route. Shall we go?" Knox took her heavy messenger bag, swung it effortlessly to his shoulder, and offered his arm. Alice let him walk her to the jet and help her up the stairway, holding the umbrella over her head. He closed the umbrella as she boarded the jet, stepped through a privacy curtain, and entered the passenger cabin, which was paneled with dark burled wood and had cushy beige leather seats. A low table held a huge tray heaped with roast beef, sliced cheese, and fresh fruit, next to a bottle of champagne cooling in an ice bucket.

"Yum." Alice glanced back at her messenger bag. "Oh, I'll keep the bag with me."

"As you wish." Knox smiled and stowed the bag on the carpeted floor, near her seat. "Would you like to change your clothes now, or would you rather we take off?"

"Let's get into the air. I'll tough it out for a while. I need to get going."

"Fine, I'll be right back." Knox closed the curtain and left, and Alice sank into the plush chair. She listened to the throaty sound of the jet engine, then the door closing, and the attendants talking to each other. She'd had to improvise since Bennie came back from the dead, but she had done well. Plan C was already taking shape. She looked outside the round window into a black hole of night.

Knox stuck his head into the cabin, through the curtain. "We're clear. Fasten your seat belt, please."

"Okay." Alice clicked the belt into place. "I don't have to wait to have a drink, do I?"

"Not at all, Ms. Rosato. Allow me."

"Please, call me Bennie." Alice watched him pluck the bottle from the craggy ice and wipe the sweating nozzle with a red napkin. The plane began to taxi, the champagne cork popped, and they both laughed.

"Ready, Bennie?" Knox picked up a glass.

"After you close that curtain," Alice answered, masking her thoughts with a smile.

Chapter One Hundred
and Six

Mary lay in her old single bed, surrounded by the shelves of high-school textbooks and faded stuffed animals. She couldn't see them clearly because it was too dark, but she knew their shapes and smells by heart. She always loved her old room and slept like a baby when she stayed over, but not tonight.

She pulled the covers to her chin, over her old Goretti T-shirt. She couldn't shake the images of the night. Judy, her eyes terrified. The flare of the gunfire. The wait at the hospital. The chill between her parents.

She was exhausted, but her mind wouldn't rest. Her mother had gone to sleep in their bedroom, and her father slept on the couch. The only other time that had happened was when he brought home live crabs. She forgave him and put the crabs in the gravy, where God intended.

Mary turned over, coming eye-level with the BlackBerry on her night table. She picked it up, checking it for the umpteenth time. Nothing from Anthony, but there was an email that hadn't been there before. It was from the realtor, with no subject line. Mary pressed OPEN:

Congrats! The buyer accepted your offer. Sorry about the delay.
All terms are fine. I'd call but it's late. Talk to you tomorrow.

She stared at the screen until it blinked off. She had just become the owner of a house that had cost her Anthony. She groaned, the only sound in the very quiet house, and it made her think about what made a house a home. It wasn't the Curb Appeal, New Fixtures, or Great Views! It was the people who lived inside.

If home is where the heart is, then the heart of the DiNunzio house was broken. Her parents' house didn't feel like a home tonight, and if she flashed-forward to her new house, it wouldn't be much of a home, either. Not without Anthony. Her heart was with him.

She knew it now, inside. She prayed it wasn't too late. She held up the BlackBerry and speed-dialed him. She couldn't give up the house, but maybe she could persuade him to live with her. Or they could talk about it, and come to an understanding. She loved him. And he loved her, right?

The phone rang and rang, but Anthony didn't pick up.

She tried again, thinking she had a wrong number, but she didn't. Then she texted: **Pls call me.**

She waited, but he didn't respond. She emailed him, too. Suddenly the phone rang, and she startled. The screen read Anthony. She pressed Answer. "It's you!"

"I was just about to call you."

"Really?" Mary scrambled to sit upright in bed. "Listen, I've been thinking and—"

"No, can I go first? I've been rehearsing this all night, since the hospital."

"Okay." Mary felt her heart hammer. "Go ahead."

"I figured something out. What I realized is that we do have a problem, but it's not about the money. You think it is, and for a while, I thought it was, too, But it isn't."

Mary wasn't sure where he was going.

"I *am* happy for all your success. I hope you make partner and get the house. I want all the best for you. I love you, Mary. I do."

"I love you, too," she said, touched.

"I know you do." Anthony hesitated. "But that's only part of it, because here's what I finally understood. To back up a minute, it's all because Judy almost died. When I saw on the news that she was in critical condition, I thought, if she dies, it will kill Mary. She can't take it, after her husband's dying."

Mary swallowed hard. She hadn't seen this coming.

"So, yes, I know you love me. But you also love him."

Mary felt her face burn.

"You bring him up all the time. It's like he's always with you, still. You compare us, in your mind. You said as much, the other day in the house." Anthony paused. "Don't get me wrong, I understand your grief. I know how grief works. My father, you know."

Mary did. Anthony still mourned his father, who had passed five years ago.

"But you don't know what it's like, from my side of the equation, to be in love with someone in grief. It's not good. I can't fight a ghost, and I don't want to. You said you can't win, but it's me. I'm the one who can't win."

Mary felt stricken. His words rang true. She hadn't seen it from his side, before.

"So here's my proposition, for us. Let's not stay apart. I hate it. I miss you."

"I miss you, too!" Mary's heart leapt up.

"But let's not move in together, either. Not until you're ready to move on. Really ready."

Mary blinked, taken aback.

"The ball's in your court. Take your time. Make sure. We'll take it slow. When you're ready, tell me. You don't have to be all the way over him, either. Just a little more than now. Sound good?"

"Great!"

"You'll know when you're ready, and the money is beside the point. It'll work itself out. Who's on the deed doesn't matter. We're who matters."

Mary heard him, maybe for the first time.

"*Capisce, cara?*"

Mary smiled. She liked it when he spoke Italian. They spoke the same language, after all. "Okay, I understand, and you're right."

"I'm sorry for what I said, when we fought."

"I'm sorry, too."

"I hate when we fight."

Mary thought of what Judy had told her. She'd had to eat a lot of crow lately, for a partner. "It's okay to fight. That's how we know we care."

"Right." Anthony fell silent a minute. "Now go to sleep."

"Talk tomorrow?"

"Yes, of course. Love you."

"Love you, too."

Mary watched the call disconnect, flopped backwards, and thought about what Anthony had said.

She fell asleep with the BlackBerry in her hand.

Chapter One Hundred and Seven

Bennie and Grady were ushered to the opposite gate with Officer Stern and Special Agent Wingate while the Philly cops, TSA, airport security, the A.D.A., and the other FBI agents whipped out cell phones and radios. Across the way, the Miami flight was boarding, the passengers disgruntled and weary.

"Sorry about that." Bennie could've kicked herself. "I thought it was her."

"Me, too." Officer Stern shook his head. "It happens."

"So what do we do now?"

"We're searching all terminals, the garage, the remote lot, area hotels and restaurants. We're checking other flights, other airports, even though it's late."

"Didn't we do that before?"

"Frankly, we're not sure what got done and what didn't. There are a lot of different agencies working the case, each with different jurisdictions. Something must've gotten missed. We didn't have much time, and this time of year, everybody's short-staffed. She could still be here."

"Not necessarily." Bennie wracked her brain. "I have to get her."

Grady glanced over, saying nothing.

"We'll stop her," Officer Stern said, with confidence. "An APB's out already. We're on it."

"But what will you do? Your jurisdiction ends in Philly." Bennie turned to Special Agent Wingate, who looked like a straight arrow, with dark eyes, short black hair, and a military bearing. "You're FBI. She's going down to the Bahamas. What can you do?"

"We'll contact Bahamian authorities and alert them to be on the lookout for her at the Nassau airport. They'll pick her up as soon as she gets off a plane." Special Agent Wingate flexed his jaw. "I understand that the Bahamian bank is freezing the accounts. In addition, we'll follow up and put them on security alert. They won't let her withdraw the money."

"What if they slip up?" Bennie looked over at the Miami gate, where the last of the passengers was disappearing into the jetway.

"They won't. They have procedures. It's not like they tape her picture on the cash register."

"But she has all my ID. She's me." Bennie made a decision. "I have to get to Nassau tonight."

"Why?" Grady looked over, alarmed. "You don't have to go yourself. The accounts will be frozen. She can't get the money. "

Special Agent Wingate nodded. "He's right. The Bahamian authorities can handle this."

"No. She'll be down there. I have to go." Bennie crossed the aisle to the Miami gate, and Grady caught up.

"Bennie, you really want to do this?"

"Yes."

"Why?"

"I just do." Bennie headed for the ticket counter at the gate, and Grady matched her, stride for stride.

"Then I'm going with you, too."

"I'd rather go alone."

"Look, I know we have to talk, and we will, but it's not safe for you to go down there."

"I'll be fine." Bennie reached the counter, which was staffed by an airlines employee. "My name's Bennie Rosato. I'm booked on this flight and I want to go."

"It's already boarded," the employee said, frowning.

"Come on, you see the situation. I have to get on that plane. It hasn't left yet."

"Hmph. May I see your ID?"

"I don't have any."

"I can't board you without ID. TSA regs."

Bennie turned to Officer Stern, who had walked up beside her. "Vouch for me, will you? I have to get on this flight."

Officer Stern addressed the employee. "This is a police emergency. She's Bennie Rosato, and she's ticketed on this flight. We'd appreciate your full cooperation."

"That's not the way we usually do it, but I suppose so."

Grady touched her arm. "What about in Miami? And Nassau? They won't let you into the Bahamas without a passport. You'll have to go through immigration."

Bennie turned to Special Agent Wingate. "Can't you help me with that? Call down to Miami and Bahamian immigration? Tell them I'll be there tonight?"

"I can call down to our people in Miami, but I can't promise they'll work with you, in the islands. I'll try my best, though."

"Try, please. I have to go." Bennie headed for the jetway door, but Grady stopped her, his hand on her arm.

"You're sure about this?"

"Yes."

"Then you'll need money." Grady opened his wallet and handed her his Amex card and all his cash. "It's six hundred and change. If they give you a problem with the card, call me."

"Thanks." Bennie avoided his eye and took off, hurrying down the jetway. Grady never would have believed that she would have three grand of drug money in her purse.

She never would have believed it herself.

Chapter One Hundred and Eight

Alice was nude in the leather seat, enjoying the afterglow. The mile-high sex had been terrific, and Knox was stepping into his pants, standing up in the moving jet. She tugged him into the chair opposite hers, and his pants were still unzipped, so she slipped her fingers inside his boxers, finding him with knowing fingers.

Knox chuckled. "I'm only human."

"Relax." Alice kept her fingers moving. "How long have you lived in Nassau?"

"All my life."

"When we land, will you spend the night with me, at my hotel?"

"Uh, well, I can't." Knox's smile faded, and Alice read his expression.

"Married? So what? All I need is information, and help. There's money in it for you, lots of money. A thousand dollars."

Knox scoffed. "I don't believe you."

Alice bent over, went into her bag, withdrew a bundle, and plopped it onto his lap. "Look, I have a bag full of dough."

"Truly?" Knox's eyes lit up and he held up money, looking at it this way and that. "Is this a thousand dollars?"

"Yes, and there's more where that came from, but I need information. BSB is the largest bank in the Bahamas, right?"

"There are many banks in the Bahamas. There's Scotiabank, First Caribbean, Royal—"

"But BSB is big?"

"Yes."

"So that means lots of people work there."

"BSB is a major employer in Nassau, yes."

"I need to find somebody who works for them. Do you know anybody who does?"

Knox thought a minute. "No."

"You sure?"

"No one." Knox looked past her, to the curtain. "I should go forward. Willa might be wondering about me."

"Okay."

"I get to keep the money?"

"Sure, and hurry back." Alice leaned over to give him a deep kiss and a final stroke, then withdrew her hand. "Can you get my clothes?"

"Sure."

"Got a cigarette up there?"

"There's no smoking on the flight." Knox smiled crookedly. "You can bum one of mine." He dressed quickly and left the cabin.

Alice poured herself another champagne, deep in thought. She'd be in the Bahamas in half an hour. The jet flew direct. A car would be waiting for her. She'd stay at a hotel near the bank, to be there when it opened. She had a great head start, and even if Bennie followed her, she'd never catch her.

Knox came back with her things, and she gave him a quick kiss, then went into the bathroom. The jet had a shower so she jumped in, shampooed her hair, dried off, and changed into the gray T-shirt and baggy shorts they'd bought her, with slip-on Keds.

She had already formulated her new plan. She'd set it in motion, as soon as they touched down.

Chapter One Hundred and Nine

Bennie shifted in her seat, her clothes still wet enough to raise eyebrows, especially in first class, where Alice had booked her ticket. She looked out of the window, and from the blackness came an image of Grady, his expression concerned as he handed her all his cash. Then she flashed on him making love to Alice, and felt a deep pang. Her emotions were coming back.

She got up from the seat, excused herself, and went forward, ducking inside the bathroom. She closed the door behind her, stuck her hand in her purse, and pulled out the Ziploc bag. She unzipped it, pleased to find the pills still dry. She popped one, bent over the tiny sink, and drank some water, then straightened up. Soon she wouldn't feel the pain in her hands or feet, or anywhere else.

On the way out, she avoided the mirror.

Chapter One Hundred and Ten

Alice looked in the mirror, applying a perfect line of black eyeliner, then waiting for it to dry. She could get used to flying private, with its free supply of toiletries. She had hardly felt the jet land and she was stalling, as part of her plan. She sprayed herself with Chanel perfume when there was a knock at the door.

"Bennie?" Knox said. "It's time to deplane."

Alice opened the door, threw her arms around Knox's neck, and gave him a long, deep kiss. "Sorry, I wanted to get all pretty for you."

"Mmm." Knox's tongue flicked inside her mouth. "You smell sexy."

"I am sexy."

"I second that. So, are you good to go?"

"Just about."

"Your car is ready and waiting. You'll have to go through immigration, but it won't take long. We have our own officer at the private airport. I'll escort you."

"Will you walk me to the car, too? I don't know where the pickup area is. I've never been."

"Certainly, I'm off for the night. Any other requests?"

"Just one." Alice kissed him again. "Send the other flight attendant home."

"She's gone. They all went."

"Even whoever cleans the plane? I don't want anybody seeing us together. My husband—" Alice broke off her sentence, and Knox's eyes widened slightly.

"Oh, I see." He glanced at her left hand. "What, no wedding band?"

"Not out of town." Alice smiled, and so did Knox.

"No worries. The service crew doesn't come until tomorrow morning."

"Good. I'll be right out."

"See you then." Knox closed the bathroom door, and Alice threw the latch to lock it, then she went into action.

She took one of the sweat socks, wet it, and wedged it around the smoke detector in the ceiling. She tore paper towels from the dispenser in fistfuls and shoved them into the wastebasket. She took the toilet paper out of the dispenser, stuffed that in with the paper towels, and put the wastebasket under the window with its plaid curtains.

She opened the matchbook, struck a match, then lit the curtains, which made a funny smell. She slid her new gun from her messenger bag and shoved it in her waistband in back. She tossed the matchbook into the flaming wastebasket, then grabbed the messenger bag, slipped out of the bathroom, and hurried to the front of the jet, where Knox stood by the open door.

"You had a cigarette, eh?" he asked, and she took his arm and pressed him toward the door.

"You can smell it, huh? Someday I'll quit."

"You and me both." Knox helped her down the stairway, and Alice looked around the airfield. It was dark, but lit enough to see a row of jets lined up next to their jet, near a silvery cylindrical fuel truck that read AVITA. The tarmac was quiet, no one was around, and not a baggage cart moving.

"Where is everybody?" Alice smiled.

"Gone to bed. Welcome to Nassau." Knox took her arm and led her toward a small modern terminal. Palm trees rustled along the concrete walk that lead to a glass double door, and the terminal's large windows showed only a single uniformed person inside.

"Only one person?"

"We're the only flight. He's waiting on us."

"Before we go through immigration, wanna stop at the bathroom?"

"Didn't you just do that?"

"Not for my benefit, for yours." Alice faked a sexy giggle. "There's one thing we didn't do, and I bet I do it better than your wife."

"Ha!" Knox laughed. "Come with me, woman."

They passed through an automatic door, which let them into a waiting room with a large screen TV in front of a leather sofa and chairs. A man in a light blue shirt was on the phone and didn't look up. Knox led the way down a hallway and went through a door that read MEN'S.

Alice followed him inside.

Chapter One Hundred and Eleven

Bennie was the first one off the plane when it landed in Miami, and she hurried down the jetway and through the door to the terminal, which was crowded with vacationers in funny hats, big families, honeymooning couples, and world-weary business travelers, all filling the air with different languages. Moms cuddled toddlers in chairs in the gate area, and students slept on the floor, their flights delayed in bad weather. Her connection to Nassau had also been delayed, and on the flight they had announced the gate number, which was only three down the hall.

She made her way through the crowd, reached the Nassau gate, and got in line at the counter to get her boarding pass. It was five people deep and manned by a single beleaguered airlines employee, so she looked around for a supervisor, but there wasn't one, so she waited. The air-conditioning had been turned off, and it smelled like body odor and patisserie hot dogs. People thronged to the gate, waiting for the boarding announcement, and by the time she reached the desk, the flight to Nassau was already boarding.

"Can I help you?" asked the airline employee, a faint sheen of sweat covering his top lip.

"My name is Bennie Rosato, I'm booked on this flight, and I need a boarding pass."

"Certainly. Your ID, please?"

"I don't have it. My wallet was stolen, and the FBI contacted you about me. They called down from Philadelphia."

The airline employee blinked a few times. "If this is a joke, I'm kind of busy."

"The FBI was supposed to call you, or someone at the airline. I just got off the flight from Philly, and they let me on without ID because I'm working with the FBI."

"If you're with the FBI, you should have identification."

"No, I'm a private citizen but I'm working with the FBI." Bennie dug in her purse and slid Special Agent Wingate's business card across the desk. "This is the agent in charge of the case. If you call him, he'll vouch for me."

"I don't have time to do that, and I can't board you without ID, no matter who says so. I don't make the rules."

"But I'm booked on this flight. You can find my name, and you know I just got off another flight, because I couldn't have gotten through security without ID, right?" Bennie sensed it was a losing cause, but she couldn't give up or Alice would be gone forever. "Just let me on. I have to get to Nassau tonight."

"I can't do that, I'm sorry." The airline employee looked at the line, worriedly. "Now, as you can see, there are so many people waiting—"

"Then give me a phone and let me call." Bennie walked around the side of the counter, but the airline employee recoiled, putting his hands up, protectively.

"Stop! You're not allowed back here."

"I just want to use your phone. I can clear this up in two minutes. I have to get on this flight."

"I'm sorry, I can't let you do that. I don't have an outside line here. The most I can do is call my supervisor, and you can take it up with her."

"Call her, then." Bennie checked behind her, and the flight was boarding quickly. "Right away."

"I couldn't reach her right away, Miss. She's on break." The airline employee wet his lips, nervously. "Why don't we put you up tonight, at the hotel near the airport, and give you a voucher for a flight anywhere in the continental United States, usable for up to one year."

Bennie turned to the next man in line. "Sir, may I borrow your cell phone, please?"

"*¿Que?*" he said, frowning, but the airline employee was already motioning him forward, speaking to him in rapid Spanish.

"Does anybody else have a cell phone I can borrow?" Bennie called to the others in line.

"Get outta the way!" an older man answered, annoyed. "We're gonna miss the flight, lady!"

"Excuse me," said a voice, and Bennie turned. Behind her stood a heavyset man with glasses and a gray-flecked beard. He had on a Hawaiian shirt and carried a Marlboro duffel bag. "Did I hear you say you need to get to Nassau?"

"Yes."

"I know somebody who can get you there."

"Tonight?"

"I can find out," the man answered.

Chapter One Hundred and Twelve

Alice tugged Knox into a bathroom stall and closed the wooden door behind them. She pressed him against the tiles, kissed him, then moved to undo his pants. "I bet I know what you want," she whispered.

"I know that you do."

Alice kissed him as she slid his zipper down. Outside she could hear shouting, so somebody had discovered the fire in the jet. Quickly she dug her fingers into Knox's crotch, got a good grip, and squeezed so hard his eyes flew open.

"Ow!" Knox yelped, bewildered.

"Do I have your attention? Our jet is on fire, and if I get lucky, it'll blow up."

Ka-boom! Suddenly, something detonated outside. Percussion shook the building. A siren went off.

"I need you to get me to my car," Alice said, holding on. "Do what I say or I'll tell your boss you set the fire. They're your cigarettes that started it, and your matches. I'll say you set it, after you raped me. I'll tell the cops, I'll tell your wife, too. Everything."

"No!" Knox shook his head. "I have a record. Please. I'll do whatever you want."

"Smart move." Alice released him. "First, get me out of here."

KA-BOOM! There was a deafening explosion, then more shouting. Another jet must have gone up, the one parked next to theirs.

"Move! Hurry!" Alice grabbed his arm, flung open the stall door, and yanked him out. "Get me to my car."

"How about another grand?"

"Done."

"This way, then!" Knox hurried from the stall with Alice, just as another explosion rocked the building. They stumbled but kept their footing, and ran from the bathroom into the waiting room.

The glass windows had blown out in the terminal, scattering shards everywhere. Smoke filled the room. On the runway raged an enormous conflagration, shooting flames into the night sky. It must have been the fuel truck that blew up. An emergency vehicle zoomed toward the blaze. A uniformed employee ran past, shouting into a radio.

Alice used Knox for interference, bolting past doors that read BOND ROOM, then MISSION CONTROL, and out the front door. The blaze superheated the air. Smoke choked her nostrils and stung her eyes.

"This way!" shouted Knox, running to the car.

Chapter One Hundred
and Thirteen

Bennie gripped the handstrap, and the helicopter left behind the funky architecture and neon lights of Miami. Her hair flew around her face, and she sat pitched forward, looking down through the windshield. The wind buffeted them, the engine rattled in her ears, and the rotors whined at a high pitch. The clouds shifted, and the moon popped into view, shining on a ripple of black water, making whitecaps like a strand of pearls.

The pilot was an older man who knew the heavyset guy from the airport, and Bennie didn't know more than that about him. He seemed to know what he was doing, his hands moving expertly over the console, with its instruments, gauges, and dials, their colorful numbers glowing disembodied in the dark.

She tried to figure out Alice's next move. The girl was probably on her way to the Bahamas, if not there already. She must have flown private. The credit cards didn't get canceled tonight because everybody had been so busy. She wondered if the FBI had called down to the Bahamas. She had no ID, no passport, and no idea how she'd get onto the island.

"Change of plans!" the pilot shouted, to be heard. "Can't land at L.P."

"What?"

"Lyden Pindling, the Nassau airport. Gotta take you to another island. Get the ferry to Nassau tomorrow morning."

"No, I have to get to Nassau tonight. That's the deal."

"Too bad. They closed the airport."

"Can't you land somewhere else on the island?"

"That'll cost you."

"I have the cash. You saw it."

"Roger that. Hang on, blondie."

Blondie. It was who Bennie had become. Otherwise, she didn't know who she was anymore. She used to fight for the law, and now she was an outlaw. She was about to enter a country illegally.

And her intent was to kill.

Chapter One Hundred and Fourteen

Alice and Knox ran to the car, amid mass confusion. Sirens blared everywhere. Smoke fogged the air. A loudspeaker barked. Airport personnel in reflective vests bolted toward the fires. At the limo stand stood a black Town Car, with its front door and trunk open.

"No driver!" Alice called out, reaching the driver's side. She caught a glint of keys in the ignition. "He left the keys. Get in."

Knox slammed the trunk closed, then jumped into the passenger seat.

Alice twisted the keys in the ignition and hit the gas. She sped out of the lot as police cruisers sped directly toward them in the same lane.

"Move over!" Knox yelled. "We drive on the other side!"

Alice steered into the other lane. "Tell me how to get out of here."

"Go left." Knox pointed, and Alice took the turn, then zoomed for the exit gate just as a red fire truck raced toward them, its headlights blinding. She veered around the fire truck and hit the main road leaving the airport, then reached a fork.

"Where now?"

"Right, then left." Knox pointed again.

Alice zoomed onto a side road and kept driving until the car rental places and businesses disappeared. She found herself in a neighborhood of small, run-down houses, their pastel hues faded and peeling. People were going to their cars and into the street to see what was happening at the airport, so she kept driving until she spotted a clearing with a dirt road. She pulled over, stopped the car, and looked over at Knox, who looked nervous in the lights from the dashboard.

"Now you gotta step up," Alice said. "I need an employee at BSB. You have to find me one."

"I know no one."

"Think harder. You have to know someone who knows some-one."

"How much is it worth to you?" Knox's eyes glittered. "I know you've got more in that bag."

"Five grand."

"Twenty."

"Ten."

"Fifteen."

Alice faked a smile. "Don't push me."

"Fine." Knox paused. "My cousin's friend might know someone, but I'm not sure."

"Then make the call."

Chapter One Hundred and Fifteen

Bennie spotted an orangey brightness blazing in the distance as the helicopter began its uneven descent. She couldn't tell what it was, but it didn't matter. The pilot flicked a switch, and a bright cone of white light shone from the helicopter onto an empty lot strewn with rubble, weeds, and broken glass.

She held on to the handstrap as the ground got closer. Winds swirled, whipping bugs into the spotlight, and the helicopter hovered, seesawing, then touched down. The pilot flashed her a thumbs-up and twisted a knob. The rotors slowed, and the whine died down and finally disappeared. The helicopter shuddered as its engine shut down.

The pilot slid off his earphones, with a broad grin. "It's better in the Bahamas."

"Where are we?"

"Adelaide, southwest of Nassau. The land belongs to a friend of mine. I'll be staying here tonight, at his place." The pilot turned. "Did you see that fire at the airport? Looks like a disaster."

Bennie mulled it over. An airport fire. Was Alice here? Was it a coincidence? "I have to get into Nassau, fast."

"My buddy and I can give you a lift there. It's half an hour by car. We got another friend, runs an all-night poker game."

"Then let's go." Bennie grabbed her purse, opened the rattly door, and climbed out of the helicopter as the pilot came around the other side, holding a canvas bag.

"Watch your step. Lots of crab holes around here. You'll see the shells, lying around. Purple, red, black ones."

Bennie saw a hole, but no crab shells. The lot was dark, and the only light came from a dilapidated clapboard house, a hundred yards away. "Is that your friend's place?"

"Yeah. Take my hand. Don't walk into a tree, there's plum and sea grapes. That's what you smell."

Bennie didn't smell anything, and she didn't come here for the flora and fauna. "Listen, there's one other thing I need."

"Sure, what?"

She told the pilot, and he didn't seem at all surprised.

Chapter One Hundred and Sixteen

Alice set the gun on the seat, near the door, while Knox talked on his cell phone to his cousin. They sat in the dark parking lot of a Chen's Food Store, a run-down affair. The store was closed so the lot was empty, but the streets buzzed with traffic heading to the airport. A light blue police cruiser tore past, its red lights flashing, then a gray cruiser with a crown on the door, which read CENTRAL POLICE. Every cop on the Bahamas had to be at the airport, and the sirens blared continuously.

"Oh, you're at FirstBank now?" Knox was saying. "Congratulations, Letty. Auntie Jane didn't mention it."

Alice whispered, "Ask her for someone who's still there. Get a name."

Knox said into the phone, "Letty, do you know anyone still there? You in touch with anyone? It's important."

Alice fished in the console and found a pen and pad with the name of the limo company.

"Who? Say again. Sure, I remember her. Do you have a phone number and address?" Knox read off the information, and Alice wrote it down. "Thanks, Letty. Love to all." He flipped the phone closed. "The name's Julie Cosgrove. I know her."

"How?" Alice set down the paper and turned the key in the ignition.

"We went to high school together. She had a crush on me."

"How do we get to her house?"

"It's near Cable, on the way to Nassau."

"Let's go. Direct me."

"Do you want to call first?"

"No, better to drop in."

"Take the first right, then." Knox opened the cell phone. "I must call my wife. What can I tell her?"

"Tell her you're helping at the airport. You'll be home by morning." Alice pressed the gas and steered out of the parking lot. She logged the address into the car's navigation system, and a white arrow popped onto a screen that was affixed to the dashboard.

"Turn right in three hundred feet," said the soft, mechanical voice.

Chapter One Hundred
and Seventeen

Bennie stood in front of an AK-47, an M3, two 30-30 hunting rifles, and three revolvers, all of which were arrayed on a grimy blanket on the ground, like a makeshift display case.

"Not much of a selection, eh?" the pilot asked, and the other man, John Something, chuckled.

"Like I said, it ain't Newark." He was a stocky young American with a shaved head and a neck tattoo that read Johnny Angel, and he had on an old-fashioned surfer T-shirt with jeans. The cinder-block shed belonged to him, and it was crammed with old lawn mowers, harrows, bush hogs, and an ancient tractor, its hood cracked open like a crab shell.

"How much is this one?" Bennie asked, picking up the Smith & Wesson. It was an older model, probably a forerunner of her own, which she kept at home in a gun safe, trigger lock and all. She'd never fired hers outside of a lesson, but it had been easy to kill the bad-guy silhouette that would come zipping up to her, his paper heart tattered into a busted star.

"The S&W?" Johnny Angel said. "Three hundred."

"Fair enough." Bennie dug the cash out of her purse, counted it off, and handed it over.

"You got six bullets in there. You need more?"

"If I do, I'm in trouble."

"Ha!" Johnny Angel laughed, and the pilot clapped him on the back.

"Thanks, man. Wanna come out with me and Tomboy? He's in the car."

"What's he doin', smokin' up?"

"What do you think?"

"Nah." Johnny Angel clucked, rubbing his grizzled chin. "I'm clean and sober, two and a half years."

"Ha! Old married man, eh?"

"You got that right." Johnny Angel chuckled again, but Bennie had slid the gun into her purse and was waiting at the door.

"You guys good to go?" she asked.

Chapter One Hundred and Eighteen

Alice stood behind Knox while he rang the doorbell of a modest house of yellow stucco. The windows were dark, and in the driveway was an old Neon with a BABY ON BOARD sign. The air smelled fragrant from a flower garden that filled the front yard, and tiny plastic starlights lit the walkway.

Alice poked Knox in the back. "Ring again."

Knox pushed the bell, and it rang just as a light went on in the second floor.

"Stick to the script," Alice said under her breath. In the next minute, a light went on beside the front door and a woman's face appeared in its window.

"Julie, it's Knox Balderston. Remember me? Can you let me in?"

"Knox?" The door opened, and Julie Cosgrove stood there in a white bathrobe. She was short, overweight, and had plain features, her dark skin pitted on her cheeks. Her hair was pulled back in a stiff ponytail, which she patted self-consciously as she smiled. "Hey, how've you been? Why're you here at this hour?"

"This is my friend, Bennie, and we have to talk to you about something. Please, can we come in?" Knox made a praying-hands, and Julie opened the door and backed up into her neat little living room.

"Been a long time. I see Letty in the market sometimes and she tells me you're doing well."

"I am, thanks. You, too?"

"So far, so good, now that I divorced Joey."

"I knew he wasn't good enough for you."

"Why'n't you tell me?" Julie shot back, and they both laughed as she gestured them into a blue patterned sofa and chairs. "Here, please."

"Letty says you got promoted at BSB." Knox sat down, and Alice followed suit.

"Yes." Julie nodded, with pride. "I'm unit manager now."

"Good, good," Knox said, and Alice lost patience with the soft sell. She leaned forward in the chair.

"Julie, I'm Bennie Rosato, and Knox and I are friends. I'm getting divorced, too, and I transferred all my money into your bank, to keep it away from my ex, who cheated on me. I want to withdraw it tomorrow morning, but I think my bank in the U.S. is going to freeze my accounts, because he wants to try to get the money, as alimony."

"My." Julie frowned, taken aback.

"Can I stop that from happening? We're talking about three million dollars."

Julie's dark eyes flared. "Are you serious?"

"Yes, very."

"You're in private banking, then. Which bank is it, in the U.S.?"

"USABank, in Philadelphia."

"I believe they're a partner bank with us, are they not?"

"Yes, they are."

"That makes it easier, if one's goal is to prevent us from freezing the accounts. Your bank, USABank, has probably already emailed us a request to put a hold on the account, because it originates with them. If one wanted to be sure that the message didn't get to us, one could intercept the email and delete it."

"How would you do that?"

"It's not difficult." Julie paused, thinking. "Simply put, that sort of email comes in to a special account, and I have access to that account. All managers do. One could just go in and delete the email.

Or it could be forwarded to the wrong department, and that would delay it until somebody figures out the mistake."

Bingo.

"In fact, that happened the other day. We didn't get a request for a transfer of funds because a manager forwarded the email to the wrong Christine. We have three Christines, upstairs. It was supposed to go to Christine G. but it went to Christine K." Julie looked sheepish. "Needless to say, our president wasn't happy."

"Look, I need you to do this for me, and I'm willing to pay you very well."

"No." Julie shook her head. "This is against procedure."

Knox patted her knee. "Can't you help us, Julie?"

"Julie, please, woman-to-woman. It's my money, and I only want to keep what's mine. Look, here's proof." Alice reached in her messenger bag, found the wallet and passport, and handed them over to Julie, who examined them and handed them back.

"It's still improper."

"But not illegal. It's not theft, since it's mine."

"The bank would never let you withdraw the full amount on such short notice, anyway."

Alice wasn't taking no for an answer. "But you could wire it to another bank, couldn't you, the same way it was wired to BSB?"

"Yes, of course, if you requested it."

"Then that's what I request, to intercept the freeze on the accounts, to fund my account tonight, and to transfer the money out immediately to a bank in Switzerland or someplace like that, where he can't get it." Alice paused for effect. "If you help me, I'll pay you $50,000."

Julie's mouth dropped open. "That's a year's salary!"

"You'll see, it can be yours in a few hours."

Knox nodded. "Do it, Jules. I am, and she's good for it. We're in it together, and if you do it by forwarding the email to the wrong department, like you said, nobody will be the wiser. You can keep your job and the money."

Julie was thinking it over, her forehead wrinkling as she glanced at Knox, and Alice could see she had to close the deal, fast.

"It's a good plan, Julie. Knox is right. It's a lot of money, and if you have a child, you can use it, right?"

"How do you know I have a child?" Julie's frown reappeared, and Alice worried she'd said the wrong thing.

"On your car, I saw a BABY ON BOARD sign."

Julie fell oddly silent.

Knox brightened. "You have a child, Jules? I have three sons."

Julie managed a smile. "I have one. James is his name, James Albert. He's two and a half years old."

"Where is he?" Knox glanced upstairs. "Asleep?"

Alice realized that there were no toys around the well-kept living room and they hadn't awakened a baby when they'd rung the bell.

Julie answered, "He's in the hospital, going on his third week. He's got leukemia."

"Oh, no." Knox touched Julie's knee again. "I'm so sorry."

"I'm praying for the best. The doctors say I should keep up hope." Julie sighed heavily, and Alice saw her opening.

"Well, then, don't you want the best medical care that money can buy? It can make all the difference in the world, can't it? If you won't do it for yourself, do it for him."

And Julie blinked.

Chapter One Hundred and Nineteen

Bennie bounced in the backseat of the Jeep as it jostled down one dirt road, then another, heading toward town. The pilot and the driver were talking in low tones, and she leaned over, dug in her purse, and pulled out her bag of pills, then swallowed the last one dry. She tossed the baggie aside.

"Here comes another," the driver said, pulling over as a car sped past. "Woohoo. Lots o' excitement. Something actually happening, besides the friggin' cruise ships."

"Breaking news," the pilot said, and they laughed.

Honk! Honk! beeped a horn, from a car behind them, then it flashed its high beams and zoomed past. Cars and trucks had been flying by all evening, speeding toward the airport, reservists and volunteers going to help.

"Can you put on the radio?" Bennie asked. "I'm curious what's going on."

The driver accelerated onto the road behind the red taillights, which were disappearing into the distance. The radio came on, the stations being scanned, then song fragments, and the news.

The male announcer said, "The status of the fire has been upgraded, and many of the first responders have been taken to the hospital, suffering from heat exhaustion. Authorities report that nine private jets and a truck loaded with jet fuel have been destroyed in a series of explosions. However, police decline to speculate that terrorists may be the culprit—"

"What a joke." The driver flicked off the radio, chuckling. "Al Qaeda, in Nassau?"

"They come for the Cuban cigars," the pilot said, and they both laughed.

Bennie kept her head to the plastic window of the Jeep, reading the lighted signs. Esso, Dream's Liquor, the Hibiscus Inn Hotel, only $29.99 a night. Grassy fields gave way to suburbs and houses, with all the windows dark and dogs barking in the yards.

"Almost there," the pilot said. "We're taking Blue Hill."

"The scenic route," the driver added, and they laughed again.

Bennie tuned them out, trying to guess where Alice would go. She'd have to stay at a hotel for the night. She couldn't present herself at the bank until morning. "Hey guys," she said, after a moment. "Do you know where the BSB bank is?"

"Sure," the driver answered. "Right in town, on Bay Street."

"Is there a hotel or two, near it?"

"Plenty. The Sheraton and the Hilton are at the head of Bay Street, then there's smaller ones, in town. Is that where we're dropping you?"

"Yes. The Sheraton."

"Sure you don't wanna come party?"

"Nah, thanks."

"Smart girl," the pilot said, over his shoulder. "When Tommy parties, he ends up in jail."

The driver laughed. "Not tonight. They've got their hands full, with this fire. You wanna knock over a liquor store, this would be the time."

His words struck Bennie as true. The cops would be completely distracted tonight. If Alice had started the fire, that could be the reason. But why, exactly? To keep the cops from the bank? To get past immigration, in case the FBI had called down?

They drove around a rotary, and another car flew by, then a blue van that read TRUST IN GOD. They passed a law school and the

College of the Bahamas, reaching the fringe of the city and a string of houses, grocery stores, and a hair salon that read Home of the Instant Weave, Whole Cap. People sat on the stoops and stood in groups on the sidewalk, talking and smoking.

Bennie eyed them. She wouldn't have a hard time finding a six-foot blonde who dressed like a lawyer.

It wouldn't be long now.

Chapter One Hundred and Twenty

Alice steered the Town Car down the dirt road, with Knox in the passenger seat and Julie in the back. It had taken a while to get in from the suburbs, but ahead she could see the tall hotels and lights of Nassau. A car behind them flashed its high beams.

"I think that car wants to pass," Julie said, tense. "Probably another one, going to the airport."

"Too bad, we're in a hurry, too." Alice wasn't kidding. Sooner or later, the limo driver would notice that his car was gone. She glanced over at Knox, who was looking out the open window. He had gotten too expensive and she knew he'd ask for more money, later. He'd outlived his usefulness, anyway.

The high beams flashed again, and Alice pulled over in front of a bright pink house and let the car speed past. She steered back onto the road, then hit the horn at the same time as she pulled her gun from her waistband, aimed it at Knox's head, and pulled the trigger.

HONK! Knox slumped instantly to the right, his blood and brain spattered over his shirt, and the car horn muted the sound of the gunshot and Julie's cry of shock.

"Shut up!" Alice grabbed the wheel and checked the rearview, where Julie had covered her mouth with her hand. "One more word, and you'll get the same. Here's what happens next. We stick to the plan, right?"

Julie remained silent, terrified.

"Say right for me."

"Right," Julie answered, her voice tremulous.

"Now, let's review." Alice tugged Knox forward by his shirt, and his body flopped over at the waist, his head bobbling in the well, his neck gone slack. She pushed the button to close the window on his side. "Julie, listen up. You there?"

"Yes."

"You and I go to the bank. You introduce me as your friend from the States. We tell the guard you left your house keys at work by accident. You were at the hospital, then out with friends, that's why we're so late. Are you with me?"

"Yes."

"We go to your office, you delete the email from USABank and do whatever else you have to do on the computer. When I know you transferred the money correctly, I'll send you your cut, and we both walk away, right? You shut up, forever."

"Yes."

"If you call the cops, at any point, even after I'm gone, I say you killed Knox, your old high-school crush. I say you were part of the bank thing, and the airport."

"The airport?"

Alice let it go. "If you talk, you go to jail, and they take your kid away from you. It's all on you."

Tears filled Julie's eyes.

"You're in deep now, but you'll get out of it if you stay quiet. Understood?"

"Understood."

"Good girl." Alice accelerated, wiping a teardrop of blood from her cheek. She checked her clothes and she was pretty clean. The only blowback was on her right hand and forearm, which she could wash off. It was lucky that Knox's window was open or it would have been a mess. "Julie?"

"Yes?"

"Tell me where we can dump this body, before he takes a shit."

Chapter One Hundred
and Twenty-one

Bennie entered the glistening lobby of the Sheraton, which was empty, and she walked to the reception desk as a young desk clerk emerged from a door behind the counter.

"Checking in?" he asked, pleasantly.

"No, I'm looking for someone named Bennie Rosato. She looks like me, she's my identical twin. Did she check in tonight? It would have been in the past few hours."

"I can't give you that information. It's confidential."

"But it's important that I see her. I have some medicine she needs and I forget where she told me she was staying."

"Hmm." The desk clerk glanced around. "Between us, I haven't seen her and I'm the only one on."

"Where are the other hotels, the chains and the smaller ones? She could be at any one of them."

"The Hilton is right next door, and there's a few others on Charlotte and Cumberland Streets. Our business district is only about ten blocks square, starting behind me." The desk clerk pointed backwards, and Bennie thanked him and left.

Outside, she scanned the street for Alice, but no luck. No one was on the sidewalk. There was almost no traffic, and it flowed one-way on Bay Street, downhill and to the left. Next door, the

Hilton was huge and well-lit, and she walked toward it, passing only a group of rowdy teenagers in oversized T-shirts. She made her way through the Hilton's parking lot and entered the lobby, which was brown, gold, and empty except for a gaggle of women in fuchsia dresses, chattering away.

The desk clerk was on the phone, but she hung up as soon as Bennie came to the desk and asked for her twin sister.

"I'm sorry," the desk clerk said. "Our guests are confidential."

"But I have some medicine she needs to take tonight."

"I see." The desk clerk bit her lip. "We're full, with three conventions and the Anders wedding. Is she with any of them?"

"No."

"Then she's not here."

"Thanks. I'll keep looking." Bennie left the hotel, went back outside, and surveyed the street. No Alice, and it was still empty. Across the way blazed the hot-pink-and-orange sign of a Dunkin' Donuts, but the store was closed at this hour, as was a Thai restaurant and a Pirate Museum flying a black skull-and-crossbones flag.

She took a left toward a stucco building that read BRITISH BANK-ING CENTRE, passed a Scotiabank, then followed Bay Street. It ran parallel to the water, guessing from the fishy odor. The night was black, the humidity oppressive, and sweat beaded on her forehead. The streetlights were few and far between, making haloed orbs, and many of the shops were covered by corrugated security gates.

She walked alone on a dark, gum-spattered pavement that ran under an overhang, past touristy T-shirt and pastel-colored gift shops, then a block of perfume shops and fancy stores like David Yurman, Fendi, and Gucci, all closed. Near the end of the block, sandwiched between a duty-free liquor store and discount jewelry store, she could see the brass letters of the BSB bank sign, the Greek columns on its façade out of place in the tropical vibe.

She walked to the bank, which had its fluorescent lights on, inside. A security guard strolled among the tellers' windows, which were festooned with turquoise-and-black crepe paper. Alice was nowhere in sight, but it made sense that she'd stay in a hotel close to the bank.

Bennie looked around. Charlotte Street lay to her right, and in the middle of the block was a lighted Colonial Inne sign. She went that way, entered the hotel lobby, and told her sick twin story to the desk clerk, who accepted a twenty for telling her that her twin sister had not checked in, though she might be at another hotel.

"Which one?" Bennie asked him.

"The Wayfarer." The desk clerk pulled out a street map, placed it on the wooden counter, and turned it around so that it was properly oriented, then drew a jagged pencil line to an X about eight blocks away.

"Do I take a cab?"

"No, you can walk it in fifteen minutes. It's off the beaten path, and many tourists favor it. The sign is small and painted pink. Just follow Charlotte, then take a right, and stay with the pencil line."

"Thanks." Bennie folded the map, went outside, and took a right. She walked a few blocks, then stopped and tried to read the map in the light from a closed restaurant, its chairs upside down on the tables. She could barely see the pencil line, so she walked left, then right, keeping an eye out for Alice.

She turned the corner, where it got darker, but there was no pink Wayfarer sign. She heard footsteps and turned, but it was a skinny man holding a cigarette that trailed a snake of smoke. She kept going down the street, then turned right. The block was deserted except for a big man in a baseball cap, walking in her direction. She saw a flash of pink at the end of the block. She couldn't read the sign but it had to be The Wayfarer.

She picked up her pace. The big man kept coming, then seemed to block her path. "Excuse me," she said, going around him, but he stepped in front of her.

"Hi, Alice," he said gruffly. The brim of his cap shadowed his face. "I'm a friend of Q's."

"Who?" Q? Bennie flashed on the name. The man Alice had pissed off, back home.

"You thought you could hide from him, by comin' down here? He's got friends everywhere, including the cops." Suddenly the man grabbed her by the shoulder, whipped out a hunter's knife, and pointed it at her chest.

Bennie gasped, terrified.

"Q wants you to know you're getting what you deserve."

Chapter One Hundred and Twenty-two

Alice followed the navigation system and steered onto West Bay Street toward Nassau. It was a winding road that ran along the beach, and the moon hung low in a black sky, making a shiny white stripe on the water. They had dumped Knox's body near a deserted construction site, and Julie had calmed down, sitting upright in back, her tears dried and her head to the window.

"Julie, we're in this together," Alice said, over her shoulder. "Cooperate and you get rid of me sooner, right?"

"Right."

"We're almost at the bank, right?"

"Right."

"Where do I park when we get there?" Alice accelerated when she saw the lights of Nassau straight ahead.

"There's a small lot around the back. I'll show you."

"Is it where the employees park?"

"No, we park on Shirley Street, remotely. But there's a small lot for deliveries, out back."

"Good girl. Don't try anything funny. The hard part is over, and now it's easy, right?"

"Right."

"Any guards on duty, and where?"

"One, patrolling inside. It's either Jonah or Floyd. I forget who's on tonight."

"Does he have a gun?"

"Yes."

"Will he walk us to your office?"

"No, he'll let me go myself."

"I'll go with you, too. By the way, no metal detectors, right?"

"None. I've been there so long they don't make me show ID anymore, and I'll sign you in under a made-up name as my guest. My office is on the third floor, above the bank."

Alice stopped at a red light, then cruised ahead, passing the Sheraton, then the Hilton. Traffic was light, and there wasn't a cop anywhere. The streets were deserted except for a few couples, their arms around each other. She steered left and right onto Bay Street. There were T-shirt shops, jewelry stores, perfume shops, and a few banks. Alice asked, "Which bank is BSB?"

"The one next to that jewelry store, on the left."

Alice caught sight of a shiny BSB sign, above weird columns. The lights were on inside, showing crepe paper and balloons, like somebody was throwing a money party.

She took a left turn, into the lot.

Chapter One Hundred and Twenty-three

Bennie screamed. The man clamped a hand over her mouth and shoved her against the wall.

She kicked him in the crotch. His eyes flared in pain. His hand fell off her mouth. The knife plunged down, cutting her shoulder.

Bennie screamed again. The man punched her in the mouth. Her head exploded in pain. She reeled backwards, dropping her purse.

"You're dead, bitch!" the man said.

Bennie fell, then she remembered. She stuck her hand inside her purse, found her gun with fumbling fingers, and fired through the leather.

Crak! The gun went off. The purse exploded like a bomb. Pain shot through Bennie's hand. She scrambled to her feet, backing away.

The man grabbed his thigh, which spurted an arc of fresh blood. He dropped the knife.

"Help!" someone shouted, from behind her. "Help, somebody! That guy's attacking that girl!"

Bennie whirled around to see another man, hustling toward her. He wanted to help, but she had to get Alice. She took off, running away.

"Miss, stop!" the man shouted. "Stop!"

Bennie ran down one street then the next, not knowing where she was going, not daring to stop. She veered around a corner, heading downhill toward the business district. She darted across a narrow street. A car swerved to miss her, then a minivan. She kept running. A taxi shot out of nowhere, screeching to a halt.

HONK! went the horn, but she kept going, back on Bay Street.

The BSB bank was straight ahead.

Bennie took a right turn and ran hard.

Chapter One Hundred and Twenty-four

Alice parked in the lot behind the BSB bank, took her messenger bag with the gun inside, and got out of the car. She was going to get Julie out of the backseat when she heard shouting. She looked up. A man was down the street, pointing at her.

"That's her!" he shouted. "She shot a guy! Get her!"

What? Alice froze, stunned. How did he know? She'd killed Knox miles away.

"Police, somebody, help!" The man kept running toward her, joined by another guy.

"Help!" Julie jumped out of the car, screaming and running for the bank. "Help, Jonah! Floyd!"

Alice took off, running full tilt. She tore down the street, but she couldn't outrun them. They were shouting, right behind her. She took a right, then a left, down one dark street after another, bolting across the road.

Honk! Honk! A bus screeched to a halt, but she kept running. She spotted an alley and ducked inside. The bus had screened her from the men.

She hid in the shadow, watching. In the next minute, the men raced past the mouth of the alley and kept running away, down the street.

Suddenly she felt something press into the small of her back. Someone lifted her messenger bag from her shoulder.

"Turn around slowly," said a voice. "I knew if I found an alley with a view of the bank, you'd drop by."

Alice recognized the voice.

It was her own.

Chapter One Hundred and Twenty-five

Bennie aimed the gun and forced Alice backwards, to the wall of the alley. There was only one way this could end. She was finally going to kill her twin.

"Bennie?" Alice put her hands up and stopped, her back to the wall. "Bennie? Bennie!"

Bennie didn't reply or waver. She advanced with the gun. Her hand was steady, her concentration absolute. The gun was still hot. She lined up its sight on her target.

"No, wait. What's the matter with you? What are you doing?"

Bennie didn't answer. Police sirens blared nearby. They would come soon. She didn't have much time. She cocked the trigger.

"Aren't you going to call the cops?" Alice burst into tears. "Please God, don't kill me!"

Bennie couldn't live unless Alice died. It was that simple.

"No, wait, please!" Alice fell to her knees. "Please, no!"

Bennie stepped close enough to stand over Alice. She aimed at her forehead. It wasn't a murder, it was an execution.

"Please!" Alice raised her hands, begging. "Please don't kill me! You can't!"

"Yes, I can." Bennie sounded matter-of-fact, even to her. "I have you in me, and you have me in you. That's why you couldn't kill me. And why I can kill you."

"No, please Bennie!" Alice collapsed in tears, doubling over, her forehead to the ground.

Suddenly there was the sound of footsteps behind her, and Bennie glanced over her shoulder. The figure of a woman appeared at the mouth of the alley. Lights from shops across the street silhouetted her.

"Benedetta, no," the figure whispered, like a prayer.

Bennie blinked. Her mother was the only person who called her Benedetta. The figure was small, about her mother's height. She could have sworn it was her mother, standing there.

Bennie shook it off. She must be seeing things. It was the pills.

"No, Benedetta," the figure repeated, with the Italian pronunciation, exactly the way her mother had said her name.

Bennie felt the words washing over her, resonating within her. Something came loose in her chest. Tears filled her eyes. The figure was backlit like an angel. Bennie wasn't imagining her. Maybe it was a vision. Her mother was an angel, come to see her. To stop her.

Then the angel stepped into the alley.

Chapter One Hundred
and Twenty-six

But it wasn't a vision, an angel, or her mother.

It was an older woman, the same size as her mother. She had a similar headful of dark hair, but her eyes glittered oddly. She must have been crazy, because she came all the way into the alley, ignoring the execution in progress.

"Go away." Bennie lowered her arm, hiding the gun. She tried to blink her tears back. "Go. Leave."

"You don't know me, but I know you," the woman said, her voice firm and strong. "I saw you tonight, earlier, at the airport. I couldn't go home and turn my back on you."

"Go away!" Bennie kept shaking her head, bewildered.

"I saw you the other day, too. On the sidewalk, yelling. You need help, and I am here to help you. My name is Fiorella."

Bennie didn't know what to do. She couldn't kill Alice, with the woman standing there. She shook her head. The tears wouldn't go away. She was thinking of her mother. She was feeling her mother's very presence.

"Benedetta, look at me. I see truth, and there is too much good in you to do this. Look at me."

Bennie couldn't look at her. She knew it was crazy. She was listening to a crazy woman having a crazy conversation, but she felt as if she were talking to her mother. She felt as if she were talking to herself. She was in a sort of dream, or spell, or maybe it was the pills, but none of it mattered any longer.

"Benedetta, look at me."

"No." Bennie was lost now, even to herself. She couldn't come back. She had crossed the line. Tears slid down her cheeks. "I'm not good. Not anymore."

"Yes, you are." The woman took Bennie's face in her hand and turned it toward her own. "I see you."

Suddenly Bennie started to cry, hoarse, choking sobs. She felt like she was breaking down, out of control. All her emotions came flooding out, and she was unlocked, her soul set free. She was surrendering to something, and she didn't know what, or who. The crazy woman. Her mother. Herself.

"I see you, Benedetta. See yourself, in my face. I look at you, like a mother. I see you, like a mother. Do you see the goodness here, and the love?"

And as impossible as it seemed, the woman was smiling at her, full of love, channeling her very mother, and in the next second Bennie felt herself collapse in the woman's arms.

Police sirens blared near the alley, breaking the spell, and Bennie came to her senses.

Alice was climbing the wall and getting away.

"No!" Bennie shouted, raising a hand. But her gun was gone somehow, and Fiorella kept a firm grip on her arm.

"Let her go. She is dead already."

Bennie heard the truth in her words, and it made her feel that she could come back, and that she already had, and she could become herself again. Because she had remembered who she really was inside, the little girl her mother had loved, all her life.

Benedetta Rosato.

And when she looked up, Alice was gone.

Chapter One Hundred and Twenty-seven

Bennie sat in a hard chair, alone in her third interview room, in almost as many days. She'd spent the night in a smelly holding cell, but the Bahamian police had fed her eggs for breakfast and fried fish for lunch, and they'd gotten her hands rebandaged, so she felt herself again. It was Tuesday afternoon, and she hadn't had any more pills, which helped, too.

She was waiting for the cops to formally release her, and her gaze wandered idly over the mint green walls, beat-up black chairs, and a metal table covered with old newspapers, blank forms, and a 2007 Nassau telephone directory. There were bars on the window, and through them she could see it was beautiful outside. A tropical sun beamed onto a windowsill cluttered with files and an old-fashioned ink pad, for taking fingerprints.

She'd been talking to the cops for hours, because under Bahamian law they could question her for forty-eight hours, with extensions to seventy-two and ninety-six hours, which turned out to be unnecessary. She'd used her phone call to contact the Philadelphia office of the FBI, who had called the American consulate. The consulate official had gotten her a Bahamian criminal lawyer, and he'd blessed her cooperating with the authorities.

So the cops had read her "a caution," their equivalent of Miranda warnings, and she'd convinced them that she'd shot the big man in self-defense, especially since eyewitnesses had seen him attack her and reported that he'd run away after he'd been shot. A search of doctors and the hospital hadn't been able to find him, and under Bahamian law, if they didn't have a complainant, they couldn't charge her, anyway. She would be fined on the weapons charge and for illegally entering the country, and in the meantime, her bank accounts had been safely transferred back to USABank. The cops were still looking for Alice, based on statements from Fiorella and one Julie Cosgrove of BSB, but Bennie knew her sister would never be found.

She's dead already.

The door to the interview room opened, and a cop in a white pith helmet stuck his head inside. He had on the smart black-and-red uniform of the Royal Bahamian Police, with a gold crown at the epaulets. "Miss Rosato?" he said.

"Yes, Officer?" Bennie rose. "May I go now?"

"Yes. Your lawyer is here, to escort you."

"My lawyer?" Bennie repeated, puzzled. "I sent him home. I can take it from here."

"Ms. Rosato?" called a familiar voice, and in the next second, Grady walked into the interview room, wearing a gray suit, a tie, and the widest smile on the planet.

"Hi, what are you doing here?" Bennie let an awkward moment pass. She wasn't about to throw herself into his arms, and Grady must have picked up on her feelings, because he didn't move to hug her.

"Of course I'd come. You have my Amex card, remember?"

Bennie laughed. "Uh-oh. I think I shot it."

Grady laughed with her, then his expression turned serious. "Did they treat you well? Are you okay?"

"Fine."

"I see you got your hand fixed up."

"For now. I have to go to an orthopedist, when I get home."

"Does it hurt?"

"Nah."

"I couldn't stand it if you were hurting, after all you've been through."

"I'm really fine," Bennie answered, touched. "I'm just waiting on the paperwork."

"I've got tickets to take you back today, and they'll let you fly without your passport, clear through to Philadelphia. It's all been greased by the FBI. They also talked to the Pellesburg police, who found the box, so they know the truth. They're not charging you with anything."

"Good."

"She buried you alive?" Grady's gray eyes went the color of steel behind his glasses. "It's inhuman that she would do that to you. You must have been scared out of your mind."

"That's not the worst part, really." Bennie tried to shrug it off, but couldn't. She'd done a lot of thinking last night, even for the short time she was behind bars. "The worst part is how much it changed me. I never thought I could be as evil as Alice. I didn't think I had that in me. But it turns out that I do."

"Who knows, maybe all of us do. Maybe any one of us, pushed to the brink, is capable of evil. Or at least revenge." Grady's voice softened. "Don't beat yourself up about it. Don't judge yourself. No one else does, least of all me."

"Thanks." Bennie managed a smile, but it felt so strange to be standing here, talking with him. She flashed on being back in the box, thinking that if she ever got out alive, she'd tell him how she felt. But for some reason, the words weren't coming to her lips.

"I do have something to say, though. I'm standing here with you now, looking at you, and I can't believe I ever mistook her for you." Grady frowned, bewildered. "I cannot believe I was fooled so easily, and I'm sorry. You must think I'm a complete idiot."

"No, not at all," Bennie said, as his words struck home. "We hadn't seen each other in a while, and if I'd let people get closer to me, especially you, then this never would have happened. So it's my fault, really. I know that now."

"Well, then." Grady's features softened, and he cocked his head.

"I propose we start over, and get to know each other better. What do you say? I'd like to give us a second chance."

"So would I." Bennie couldn't say more, except to throw her arms around Grady and relax into his embrace like it was the most natural thing in the world.

Because, suddenly, it was.

Chapter One Hundred and Twenty-eight

Bennie, Grady, and Fiorella arrived in the Philly airport and joined the stream of tourists, vacationers, and business travelers heading down the hall to the terminal exit. They passed a souvenir cart, a soft pretzel stand, and finally, the Miami gate.

Bennie smiled, catching Grady's eye. "Remember the last time we were here? Not my finest moment."

Grady chuckled, throwing an arm around her. "Beg to differ. That kid had it coming."

"Look!" Fiorella pointed down the hall, where Mary, her parents, and The Three Tonys stood, waving at them and holding flowers and balloons.

"YO, BENNIE!" The DiNunzios and Mary rushed forward to meet her at the exit, startling the TSA guard and causing heads to turn.

"*Benedetta!*" Mrs. DiNunzio reached up for her.

"Bennie!" Mary squealed, and Bennie gathered them up in a big hug, then released them.

"Hey, Mary! Or should I say, partner? Congratulations!"

"Wow!" Mary's lips parted in happy surprise. "Partner works for me, but did you just call me by my first name?"

"I sure did, and why not? It's about time, don't you think?"

"Sure!" Mary beamed.

"How's Carrier? I mean, Judy?"

"She's great! She says hi, and she'll be back at work in two weeks."

Bennie wanted to hear more, but she and Mary got distracted by something happening between Mrs. DiNunzio and Fiorella, talking in front of Mr. DiNunzio and the Tonys.

"*Grazie,* Donna Fiorella." Mrs. DiNunzio stood next to Mr. DiNunzio, who had his arm around her shoulder. "You save Benedetta. *Mille grazie.*"

"You're welcome." Fiorella nodded in acknowledgment. "Do you still believe I'm not a good woman? Or have I redeemed myself?"

"You are good!" Mrs. DiNunzio answered, and the two women hugged like old friends. When they broke their clinch, Mrs. DiNunzio's eyes were glistening. "So, why you come back, Fiorella?"

"I've decided to move to Philadelphia."

Everyone looked dumbstruck, except for Mr. DiNunzio, who grabbed one of The Tonys by the shoulder and tugged him over to Fiorella. "FIORELLA, YOU REMEMBER MY BUDDY PIGEON TONY LUCIA? HE CAN SHOW YOU AROUND TOWN."

Fiorella extended a hand to Pigeon Tony, with a seductive smile. "How very nice to see you again."

Bennie returned to Mary. "Mary, did you buy a house? Grady told me everything that's been going on."

"Yes, I'm a new homeowner, and Anthony and I are doing great, too."

"Congratulations on that, too! Are you guys going to live together?"

"Not yet." Mary shook her head, smiling. "We're taking it slow."

"Good. Tell Anthony I said hello, will you?"

"You can tell him yourself. He's here, and he brought a friend."

Mary stepped aside with a flourish, and her parents, Fiorella, and The Tonys cleared away. Anthony emerged from the back of the crowd, holding a leash, and at the end stood Bear, wagging his tail. His belly had been shaved and two of his legs had a bandage, but when he saw Bennie, he scampered stiffly to her, in delight.

"Bear!" Bennie felt tears come to her eyes. "Look at you, pal!"

Grady beamed. "I couldn't bring myself to put him down and I asked them to do the surgery. I had to make secret phone calls to see how he was, but I didn't want to tell you until he was out of the woods."

"I love you!"

"Me or the dog?" Grady asked, but Bennie had knelt down and was burying her face in the dog's thick ruff. She kissed his muzzle and caught a whiff of his breath, which smelled suspiciously of peanut butter. She laughed, stood up, and took his leash.

"Let's go home, gang," Bennie said, her heart full and happy.

"Arf!" Bear barked, and everybody laughed.

Acknowledgments

Think Twice is a thriller with gunplay, chase scenes, and bad girls, but at its warm and gooey center, it's a story about the power of a mother's love. So first, thanks go to my mother, Mary Scottoline. She's the strongest person I know, or could even imagine, and has triumphed over so much adversity to become the woman she is that I can't decide whether I love her more than I admire her, or the other way around. She's the reason I started writing, because I wanted to see in books the kind of strong, smart, and funny women I saw in life. And ultimately, I'm so grateful for all she has done for me, my daughter, my brother, and my friends. All the good parts of me are from her, and frankly, so are the bad parts, which are way more fun. Thanks, Ma.

I'm a big fan of thank you, and after sixteen novels, I'm lucky enough to have a SWAT team of go-to experts to answer all of my hard questions, though any mistakes are mine. For legal and police procedures, I always turn to Glenn Gilman, Esq., and Detective Art Mee, who never let me down. Thanks, gentlemen, once again.

For medical issues, thanks to Brad Zerr and Tina Saurian. For financial and banking issues, thanks to the folks at PNC, Rick Monterosso and Marlene McCafferty. And for law firm finances, thanks to my BFF Franca Palumbo, Esq., now of her own law firm, Thalheimer & Palumbo. Congrats, Franca!

Big hug to the University of Pennsylvania School of Veterinary Medicine and to the brilliant Jolie Demchur, who can tame the wildest of horses and helped me so much with all matters veterinary.

Think Twice took me off the reservation big time, for a research trip to Nassau, Bahamas, where everyone was enormously helpful and friendly. Thanks so much to Officer Antonio Bain, of the Royal Bahamian Police, who answered all of my questions and took me on a tour of the police station in Nassau, and huge thanks to Wilbert Moss, an expert criminal defense attorney, who spent so much of his valuable time teaching me the intricacies of Bahamian criminal law. Thank you both so much for your expertise and hospitality.

On the publishing end, thank you to the gang at St. Martin's Press, starting with my editor and coach, Jennifer Enderlin, who improved *Think Twice* so much, in addition to coming up with the title (again!). Thanks for everything to John Sargent, Sally Richardson, Matthew Shear, Matt Baldacci, Jeff Capshew, Nancy Trypuc, Monica Katz, John Murphy, and John Karle. Thanks to Michael Storrings, for a great cover design! Also hugs and kisses to Mary Beth Roche, Laura Wilson, and the great gang in audio. I'm indebted to all of you.

Thanks and big love to my genius agent, Molly Friedrich, to the Amazing Paul Cirone, and to the lovely and talented Lucy Carson.

My wonderful assistant and bestie Laura Leonard is invaluable in every way. Thanks, sweetie, and especially for going to Nassau with me as one of our continuing excellent adventures. Nobody is better on a research run than Laura, and plus, she's fun!

Finally, biggest thanks and love go to my remarkable daughter, Francesca, a writer herself, who helped me with this book, as well as our dogs, cats, and a very stubborn pony, who shall remain nameless.